C000253358

RISE OF A WIZARD QUEEN

FATE OF WIZARDOMS: BOOK 5

JEFFREY L. KOHANEK

© 2020 by Jeffrey L. Kohanek

All rights reserved. No part of this book may be reproduced, stored in a retrieval system or transmitted in any form or by any means without the prior written permission of the publishers, except by a reviewer who may quote brief passages in a review to be printed in a newspaper, magazine or journal.

The final approval for this literary material is granted by the author.

First Edition

Print ISBN: 978-1-949382-27-3

This is a work of fiction. Names, characters, businesses, places, events and incidents are either the products of the author's imagination or used in a fictitious manner. Any resemblance to actual persons, living or dead, or actual events is purely coincidental.

PUBLISHED BY JEFFREY L. KOHANEK and FALLBRANDT PRESS

www.JeffreyLKohanek.com

ALSO BY JEFFREY L. KOHANEK

Fate of Wizardoms

Book One: Eye of Obscurance

Book Two: Balance of Magic

Book Three: Temple of the Oracle

Book Four: Objects of Power

Book Five: Rise of a Wizard Queen

Book Six: A Contest of Gods

* * *

Warriors, Wizards, & Rogues (Fate of Wizardoms 0)

Fate of Wizardoms Boxed Set: Books 1-3

Runes of Issalia

The Buried Symbol: Runes of Issalia 1

The Emblem Throne: Runes of Issalia 2

An Empire in Runes: Runes of Issalia 3

Rogue Legacy: Runes of Issalia Prequel

* * *

Runes of Issalia Bonus Box

Wardens of Issalia

A Warden's Purpose: Wardens of Issalia 1

The Arcane Ward: Wardens of Issalia 2

An Imperial Gambit: Wardens of Issalia 3

A Kingdom Under Siege: Wardens of Issalia 4

ICON: A Wardens of Issalia Companion Tale

* * *

Wardens of Issalia Boxed Set

JOURNAL ENTRY

Ah. I see you have returned, undoubtedly riveted by the gripping story, curious to discover what fate awaits the wizardoms. Gladness fills my soul to have your attention, for much has yet to be revealed.

As you have discovered, with each stanza comes new twists in the chronicle of the Eight Wizardoms. Incredible truths and frightening conspiracies will be exposed, some of which you may have guessed, others sure to surprise. Still, once aware and blessed with a new perspective, I believe you will realize the story has been heading toward such an end all along.

Before we resume the tale, let us reflect on what has been revealed thus far.

A menagerie acrobat named Rhoa stole the amulet known as the Eye of Obscurance, the same one pursued by master thief Jerrell Landish. Jerrell, who goes by the name Jace now, agreed to track down this acrobat, claim the Eye of Obscurance, and use it to assassinate Lord Taladain, the Wizard Lord of Ghealdor.

Jace eventually caught up with Rhoa's menagerie outside of Starmuth, where he agreed to team up with Rhoa and a dwarf named Rawk, all sharing the goal of killing Lord Taladain. Soon afterward, the trio met me in a small Ghealdan village, where I, Salvon, invited them to ride with me to Fastella. With my assistance, the four of us laid plans for Lord Taladain's final performance.

Taladain's daughter, Narine, returned from the University as a master wizardess, seeking to become an asset to her father. Unfortunately, her brother, Eldalain, viewed her as a threat.

While Prince Eldalain was away, we delivered a memorable troupe performance for Lord Taladain, killing the man in the process, an act made possible by the Eye of Obscurance. In the process, it was discovered that Rhoa possessed a natural immunity to magic.

To escape her brother's wrath, we smuggled Narine and her bodyguard, Adyn, out of the city, but our small group did not remain together for long. High Wizard Charcoan's soldiers attempted to arrest Narine, forcing Jace, Narine, and Adyn to flee Starmuth on a ship bound for the Farrowen city of Shear, while the rest of us journeyed by land toward Lionne.

Rhoa, Rawk, and I were soon captured by Captain Despaldi and brought to Marquithe to face Lord Malvorian, ruler of Farrowen. After escaping our cells below the Marquithe Palace, we discovered Rawk's uncle, Algoron, secretly working for Malvorian.

We were led to Malvorian's throne room, discovering Jace, Narine, and Adyn already there. A confrontation of magic, swords, and death ensued. While we defeated Malvorian, Thurvin, and Despaldi, Jace was severely wounded in the process. As destiny would have it, Narine acquired an enchanted bracelet, enhancing her magic and enabling her to save his life. Malvorian was not so lucky.

Our party of heroes escaped the city, on the run once again. With two wizard lords dead, a shift in the balance of magic occurred. Creatures of legend, mighty and dangerous, began to appear – something unheard of for two millennia.

Upon reaching the Pallanar border, we sought the assistance of a retired soldier named Brogan Reisner and his archer companion, Blythe. Despaldi was chased off, and we journeyed to Illustan, the capital of Pallanar.

While meeting with Wizard Lord Raskor and his wife, Ariella, a dragon attacked the city. The wizard lord confronted the beast, unaware of dragons' immunity to magic. With quick thinking, Narine crafted an illusion and led the dragon from the city, saving the populace. Strangely, Raskor eventually succumbed to wounds inflicted during the confrontation.

All the while, the Farrowen Army captured the Ghealdan cities of Starmuth and Marquithe, converting the purple flames of Gheald to the blue of Farrow, redirecting the prayers of Devotion to Lord Thurvin, the new Wizard Lord of Farrowen, feeding the wizard's power. Dorban was eventually added to the list, the city captured because of the heroics of Lieutenant Garvin and a thief named Rindle.

After Lord Raskor's demise, a Seer named Xionne and her dwarf guardian, Hadnoddon, arrived in Illustan, demanding we all accompany her on a journey to the legendary city of Kelmar. With an escort of Pallanese soldiers, we sailed to

Eastern Pallanar and made for the Frost Forest. A trio of wyverns attacked at night, the skirmish killing all but one of the soldiers and nearly costing Brogan his life.

When our heroes arrived in Kelmar, the Seers guided them through prophecies until the truth was revealed – the Dark Lord, Urvadan, rises with the desire to extend his dominion over mankind. After surviving a darkspawn attack, the Seers sent our heroes in different directions with the objective of recovering two enchanted items, each hidden in a different corner of the world.

Jace, Narine, Adyn, Hadnoddon, and I headed north in search of the Band of Amalgamation. During our journey, tragedy struck, killing our escorts and forcing us to take an underground path through the lost dwarven city of Oren'Tahal. There, we came upon darkspawn using a sacred forge to craft weapons to use against mankind. A confrontation ensued, the darkspawn dying at the hands of our heroes. Unfortunately, I, Salvon the Great, was also lost when I fell into a pit of lava.

The remaining members journeyed to Tiamalyn, where Jace was held captive, forced into a fight to the death to prove his innocence. Incredibly, he defeated eight seasoned warriors before a stadium of thousands. Freed, he and the others continued north until they reached the Enchanter's Isle. They snuck into the Enchanter's stronghold and recovered the Band of Amalgamation. Another wizard lord died in the process, destroyed by a fellow Enchanter who had embraced the dark art of sorcery.

As our heroes made their escape, Despaldi and the remaining Fist of Farrow attacked before they could depart. Fresh off killing the Wizard Lord of Orenth, Despaldi and his magically augmented crew became overly confident, underestimating the power of destiny. Jace, Narine, Adyn, and Hadnoddon survived the battle, slaying the dastardly Despaldi, but at significant cost to Adyn. Desperate to defeat the magic-imbued attackers, she donned the Band of Amalgamation, which transformed her flesh into metal.

Wounded and worn from the battle, with Narine remaining unconscious, they boarded a ship with the promise of free travel to the destination of their choice. Unfortunately, it was a trap. Drugged, they now sail toward an unknown destination.

The other group of heroes, which consisted of Rhoa, Rawk, Algoron, Brogan, Blythe, and a host of dwarven escorts, headed toward the unmapped southeast in search of the Cultivators, a race last seen two thousand years earlier. With Rhoa's immunity to magic, they found the golden forest home of the Cultivators, who turned out to be elves. Calling themselves the Silvan, the elves refused to help our heroes with their search for the Arc of Radiance, instead incarcerating them. But a darkspawn attack changed everything. Freed, our heroes helped fight off the attacking goblins. Driven by urgency, Blythe used a golden longbow, the arrows of light felling darkspawn by the dozens. The enchanted bow bound itself to her, changing her eyes to gold, her nature altering to half-human, half-elf.

Knocked unconscious during the battle, Rhoa was captured and dragged off to a cave where darkspawn intended to sacrifice her to their god, unaware of the dragon living there. The dragon killed the goblins, freed Rhoa, and returned her to the elven forest. To thank her for recovering a lost treasure, the dragon gifted Rhoa with a horn to use when in dire need.

The elves, shaken and fearful after the darkspawn attack, abandoned their dying forest and returned to their forest of old – the Silvacris, which had remained frozen for two thousand years. Upon their return, the forest bloomed to life, reconnecting with the elven magic. To repay the debt of having saved his life and his home, the son of the elven queen joined our heroes, and the squad set off on their next quest.

While all this was occurring, Queen Priella, the last surviving offspring of Lord Raskor and first female wizard lord in a thousand years, plotted, with the desire to expand her rule. Unprecedented, she divined a means to leave her city of Illustan while remaining able to collect the prayers of her people each evening. With her crystal throne mounted on a wagon, she and her army marched north, through the snow-covered mountains, to the Farrowen city of Marquithe. There, she met with Thurvin – a wizard lord who wielded the power of two wizardoms – and bewitched him with the long-forbidden spell of compulsion. What scheme drives this wizard queen and her army?

Thus, the world has been thrown into chaos – five wizard lords dying in a short span, three thrones remaining unclaimed, and one wizard wielding the power of two wizardoms. The Murguard was crushed, darkspawn no longer contained to The Fractured Lands. All of Kyranni has fallen, save for Anker, the capital city, which is protected by Lord Kelluon. Should Kelluon and his city succumb, the darkspawn invasion will advance uncontested…until they meet another wizard lord.

And, so, our story continues…

-Salvon the Great

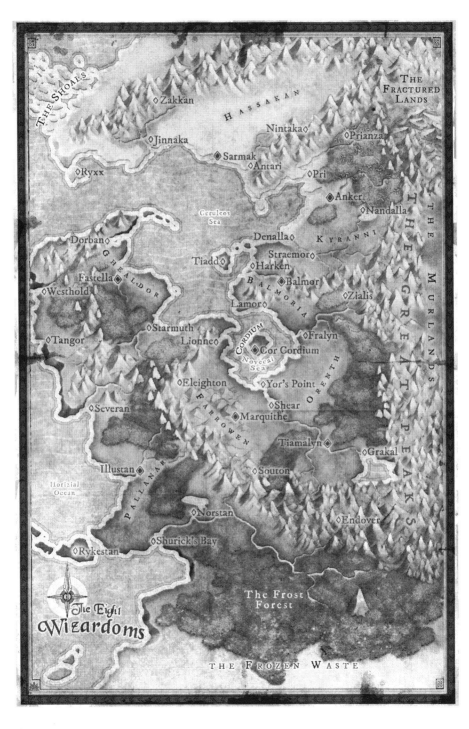

The Eight
Wizardoms

PROLOGUE

H'Deesengar sat upon his stone throne in the Temple of Tenebri, deep below the city of Murvaran. The demon lord hated both the throne and the underground temple in which he lived – his prison.

Twenty-five hundred years had passed since Urvadan captured H'Deesengar and began using the demon lord's magic to advance his schemes. Among other things, H'Deesengar gave birth to darkspawn – goblins, ogres, and trolls, all to feed the god's elaborate agenda. Five hundred years after that, Urvadan's plans finally came to fruition, capturing the moon to feed his own magic, breaking the world in the process. The event had all but consumed the demon lord, sapping him of his magic. Worse, when H'Deesengar was at his weakest, he was attacked by a band of heroes and slayed...or so they thought.

As a being of netherworld magic, H'Deesengar remained little more than a memory, slowly regaining power. Two centuries passed before his consciousness rematerialized, three more by the time his magic fully returned.

Unlike the years prior, Urvadan had abandoned the temple to live in the city of Murvaran, beneath the moon that fed his might. To contain H'Deesengar, Urvadan crafted an ingenious spell, encasing the demon lord. Although trapped, the demon lord's mind was no longer a slave to the Dark Lord's will, allowing him to exert his magic toward his own agenda, rebuilding his darkspawn army, adding new elements to ensure success when his time arrived.

Shaman magic was one of the demon lord's gifts to the world, enabling him to instill an intelligence goblins otherwise lacked, providing a means to control mindless monsters. Wraiths were another such gift – his means of trapping the souls of sacrificed humans. Stuck within this plane of existence, they were mindless creatures driven by the hunger to feed on the souls of mankind.

His final gift was inspired by Gyradon, the dragon that had accompanied the heroes who nearly killed H'Deesengar. Impressed with the creature's majesty and magic, the demon lord created beings of a similar nature. Thus, wyverns were born.

Across the underground temple, a shape emerged from the shadows, stirring H'Deesengar from his musings.

A goblin shaman, wearing a necklace of human bones around its neck, climbed the stairs. It kneaded its hands in worry, bulging red eyes flicking about, never meeting the demon lord's gaze. Just beyond the eight-pointed star etched into the dais and surrounding the throne, the creature knelt, bowing, face and arms resting on the cavern floor. In the past, each point of the star had shone with a light of a different color, one sometimes darkening for a short time before returning to life. Of late, more gems had gone dark than any time since his rebirth. Only five stones shone – light blue, dark blue, red, orange, and yellow.

The prostrated minion spoke in its guttural, stilted language.

What it said made H'Deesengar frown. "I do not care if a wizard lord protects the city. You must capture Anker, and you must do so quickly."

Twenty days had passed since his army first attacked the capital city of Kyranni. Four times, his horde had faced Kelluon and the city soldiers, failing each time. H'Deesengar had lost twenty thousand goblins in the process, including a hundred of those gifted with his magic. Worse, sixteen rock trolls had died. The big, stupid monsters were difficult to replace, each taking decades to gestate.

"Vezkalth!" he shouted.

A goblin with black skin hurried from the side of the temple, climbed the stairs, and knelt on one knee, head bowed. "Yes, Master?"

"How many can we send?"

Vezkalth replied, "A fresh clutch hatched thirteen days past, the largest yet – thirty thousand, hungry and ready for battle."

"And those that appear capable of accepting my gift?"

"I have chosen the three hundred most likely candidates."

The demon grinned, a sight likely to stir terror in any being present. "Send them in."

As Vezkalth rushed off, H'Deesengar leaned forward, speaking to the prostate shaman before him. "You will lead this force back to Kyranni and rejoin the main host."

"Yes, Master," the goblin said. "However, less than six thousand remain."

"What?"

"Some of my brethren decided to turn south, toward the land of Bal, in the hopes of finding easier quarry."

"How many?"

"Eight thousand. Ten at most."

The demon lord growled. "And what of the trolls?"

"The last four are in Kyranni with those that control them."

H'Deesengar sat back. "At least the trolls remain."

With the trolls, backed by magic and a timed assault of thirty-six thousand minions, the horde should be able to claim the city. *Kelluon is the key.* The wizard lord needed to die. *If only I could face him myself.*

The demon lord extended a hand, the energy field surrounding him shimmering when he touched it. Unlike centuries past, it gave when pushed, flexing but not breaking. He did not understand the nature of the magic holding him, but it was weakening. And he could guess at why.

Yes. Kelluon must die.

Vezkalth reappeared, a host of wide-eyed goblins following.

"Go and wait near the portal," the demon lord growled, the goblin shaman rising to its feet before scurrying away.

Vezkalth stopped before the throne and bowed, hundreds of goblins clustered on the stairs, fear in their eyes. "The candidates, Master."

"Stand aside, Vezkalth."

The black-skinned goblin moved to stand to the side of the throne, careful to remain outside the star on the floor. H'Deesengar stood and extended a hand, drawing in magic, the air above the goblins turning a dark purple. Slowly, he lowered his hand, the blanket of magic descending, the goblins inhaling the murky mist, eyes bulging, hands going to their throats. They began collapsing, bodies convulsing, kicking and squirming on the stairs before falling still. When the cloud of darkness cleared, two-thirds of the goblins lay dead, fewer than a hundred remaining upright.

Vezkalth whistled. Seven black-skinned goblins rushed into the room, each carrying an armful of necklaces made of dozens of human bones. They climbed the stairs and began slipping them over the heads of the newly enchanted goblins. By wearing the necklaces, those goblins would control a host assigned by blood. With their newfound magic, they would lead the army against mankind.

1

ALONE

Rhoa Sulikani climbed the steep stairs, opened the hatch, and emerged on the ship's deck. Wind blew, her hair and cloak fluttering wildly. She closed the hatch and turned toward the rail, spotting a lean form standing near the prow. With excellent balance honed from years of acrobatics training, she crossed the angled deck, the ship rising and falling as it cut through the waves. Spray burst over the starboard side each time the bow crashed down.

She drew close to the port side rail, slowing as she approached. He turned toward her, golden eyes measuring, platinum blond hair tied back in a tail, chiseled face like porcelain.

"You are welcome to join me, Rhoa Sulikani," Tygalas said.

She leaned against the rail, narrowing her eyes at the elf. "Every time I come on deck, I find you here."

"I have little love for tight spaces. The cabins below feel stifling, the wood bereft of life." He peered out over the water, the island of Rykestan on the southern horizon. "The sea is frightening, yet thrills me at the same time." He shook his head. "I never imagined how endless it would appear and how much energy it contained."

Rhoa thought back to their journey through the Frost Forest. While frozen beneath a layer of ice for centuries, the woods had been lifeless, lacking even birds. The return of the elves breathed life into the forest, transforming it into the lushest Rhoa had ever seen. Within the first day of travel, they had seen dozens of animals, ranging from squirrels to birds to deer. Where the creatures had come from, she had no idea. The fact they had appeared so quickly was astonishing.

After leaving the forest, they made the downhill trek to Growler's Rock, arriving late in the evening three long days after leaving the reborn elven city of Silvacris. During that time, Tygalas had changed, his easy-going manner shifting to something else.

"You have never before left your forest, have you?" Rhoa asked, realizing the truth.

He sighed. "I have not. I had no idea how difficult it would be. The disconnection from the trees, my people... I am incomplete."

"Do you regret joining us?"

The elf shook his head. "No. It is my burden to bear. Sometimes, duty can be the heaviest weight of all."

She put her hand on his, hoping to help him feel at ease. "We are thankful to have you with us."

He looked at their hands. "It is kind of you to say so, but I doubt everyone feels as you do."

Rhoa frowned. "What do you mean?"

Tygalas shook his head and turned away. "Never mind. Perhaps it is mere paranoia. After all, I have had little experience with humans...or dwarfs. Before you arrived, I had never seen either in my ninety-three years."

Ninety-three? Rhoa shook her head in wonder. The elf appeared no older than her own age of nineteen years. Then she realized she had missed a birthday.

Twenty, she corrected herself. *You are now twenty.*

Prior birthdays had been spent with the troupe members in Stanlin's menagerie. For ten years, those people had been her only family, and she suddenly missed them. A tear ran down her face. *Will I ever see them again?*

"Did I say something wrong?" Tygalas asked gently. "If so, I apologize. I know little of your ways."

"No." She wiped her cheek and chuckled. "It was just a painful memory."

He smiled. "If you would like to remain and talk for a while, I would welcome the company."

She returned the smile. "I would like that."

~

Rawkobon Kragmor huddled in the dark cabin, fists clenched on the table before him. Having no windows, only a thin slice of light seeped beneath the door. It was more than enough for his light-sensitive eyes to see the small room clearly, both bunks empty, as was the chair across from him, no different than two hours earlier.

The sound of laughter arose from the neighboring cabin, Brogan, Blythe, and Filk responding to something Lythagon said. The display of camaraderie taunted him, but he refused to investigate. *If they wanted my presence, they would find me.* Nobody ever had...except for Rhoa. Now, even she had left him alone.

Rawk had been inspired by Rhoa, making him wish to be something other than the outcast he had been most of his life. He was trying, but he had begun to wonder if it was too little, too late. Meanwhile, Algoron remained in their cabin, alone, often sleeping. His uncle seemed to have given up attempting to fit in with others, but Rawk had not. He just had no idea where to begin.

Footsteps pattered down the stairs and into the hold, the hatch thudding closed. The sound of steps continued down the hall and stopped outside the neighboring cabin. Rhoa's voice came through the door, followed by her laughter. The door opened, light invading, forcing Rawk to shield his eyes and blink as his vision adjusted. Rhoa fumbled with the enchanted lantern on the wall, azure light flaring to life, Rawk squinting. To her, the light was dim. To him, it was as bright as the sun.

When she saw him sitting there, Rhoa gasped, hand flying to her chest. "Rawk! You scared the blazes out of me. Why are you sitting in the dark in my cabin, alone?"

"Alone," he repeated. It was a nasty word, a hateful word, a word used far too often around him.

She closed the door. "Yes. Why are you in here? Is everything all right?"

"Where were you? I waited for hours."

Her brow furrowed. "I was on deck, speaking with Tygalas."

Rawk frowned. "The elf?"

"Yes." She sat across from him. "I do believe he is an elf."

Here was Rawk, sitting alone in the dark while she was with Tygalas. An ache settled in, one familiar yet foreign at the same time. Envious of others such as Lythagon and Filk, Rawk had long felt like an outsider among his own people. Now his envy twisted to jealousy, leaving a dark pit in his stomach, which filled with an ugliness he wished was not there.

"I am here now," Rhoa said softly. "Did you wish to talk about something?"

"I..." *Feel sick. Am sick.* He rubbed his eyes and stood. "I am tired and am going to bed. Perhaps we can talk tomorrow."

He left the room, closing the door behind him, his back to it while he stared at the floor. Laughter came from the door down the hall, the sound a dagger to his troubled soul. Sighing, he opened the door across the hall and entered the dark cabin he shared with Algoron.

2

ABDUCTED

J ace gasped, his back arching off the bed, muscles contracting, fists clenched at his sides. The moment passed, his body relaxing as his breathing calmed. He blinked, eyes opening to dark wood slats just above his face, illuminated by a pale blue aura. When he turned toward the light, he saw a pretty blonde standing beside him, her cerulean eyes filled with concern.

Narine.

His position was even with her head as he glanced around, the room small, dark, and made of wood. Another set of beds stood along the opposite wall, the upper bunk empty. Hadnoddon rested on one elbow in the lower one, the dwarf peering up at him.

A ship… I'm on a ship. His thoughts were muddled, memory fuzzy.

Then, sitting in a chair across the room, he saw Adyn, naked and bald, her skin the color of charcoal and covered with narrow lines, as if she had been constructed of strips of metal. On her arm was a golden circlet…

The Band of Amalgamation.

Memories flooded in – the mission to find the object of power, sneaking into Cor Meum, Lord Belzacanth's death, finding the Band in the Repository, the confrontation with Despaldi and his men. What occurred afterward, he could not recall.

"There you are," Narine crooned, a gentle smile on her face. She then raised her voice. "He is awake."

"Good. Now we can get to the bottom of this," Adyn said.

When Jace tried to sit up, he found his movements restricted. "Am I tied up?" he mumbled.

Narine tugged the blankets free, untucking them from his bunk. "Sorry. I didn't want you to fall if you woke abruptly, so Adyn and I tucked you in, securing your covers to hold you in place."

He swung his legs over the bed, placed his foot on the bottom bunk, then the floor, and stumbled to a knee. The cabin tilted, his head pounding. He winced, eyes focusing on the bed before him and what lay beneath it.

"Why are there broken pieces of wood stuffed under this bunk?"

Hadnoddon chucked. "That was Adyn's handiwork."

"Hush now," she warned.

The pieces consisted of stained spindles and sanded boards. *Furniture*, he thought. *Broken furniture*. More memories surfaced – boarding a ship, a cup of swoon, Adyn passing out and falling over the table, destroying it. It was the last thing he could recall.

Jace rubbed his temple, eyes narrowed. His head pounded, as if he had taken a beating. "I think we were drugged."

Hadnoddon snorted. "There is no *thinking* about it. Quiarre, the sailor who brought us on board, drugged us for sure."

"With you finally awake," Adyn said, "maybe they will explain why we were abducted and are bound for Hassakan."

"Hassakan?" Jace asked, shaking his head with a wince. "I am not going to Hassakan."

Narine extended a hand and helped him to his feet. "Let's hear what they have to say."

Jace recalled the end of the skirmish with Despaldi – Narine passing out, him carrying her down to the docks...

"Are you all right?" He rested a hand on her hip, partly to steady himself, partly because he wanted to touch her. "You fainted after we faced Despaldi and his men."

She smiled. "I am fine. I simply overexerted my magic and needed rest. Good thing, too, because I had to use it just to wake you."

"What about the others?" He glanced at Adyn, then Hadnoddon.

Hadnoddon said, "I was the first to wake. Adyn woke soon afterward. It took a while for Narine to respond, but you just kept on sleeping."

A knock sounded, the door opening before anyone could respond. A swarthy man wearing a turban stuck his head in, smile stretching across his face, teeth bright against his dark skin.

"Ahh. Mister Landish is awake. Excellent."

Jace stepped toward the door, his fists clenching. "You drugged us."

Adyn stood and placed a metal hand against Jace's chest. "While I understand your desire to punch this man, it will do no good."

Hadnoddon grunted. "We have already been through this. She had to stop me from pummeling him a few hours ago."

Jace turned to Adyn. "Since when are you the voice of reason?"

The woman's silvery eyes almost stared right through him before she replied. "Yes. In the past, I would have reacted with more emotion. Perhaps you have noticed... I have changed."

The alterations to her appearance were obvious, but he realized other changes may have taken place. A pang of guilt twisted his gut at his lack of concern for her.

"I'm sorry. Is there anything I can do?"

Adyn shook her head. "Don't be sorry." She lowered her hand and stepped back. "I have come to grips with it. In addition, I discovered a sense of calm inside me, the heat of my emotions now a simmer. It leaves my thinking less clouded."

Jace arched a brow at Narine, but she did not notice, instead staring at Adyn with obvious concern. He put his arm around her shoulders while turning toward the man at the door.

"All right, Quiarre. Why did you drug us? What is this about?"

The man bowed. "If you would come with me, all will be explained."

He led them down the narrow corridor and up the stairs, opening the hatch at the top. Bright sunlight streamed in, joined by the rush of the surf. Quiarre climbed out, Jace and the others following.

When he stepped on deck, Jace peered up at the sun, quickly deciding it was mid-day. A slow scan from horizon to horizon revealed nothing but sea in every direction.

"Where are we?" he asked.

Quiarre turned toward him as the others gathered. "We are two days out from Cor Cordium, somewhere between the Ghealdan coast and the island of Tiadd."

Before he could ask the next question, Quiarre strode toward the stern. Jace glanced at the others, Narine appearing apprehensive, Adyn's expression unreadable. Hadnoddon gave him a shrug and followed the first mate.

As he approached the rear of the ship, Quiarre waved to the woman at the wheel. Seeing a female steering the ship gave Jace pause. She was handsome with long, black hair, coppery skin, and brown eyes, wearing striking, unique clothing – black, wide-brimmed hat with a red feather that matched the bright tunic she wore beneath her black leather vest. Her skin-tight breeches were black, tall boots brown to match her belt. Much like Quiarre, a curved scimitar rested in the sheath on her hip. Eyes fixed on Jace, a smirk lifted her lips. She was tall for a woman, her body appearing lean and strong, despite being approximately ten years his senior.

Quiarre knocked on the door beneath the quarterdeck, waited for a breath, and entered. Jace and his companions ducked inside, the room dark, save for a small window at the far end. Along one wall sat a bed, cabinets above it. A table and chairs were positioned at the foot of the bed, and a long desk occupied the wall opposite, the desktop covered in maps. A man sat at the desk with a feathered pen in hand, scribbling notes into a journal.

When the door closed, the room darkened further, the man turning toward them. Wearing red and black robes, his skin was swarthy, eyes dark, hair black, with a black beard as thick as Hadnoddon's. The man wore an odd type of jewelry – a series of gold chains connected to a ruby bracelet at his wrist, the chains crossing the back of his hand to a ruby ring on his small finger.

Quiarre bowed. "I have delivered our guests as requested, Master Chandan."

Narine dismissed her worry for Jace, who now seemed himself, no apparent lingering effects of the drugs. Instead, she focused on the man named Chandan. His robes and bearing screamed wizard, but he held no magic, at least not at the moment. Still, she remained wary.

"You call us guests?" Jace snorted. "Unless things have changed, Hassakani do not drug their guests and hold them captive against their will."

Chandan chuckled in a deep voice. "How droll, Mister Landish. The notoriety of your sharp tongue competes with the outrageous nature of your exploits. I see such reputation is well-earned."

"How do you know my name?"

"You have been known to us for some time. More importantly, we now seek your services." He gestured toward the four chairs around the table. "Please, sit."

Jace grimaced at Narine.

She whispered, "It doesn't hurt to listen."

He nodded and pulled out a chair for her before seating himself. Hadnoddon joined them, while Adyn stared at the fourth chair.

"Will it hold my weight?" the bodyguard asked.

Chandan chuckled. "Yes. The Band of Amalgamation has changed your body, making it far more dense. However, the chair is new and well-made. I suspect it will hold."

Adyn sat carefully, the chair creaking but not breaking.

Narine narrowed her eyes, studying the man. *He knows about the Band and what it does.* Her wariness seemed to increase with each sentence he uttered.

"All right," Jace said. "Who are you, and what do you want with us?"

"Have you ever heard of the Order of Sol?"

Jace cast a questioning look at Narine. She shook her head, the name unfamiliar.

The man continued. "Most have not. You see, the Order is a secret society tasked with protecting the most dangerous of secrets."

I knew he was trouble, Narine thought.

"What sort of secrets?" Jace asked.

Chandan grinned. "The ever-curious thief. I am not surprised you wish to know."

"Now you are just trying to irritate me."

The big man laughed and sat forward. "The greatest secret of all is the Order itself. It exists everywhere, with agents hidden throughout every wizardom. Some appear poor, others wealthy. Some are wizards, others are not. You see, they watch and collect information, funneling each new discovery back to the brotherhood. Those discoveries deemed too dangerous are confiscated, and we do everything in our power to erase them from history."

He reached over to the desk and opened a drawer. From it, he removed a black book, the cover embossed in golden runes. It was immediately familiar.

Narine gasped. "You stole my book!"

Chandan waggled a finger at her. "Tsk, tsk, Princess. This was never yours. You stole it from the Seers, did you not?"

"How did you know?" Narine had not told anyone. She doubted Jace would have said anything. He'd been unconscious for the past two days.

"I told you, the Order is everywhere."

Hadnoddon growled at Narine, "You stole from the Seers?"

She shook her head. "We–"

Jace put his hand on Hadnoddon's arm. "Focus. We are not the enemy here."

"Neither are we," Chandan replied. The wizard looked down at the book in his hands and set it on the desk. "In stealing this, you actually did the Order a favor. The Seers should not have had it in the first place. Better for this particular secret to remain so."

Narine grew nervous and threw a worried glance at Jace. *What will they do to those who know about the contents?*

Chandan shook his head, as if reading her mind. "Don't worry, Princess. The constructs you and the thief have gleaned from the book will do little harm, unless you intend to share the information with others. Based on your recent history and the future awaiting you, I suspect it unlikely."

Narine bit her lip and collected her thoughts. Questions seemed to be mounting, so she sought to stem the tide. "You appear to be part of this Order of Sol. What does a secret society have to do with us?"

"Ahh…" Chandan nodded. "Now you are asking the right questions. Unfortunately, that particular answer must wait a bit longer."

Rolling his eyes, Jace asked, "What *can* you tell us?"

"I can tell you we are bound for Ryxx."

Narine sucked in a breath. "Whatever for?"

"You have heard of it."

"Yes. It's an island off the coast of Hassakan…an island run by pirates."

While at the University, Narine had studied Hassakan and its cities. The history of Ryxx was filled with turmoil, the other wizardoms choosing to avoid the waters near the island, treating it as if it were part of the Shoals. Nobody, other than pirates, dared to sail into the Shoals.

Chandan shrugged. "More or less."

She crossed her arms. "It is reputed to be a nasty place, visitors likely to be robbed or murdered."

"A well-earned reputation."

Jace asked, "Why Ryxx? Why us?"

"You and your companions' skills are required, Mister Landish." He sat forward. "You are going to execute a mission for the Order. Once complete, you will receive all the answers you wish, perhaps including those to questions you have yet to comprehend. Besides, the Order can offer the princess the opportunity to recover the secret of the eighth family of constructs."

Narine's brow furrowed. "There are only six major constructs." She had trained in each type, memorizing them to perfection.

Chandan laughed. "Did you forget?" He reached over and lifted the book of magic from the desk. "In these pages, you discovered the construct of augmentation, the seventh major construct."

Narine and Jace had only tested two of the augmentations, but both had worked brilliantly. "Fair point. What of this eighth construct? What is it?" She could not keep the eagerness from her voice.

"Oh, no. Not yet, Princess. The lot of you have a task to complete before further answers can be shared."

"Which is?" She really wanted to know about the eighth construct.

"You must rescue someone held captive by High Wizard Kalzan."

Jace shook his head. "While I am sure Narine is eager to discover a new use of magic, it is hardly worth risking our lives just to save someone we do not know."

"Ahh. You require additional motivation." Chandan leaned forward again, grinning. "You see, the person held captive is the sister of Sarazan, Wizard Lord of Hassakan."

Narine inhaled sharply. "Princess Sariza?"

Over two years had passed since she had seen Sariza. When the elder princess had graduated from the University, Narine had lost her only friend from the school. Sadly, it was not until Sariza's final year that they grew close.

The man turned to her. "Yes. We are aware of your relationship with Sariza. If Mister Landish does not free your friend, she will meet a dire fate."

Jace sat back, considering the situation. "Why us? Couldn't Sarazan just send the Redwing Guard or the Crimson Knights in to save her?"

"He could, but not without destroying his treaty with Ryxx."

He narrowed his eyes. "Why? What terms would protect Kalzon?"

"When Sarazan claimed the throne six years ago, he did so as the only applicant, even though Kalzan held a stronger position and was deemed more likely to rise to wizard lord."

Narine could not imagine a powerful wizard conceding the throne to another, discarding the chance to wield the magic of a god. "Why would Kalzan allow it?"

"In exchange for Kalzan removing his name as an applicant, Sarazan promised his sister's hand on her twenty-fifth birthday. Should the wizard lord break his promise, every pirate on Ryxx would rebel against Sarazan, certain to attack any ship flying Hassakani colors, as well as those bound for ports of the wizardom."

3

POTENTIAL

From beneath the shade of a canopy, Priella Ueordlin stared out over the rolling hills of Farrowen. Brown patches of plowed fields and copses of trees interrupted the plains of yellow grass that stretched off into the distance. A ribbon of gray ran east, the stone roadway meandering around trees and between farms until it was obscured by the rays of the rising sun. Infantry marched along the road, six thousand of Pallanar's finest and a thousand Farrowen soldiers, all bound for Orenth. When the rumble of horses came from the city, Priella stepped out into the sunlight to see who approached.

A few dozen Midnight Guard rode toward camp, or what remained of it. All tents had been struck, save for her own, wagons and horses prepared for travel. Four hundred Pallanese Cavalry remained, equal to the number Lord Thurvin was to send with her. The commitment would leave Marquithe with six hundred guards to hold the city should the need arise.

A train of wagons followed the Farrowen Cavalry. Rather than stop at the camp, they continued, many soldiers staring in Priella's direction as they rode past. She read expressions ranging from determination to resentment. However, none would dare cross her or her new slave. Not with her magic, and certainly not with his.

She smiled. *Thurvin is no longer even aware of how I am manipulating him.*

At the start, capturing one's mind was akin to a brutal assault, dominating their will and forcing them to comply. Over time, she had discovered her subjects no longer fighting her control. She was careful to remain subtle while planting ideas to align their ambitions with her own, the subjects acting of their own free will but according to her agenda. *Compulsion*, she thought. *With it, I could claim the world as my own.* The idea of every person among the Eight Wizardoms worshiping her, loving her, adoring her... It was tremendously alluring.

She thought of her mother and the men from the Illustan Wizard's Council. The influence she levied upon each of them had waned over time due to the strength of their magic, and Lord Thurvin was vastly more powerful.

I must watch him closely.

A horse trotted off the road and settled just strides from her tent, while the cavalry and trailing supply wagons continued north. The rider wore Midnight Guard armor, his dark blue cape draped behind his saddle. A star embossed on his breastplate marked him as a captain. He pulled his helmet off and rubbed a hand over his shorn scalp. Priella recalled Thurvin talking to the man the prior evening.

Quiam. His name is Quiam.

"Greetings, Your Majesty." He had a round head and thick, black mustache.

Priella nodded. "Captain Quiam." She intentionally used his name. Her father had always taught her to file names away. His voice echoed in her head *"Citizens or soldiers, it does not matter. All are more likely to remain loyal if you recall his or her name."* She frowned, noting a missing figure. "Where is Lord Thurvin?"

"He remains at the palace, resolving some last-minute issues."

Priella pressed her lips together, ire stirring. "You are to ride ahead?"

"Yes. I am to escort our forces and organize camp this evening." He gestured toward a covered wagon amid the others. "I am also to protect the Throne of Farrow."

"So, he was successful in removing it." She allowed a smile. At least something had gone as planned.

"It was an amazing sight to witness..." Quiam stared at the covered wagon as he spoke. "To see Thurvin float through the air on a throne made of crystal..." He shook his head. "When the morning sunlight shone upon the object, it appeared like a glowing block of ice. The throne is a thing of beauty and wonder, never before seen by any save for past wizard lords." His voice was thick with awe.

"I suggest you ensure nobody touch the throne, Captain."

He turned toward her. "As per Lord Thurvin's orders."

"I ordered the same thing among my army. Yet one wagon driver could not resist the temptation."

"I assume you punished the man."

She shook her head. "There was no need. One touch vaporized him, only a smoldering pile of clothing remaining."

Quiam's face grew pale. "I...see." He slipped his helmet over his head. "I had best be off. I will report when we gather at camp tonight."

"Safe travels, Captain."

When the man reined his horse around and rode off, Priella spun and crossed the trampled grass, heading toward the waiting carriage. Bosinger Aeduant stood beside it, conversing with the driver. Six feet tall with a muscular build, a sword on one hip, dagger on the other, his armor a blend of leather and metal plates, one might assume him to be nearly as lethal as he was in reality.

As her personal bodyguard, Bosinger's intense gaze fixed on Priella as she approached. He always seemed to be watching her, his hand never far from one hilt or the other. She suddenly realized she had never seen him without weapons or armor, despite knowing him for most of her life.

"Bosinger," she said as she approached. "I need to return to the palace."

He grunted. "By carriage?"

"Send the carriage ahead. We can ride on horseback. It will be easier to catch up to the army once we leave the city."

The bodyguard whistled, a shrill sound drawing the attention of a man standing beside six horses munching on long grass. Relecan had been horse-master for Priella's father for as long as she could recall. The man had insisted on joining the campaign, promising to personally care for her horses, as well as her carriage.

Bosinger held up two fingers, and Relecan nodded. He gathered the reins and led two horses over.

The horsemaster bowed. "Your mounts, My Queen."

"Thank you, Relecan," she replied and climbed into the saddle. "You and my carriage may depart. I will see you at camp tonight."

He handed her the reins, while Bosinger climbed into the other saddle. "Yes, My Queen."

Without waiting, Priella turned her mount toward the city and kicked the horse into a trot. The bodyguard rode at her side, eyes narrowed, his free hand on his thigh, just inches from the hilt at his hip. They passed through the gate unchallenged, the guards on duty watching them but saying nothing.

Do they understand their wizard lord has plead fealty to me? Does that guarantee their loyalty? I must remain wary of betrayal, she reminded herself. With her newfound abilities, it was easy to believe she was invincible. *Pherelyn thought so, as well.*

The city seemed unaffected by the prospects of war. Farmers selling produce, shopkeepers peddling wares, citizens with coin to spend milling around, all appearing as if nothing of import had occurred. *Why would they care? The war is occurring on foreign lands rather than coming to their own front door.*

Her thoughts then shifted to the various pieces on the gameboard and their movements.

The Pallanese force – Gleam Guard elites, cavalry, general infantry – now marched toward the Orenthian border, joined by the Marquithe Midnight Guard. Additional Pallanese forces had sailed from Norstan and Severan, bound for Fralyn. It was a long journey, those coming from Norstan likely to be on the water for nearly three weeks. Half of that time had already passed. Those ships would arrive before the main force, unless she could find a means to take Tiamalyn and Yor's Point quickly.

They reached the palace and, again, entered the gates unchallenged. Rather than head to the stables, she led Bosinger straight to the door nearest the throne room and dismounted.

Priella approached the guard standing outside the door. "Watch our horses. If anything should happen to them, your life will be forfeit."

The man's eyes widened, jaw working but no sound coming out. She continued past him before he could form a reply.

Inside, they followed a short corridor connecting to the receiving hall and headed straight toward the closed doors of the throne room.

"Your Majesty," said a guard beside the door. "Lord Thurvin is inside. He said you, alone, would be allowed to interrupt."

"Good, because I intend to do so." Priella waited while Bosinger opened the door.

"Your bodyguard must remain out here," the guard said.

"He goes where I go." She walked past Bosinger and down the aisle.

Thurvin sat upon his throne, in conversation with a small man dressed in dark clothing. The man stopped talking and looked over his shoulder. His dark hair was a mess, smudges on his hands and face making him appear as if he had not washed for weeks. He scrutinized Priella with narrowed eyes, his big nose hooking over a dark mustache.

Similar to the other man, the wizard lord was small of stature with a mustache and shoulder-length brown hair. Middle-aged with squinty eyes and a stern frown, few would call Thurvin Arnolle attractive. None of that mattered, for his magic was what made him useful. Still, why did he not comply with her wishes?

Thurvin, dressed in robes of midnight blue with patterns of silver on the cuffs and collar, sat back and smiled. "Ah, Queen Priella. I am glad you decided to join us. Meet Jezeron, the head of my information network."

"Sire!" Jezeron said, aghast. "Is it wise to reveal my role?"

Thurvin frowned. "I…"

Sensing his hesitation, Priella sought to redirect his thoughts. "The army marches. Were you not supposed to depart with them?"

"Yes. But I needed to ensure information continues to flow toward me while I am away." His scowl relaxed. "In fact, Jezeron just disclosed some rather pleasant news."

"Do tell."

"Another wizard lord had died."

Another one? Priella thought about those who had recently passed – Taladain, Malvorian, and her own father, Raskor. To lose three in a decade was unprecedented. *But now four in two seasons?*

"Who?"

"Horus."

Careful to maintain a stoic exterior, she marveled at her luck. "The throne of Orenth sits unclaimed?"

"Yes." Thurvin rubbed his hands together. "By my hand."

Her eyes narrowed. "How so?"

"Assassins, of course."

"You expect me to believe ordinary men could kill a wizard lord?"

He grinned. "Oh, they are not ordinary."

"Explain?"

"Ahh." The wizard lord wagged his finger. "Not all secrets are ripe for sharing."

I am losing him, Priella thought. She embraced her magic and roared, "Out! Jezeron, Bosinger, I wish to speak with Lord Thurvin alone." Her angry tone left no room for negotiation.

Jezeron's narrowed eyes flicked from Priella to Thurvin, but he did not move until the man on the throne nodded. As Bosinger escorted the man from the room, Priella pictured the construct she wished to cast. The door closed, leaving the two of them alone. She stepped upon the dais, Thurvin tensing but not yet drawing upon his magic, she still holding on to hers.

If I can just touch him, she thought.

"I am impressed, Lord Thurvin," she crooned.

"What do you mean?"

Priella took a step closer, a finger trailing down her neck, toward the deep neckline of her dress. "By eliminating Horus, you have made our goal easier to attain."

She placed her hand on the arm of the throne, her fingers mere inches from his. The man's eyes followed her other hand as it traced past her collarbone and down the gap between her breasts, his gaze filled with longing.

Priella lowered her voice to a whisper. "I must know. How could ungifted assassins kill a wizard lord?" She leaned forward while sliding the hand on the throne arm closer, fingers touching his as the construct materialized, her magic flowing into him, easing his worries.

You have nothing to fear from me, Lord Thurvin. Everything you ever desired will come true by following my wishes.

The man swallowed visibly, staring down the front of her dress, oblivious to her coercion. "Yes… You see, I have discovered how to gift others with magical abilities, changing ordinary soldiers into lethal weapons."

She planted one last seed into his mind, hoping to solidify his loyalty. If needed, she would take physical action to seal his fate, but only as a last resort. At twenty-four, she remained a virgin, and the thought of him being her first sickened her.

Stepping back, Priella narrowed her eyes, turning his statement over in her head. "I mastered all constructs taught at the University. None pertain to gifting others magical abilities."

He smiled. "This is a new discovery called augmentation. I found these new constructs in a journal and gifted five of my best soldiers with a unique type of magic, enabling me to extend my abilities beyond Marquithe.

"These men were to confront Horus with a coordinated attack. None would suspect unarmed, non-wizards to have such abilities. Apparently, the surprise assault worked, for Horus is dead, the emerald flames in the Tiamalyn Tower of Devotion now dormant."

She considered the revelation and wondered how she might use it to further her objectives. *I need him to give me the book.* "I saw your throne leave the city. I trust you had no difficulty removing it."

He grinned. "Once you described how, the execution was child's play. I must thank you for freeing me from the prison I had crafted for myself."

"It was the same prison occupied by all wizard lords before you. However, your magic is no longer bound to Marquithe. You no longer have need for this journal you describe. Perhaps you could gift it to me to study?"

Thurvin nodded. "Very well. It is in my chamber." He rose from the throne. "As you say, I no longer have need of it. Besides, with Horus dead, I will soon wield the magic of a third god."

"You intend to claim Tiamalyn as your own?"

Stepping off the dais, he headed to the back of the room with her at his side. "The plan is already in motion. A week past, I sent a pair of men to take the tower and convert it to Farrow." They stepped on the lift. Thurvin embraced his magic, the lift rising. "If successful, my power will rise once again, fed by the prayers of another great city."

Priella considered his scheme and how it fit with hers. His magic was to be her tool, a powerful weapon to wield, placing him in danger while she operated from a distance. *Three wizardoms' worth of magic should suffice.*

"Very well," she said as the throne room faded from view, obscured by stone blocks. "You shall claim the cities of Orenth, save Grakal. It is too remote and too small to trifle with. However, when we conquer the cities of Balmoria, those prayers belong to me."

"As you wish."

"Soon, we will both possess everything we wish."

The lift stopped and they climbed off, heading down the corridor, toward Lord Thurvin's chambers.

In a musing tone, Thurvin said, "Since taking the throne, I have been bound to Marquithe – trapped with no means to escape." He paused outside his door, turning toward her. "With my throne mobilized and my bonds removed, I have never been so excited to travel."

She allowed a smile. "I am happy to have you join my expedition."

The man grinned while making a fist, knuckles turning white. "At last, the world will understand the expanse of my might."

"Speaking of the world, how soon do you think you will acquire the Tiamalyn Tower of Devotion?"

He opened the door and led her inside. "The men I sent to claim it are resourceful, but such things take time. In this case, they are to take it with guile. Why send an army to take the entire city when all I need is the tower?"

Priella nodded in agreement. "Fair point."

"If nothing has occurred when we reach Orenth, I will lead a contingent to claim the tower myself."

She followed him into his study. "Very well. Just remember, the Darkening approaches. We cannot risk another wizard claiming the throne."

Thurvin stopped at his desk and picked up a black book, his hand running over the cover, eyes staring into the distance. "That throne will remain vacant for centuries. Those prayers are mine, and when their magic feeds my own, I will be unstoppable." He held the book toward her. "Take it. As you said, I have no use for such things any longer, not when I can crush armies with my magic alone."

He left the room with her holding the book, wondering if she could maintain control over him when his power reached its full potential.

4

RECONNAISSANCE

The pale light of the full moon illuminated the plaza outside Tiamalyn Palace. From the shadowy recess of a doorway, Lieutenant Trey Garvin watched as a pair of guards marched along the palace outer wall and turned at the corner, the sound of their footsteps fading. Another pair of guards on patrol passed the palace gate, nodding to companions stationed there, and continued onward.

Movement appeared at the top of the wall, a dark silhouette moving in a crouch. The thin line of a rope dropped down, followed by the man lowering himself, hand-over-hand, to the ground. Grabbing the rope above him, the thief gave it a tug, a ripple running upward. He repeated the motion until the top end broke free, the grappling hook at the end sailing through the air.

Catch it, Garvin thought, imagining the noise of the hook landing on the brick-paved street. *You need to catch it.*

The thief darted into the street, arms outstretched, chasing after the falling metal hook. Too slow or too late, it did not matter, Garvin's fear coming to fruition.

The hook struck the ground, the metal-on-stone clatter echoing in the night. The patrolling guards stopped and spun around, pausing briefly before they burst into a run. Around the corner, the intruder scooped up the grappling hook and dashed across the open space, heading toward the nearest cross-street while reeling in the trailing rope. Garvin's eyes flicked from the two soldiers to the fleeing man, measuring the distance. It would be close.

Just as the two soldiers rounded the corner, the other man disappeared into the shadows. The guards stopped, gazes sweeping the area between the palace wall and the nearest buildings two hundred feet away. The night fell quiet, neither moving for a few moments. Each pointing in a different direction, the guards argued, voices muffled by the distance. After a brief conversation, they resumed their patrol.

With the men's backs to him, Garvin emerged from the shadows and walked down a street lined by enchanted lanterns. His gaze settled on the massive building at the end marking the center of Highmount, the upper portion of Tiamalyn. The Bowl of Oren was an easy landmark to note. The five-story-tall, circular structure was impressive, even when cloaked in shadows.

Minutes later, he reached the arena and circled it, the tall, white columns along the exterior painted a pale blue by the moonlight. Three days a week, gladiators battled against one another for the entertainment of the wealthy. The next duels were to occur tomorrow. Garvin had attended a handful of those events over the past week and found them mildly entertaining. While brutal and bloody, the gladiator fights lacked the raw, frenetic nature of a true battle. In his experience, it was rare for one-on-one fights to occur in the real world, and certainly none lasting as long as the arena duels. What interested him more were the stories repeatedly told in the city – tales of a small thief with superior speed and guile who defeated eight seasoned gladiators. The citizens were convinced the man had been blessed by Oren himself, gifted with some sort of magic to prove his innocence against the charges he faced. The only subject discussed as often in Tiamalyn was conjecture surrounding the recent death of Orenth's ruler, Lord Horus. Garvin wanted to know...*needed* to know the truth behind the wizard lord's demise.

He reached a corner, headed down another street, and ducked into the fifth building on the left.

The inn was quiet, tables empty, the barmaid and owner busy cleaning. Both glanced up at him and returned to their business, used to his comings and goings at odd hours. He climbed the stairs to the third floor and returned to his room at the end of the hallway. Unlocking the door, he opened it just as a man slipped in through the window.

Garvin shut the door, locking it. "That was sloppy."

Rindle slipped the coil of rope off his shoulder and tossed it onto his bed, the grappling hook bouncing before it settled. "I didn't expect the hook to sail quite so far from the wall."

"You had *some* luck. The guards gave up quickly, likely deciding the noise was nothing of concern."

"That's good." Rindle sat on his bed with a sigh and began pulling off his boots. "I believe I have a means for us to reach the tower."

"Even better," Garvin said as he removed his coat. "Explain."

"I was able to reach the palace roof. The tower stands no more than a hundred feet above it. The walls are impossible to scale, and the lift is out of the question, but if we can get a ballista and rope to the roof, I believe we can climb up."

Brow arched, Garvin replied, "A ballista? How are we going to get something so big into the palace and up to the roof?"

"That is the trick." Rindle stretched his toes, now free of the boots. "I have a plan for that, as well. It involves the Bowl of Oren. We will need to do some reconnaissance tomorrow before we can lay out the full plan. We will then procure the necessary equipment and should be able to complete the mission two days later, after the final bouts of the week."

With a sigh, Garvin sat on his bed. "Three more days." Having lived the life of a soldier for half his life, he had learned the value of patience. Still, he longed to be free of the gem, to shed the yoke of duty he no longer wished to wear.

"I learned something else of note," Rindle said.

"Which is?"

"A man survived the attack that killed Lord Horus. He was there, saw everything."

Garvin leaned forward, gaze intense. "Who? I would like to question this man."

The thief shook his head. "You aren't going to like it much."

"Just spit it out."

"Apparently, Chancellor Kylar Mor, a powerful wizard, interrupted the assassins but paid a price in the process. Word among palace staff is the man can no longer use his magic."

"That's good. We will track him down and question him without worry."

"Not quite. From what I heard, the wizard has gone mad. He is seldom coherent, often babbling nonsense and drooling like a babe fresh from the teat."

Garvin frowned. "That is not ideal. Still, he might have answers. I must know."

"Perhaps we should plan a visit."

"Yes." Garvin nodded. "But not until we complete our mission. Once the tower has been claimed, I will have fulfilled my duty. We can then track down Mor, get some answers, and decide on our next step."

"You are sure? This is the end of it?" Rindle asked in a soft voice.

Garvin dug into the pack beneath his bed and pulled out a sapphire the size of his fist. Twisting it in the light, he glared at his burden, eager to be free of it. "Lord Thurvin has the other gems. He can find someone else to claim other towers. Once we replace the emerald in the tower with this sapphire, we shall disappear. He will get what he wishes and should quickly forget about us."

"Then what?"

Do I pursue Despaldi? Should I return to The Fractured Lands? Could I just become a thief like Rindle? Garvin had never given much thought to life outside the military.

"We shall see what the future holds."

5

ARRIVAL

Brogan Reisner waved at the four soldiers beside the gates to Illustan, his mouth turning down into a frown after passing them. Each was obviously older than his own forty-two years, two of them gray and wrinkled. It struck him as an odd sight, for gate duty usually fell to younger soldiers. His gaze flicked up to the Tower of Devotion above the hilltop palace. The ice-blue flame burned once again, but something about it seemed off, the fire a flat ring without the usual sparkle.

Blythe walked beside him, her expression determined, her golden eyes – eyes of another person from another race – focused on something unseen. The Arc of Radiance was slung over her shoulder, the bow shimmering with a golden aura. It was somehow now a part of her. While the woman had changed, he still loved her...always would, even if she eventually realized just how big a mess he truly was.

To his other side was Tygalas, the newest member of their party. The hood of his cloak covered his head, the cloth hiding his pointed ears, shadows obscuring his almond-shaped, golden eyes. The elf gripped a staff of golden wood in his hand, the butt thumping against the street with each stride.

Rhoa, Rawk, and Algoron trailed behind them, none of the three standing taller than five feet – Rhoa lean and athletic, the two dwarfs, stout and thickly muscled. Despite her small stature, Rhoa had proven herself a feisty and loyal companion. Similarly, Rawk and Algoron had Brogan's full trust, the two stone-shapers quiet and reliable. The pair of dwarfs at the rear were another story. Yes, they had proven they could fight, but Lythagon and Filk were anything but quiet. The pair joked and made inappropriate comments as if unaware of the people around them.

The streets were covered in shadow, citizens strolling in all directions, heads down, thoughts seemingly elsewhere. They crossed the central square, which was occupied by carts and wagons, farmers and merchants packing up their wares. All seemed normal, but somehow subdued.

After the square, the streets became an incline, rising to homes built on the hillside below the palace. Eventually, those streets ended at a staircase heading up in a series of switchbacks. The climb was long, the stairs taking them past Parwick's Den, noise from the gathering crowd coming from within. The sound of laughter tugged on Brogan. Many years ago, Parwick's had been a favorite haunt, a place of fond memories. Two decades had passed since he had last visited the taproom.

I miss you still, Rictor. Thoughts of the prince, once his best friend, stirred the well of regret he had tried to bury.

"You are scowling again," Blythe noted.

He gave her a sad smile. "Memories. This place holds many. Most are fond, yet somehow poisoned."

Rather than chastise him, she took his hand, the two finishing the climb together in a silent connection.

They strode across the road, toward the palace gates. Nearing, Brogan's scowl deepened.

Two overweight soldiers converged to block their progress. "Greetings," one said in a grizzled voice. "What business do you have at the palace?"

Brogan narrowed his eyes. "Orvan?"

The man stepped closer, peering at him, recognition flashing in his gaze. The stubble on his face was gray, lines marking his advancing age, but it was him. "Brogan Reisner? I haven't seen you in…"

"Twenty years."

The man pulled his helmet off and ran his hand through his thinning hair. "So long?" He shook his head. "I lose track of years. By the gods, it has been a decade since I last wore this armor."

"Why are you working the gate anyway?"

"Someone has to."

"Where are the other guards?"

"Gone. Every soldier who could march has left the city."

Brogan looked at Blythe, her eyes reflecting concern, then turned back to the guard. "Gone where? Why?"

Orvan slid his helmet back on. "I cannot say. It is not my place to share such information."

Frustrated, Brogan was about to push the subject when Blythe interrupted. "The tower flame burns again. Who is the new wizard lord?"

The old man smiled. "You don't know about our new queen?"

"New queen?" Brogan asked. "What of Ariella?"

"Oh, she is still here."

"Can we speak with her?" Rhoa asked. "We have returned from a mission on her behalf."

The man shrugged. "I can escort you inside and send her a message, but it is up to Ariella to decide."

Brogan nodded. "Fair enough."

Orvan spoke to the other two guards before leading them through the gate, the man moving at a methodical pace, walking with a noticeable limp. Once inside, he sent a page to inform Ariella of their arrival. Uncomfortable minutes passed, the group standing quietly, the old man leaning against the wall, seeming as if he were about to fall asleep. When the page finally returned and agreed to lead them to Ariella's room, Brogan sighed in relief.

The young page led them up the stairs and down a corridor, past the room Brogan was expecting. At a door across the hall, he knocked. Moments later, Ariella opened the door, gray-streaked blonde hair piled on her head, no crown visible. She wore a simple, pale blue dress with white lace and ruffles. Her face broke into a smile, eyes filled with relief.

She burst forward and hugged Brogan, squeezing him tightly, her head buried in his shoulder. He held her gently, unsure of what to say. Blythe rubbed the queen's back, eyes pained. After a minute, Ariella stepped back and wiped her eyes.

"You must excuse me. These past few weeks have been difficult and... I had not expected to see you again." She backed away, smoothing her dress. "Please. Come in."

While luxurious, the chamber was less than half the size of the one Ariella had shared with her husband. Brogan's thoughts shifted to his last days spent with Raskor. *At least Raskor had found it in his heart to forgive me before he died*. There was a time Brogan had seen the Wizard Lord of Pallanar as a father-figure. Being banished had crushed Brogan's soul, or what remained of it after Rictor's murder. The following years were filled with dark moments and even darker thoughts.

Blythe squeezed his hand, drawing his attention. He turned his scowl into a smile and entered the room. The others filtered in, Blythe and Rhoa each hugging Ariella, the dwarfs appearing uncomfortable, their gazes elsewhere. Tygalas was more difficult to read, his head still shadowed by the hood of his cloak.

Ariella stared at Blythe, brows furrowed. "What happened to your eyes?"

"It is a long story, one that can wait," Blythe replied before introducing Lythagon, Filk, and Tygalas.

Ariella gasped when the elf lowered his hood.

"Yes," Brogan said. "He is an elf…a Silvan. However, the stories do them injustice. We discovered that the Cultivators are, in fact, elves. During our stay in their forest, it was clear they do not trust humans, but I also saw little evidence of them eating human babies."

"*What*?" Tygalas exclaimed, his face twisting in disgust. "That's revolting. Why would anyone invent such a monstrous tale?"

Lythagon and Filk both laughed, drawing a frown from the elf.

Blythe placed a hand on Tygalas' shoulder. "From what I can tell, both of our peoples have a misconception of the other. Perhaps we can help to change those perceptions for the better."

He nodded. "Yes. I would like that."

Blythe turned toward Ariella. "You appear tired, My Queen. Perhaps we should sit." She took Ariella by the hand and led her to the sofa, the two of them sitting.

Brogan stood in front of the two women, his gaze going out the window and to the pale blue fire at the top of the tower. "The flame of Pallan burns once again. Who is our new wizard lord?"

A cloud came over Ariella's features, the light in her blue eyes dimming, the lines on her face deepening. "Much has occurred since we last spoke. I fear what the future holds."

He knelt before her, taking her hand. "Please, tell us what has happened."

Her eyes were downcast as she spoke. "Shortly after your departure, my daughter returned from the University."

"Priella," Brogan said, recalling her as a red-haired toddler. Over twenty years had passed since then. "How is she?"

"She changed during her time in Tiadd. The curse…" Ariella raised her head and gazed into Brogan's eyes. The curse was something he knew well, a thing he had endured for decades. A burden he and Priella understood unlike anyone else. "Since Serranan's death, her life has been difficult. The people blamed her for our family's troubles, bitterness cooling her heart and hardening her exterior. Her stay at the University only made it worse, her self-isolation while harboring a hatred for the world around her. Worse, I blame myself for not protecting her, not forcing the citizens of Pallanar to cease the rumors, to set aside their superstitions rather than blaming a little girl for the troubles of a wizardom." A profound sadness seemed to have seated deep inside Ariella. "I am to blame for what has come to pass."

Brogan wished to tell her she was wrong, to stop blaming herself, but he could not say the words…not when they were lies. Regret was something he understood too well. *How can I pretend to help when I have yet to resolve my own regrets?* Instead, he focused on the present.

"What happened?"

Ariella sighed, looking down at the floor once again. "Against my wishes, and those of the Council of Wizards, Priella used guile to place herself among the applicants at the Darkening ceremony. Worse, Pallan chose her." She lifted her gaze. "He chose a woman to gift his power. Priella is now Queen of Pallanar."

Chills ran down Brogan's spine and left him unable to speak, able only to think of Pherelyn.

Ariella continued, tears tracking down her face. "She wields magic long forbidden and has forced her people to love her, our wizardom's leaders to bend to her will. Even now, she marches north with our armies, intent on conquering the world."

6

FUNNER

With dusk upon Illustan, enchanted lanterns lit the streets, the walls glowing like ghosts as the western sky grew darker. From a warm chamber in the palace overlooking the city, Brogan stared out the window and wondered if the world had gone mad. Over recent weeks, his peaceful existence had been turned upside down, and he feared the next surprise awaiting them.

The door opened, Blythe and Rhoa entering. The latter headed off to the adjoining chamber, while Blythe settled on the bed with a sigh.

"After much consoling and some hot tea, the queen has fallen asleep," she said. "I just hope she remains so until morning. I fear she has slept little as of late." She looked up at Brogan. "Did you notice her hair? I am positive it had less gray when we left Illustan, which was only five weeks ago."

He shrugged. "I couldn't tell you. I am not one to ask about such things."

At a knock on the door, Brogan crossed the room and pulled it open.

"Hello, Brogan." Lythagon glanced at the dwarf standing beside him. "Filk and I spotted a tavern as we approached the palace. With all that has happened, we thought a night out might be in order."

Brogan nodded. "Yeah. Parwick's Den. It's a good place to spend an evening."

Filk grinned, his teeth white amid his thick, black beard. "Would you join us?"

"I…" Brogan turned back toward Blythe in the hopes of her giving him an excuse to say no.

She smiled at the dwarfs. "He would love to."

Brogan glared at her, hoping she would get the message. She did not.

Blythe stood and strolled to the door. "You two go on down to the entry hall and wait. Brogan will be along soon."

"Brilliant!" Lythagon said, the two smiling dwarfs walking down the corridor as Blythe closed the door.

He turned toward her. "Why did you tell them I would join them?"

"Because you need a diversion."

"I don't want a diversion. I just want to sit here and–"

She gripped his coat and pulled him toward her. "You need to stop thinking about the past, while also taking a break from the troubles of today." With another tug, she brought his face to hers, their lips meeting in a quick kiss. She released him, straightening his coat while giving him a smile. "Go have a few drinks with those two boys. Who knows? You might even have fun if you allow it to happen."

He frowned. "What about you?"

Blythe glanced at the adjoining room. "I will be with Rhoa. There are times women prefer to be alone with other women." Her gaze shifted back to him. "As you know, there has been little chance of that over the recent weeks."

"Very well."

He fished for his coin pouch. It jingled, but he could not have much more than a silver remaining. It was among the reasons they had chosen to sail to Illustan, lacking funds to go much farther.

Blythe patted his cheek. "Go on and spend it. Ariella promised us funds and a ship. We will leave in two days. Until then, enjoy yourself."

Brogan opened the door, and she shooed him out into the corridor. "Why do I feel like you are trying to get rid of me?"

"Because I am. I will see you in a few hours." She smiled. "Don't worry. I will be here waiting for you."

Blythe Dugaart closed the door, the room falling quiet, Brogan's heavy steps fading down the corridor. Her heart was overjoyed to have his affection after so many years of wishing for more than friendship. However, she was concerned. His dark moods seemed less common as of late, but the pain of his past lingered and seemed at its worst when he was in Illustan.

I did the right thing, she told herself. *Those two dwarfs are unlikely to let him brood, and that is worth a night apart.*

She crossed the room and knocked on the door to Rhoa's chamber.

"Who is it?" Rhoa's voice came from inside.

"It's me. May I come in?"

"Yes."

Blythe opened the door just in time to glimpse the black book Rhoa stuffed beneath her pillow.

The petite, copper-skinned woman sat on the bed, her leather coat off, wearing a burnt orange tunic. Her dark hair was wet at the front, water droplets visible on her shirt. A washbasin, soap, and towel rested on the table along the wall. Other than the bed and table, a wooden chair was the only other furniture in the small room. Blythe pulled up the chair and sat across from Rhoa.

The younger woman's brow furrowed, her dark eyes questioning.

"It is time we talked," Blythe said.

"All right...," Rhoa replied carefully. "About?"

"About your secrets. Keeping them is unhealthy, and I worry about you."

Rhoa swallowed. "What secrets?"

"Let's begin with the journal."

The acrobat's gaze flicked toward her pillow.

"Yes. *That* journal."

Rhoa sighed. "I haven't even read the entire thing. Not yet. It...was Salvon's."

Blythe nodded. "I suspected as much. He was clearly fond of you."

Her face turned red as she snarled, "He *betrayed* me!"

"What do you mean?"

Rhoa pulled the book from beneath the pillow and placed it in her lap, looking down at it. "Ten years ago, my parents were taken from me, selected in the lottery as sacrifices for the Darkening in Fastella. But he made it happen."

Blythe frowned. "How?"

"I'm not completely sure, but his journal says..." A tear trickled down her face. "The old man intended for it to happen. He wanted me to hate

36

Taladain. He knew magic could not affect me and sought to turn me into a weapon designed to kill a wizard lord."

"To what ends?"

"To upset the balance of magic. To initiate a series of events that would throw the world into chaos."

Blythe could not believe what she was hearing. "Why would he do such a thing?"

Rhoa shook her head. "I don't know. In truth, much of what I have read does not make sense. It includes odd notes of places and events that appear harmless and disconnected. Only a few passages mention me and how he destroyed my life."

Rising to her feet, Blythe stood before Rhoa and hugged her head to her midriff, the younger woman wrapping her arms around Blythe's waist. "I will read through the journal with you. Perhaps we can make some sense of it and discover the truth…together."

The dull hum of chatter came from inside Parwick's Den. Pausing outside the door, Brogan glanced toward his companions, the two dwarfs and Tygalas, the latter having encountered Brogan in the palace corridor before they left. When he had told the elf where he was headed, Brogan never suspected he would choose to join them. He pushed the door open, the noise from within the tavern coming to life.

Parwick's had long been a favored spot among the palace guard due to its position high on the hillside. However, the clientele often skewed young, certainly younger than it did this evening when Brogan found himself among the male patrons. Of course, there were still young women, but most were clustered in a group rather than on a man's knee. At least those who did not offer their company in exchange for coin.

Brogan sat at an open table positioned below an enchanted lantern. The elf, his hood raised, sat beside him, the two dwarfs sitting on the opposite side of the table.

A thin, blonde woman with a blue apron over her gray dress hurried past, stopping when Brogan caught her arm. She looked at him over her shoulder, and he held out a half-silver.

"Four ales, plea–"

Before he could finish, she snatched the coin and was off again.

"Ales?" Lythagon asked. "What are ales?"

Tygalas lowered his hood. "Yes. What is this *ale* you speak of?"

"You haven't heard of ale?" He turned from the elf to the two dwarfs. "What do you drink in Kelmar taverns?"

"Ludicol, of course," Filk said.

"Never heard of it."

"It's a warm drink. Five cups will have your head spinning. Eight might cause you to stumble."

Lythagon snorted. "I drank twelve cups once." He grinned. "I don't recall anything from that day."

Tygalas asked, "If you can't recall anything, how do you know you drank twelve cups?"

The dwarf appeared put-off. "I just know. It's a famous story. My comrades tell it, so it must be true."

Brogan was a big man, and he knew he could drink more than most of his fellow soldiers. However, he knew nothing of dwarfs or elves and wondered if alcohol affected them all the same. Yes, the dwarfs were thickly built, but he still outweighed them by a fair margin, likely weighing two times as much as Tygalas.

He explained. "We humans have various kinds of drinks. Swoon is the strongest. Even a small cup can affect you. Brandy is not quite as strong, wine even less so. Of them all, ale is weakest."

Lythagon jerked back in surprise, his voice rising. "Then why did you order ale? We should be drinking swoon!"

Brogan shook his head, chuckling. "Let's not get ahead of ourselves. Ale may not be so strong, but it is tasty, fermented to create bubbles."

"Bubbles?" Filk asked.

"Yeah, the bubbles..." Brogan paused, struggling to find the right words to explain ale.

The barmaid saved him, the young woman appearing with four mugs in hand, placing them on the table before bustling off. Each of them grabbed one, the two dwarfs giving the foam-topped mugs a sniff, the elf wiping his finger across it before bringing the brown-tinted foam to his nose. His face wrinkled, expression sour.

Brogan laughed and patted him on the shoulder. "Try it. It'll taste odd at first, but the more you consume, the more you'll like it." He lifted his tankard. "Before we drink, we often make a toast by tapping mugs together. For instance, let's toast to making it this far and for our good health."

The dwarfs glanced at each other, shrugged, and slammed their tankards into Brogan's, foam and beer spilling on the table.

"Whoa! Not so hard. Look at how much you spilled."

"I've got this." Filk set his mug aside, bent over, and began licking ale from the table. "Mmm. This is good." He sat up moments later and grinned, his black beard thick with foam, a glob of it on the end of his bulbous nose. "How do I look?"

Brogan laughed heartily, reached across the table, and clamped a heavy paw on Filk's thick shoulder. "You look like a fool!"

The dwarf nodded. "Good." Then he proceeded to pour ale down his face, his tongue flicking out, lapping it up like a dog.

They all laughed, Brogan forgetting the troubles of his past, both recent and distant, if even just for a night.

In the light of an enchanted lantern, Blythe poured through the journal, Rhoa at her side. Many of the passages meant nothing to her, the ones Rhoa had noted only making sense after explanation. Once revealed, she understood why the young woman had been so upset.

When a paragraph struck a chord, Blythe's eyes widened. "Listen to this."

Rhoa leaned close, listening while Blythe read the section.

"I returned to the cabin today and found it empty. A grave marker stood behind the building. The man appears to have finally died, the building abandoned. I must locate the hunter and the ghost who follows her. Without a defined path, I will convince her to follow me."

Blythe sat back, frowning. "This could be about my father's cabin. Salvon never told me he visited it before he met me. I wonder if he knew my father."

"I get the feeling Salvon knew far more than we ever suspected."

While Blythe did not reply, she agreed with Rhoa's assessment.

Minutes passed while Blythe continued reading, stopping when she arrived at another passage describing familiar events. Shocked, she read the section again and sat back.

"What is it?" Rhoa asked.

"*He* did it," Blythe breathed.

"Did what?"

Blythe tapped on the open page. "Salvon set the moar bear after Brogan by hiding the mother bear's cub and leaving one of Brogan's gloves behind. The den was only a mile from his cabin. The bear followed the scent and attacked. Salvon and I heard Brogan's screams." She shook her head, a tear tracking down her face. "We came upon a scene from a nightmare, the bear on top of Brogan, him covered in blood. It took six well-placed arrows to chase the bear off, the beast eventually succumbing to its wounds." She sighed. "Brogan was lucky to survive and only did so with Salvon's help."

Rhoa's brow furrowed. "Why would Salvon arrange a bear attack only to save Brogan's life?"

"Why indeed." Blythe shook her head. "I can't believe he used me like this." She was on the verge of tears again.

Rhoa put her arm around Blythe, her head on her shoulder. "He used both of us. Likely others, as well. I just wish I understood why."

～

The crowd clapped to a beat, Brogan and Tygalas joining them, both smiling. Lythagon and Filk stood on the long table in the middle of the taproom, backs to each other as they danced in a crouch, arms crossed while they kicked their feet in time with the clapping. Still with their backs to each other, they began to spin, shouting, "Ho! Ho! Ho!" while thrusting their hands toward the ceiling.

Brogan downed his ale and wiped his lips clean. He had lost count of his mugs, the suds flowing down his throat with ease. Even Tygalas seemed to be having fun, yet Brogan was taken by surprise when the elf jumped up on the bar. He danced along the top, easily avoiding the mugs resting there, his steps light, as if he weighed nothing. When he reached the end, he leapt and gripped an overhead beam, pulling himself onto it while the crowd watched. When Lythagon saw the elf above, he stopped dancing, sending Filk stumbling backward. The dwarf fell off the table to land on the floor.

Above, Tygalas jumped up, spun, and landed lightly on the beam. Another leap carried him to the next beam, ten feet away. He landed with ease, eliciting a round of cheers. The elf then dropped down to a tabletop and danced, waving for Lythagon and Filk to continue. Filk hesitated for a moment before climbing back on the table to rejoin the dance, all three tapping their boots each time they kicked, switching legs and hopping to the beat set by the crowd.

Brogan laughed and clapped with them, stopping only to order another round from Ellie, the barmaid. He could not recall the last time he had such fun.

~

Blythe woke to a horrible sound from the corridor outside her room. She sat up in the bed, the room dark as she stared toward the door. The singing was atrocious, multiple deep voices shouting more than singing, all at a different pitch. The song ended, followed by laughter and goodbyes. Someone collided into the door with a thud, the handle turning, Brogan stumbling in.

He stood, swaying in the light from the corridor before closing the door, the room darkening again. Her vision had grown keener since her transformation, making it easy to see the man as he fumbled around, searching for the chair.

"You apparently had a good time," she noted.

Startled, he staggered and fell over the chair, both crashing to the floor.

He groaned, holding his shoulder as he rolled to his back. "That hurt."

Reaching for the enchanted lantern on the nightstand, she activated it, the room illuminating with pale blue light.

"Do you need help?"

With obvious effort, he stood the chair upright and sat heavily, wobbling as he pulled off a boot. "No. I don't think tho," he slurred.

"Just how much did you drink?"

He looked at her with bleary eyes. "Don't know." His body swayed on the chair. "Just enough, I would think. Maybe ith good we ran out of coin."

She arched a brow. "You spent five silver pieces on alcohol for the three of you?"

Brogan held up a hand with fingers extended, narrowing his eyes while focusing on his own hand. "Four. Tygalath joined uth."

"If you are like this, I'm afraid for him."

He shook his head, wobbling as he pulled off his other boot. "I think he'th fine. Didn't theem tho drunk to me. Just funner."

"Funner?"

"Yeah. Funner."

"I don't think that's a word."

Standing, staggering as he did so, Brogan tossed his coat aside and fell onto the bed, face-first. He turned his head toward her, his breath reeking of alcohol.

"It ith a word now," he mumbled.

Blythe frowned, rethinking her suggestion for him to join the dwarfs for drinks. A rumble arose, a snore emerging, the man still clothed and on top of the covers.

"Wonderful." With a sigh, she turned out the light.

7

FRIENDSHIP

Rhoa climbed from the carriage and peered over Illustan Harbor. The morning sun shone upon the docks and the vessels moored there, the tall city walls casting the dock warehouses in shadow. She turned as Blythe emerged from the same carriage, followed by Rawk and his uncle, Algoron. It had been a quiet ride through the city while Rhoa reflected on her conversation with Blythe the prior evening. Sharing the shocking passages in the journal had been cathartic, as if Rhoa had shed a burden. In fact, she felt better than she had in quite a while…with the exception of her ride on the back of a dragon. Little could compete with such a wondrous experience.

Two other carriages stopped near her own. An aged guard climbed from one before helping Queen Ariella do the same. From the other, Lythagon and Filk emerged, the two laughing. Tygalas climbed out next, the elf squinting in the light, adjusting the hood drawn over his head. Brogan came out last, appearing bleary-eyed and disheveled. The group gathered on the docks, standing in shadows.

Blythe leaned close to Rhoa and whispered, "Brogan is regretting his lack of control last night."

Rhoa covered her smile with a hand while Ariella faced them.

"It was not so long ago you departed from this very same pier. Then, you were on a quest for answers, and I was able to provide an armed escort. Much has changed since that day, but your quest remains as important as

43

ever. Should the Dark Lord succeed, we are all doomed." She closed her eyes for a breath before resuming. "I regret I cannot offer you an armed escort this time, but I can offer you passage to Balmor. I can also offer you this." She held out a leather purse.

Brogan accepted it, mumbling, "Thank you, My Queen."

She smiled. "You look dreadful, Brogan."

He snorted. "Only dreadful? I feel many times worse than dreadful." He turned toward Lythagon and shook his head. "I just wish some of us were less chipper this morning. It seems unfair for me to suffer alone."

The dwarf grinned. "We dwarfs are a hardy lot."

Tygalas put a hand on Brogan's shoulder. "I, too, feel miserable." He cocked his head. "If this happens when you drink ale, why do it?"

Brogan chuckled softly. "Didn't you have fun last night?"

"Well, yes."

"That's why."

A soldier took something from the queen's carriage and handed it to her. Ariella turned toward Blythe and held out a long strip of black cloth.

"What is it?" Blythe asked.

"I had a cover made for your bow." Ariella gave her a wry look. "You cannot go around with a glowing bow on your shoulder without attracting far too much attention."

"Good point," Blythe said, accepting the cover before sliding the bow off her shoulder. It fit over one end, then the other, cinching together with a pair of straps. "Perfect fit."

"I had my seamstress work on it last night."

"Thank you, Ariella," Blythe said, placing a hand on the woman's arm.

The conversation tailed off, the group saying goodbye to the queen before heading down the quiet pier. At the far end, a familiar man with a gray-speckled brown beard and weathered face stood, arms crossed over his chest, feet spread shoulder width apart. The ship beside him was familiar, as well, the hull standing high above the waterline, the words *Sea Lord* painted along the stern.

"Greetings," the man said as they approached. Removing a hat with fur earflaps and straightening his brown hair, he flashed a grin. "I recognize some of you, but see new faces, as well. I am Captain Helgrued." He gestured toward the ship to his left, the plank rising from the dock to the deck. "*Sea Lord* will be your new home for a while. With this small a group, we'll only have to house two people per cabin for this trip, and two of you will have private rooms."

Brogan extended a hand, the two shaking. "It's good to see you again, Helgrued. I assume you know our destination?"

"I was told you seek passage to Balmor, the very same port I have been assigned."

"You were already bound for Balmor?"

"Yes. I am to deliver food there."

Blythe cocked her head. "That seems awfully convenient."

The captain grinned, revealing a gold tooth. "Timing is right, too. Had you arrived a day later, I'd be gone by now."

Brogan asked, "How long will the trip take?"

"If all goes well, twelve days. Longer if we encounter bad weather or unfavorable winds."

Rhoa had never spent so much time on a ship. In fact, her journey from Illustan to Growler's Rock and back had been her only voyages. She thought of Rawk and wondered how he would fare.

Brogan sighed. "All right." He turned toward the others. "You heard the man. Climb on board so we can set sail. The sooner we depart, the sooner we reach our destination."

Rhoa climbed the plank first, glancing down at the evenly spaced openings along the sides of the hull, oars sticking through them. She stepped onto the deck, sailors moving about as they prepared to set sail. Five weeks had passed since *Sea Lord* had taken them to Growler's Rock, much occurring during that short span. Of the ship itself, nothing had changed.

The masts were thick – one at the bow, one mid-deck, one near the stern. Coils of rope, barrels, crates, and hatches stood upon the broad deck. Two stairwells rose to the quarterdeck at the stern, a door beside each – one to the captain's cabin, the other to the galley.

With Rhoa in the lead, they descended below deck to choose their cabins, Blythe opting to share one with Brogan, allowing Rhoa to have a cabin to herself. She quickly stored her things in the room and went back up on deck, eager to spend time in the sun.

She emerged from the stairwell as the ship drifted from the pier, the sound of a drum coming from below deck, oars sliding through the water with each delayed beat. The ship turned east, toward the wide mouth where the river met the ocean. The water was calm, the morning peaceful.

Rhoa turned and saw Rawk at the port side rail. She crossed to join him, noting his firm grip on the wood, knuckles white. "I'm surprised to see you out here."

He glanced toward her. "We are to be on this ship for many days. I must try."

Rhoa knew of Rawk's fear of the sea. In their prior two journeys, he and Algoron had spent the entire time in their cabin. Yet she sensed something more in this abrupt change.

She put her hand on his back. "What's wrong, Rawk? Did something happen?"

He stared toward the city walls slipping past, the ship easing toward open water. "Lythagon and Filk went out with Brogan and Tygalas last night."

Rhoa chuckled. "It appears as if Brogan got the worst of the bargain."

Rawk did not laugh with her. Instead, he appeared saddened.

She frowned. "You are upset about them going out?"

His lips pressed together, gaze fixed on the far shore of the bay. "Although I am a dwarf, I am not like Lythagon and Filk."

The difference had been obvious from the start. Rhoa shrugged. "They are boisterous, obnoxious, and appear focused on themselves. You are quiet, thoughtful, and kind-hearted."

He turned toward her. "You don't understand. Look at them. They are normal. *I* am the one who never fit in with my brethren, never invited to eat or drink with them, forever excluded. You treated me differently. You accepted me, as did the others, and for a time, I felt as if I belonged.

"Since the dwarfs from Kelmar joined our group, the lie I had built around myself has begun to crumble." He sighed. "It is as if I am back in Ghen Aeldor. I can almost hear the taunts labeling me as a freak."

Tears blurred Rhoa's vision, her heart breaking for her friend. She wrapped her arms around him, squeezing. He held her gently with one arm, the other still gripping the rail.

After a moment, Rhoa stepped back and wiped her eyes. "This is why you are out here? To face your fears in order to prove something?"

"I just want to fit in." His voice was barely audible above the rush of the water along the hull. "Being different is a lonely business."

She thought of his uncle, hidden away in the cabin below. "Algoron seems different, as well."

He put both hands on the rail and stared toward Illustan as the ship turned toward the ocean. "Yes. However, his company offers me little solace, reminding me of what I will become should I continue down the same path."

Rhoa struggled for the right words but soon gave up. Instead, she stood beside him while sailors scrambled around the ship, adjusting lines and unfurling sails. She decided to remain at his side for as long as he could endure being surrounded by water. If he wanted to face his fear, he would not do it alone.

8

DISTRUST

Narine ascended the stairs and climbed on deck, lit brilliant in the morning sun. She scanned the horizon. No land in sight, the seas calm, the blue sky dotted with puffy, white clouds. Her gaze settled on the forecastle at the bow, two rough sailors standing upon it, staring at her with dark eyes and creepy smiles. One man had a cloth tied to his head, a ring in his nose, a scar on the side of his face. The other was bald, his scalp covered by tattoos, a thick, black beard hanging to his bare, barrel chest. When she looked at them, their smiles widened.

She spun away and hurried across the deck, heading toward the rear of the ship. The two men laughed, the sound taunting her. Her magic would protect her, but something about the men made her feel as if they stripped her clothes off with their eyes, their imaginations doing unspeakable things to her body.

Harlequin stood at the helm of *Hassaka's Breath*, the female captain chatting with a sailor, who then gripped the rigging and scrambled up the mizzenmast. Seeing the woman alone, Narine decided it the perfect time for a quiet conversation to see if she could learn something useful.

Holding to the starboard rail, she made her way toward the stern, spotting Jace near the port side rail in conversation with six sailors. Quiarre stood beside him, grinning. *Jace must be digging for information, as well.* The thought made her smile. He was clever and likely to trick the men into revealing something.

She climbed the stairs to the quarterdeck, the woman at the helm staring at her, a brow raised beneath her black, brimmed hat. While Narine would never wear such a flamboyant hat, she had to admit, the woman appeared dashing – an intriguing image of a strong, imposing female.

Narine stood at the rail and smiled. "Good morning."

The taller woman nodded. "'Tis a good morning. Sun's up, winds in our sails, and the sea beckons."

Narine turned toward the water as three gulls dove down, disappearing below the surface, one resurfacing with a fish in its beak. "While I find beauty in the sea, my stomach often disagrees."

The captain snickered. "Which explains why Quiarre was cleaning up after you the entire first day. You half-filled a bucket with chum."

Narine grimaced. "I had thought perhaps I had avoided the illness this time."

"Oh, you may have been unconscious, but you were still plenty ill."

"I should have guessed." Narine recalled the nasty taste in her mouth when she finally woke, now understanding the cause.

Jace and the sailors crossed the deck and surrounded the main mast, Quiarre pointing at it, the distance and the noise of wind and surf too much to allow Narine to hear what was said.

"Is he truly Jerrell Landish?" Harlequin asked.

"Jace?" Narine looked at him dressed in his tight breeches and black coat, wearing a knowing smirk as he spoke with the sailors. She smiled. "Yes. He is truly Jerrell Landish."

Harlequin stared toward Jace, her hands still on the wheel. "From the stories I have heard, I thought he would be a larger, more impressive man."

Chuckling, Narine shook her head. "Don't allow his height to deceive you. He is…" She struggled to find the right words. "Frustrating and clever, outrageous and hilarious, selfish, yet selfless. He is the most amazing man I have known, but I am often bewildered as to why I am drawn to him so."

The captain stared at Narine for a long moment. "You love him."

"I…" There was no point denying it. "I do. Sometimes I wish otherwise, but I cannot help myself. I think I have finally stopped fighting it."

Jace and one of the sailors split off from the others. The man stood a head taller than Jace, was sinewy with coppery skin, his hair tied back in a tail. He wore an unlaced vest and loose trousers tucked into knee-high boots. The two of them walked toward the quarterdeck and stopped just below the helm where Harlequin stood.

Now that Jace stood much closer, Narine heard him say to the sailor, "Three throws. You go first."

The other man nodded and drew a dagger from his belt, eyeing the mast thirty feet away. On it, Quiarre traced a circle in white, marking it with two crossing lines that intersected in the middle of the circle. When Quiarre stepped aside, the sailor threw.

The first blade struck just inside the bottom of the circle, his second throw to the right of the intersecting lines. His third throw struck just to the left of the lines, but all three were within the target.

Harlequin gave Narine a sidelong glance. "Will he best Korrik's throws?"

Narine smiled. "If he wants to win, he will do so with ease."

The captain arched a brow. "Truly?"

"Yes."

"And if he loses?"

"He does so on purpose, likely part of some scheme to manipulate the man or to get the others to increase their bets."

Harlequin chuckled. "My kind of man."

The sailor moved aside, and Jace took position, drawing the dagger on his hip. He cocked and threw. Before the blade struck, he drew the two from his sleeves and tossed them in rapid succession. All three landed inside the circle, an inch apart, forming a perfect triangle surrounding the intersecting lines. The sailors emitted exclamations, Quiarre clapping vigorously, a massive grin on his face. Coins exchanged hands, Jace and Quiarre receiving them from the other men.

"He clearly wanted to win," Harlequin said, a smile on her face. "How interesting."

Narine's grin slid off her face as she watched Harlequin stare at Jace, a smirk on the other woman's lips. Forgetting why she had approached the captain in the first place, her gaze turned toward Jace, who grinned broadly and looked far too handsome.

She hurried down the stairs and went straight for him.

"Narine," he said as she drew near. "Did you see my throws?" He slid one blade into a sheath hidden up his sleeve. "I won us two silvers."

Without a word, she gripped his arm and dragged him toward the stern.

"Wait!" he said. "Where are we going? I was going to have them place another bet."

She stopped and turned around, eyes narrowed at the woman at the helm, a smirk still on Harlequin's face as she watched from across the ship. Narine set her jaw and glared back, defiant. She then gripped Jace by the coat and pulled him close, kissing him, hard. When she released him, Harlequin was still staring.

He smiled. "While I'll not complain, what was–"

"You are to remain below deck until we reach Ryxx."

Taken aback, the smile fell from his face. "What? Why?"

"Because...I don't trust this crew. They appear...unsavory."

"They are supposed to, Narine. We are heading to Ryxx, and the crew is meant to appear as pirates."

"Well, it doesn't mean we need to socialize with them." She took his hand and pulled him down the stairs.

He followed, a frown on his face. "We don't land at Ryxx until late tomorrow. What are we supposed to do until then?"

She stopped in the corridor and kissed him again, her hand running down his chest. Moving her mouth to his neck, she continued to kiss him, her hand trailing south until he moaned.

"Where are we to go?" he whispered. "We share a cabin with Adyn and Hadnoddon."

Narine pulled back and frowned. "We can send them away for a bit." She smiled, kissing him again before whispering, "Regardless, I'll make it worth your while to remain below deck."

9
―――――

BURDEN

Cheers echoed in the streets outside the Bowl of Oren. Despite the noise from inside the stadium, the area outside was strangely quiet, occupied only by city guards and empty carriages. Some of the guards took their duty seriously, patrolling the area, alert as they protected the carriages parked there. Most gathered in clusters, talking, joking, laughing, no different than they had since Garvin and Rindle had arrived in Tiamalyn. Such behavior, once a trend was established, was predictable.

Standing in the shadows of a doorway, Garvin peered across the square, the ballista resting beside him, point down. The rear of five parked carriages faced him, the drivers off to the side in discussion, waiting for the stadium bouts to finish. A pair of guards strolled past the shadowy recess where Garvin waited. He hefted the ballista with a grunt.

This thing is heavy.

"Ready?" He nodded to Rindle, who had a coil of rope with a massive, hooked bolt at one end draped over his shoulder.

"Yes. Let's go."

Mindful to keep the carriages between him and the drivers, Garvin strolled across the plaza, toward a white coach with gold wheels. The carriage was ostentatious to be sure, but it was easy to pick out from the others, for which he was thankful. Rindle at his side, the pair walked with a purposeful stride, just shy of running. He glanced from side to side, worried someone might stop them. The patrolling guards' backs were toward them, carriage drivers laughing at something, another cluster of guards kneeling in a circle as they threw dice. None looked in their direction.

The duo reached the white carriage without issue. Rindle opened the rear compartment and stepped back, lifting the coil of rope off while Garvin quietly set the ballista into the opening. The thief shoved the rope and bundle in before quietly closing the door.

Another cheer arose from the bowl, the noise masking his movement as Garvin gripped the rear carriage rail and slid underneath, shimmying feet first across the bricks until the rear axle was above his head. He quickly disconnected the four extra belts from his torso and began looping them over the axle. A sideways glance revealed Rindle doing the same to the front axle. When finished, each axle had two belts secured to one another in a large loop and two other belts in smaller loops.

Noise rose again, then footsteps and the hum of chatter as people poured out of the stadium. Knowing he had little time, Garvin slid his arms and head through the larger loop, pulling it down until the leather strap was across his lower back, holding him inches above the ground. He then hooked a boot into each of the smaller loops at the front axle, using them as stirrups. Rindle did the same, his upper body strapped to the front axle, feet beside Garvin's head. With them both secure, they waited with their backsides resting on the ground.

The clanking of armor drew near, a dozen leather boots leading a pair of slippered feet beneath a black dress, trailed by green wizard robes, swishing with each step. The woman in the dress would be Queen Grenda, the man, Kollin Mor, Kylar Mor's son. The pair had attended the gladiator fights consistently since Garvin and Rindle first arrived in the city.

Predictable patterns, Garvin thought. *The skills of a good thief are not so different than a talented soldier. We both track patterns, seek weaknesses, and exploit them. Thieves are merely paid much better for their efforts.* The idea of working for himself became more appealing every day.

The carriage rocked as the queen and wizard climbed in, shifting even more when the soldiers escorting them climbed on top. Garvin lifted his backside off the ground, abdominal muscles tight. The thief beside him did the same. With a shout and a snap of the reins, the driver urged the team forward, the carriage making a rounded turn before the horses pulled it down the street at a trot.

The palace was not far, but holding the stiff position required effort, the strain on his back leaving him wishing it were even closer. Grunts came from Rindle, the thief's backside dipping to drag along the pavement just before the carriage came to a stop. Garvin relaxed, enjoying the brief respite as the palace gates opened. When the carriage resumed, both men lifted themselves up and held steady as the carriage headed toward the palace stables.

∼

Garvin huddled in the dark coach house storage closet, listening, waiting. It had been a long afternoon and even longer evening. He was a patient man by nature, which was good in this case. The life of a thief turned out to require as much patience as that of a soldier.

A noise came from within the coach house where he hid. He leaned forward and peered through the cracked-open closet door. A shadow moved, soft footsteps approaching. His hand went to his dagger, drawing it slowly. The door opened, Garvin prepared to strike.

"It's me," Rindle whispered just in time.

"You should have said so earlier," Garvin warned. "I almost sliced your throat."

Rindle's smile flashed in the gloom. "You could have tried."

Garvin sighed as he slid his dagger into its sheath. "Let us not get into that debate. What did you see?"

"Much of the palace is dark, the guards on duty reduced, rounds just completed. It will be a while before they make another round."

"Good. Let's get to the roof and do this." Rising to his feet with the belts in his hand, Garvin turned his back to Rindle. "Help me strap this thing on."

The thief placed the ballista against Garvin's back and began strapping it with the belts as they had practiced. While not exactly comfortable, it was the easiest way to carry the heavy weapon. When finished, Rindle hefted the coil of rope and looped it over his head and shoulder.

"Mimic my actions and remain quiet," the thief said. "I hope you are ready for the climb."

"Just lead the way."

They scurried past the parked coaches, pausing at the door before stepping out into the moonlight.

Rindle led him along the coach house wall and ducked through a gap in the hedges. They passed through a garden to a moonlit courtyard – a bright contrast to the shadows of the surrounding trees. Hugging the narrow shadow along the palace wall, they crossed another courtyard and slipped through a gap between two shrubs. The rushing sound of water came from ahead, growing louder as they progressed deeper into the palace grounds. By the time they reached the rear of the palace, the noise of the waterfall was prevalent, completely masking their footsteps.

Rindle stopped with his back to the wall and peered around the corner. On this side of the palace, the outer wall surrounding the palace grounds was no more than four feet away, leaving a gap between it and the building itself. A moment later, he signaled for Garvin to follow, the pair rounding the corner and hurrying down the narrow gap between the two walls.

The thief glanced up repeatedly as he ran. Fifty paces in, he stopped, turned toward Garvin, and leaned close, speaking over the sound of the waterfall. "This is where we go up. We will rest on the fourth-story balcony, which is even with the top of the outer wall. From there, the climb gets difficult. Also, the wizard lord's chambers are above, so remain quiet."

"Lord Horus is dead," Garvin reminded him.

"Yes, but the queen is not. She was inside the night I scouted. I saw her through the open balcony door." Rindle grinned. "She is one spectacular woman."

Garvin grunted. "Focus on the mission. You can worry about women later, when we are free of this burden."

The thief nodded, put a palm against the outer wall and the other against the palace itself, and jumped up. Applying pressure with his boots and hands against the opposing walls, he hopped up and up, quickly rising toward the balconies above.

Following suit, Garvin began the climb, careful to reach up in small bursts, quickly becoming aware of the extra weight the ballista added. As he rose higher, the noise of the waterfall grew louder. He looked up, the top of the outer wall growing closer, Rindle climbing over the balcony rail across from it. When Garvin's hands were above the rail, he pushed hard against both walls to brace himself and slipped one boot on the balcony railing. He then gave a push, his arms flinging forward to grasp the rail. After pausing for a breath, he swung his leg over and climbed on.

"That was the easy part," Rindle said softly. "Rest up a bit before we resume."

Rather than reply, Garvin rested against the rail, back bent and hands on his knees as he gathered his breath. Rindle crossed the balcony, climbed up to stand on the rail, and gripped the stones jutting out from the palace wall. As the thief began his climb, Garvin blew out a breath and strode across the balcony, watching where Rindle found his grip. He then looked down, the drop easily enough to kill him. To make matters worse, he had the heavy ballista on his back.

Gods, give me strength, he thought as he climbed on the railing. By then, Rindle was even with the top balcony and nearing the roof.

Garvin reached out and found a grip with each hand, then one for his boot, and began to climb. One stride up, he heard a noise, the door to the upper balcony opening, a young man wearing nothing but his smallclothes stepping outside. Not moving, Garvin clung to the wall, fearful the man might turn and spot him.

A dark-haired woman emerged, dressed in nothing but a gossamer robe open at the front. She had long, dark hair and the body of a goddess, curvy with a slim waist.

"What is wrong, Kollin?" she asked.

The young man stared toward the waterfall and shook his head. "It feels wrong. This chamber... It is intended for the Wizard Lord of Orenth."

The woman slipped her arms around him from behind, her fingernails tracing across his lean torso. "Have you forgotten? Horus is dead."

"Yes, but a new lord will arise. The Darkening is only days away."

"That man will be you, Kollin."

He turned toward her. "What of my father? His magic and experience would be of more value to Orenth."

She gave him a level glare. "Your father has gone mad, his skill significantly diminished. You know this as well as anyone. Oren would never bless someone with such issues." The woman gripped his chin, drawing his face toward hers. "You will be wizard lord, and I will be your queen. With me at your side, you will find the same success Horus had these past ten years."

Please, go back inside, Garvin thought, his fingers cramping.

"What of our age difference?"

She shrugged, reaching down as she bit her lip. "One day, I will die, and you will find another." Her hand slipped inside his smallclothes. "Until then, I will reward you every day for making me your queen."

"What of my...problem?" His voice sounded pained. "Even you... If someone with your beauty and talents cannot help me, what hope do I have?"

She crooned, "You have found other ways to satisfy me thus far. When you possess the power of a god, you will be able to heal anything...even this."

The pair kissed, her moaning as she dragged him back inside. Once the door closed, Garvin resumed his climb, his muscles weary, each reach requiring concerted effort. When he reached the clay-tiled roof, Rindle helped him over the edge. He lay on his side, panting, clenching and unclenching his hands, while the thief released the straps from his torso. Only when the ballista was off his back did he rise to his feet, scooping the weapon up and following Rindle across the roof.

The tower above the palace was dark, as it had been since they arrived in Tiamalyn. Even so, the full moon shining off the alabaster tower wall made it appear to glow in the night. The apex was ten stories above, open at the sides, topped by a green dome supported by eight white columns.

Rindle stopped ten strides from the tower and pointed. "If we can get the hook to loop around a column, it should catch." He turned toward Garvin. "We'll just have to hope we don't make too much noise."

"Leave the shooting to me," Garvin said. "I have more experience with ballistae than most could claim." It was among the skills acquired during his time in the Murguard.

He set the ballista down and began cranking the launch mechanism, slow but steady to limit the noise. When it was fully cocked, he took the hooked bolt from Rindle and placed it into the launch channel.

"Stand in front of me. I'll use your shoulder to hold it steady," Garvin said as he lifted the oversized crossbow.

Rindle stood in front of him, holding one end of the rope in his grip. With the front of the ballista resting on the tall thief's shoulder, Garvin squatted and took aim, the rope dangling from the bolt, the remaining coil on the roof tiles beside him. He took a deep breath, held steady, and pulled the trigger. A *twang* resounded, the noise far louder than he might have wished. The bolt flew high, arcing as it lost momentum, and sailed through a gap beside one of the columns. The metal bolt swung around the thick post, the hook looping around the rope. Rindle pulled tightly to set it.

The thief turned toward Garvin. "Nice shooting. It was noisier than I would have preferred, but it could have been much worse."

"Thanks." Garvin took the rope and approached the tower. He slipped his boots off and set them aside, his gaze going toward the tower above. "Tug on the rope if anything goes wrong."

Without waiting, he gripped the rope in both hands, put his bare feet against the tower, and began his climb. Immediately, he was reminded of the capture of Starmuth, the ascent up the obelisk almost exactly like this climb. It had been the first city he converted to Farrow, back when he believed in his cause. Now, he wished to be done with the entire thing.

By the time he reached the top, his arms and shoulders ached. He climbed over the tower rim, noting the lack of flames surrounding it. Similar to the tower in Fastella, a crystal throne sat upon a dais in the center. The difference was this throne held a green emerald rather than a purple amethyst.

Garvin removed the sapphire from his inside coat pocket, eyeing it in the moonlight. *If I were to smash this, I could prevent Thurvin from gaining more power.* He knew the act would be a death sentence should the wizard lord ever catch him. Worse, he suspected it would merely delay the inevitable. With a sigh, he shook off the idea and reached for the emerald.

It was wedged in tightly, refusing to break free. He drew his dagger, stuck the tip between the gem and the throne, and pried it free. The stone popped out, and Garvin snatched it just before it struck the seat of the throne. He pocketed the emerald and lifted the sapphire to the opening, pausing for a breath before inserting it. The jewel snapped into place. He stepped back. A deep blue glow emerged in the stone and spread throughout the throne. The tower rim burst into flames of dark blue, the light simmering to a shimmer. He hopped over the flames and lifted the rope, prepared to climb down.

A ray of blue light streaked across the sky, coming directly toward Garvin. He leapt off the tower, rope gripped tightly. The azure beam struck the tower, the flames erupting to an inferno as Garvin fell. He twisted, lifting his legs just in time to brace himself as he slammed into the side of the tower. The rope jerked from his grip. He fell backward, his stomach rising into his throat as he imagined his splattered corpse on the rooftop. However, it seemed fate was on his side, because his leg twisted in the rope, a coil tightening around his ankle. The rope stretched taut, stopping his fall with a harsh lurch, his side slamming into the wall.

Upside down, he scrambled to grasp the rope, his grip tightening just as his foot came free. His body flipped, legs flinging wildly as he swung from the rope. Finally, he settled himself, heart racing.

Panting from his near-death experience, he began his descent, thoughts of the tower receding as those of Despaldi returned.

I must find him.

10

ECSTASY

Ecstasy. It consumed all, Thurvin Arnolle basking in the rapture of Devotion, surrounded by a blaze of blue. Prayers from across two wizardoms flowed in and fed his power, rising to levels beyond any wizard who had ever lived. Time became irrelevant, the bliss all-consuming. Just as the flow began to wane, a new burst of energy struck, the torrent of new prayers rushing in so intensely, he lost control. Magic began to release from his body in sparks and fits of raw energy. He struggled against the deluge, fearing it might destroy him. With focused effort, he regained control. The eruptions of power ceased, the magic filling his core as he fought to contain it. Teeth clenched, screams blasted from his lungs, nails digging into the crystal arms of his throne.

Finally, the flow of prayers slowed, the tension in his body easing with it. Blowing out a breath, he withdrew his connection with the sapphire in the throne, ending Devotion. The azure flames faded, his surroundings again becoming clear. Fire licked his legs, setting his robes ablaze, the wagon beneath the throne burning. Rather than panic, he encased the wagon and himself within a shield of solidified air and sucked the oxygen away, simultaneously casting a construct of repair to heal his wounds. The fires dwindled and died in moments, black smoke swirling from the singed hem of his robes. A loud *crack* sounded, the wagon bed breaking, the heavy crystal throne falling through. It dropped only a few inches before stopping. Still, the wagon was destroyed.

Thurvin dismissed the shield, cool evening air rushing in. He gasped, taking in a deep breath before climbing off the throne and jumping down to the long grass. Frightened, wide-eyed soldiers stared at him from a distance, nobody moving, the camp oddly silent. Smoldering corpses, probably more than two dozen men and horses, were strewn on the ground, destroyed by his magic.

Queen Priella walked toward him, the woman not bothering to cover the exposed skin of her shoulders, arms, and upper chest, despite the cool weather. The glow of magic surrounding her informed Thurvin she used it to warm herself. It took little effort, especially after Devotion.

"Explain yourself, Lord Thurvin!" she demanded. "I heard the screams from across camp." Her gaze swept the area as she stopped a stride away. "Why would you attack your own men? We need these soldiers *alive*."

He shook his head, which caused him to stumble. A thick dizziness lingered, remnants from the power surging through his veins. "It was an accident."

Her brow furrowed. "Explain."

"As I neared the end of Devotion, a surge of energy struck. It was significant, similar to when Fastella fell. Added to the prayers already flowing in, it briefly overwhelmed me. Some of it slipped out before I was able to regain control."

"Additional prayers?" She stared at him with narrowed eyes, slowly reaching out to touch his arm. The anger fled from her voice, shifting to a soft, soothing croon. "Your men must have converted the Tower of Devotion in Tiamalyn."

Thurvin's eyes widened. "Yes! That must be it!"

"The additional magic... You can handle it?"

He set his jaw. "I can and will." The power was his to wield.

She arched a brow and turned toward the nearby corpses, some still smoldering. "It appears you have approached your capacity."

Stopping now was unthinkable, the very notion causing him to panic. Quickly, he regained control, determined to squash any doubt. "Nonsense. I was just...unprepared. It will become easier to manage with each successive Devotion."

"If you are so sure, you should have no issue with claiming Yor's Point tonight as planned."

The thought of adding more prayers, even if Yor's Point was a small city of only eight thousand citizens, had him both eager and concerned. Still, she had promised him the cities of Orenth should he prove capable. It would be the extent of his direct rule, but thrice more than any wizard in history. He was determined, unwilling to relinquish even one city.

"We will proceed as planned. When I begin Devotion tomorrow evening, it will be with two Orenthian cities in my grasp." He stormed off toward his tent.

Torches stood outside the entrance, amber light flickering off the armor of two guards posted there. Also visible in the torchlight, the flag of Farrowen rippled in the breeze, the dark blue fabric graced by a silver bolt of lightning.

Thurvin walked past the guards and ducked inside, an orb of light appearing above his open palm, illuminating the interior, the ground covered in carpets. A large chest, a table, a chair, and a pallet covered in blankets and pillows occupied the tent. He went directly to the chest, threw it open, and withdrew a gem the size of his fist from a padded leather sack. Holding it between two fingers, he examined the sapphire. It was a perfect octahedron. With it in his grip, he stormed back outside and turned to his guards.

"I will be away for a few hours. Nobody is to enter while I am gone."

The two men nodded, one replying, "Yes, Your Majesty!"

Thurvin walked across camp, weaving his way past hundreds of tents and dozens of campfires, often accompanied by the smell of meals cooking. He then realized he had not eaten since lunch. It did not matter. He had no time to sate his hunger, at least not the hunger in his stomach. Another type of hunger drove him, one he might never satisfy.

Soon, the ground became a decline, the hillside gradually rounding until a strip of black appeared in the moonlight, rippling reflections dancing upon the surface. *The river.* In the darkness, he spotted Graybeard Bridge a mile away. The bridge had stood for millennia – a Maker-built structure from another era. It connected Farrowen to Orenth, a major trade route and the only means to reach the neighboring wizardom without a boat or ferry. He spun around to face the other direction where the river flowed toward the Novecai Sea...and his destination.

Thurvin cast a shield of solidified air, shaping it into a sphere twice his height, encompassing him. Using his magic, he lifted the sphere into the air and propelled himself forward, hovering hundreds of feet above the river. Inside his protective bubble, he sped north.

The lights of Shear passed below. The new portion of the city rested upon a bluff, the old on a flat strip of land between the cliffside and the river. As a Farrowen city, the Obelisk of Devotion burned with a blue flame, sparking the blaze of satisfaction Thurvin felt each time he claimed a new city. Shear had been among the first, along with Marquithe, Lionne, Eleighten, and Souton, all falling to him the day he assumed the throne of Farrowen. The cities of Ghealdor followed, beginning with Starmuth. Ten more weeks passed before his forces had claimed Tangor, the fifth and final Ghealdan city, giving him the power of two wizard lords. Still, it was not enough.

Thurvin followed the waterway as it widened, appearing like a long, meandering lake surrounded by tall cliffs. The dark cliffsides sped past as he flew many times faster than the fastest horse. Soon, lights appeared ahead, marking another city. Docks lined the shoreline, the smaller ones occupied by fishing vessels, the larger with ships moored for the evening. *Yor's Point.* He had reached it in less than two hours – a trip that would have taken two days by carriage.

He lowered himself, guiding the bubble toward the city walls where torches burned, the dark silhouettes of guards patrolling. None noticed him. Why would they bother to look up? What could they do if they had?

Nobody can stop me.

The sphere sailed over the city, rising along the hillside, hovering no more than twenty feet above the rooftops. A tall, thin spire, pale in the moonlight, beckoned. He directed the sphere toward it, slowing as the obelisk took shape.

Fifteen feet across at the base, the obelisk stood two hundred feet tall in the heart of the city square. To one side of the square was a guarded wall surrounding the city castle, two enchanted lanterns alight just outside the closed castle gate. The square was quiet, the streets blanketed in shadow.

Thurvin smiled, realizing nobody had yet noted his presence. *Think of the surprise when the citizens wake. A fervor will run through the city.* He wondered how the people might feel about waking to a new god. *Will they feel grief for Oren? Do they even care?*

Dismissing such thoughts, he altered the shape of the sphere, opening it at the top and lowering the sides until it was nothing more than a three-foot disk beneath his feet. The ocean breeze struck, his robes rippling, hair fluttering, but he retained his balance and control.

He moved the disk beside the obelisk, rising until he stood just below the peak. A shadowy recess was carved into the sloped tip. Thurvin reached inside, his fingertips finding the smooth, angular surfaces of a gem. He gripped it, pulling, rocking, twisting until it came free. He withdrew the jewel and looked at it in the moonlight, the emerald appearing black. From the pocket of his cloak, he withdrew the sapphire and held it beside the other gem, appearing identical in shape and size, differing only in hue. After placing the emerald in his pocket, he cast an orb of light, revealing the perfectly spaced mounting inside the opening. With care, he set the sapphire inside and snapped it into place.

The gem sprang to life, a shimmering azure aura emitting from it, appearing as if a burning flame.

Thurvin drew back. "It is done." He grinned. "So simple, so quick." Shaking his head in amazement, he stared at the burning flame. "It is beautiful."

Shouts and cries of alarm came from below, the castle gate opening and armed soldiers rushing out. As quick as a thought, Thurvin extended his shield around him, reforming the sphere just before a foolish soldier raised a crossbow and fired, the bolt shattering against the shield. Thurvin formed a construct and unleashed a bolt of lightning, striking the man's breastplate and blasting him across the square.

"Behold!" he shouted. "I am Lord Thurvin, your new wizard lord. The flame has returned, but it burns blue. Oren is dead, your prayers lost to him. Praise Farrow, for he is your new god!"

The soldiers looked at one another, confused.

Thurvin scowled, muttering, "I don't have time for this."

He sent himself toward the castle, passing over the wall, archers loosing toward him, arrows sailing wide of their mark. Spying a third-story window lit with an amber light, he steered toward it. Inside, people sat around a long table, laughing, eating, drinking. Without slowing, he made for the window, the glass exploding inward when his shield struck. Shards scattered across the room, some finding flesh. A woman cried out, a chunk of glass sticking from her back as she staggered from her chair. A man in robes pulled a shard from his cheek, blood oozing from the wound.

Dismissing the shield, Thurvin landed on the floor and straightened his robes. The glow of magic enveloped the man at the end of the table, an energy construct forming. Before he could release it, Thurvin wrapped coils of magic around the wizard, binding the man's arms to his sides, lifting and pinning him to the wall.

Thurvin strode toward the other wizard with a menacing glare. He was in his early thirties with brown, curly hair, face covered in scruff. His robes were black with emerald trim.

"High Wizard Paloun, I presume."

The other man squirmed, unable to move. "What is the meaning of this?"

Thurvin gestured toward the window, the blue flame atop the obelisk visible. "Behold. Yor's Point now belongs to Farrow." He tapped his chest. "I, Lord Thurvin, am your new master."

The color in the man's face drained away. "Lord Thurvin?"

"Yes." He drew in more magic, his skin alight to anyone who had the gift. "My power is unequaled, fed by the prayers of Farrowen, Ghealdor, and your very own Tiamalyn. Soon, the remainder of Orenth will fall to my might."

"What… What do you want with us?"

"I want you to obey," he growled.

"Anything."

"My mistress, Queen Priella of Pallanar, requires you and your soldiers join us. The combined might of Farrowen and Pallanar march across Orenth, bound for Balmoria. Gather your forces, every soldier and wizard you can spare, and sail to Fralyn. Meet us there in five days. If you fail to appear, we will return and crush you."

As his anger cooled, the smell of the interrupted meal caught his attention. He turned toward the table, three guests still seated, their eyes round with fear. Four full chickens sat on the table, along with potatoes, corn, and freshly baked rolls. Some of the wine goblets had tipped over, staining the linen tablecloth dark red.

"Your dinner party appears ruined. Unfortunately, it was never meant to be. We are at war and have no time for such frivolities."

He tore a leg off one of the chickens and took a bite. With his other hand, he lifted a goblet, draining the contents. Slamming the empty goblet down, he turned toward the window and burst into a run. Leaping, he sailed over the broken glass and reformed his shield, directing the sphere toward the river as he sped into the night.

11

LONGING

Priella leaned over the neck of her galloping horse, trailed by five hundred mounted soldiers, Bosinger at her side. The countryside sped past – trees, farms, fields, and vineyards. From time to time, the river appeared on her right, only to fade at the next bend.

The sun edged above the trees to the east, a quarter of the way into the sky. The moon hovered just north of the sun's path, the Darkening soon coming to Tiamalyn.

It had already been a long morning, having set out an hour before sunrise. One day was all she had, for she was determined to return to camp before Devotion. The thought of missing it for even a single night left her cold and wanting.

Her horse climbed a small rise, rounded a bend, and emerged from the forest. The view opened, the morning sun shining upon the white walls of Tiamalyn. Highmount, the upper portion of the city, overlooked the valley.

He lives there, she thought. His dark hair, amber eyes, and chiseled face materialized in her mind. Many nights, his face had occupied her dreams. Rare were the days when images of him did not creep into her head, even after he had left the University.

She pressed her lips together in resolve. *Focus on your objective, Priella. He never had time for you before, and you have no time for him now.*

Dismissing such thoughts, she slowed her horse to a trot, her escort doing the same.

Theodin brought his mount beside hers. "City guards should have observed our approach by now. Regardless of who runs Tiamalyn, foreign armies are seldom a welcome sight. They are sure to prepare an unkind reception."

"It does not matter. The show of force is a reminder of my position and will give them something to think about." She turned toward him. "Choose five soldiers to accompany us into the city."

He nodded. "Yes, My Queen." Theodin slowed his mount, leaving her and Bosinger alone.

The trotting horse brought her closer to the city, the misty falls visible beyond the docks. A mile across and hundreds of feet tall, water flowed over the cliff with a roar that could be heard from a mile away. The morning sunlight cast a rainbow in the mist below the falls.

Beautiful, she thought, allowing herself a rare moment to enjoy such things. The moment passed too quickly, the walls soon obscuring the view as she drew near.

Outside the city gate, guards with green capes and green crests on their helmets formed a line across the road, six men deep. Dozens more with bows, arrows nocked, stood upon the wall.

Priella stopped her horse a few hundred feet from the wall, just at the edge of the archers' range. Bosinger stopped beside her, the other riders settling behind them.

"It appears we have captured their attention," she noted.

"As I suspected," Bosinger replied, loosening his sword. It was his habit when confronted with potential danger, which seemed to be a frequent occurrence of late.

Theodin rode up, stopping beside her.

Priella turned toward her captain. "Make sure your men keep their weapons sheathed. I don't want any misunderstandings. We are here to recruit, not slaughter."

Theodin dipped his head. "Understood, My Queen."

She kicked her horse into a trot, Theodin and Bosinger riding at her side, twenty riders in tow. A man in green leather armor adorned by gold-tinted plates circled the ranks standing on the road and stopped before them, feet spread, arms crossed over his chest.

Priella slowed her horse. "Greetings. With whom do I speak?"

The man shouted back, "I am Sergeant Paello of the Fifth Phalanx."

"Greetings, Sergeant. I am Priella Ueordlin, Queen of Pallanar."

"I had heard rumors of a woman now ruling Pallanar. Do you possess the power of a wizard lord?"

"I do." She grinned. "Would you care for a demonstration?"

A nervous rustle ran through the ranks behind the sergeant. He turned toward his soldiers. "Hold steady!" The man turned back toward Priella, eyes narrowed. "Your soldiers are not allowed in the city."

"I have not come to attack Tiamalyn, Sergeant."

He uncrossed his arms. "If not, why did you bring an army?"

She laughed, hard and loud. "This is just an escort, a tiny slice of my army." Her expression grew serious. "The bulk of the army marches across Orenth as we speak, soon to be joined by the Orenthian garrison at Yor's Point."

The man's gaze flicked from person to person, his arrogance gone. "What would you have of Tiamalyn?"

"I request an escort to meet with whomever rules the city. As I understand it, Lord Horus no longer sits upon the throne." She gestured toward the tower high above the bluff. "The Tower of Devotion burns with the blue of Farrow. I know the truth behind both events and am here to share such information."

The man scowled. "This is a peaceful visit?"

"Yes."

"Very well. Have your main force retreat to the tree line, then we will open the gate."

She turned toward Theodin. "Do as he says."

Theodin called out orders, the force turning and riding back to the tree line. Sergeant Paello called for the gate to be opened, his men parting as he led Priella and her seven-member escort into the city. Inside the gate, Paello spoke with another soldier and mounted a horse. A contingency of two dozen mounted guards waited.

He expected to escort us the entire time. She wondered if Paello had come up with the conclusion himself or if someone else had given the order.

They rode through the city, citizens stopping to watch her passing – the men with mouths gaping and gazes filled with longing, the women staring in narrow-eyed jealousy. Priella smirked at the effect of her illusion. She glanced down at her plunging neckline, breasts bouncing to the rhythm of her trotting horse. *I do so enjoy the attention.* She could be honest with herself. *After all, why else would I constantly don this appearance?* In truth, she did not need it to bend others to her will. Not when she could influence their minds using more subtle methods.

The city itself was a curiosity to Priella, the buildings small and cramped, the streets narrow, alleys filled with refuse. It did not feel like a great city. The citizens were all dressed like commoners, none appearing wealthier than an average merchant, most appearing like beggars.

They came to a street with an incline, running along the wall on the opposite side of the city from the river. An elegant carriage rode toward them, the driver dressed better than anyone in the lower portion of the city. The climb was steep, the buildings along the roadway nicer than anything she had seen below. When they finally reached the top of the bluff and the road leveled, she discovered that Highmount, the upper district, was diametrically opposite from the district below.

Broad, red-bricked streets ran between alabaster buildings with red-tile roofs. To the south side of the road stood walls with barred gates surrounding massive mansions amid green grounds, trimmed shrubs, and white statues. Each was built along the bluff's edge, gifting the owners with a view of the lower city and the valley beyond.

To the other side of the road was an enormous circular structure with numerous arched entrances. Tall pillars supported the upper reaches six stories above. *The Bowl of Oren. It can be nothing else.* She wished she could watch a duel in the famous stadium, but it was not meant to be. Not today. Her throne awaited her return.

The small procession continued down the street, toward the palace, the tall, white spire above it burning with the blue flame of Farrow. Envy welled up inside her, craving the power Thurvin held in his possession. She squashed it, telling herself, *He is my tool, which makes his magic an extension of my own.* Still, she longed to claim the power of additional prayers for herself.

Sergeant Paello stopped outside the palace gate and spoke to the guards on duty before riding past. The man led them down a drive lined by tall, narrow pines trimmed to appear like arrows pointing to the sky. A spectacular fountain loomed ahead – giant wedges of white marble piled thirty feet high, the water trickling down from one wedge to another, ending in a pool filled with orange and gray fish.

They turned at the fountain and entered a stable yard, two tanned, shirt-less men running out to take their horses. Both had lean, muscular frames, appearing similar to her own age of twenty-four. A young man with long, brown hair tied back in a tail accepted the reins from Priella's outstretched hand. She watched his amber eyes as she climbed down, the man's gaze lingering on her exposed cleavage.

With a smile, she ran a finger down his sculpted chest. "Take care of my horse."

The man stammered, "Yes, um…"

"She is a queen," Bosinger growled. "No other title will do."

Wide-eyed, the young man bowed, backing away. "Sorry, My Queen."

Priella snickered. "How apt. I *am* your queen."

Paello frowned. "Ignore Talmak. He is a mere stable boy." The man waved them along. "Come."

They entered the palace and followed a long corridor to an open hall. Paello approached a gray-haired man dressed in a green doublet with white ruffles.

"Fertello." The sergeant extended his arm toward Priella. "The Queen of Pallanar wishes to speak with Chancellor Mor."

Fertello's eyes widened for a moment before he recovered. The elderly man shook his head. "Regretfully, the chancellor is not seeing anyone today."

Priella stepped before the man and arched a brow. "I suggest you recon-sider your response, or it will be the last poor decision you ever make. I will see him, and it will happen today."

Kneading his hands, the man swallowed hard and cast a glance toward Paello, twenty armed soldiers standing behind him.

The sergeant shook his head. "She sits upon the throne of Pallanar. If she wields the magic of a wizard lord, what can we do to stop her?"

Priella smiled. "Nothing."

"But…," Fertello stammered.

"Watch!" Priella sneered. She turned toward the soldiers standing ready and chose the largest one, a man standing well over six feet and as broad as a house. "You. Die." As she said the words, she used a construct of compulsion.

The man stiffened and fell forward, smashing face-first into the marble floor. Blood ran from his nose, pooling under his head, as another soldier knelt beside him and turned him over, his empty eyes staring at the murals on the ceiling.

"You see," Priella said, burying any guilt over the action. Time was short and too much was at stake. Many others would die before she was finished. "With one word, I could fell every person in this room. Are you certain you wish to test me?"

Fertello shook his head frantically and backed away. "Please, forgive me, Your Majesty. I will lead you to him straight away."

He turned and crossed the room, Priella following, Bosinger and Theodin a step behind. Sergeant Paello and the remaining guards trailed at a distance. They entered a corridor and turned a corner. Fertello stopped at a door and opened it to the sound of birds singing.

"Outside?" Priella asked.

"Yes. The Chancellor is in the garden, enjoying the view." Fertello shrugged. "It helps keep him grounded. Few things do these days."

What does that mean?

The door across the corridor opened and a tall wizard stepped out. The young man had dreamy, dark eyes, a square jaw, and a tanned complexion. He looked as dashing as ever, his green and white robes fitting perfectly over his broad shoulders, sash cinched around his narrow waist. Only his hair had changed, the long locks trimmed, bangs combed to the side.

"Kollin," Priella breathed.

He arched a brow, his eyes sweeping her body. "We cannot have met. I would never forget a woman as striking as yourself. How do you know me?"

Her hand went to her chest, drawing his gaze. The look of longing on his face was her most rewarding moment since taking the throne, all save for Devotion. Nothing could match that.

Fertello replied, "This is Queen Priella of Pallanar. She has come to see your father."

Kollin's brow furrowed. "Priella? You... You have changed."

"For the better, I would hope."

"Certainly." He stepped closer and stared into her eyes. "If you wish to see my father, I will accompany you."

She smiled, her heart racing. "I would welcome your company."

A woman emerged from the doorway behind Kollin. She had long, black hair held back by a golden crown covered in emeralds. Her dress was even more revealing than Priella's, exposing a scandalous amount of her tanned, plentiful chest.

The woman pursed her lips, her scrutinizing stare running up Priella's body. "Who is our visitor, Fertello?"

"Queen Grenda." The man bowed. "Let me present Queen Priella of Pallanar. She was just about to meet with Chancellor Mor in the garden."

The woman arched a brow. "Interesting." She took Kollin's arm, pulling his elbow against the side of her chest. "I believe I will join you."

12

INTERROGATION

G arvin followed Rindle along the rocks, the city wall to his right, the raging river to his left. The roar from Tiamalyn Falls was deafening, the white-capped water flowing over the edge just ahead. The rocks were slippery, each step having to be carefully placed. The pair was masked by the shade of the tall, alabaster wall, the mid-morning sun yet to crest the structure.

They passed the point where the river dropped over the edge, spray swirling in the air. Garvin peered down. It was a long drop, difficult to survive, most likely to result in a flattened corpse even when landing in the water. He turned from the river as Rindle eased around the bend of the city wall.

The lower portion of Tiamalyn lay below, hugging the riverfront. A low wall ran along the top of the bluff, allowing a view of the vista for those inside the grounds. Rindle stopped near the wall and swung a coil of rope from his shoulder, a metal, three-pronged hook tied to one end. The thief climbed on the tallest rock and stared up at the wall, the top twenty feet above. He gripped the rope a foot from the hook and began to swing it around, a *whoop, whoop, whoop* sound coming from it. With an upward lunge, he released it, the hook sailing up and arcing toward the wall. It cleared the edge and disappeared. When he pulled back, a clatter came from above, the hook digging in.

A few tugs seemed to satisfy Rindle, who then glanced toward Garvin. "Ready?"

"You are sure about this?"

"The maid says he spends every morning in the garden. Always alone."

Standing on the narrow ledge, Garvin glanced down at the lower portion of the city, the fall hundreds of feet. "I feel exposed up here. If anyone looks up and sees us…"

"We are in the shadows." Rindle pointed toward the falls, sunlight casting a rainbow in the swirling mist. "The sun will soon crest the building, but while we are obscured, anyone looking up here will be blinded. However, the moment will soon pass, so we had best hurry."

Garvin took the rope from Rindle, placed a boot against the wall, and began the climb. Hand-over-hand, he went up the wall, lunging at the top to get a grip before pulling himself up. He peered over the edge into a quiet garden filled with sculpted shrubs and tall, narrow trees. White statues stood amid the greenery, multi-hued flowerbeds at the foot of each. Nobody was in sight, no sound other than the roar of the falls and the chirping of birds from the garden. He pulled himself over the edge and dropped down to the turf four feet below. Beyond the garden was the palace, his position in the corner providing a view of the narrow gap between the building and the outer wall they had scaled up just days earlier. Squatting, he hid behind shrubs while Rindle climbed up.

Once in the garden, the thief hurried along the wall at a crouch, Garvin creeping behind him, the pair using surrounding shrubs as cover. They soon came to a brick-paved path lined by hedges. Following it, a white structure came into view.

It was a raised dais with a bench facing the city. Pillars connected by arches surrounded the dais, but it had no roof. A man in white robes sat alone on the bench, hands covered by the loose sleeves of his green robes. He was middle-aged with dark hair and eyes, face drawn in a frown as he stared out over the city and the valley beyond.

Rindle whispered, "He appears to match the description."

"I don't see anyone else."

"How do you wish to do this?"

"Let's start with a simple conversation." Garvin pointed to the right. "Circle around and approach him from the rear. Draw your weapon as encouragement, but don't poke any holes through him. Let me do the talking."

When the thief nodded and slunk off, Garvin turned his attention on his quarry. He sought answers, nothing more. However, the man was a wizard, which complicated things. He closed his eyes and said a silent prayer, hoping the rumors were true. Finally, he took a deep breath and stepped out, approaching as if he were on a simple stroll through the garden.

At first, there was no response, the wizard continuing to stare into space. Then he glanced to Garvin, who flashed a smile. The man's gaze flicked away, returning to the city.

"Good morning," Garvin said in a friendly tone.

No response.

He tried again. "You must be Kylar Mor, Chancellor of Tiamalyn."

The man's eyes shifted, focusing on Garvin. He laughed, loud and boisterous – the sound of madness. "I am not the man you seek. He is dead." The wizard lifted his arms, sleeves slipping down to reveal his hands.

A chill ran down Garvin's spine, his stomach twisting. The man's hands looked…melted. Fingers gone, skin taut and glossy, bleeding in areas where it had split, exposing raw flesh.

"What happened to you?" Garvin breathed.

The man laughed again. "I was so sure of myself, bolstered by the strength of my magic. In all of Orenth, my abilities were second only to Lord Horus." He shook his head and stared at the scarred, twisted stumps on his wrists. "Horus was already dead, yet I entered the fray. I killed one of his assailants, but it cost me everything."

Rindle approached the man from behind, his rapier drawn.

Garvin shook his head and motioned for Rindle to stand down. "So, you *are* Kylar Mor."

"I…was."

Garvin squatted before the wizard. "The men who attacked Horus… I am searching for them. Where did they go?"

The wizard just stared at his deformed hands, despondent.

"Chancellor Mor," he said more firmly. "I search for Despaldi. Where did he go?"

Mad laughter burst from the man, eyes bulging. "Landish! They pursue Landish. Finally, the bloody thief will receive his due."

Rindle's brow furrowed. "Jerrell Landish?"

76

The wizard hooted, not bothering to turn around to see who spoke. "The very same! He cannot escape this time. Not against men able to kill a wizard lord!"

The thief appeared concerned.

Garvin adjusted his tactic. "This thief Despaldi pursues... Where did he go?"

The man's laughter settled, head shaking. "Princess Narine tricked me. She performed some witchery on the thief. It is the only answer. He could not have otherwise survived against eight gladiators."

"What does Princess Narine have to do with Landish?"

"She loves him."

Rindle guffawed. "Jerrell with a princess?"

The wizard ignored the comment. "When he survived, I lost my wager and was forced to provide them transport. It was the last command Horus ever made."

Frustrated, Garvin gripped the wizard's forearms. "Focus. Tell me. Where did Landish go?"

"Same as I told Despaldi... Landish wished transport to Cor Cordium."

Motion out of the corner of his eye caught Garvin's attention. He turned as a cluster of people approached the dais, led by a beautiful woman with a silver crown nestled in her red hair.

A man in a green doublet pointed. "Intruders!"

Rindle turned with his sword, prepared to fight. His eyes went blank, sword falling from his grip and clattering to the dais. Garvin spun around to run but was lifted off the ground, his arms bound to his sides.

The red-haired woman strode toward them, full lips curved up in a smirk. "Well, well, well. It appears we have captured a pair of rats in the palace gardens."

Priella stopped strides away from the man seated on the garden bench, who she assumed was Kylar Mor. The thin man behind him stared into space, his mind captured with her magic. The other man, handsome and athletic, was held in the air by Kollin's spell.

Fertello rushed over to the sitting man, placing a hand on his shoulder. "Is everything all right, Chancellor? These men... They did not hurt you?"

Kylar Mor stared into space as if he'd heard nothing.

"What's wrong with him?" Priella asked.

"My father..." Kollin ran his hand though his hair. "He is ill. I fear he may never recover."

Chancellor Mor turned toward his son and held up twisted stumps of hands. "This cannot be healed. The most gifted wizardesses in Tiamalyn have tried."

Priella frowned in thought.

Kollin approached the man suspended in the air. "Who are you? What do you want with my father?"

The man squirmed and tried to free his arms, to no avail. "I was merely seeking information."

"Regarding?"

"The men who killed Horus."

Kollin's eyes narrowed. "Why?"

"I pursue them."

"They left for Cor Cordium over a week past."

"So your father says."

"And this is all you wished to know?"

"It is. In fact, we were about to leave when you arrived."

Kollin glanced toward Priella, who took the opening.

"What is your name, soldier?"

"Garvin. Trey Garvin."

She nodded at the man staring into space. "And his?"

"He goes by the name Rindle."

She smiled. "You are Lord Thurvin's men."

He blinked. "What makes you think so?"

"Lord Thurvin has mentioned you."

She released her grip on Rindle, who staggered, blinking as his mind recovered. With a wave of her hand, she said to Kollin, "Release him. These men will present no harm, nor will they attempt to flee. If they do..." She grinned, "they will regret it."

Kollin lowered Garvin to the ground, releasing him, the man staggering before regaining his balance.

Priella turned her attention to Kylar Mor. "Chancellor, the Tower of Devotion burns blue, the prayers of Tiamalyn now belonging to Lord Thurvin of Farrowen, who has plead fealty to me; therefore, your city is mine to command. Whether it happens with your compliance or not, it *will* happen. Comply and you will be rewarded, for I have little time for anything less than obedience."

He held up his hands again. "What does it matter? I can do nothing to stop you. My magic is useless."

"If I were to heal your wounds and place the city in your hands, would you commit your forces to my cause?

The man laughed. It was the sound of madness. When he saw the look in her eyes, he calmed. "If you can heal my hands, you can have anything you wish."

Priella smiled, her gaze shifting to Kollin, who watched his father, brows furrowed in concern. "I accept those terms."

Garvin watched curiously. He had been healed by magic numerous times – gashes knitted together, broken bones repaired, searing burns cooled. All left scars, but none approached the damage done to Kylar Mor's hands.

Queen Priella squatted before Mor and held out her hands, the man placing his twisted stumps onto her palms, her eyes closed. She remained still for a long moment, nothing happening. Mor suddenly jerked upright, his back arching, eyes bulging as his mouth opened in a silent scream. The nubs of his knuckles stretched, bones breaking through the skin. Raw flesh wrapped around the bones as they extended and grew, pale fingernails at the ends. The scarred skin on his hands peeled off and fell to the ground, fresh skin weaving together, spreading across his hands in moments.

He gasped for air, body sagging, as if exhausted. Priella opened her eyes and rose to her feet while the wizard stared at his hands in wonder, clenching and unclenching them. Then he began to cry.

"It is done," Priella said.

"His madness?" Kollin asked.

"I repaired that, as well."

"H-how?" Kollin stammered. "Regrowing appendages, healing mental defects... Both are impossible."

"Did you not see his fingers grow before your eyes?" She smiled. "I wield the power of a god, Kollin. The first woman in a thousand years to do so."

Kylar Mor continued to flex his fingers, the man still weeping. Then his hand lashed out, a blast of lightning arcing across the garden and striking a tree, thunder echoing as the tree cracked and toppled, the bark burning where the lightning had struck.

"Ha-ha!" Kylar Mor stood, grinning at his repaired hands. "I am whole again."

"We had a bargain, Chancellor," Priella said. "Your mind and magic are returned. I will now have my compensation." She narrowed her eyes toward Kollin. "How many soldiers are stationed in Tiamalyn?"

He shrugged. "Perhaps three thousand."

"Send twenty-five hundred north. They are to join my army in Fralyn within the week. Gather every bit of food you can spare and ship it with the force. Lastly, I want a list of every wizard and wizardess in the Tiamalyn Guild. You are to notify them that they have been enlisted. Any who don't report by the time the army reaches Balmor will be considered an outlaw and will answer to me." She glanced toward Grenda, who stared at Kollin. "Your son will accompany me. You and Queen Grenda will remain to govern the city jointly."

The man scowled. "I cannot–"

She gave Kylar a threatening glare. "Your hands are whole again, through the power of my gift. If you do not comply, not only could I reverse the process, but you could lose far more."

He nodded, swallowing. "Very well."

Priella smirked. "I am glad we have come to an accommodation." She turned toward Garvin and Rindle. "You two are coming with me."

"I had hoped to–" Garvin began, but stopped when he saw the fire in her eyes. "Yes, My Queen."

"Excellent." She turned toward the Tower of Devotion. "Lord Thurvin said you were capable. It appears you are intelligent, as well. I have need of such soldiers."

She spun around. "Gather your things, Kollin. I am going to eat, then we depart. We have an army to catch."

When Priella headed toward the castle, Queen Grenda's gaze followed, eyes narrowed in undisguised hatred.

13

PIRATES

Standing on the forecastle, Jace stared toward the island of Ryxx, his fingers absently toying with the blade hidden in his sleeve. While Narine had made his time spent below deck well worth the seclusion, fresh air was welcome.

The island rose high above the water, puffy clouds hugging a pair of jungle-covered peaks at the center. The harbor occupied an east-facing bay with a long, curved peninsula looping around the south side. Battlements ran along the peninsula, walls and short towers with catapults and ballistae mounted to the bulwark. At the end of the peninsula was a tall tower with mirrors at the top, men moving them and flashing a signal to the approaching ship.

Captain Harlequin shouted orders from the helm. Quiarre repeated them, the call going to the men on the main mast. A flag was attached to the top of the mast and hoisted up, rippling in the breeze, red fabric with a black bird of prey in the center. The mirrors on the tower stilled. As *Hassaka's Breath* rounded the point, the city of Ryxx came into view.

Dozens of ships occupied the harbor, masts all topped with the same red and black flag. Two ships sailed out as the vessel Jace stood upon drifted in.

Surrounded by steep hillsides, the city itself was nestled in a bowl at the bottom, just above the water's edge. A castle stood upon the hillside north of the city, overlooking the bay, machines of war lining the battlements.

Compared to the towering walls of great cities such as Fastella and Marquithe, the walls of Ryxx were mundane, none rising more than two stories. Still, Jace had never seen a harbor with such daunting defenses. Taking the city would be easy for invaders willing to pay the steep price to reach land.

Harlequin called for the sails to furl, the sailors responding with efficiency. The ship slowed, drifting in between two others moored a few hundred feet from shore. The anchors were lowered, one at the bow, another at the stern.

While the sailors prepared the longboat, Jace stared toward the castle on the hillside. It reminded him of Montague's outside of Lionne – standing above anyone approaching, making it difficult to sneak inside. It was by far the most defensible position on the island. Somewhere inside, Sariza waited to be rescued. He grimaced, having once performed a similar deed. The escapade had gone poorly, only yielding positive results after numerous twists and turns nearly ending in failure.

When he heard approaching footsteps, he turned to find Adyn, Narine, and Hadnoddon climbing the forecastle stairs.

When she reached the top, Adyn extended a hand toward him. "Here is your pack."

He accepted it, noting the black gloves covering her hands, red tunic over her torso secured at the waist by a thick, black belt. She wore matching black boots, turned down at the tops, brown breeches covering her legs. With the hood of her black cloak up, only the metal of her face was visible.

Jace nodded in approval. "Keep your hood up and we should avoid notice."

Narine put her hands on her hips. "Don't you think we know that?"

He grunted. "I suppose."

"So, you like her outfit?"

He shrugged. "Yeah. Looks great."

"That didn't seem sincere." Narine sounded hurt. "I spent a lot of time digging through Harlequin's things to choose just the right look."

Jace glanced toward the ship's captain at the helm at the far end of the ship. "She is roughly the same size as Adyn. I should have thought of it myself."

Narine prodded him. "I guess *you* can't think of everything."

"No." His gaze returned to the castle on the hillside above. "At the moment, I have bigger problems than worrying about Adyn's wardrobe."

Quiarre, bracketed by two sailors, stopped at the bottom of the stairs. One sailor was tall, bald, and thickly built, shirtless, tattoos on his face. The other was even taller but lean, with long, black hair and a curved mustache that draped past his chin.

The first mate waved. "Please, come down, Mister Landish." He then turned and headed across the ship.

Jace descended, he and his companions following as Quiarre angled toward the boat hanging over the edge of the starboard rail.

Stopping near it, Quiarre flashed a toothy grin. "The longboat is ready. Climb on, and I will escort you to the city."

"Thank you, Quiarre," Narine said.

He waggled a finger. "Not you, Princess. You will remain on the ship." He gestured, and the two sailors stepped forward, each man grabbing Narine by an arm.

Adyn had her swords out in a flash, tips inches from each of the sailors' chests. "Let her go."

Quiarre shook his head. "They cannot."

"Why are you doing this?" Jace asked. "This wasn't part of the agreement." He crossed his arms, prepared to grab the knives hidden up each sleeve. The hair on his arms stood on end as Narine gathered her magic.

She suddenly floated up, arms and fists pinned against her sides, grunting and struggling to move. In a flash, she flew across the deck, jerking to a stop at the top of the quarterdeck stairs. Harlequin drew a dagger and held it to Narine's neck. Jace then noticed Chandan standing outside the captain's cabin.

"Sorry, Princess," Chandan said, his hand outstretched toward Narine as he held her with his magic. "I cannot allow you to use your gift."

I should have guessed he was a wizard, Jace thought.

"Careful, Jerrell." Harlequin gestured toward the main mast. Jace looked up and saw two men holding crossbows, bolts loaded and aimed at Narine. "It would be heartbreaking to witness the woman you love killed because of your misstep." She sheathed her dagger, produced a black sash, and began binding Narine's hands behind her back.

Chandan released Narine, her slippered feet landing on the quarterdeck. He then strode across the deck, stopping before Jace, gaze intense.

"As you can see, Mister Landish, fighting at this point would be a poor decision. I suggest you accept your quest. Return with Sariza, and Narine will go free."

The two sailors met Harlequin at the bottom of the stairs. She handed Narine to them and approached to stand at Chandan's side.

Jace replied, "I need her help, Chandan. If you want Sariza alive, Narine's talents would tremendously increase our odds of success."

The wizard smiled. "Perhaps, but I know you have executed similar contracts without the assistance of magic. You will have to do so again. Harlequin will join you. I suspect you will find her knowledge of Ryxx, the castle, and Kalzon all invaluable to this venture." His grin widened. "She will also ensure you remain on course."

Frustration arose, Jace gritting his teeth and clenching his fists. He hated being manipulated. Worse, Chandan had discovered a weakness and exploited it, using Narine's life to extort him into complying.

Adyn stared at him, tense and waiting for his response, her swords remaining ready. A grimace twisted Hadnoddon's face, the dwarf appearing prepared to chew through metal. All it would take would be a single word or action from Jace, and they'd both fight. He might be willing to risk the others, but not Narine. She would be the first to die. *This is why I work alone.* A similar situation from his past had ended poorly. He had lost a friend that day. Despite the passing of years, the wound remained tender, the loss something he had never spoken of since.

Finally, he sighed. "Fine." He pointed toward Chandan. "But if any harm comes to her, I will cleave off your manhood and feed it to Harlequin while you watch."

Chandan's eyes widened, the wizard glancing toward the captain at his side.

Harlequin smirked. "You must admit, he has a flair for the dramatic, even if it would be nothing more than a light snack."

Chandan snorted. "How droll."

The wizard crossed the deck to the two sailors holding Narine. Gripping her upper arm, he pulled her close. "Do not worry, Princess." Chandan glanced back at Jace. "You will remain with me in the captain's quarters where you will be safe while the others go about their business."

The wizard ducked into the cabin beneath the quarterdeck, dragging

Narine with him. She cast a worried glance over her shoulder just before disappearing from sight. When the door closed, Quiarre turned to Jace.

"I am sorry it had to come to that, but this quest requires your utmost effort. Come. The longboat is ready." Without waiting for a reply, Quiarre climbed over the rail and stepped into the boat.

Harlequin approached and put a hand on Jace's chest, crooning softly into his ear. "Come along, my little thief." She then followed her first mate into the longboat.

"I don't like the smell of this." Hadnoddon scowled. "Let's get off this ship and back on solid land. I could use a drink."

Moments later, Jace stood at the rail, alone, the others in the longboat, waiting, while he stared toward the captain's cabin. When he turned toward the longboat, his gaze met Harlequin's. Her smirk remained. He wondered if it was due to confidence in their mission or something else. Worry twisted his innards as he gripped the rail. Even before the sailors had taken Narine, the entire situation had felt off, irritating him like an itch he couldn't scratch. Yet he could not figure out exactly why.

Once Jace climbed into the longboat, joining Adyn, Hadnoddon, Quiarre, Harlequin, and two other sailors, the winches were released, the pulleys squealing as the boat dropped toward the water. It stopped with a jerk just above the surface before lowering slowly. Once floating, the boat was disconnected, and the two sailors rowed toward shore.

As they neared shore, the warmer it became, the sea breeze blocked by the surrounding city and the hills beyond. With concerted effort, Jace tore his attention from the receding ship, dashing his concerns for Narine and focusing on the approaching city.

The buildings were all made of tan stone, as was the two-story-tall wall. Strangely, no guards stood at the gate. He looked closer, realizing there *was* no gate, only an open archway, sailors dressed in loose clothing passing through, all with the black hair and coppery skin of Hassakani.

We are going to stick out, he thought. He hated being noticeable, preferring to blend in, his appearance unremarkable and unmemorable until it was too late for his targets.

The boat drew near the docks, Adyn grabbing a post and pulling the bow close.

"Get out," she said.

Jace, Hadnoddon, and Harlequin climbed onto the dock before Adyn joined them. Quiarre pushed the boat away, it drifting out while the men on the oars turned it around.

"How will we get back to the ship once we have her?" Jace asked from the dock.

Quiarre pulled a clump of red cloth from his tunic and tossed it to him. "Wave this from the docks and we will come."

The sailors set to work, rowing in unison, propelling the boat back toward the moored ship.

Quiarre raised his voice. "Focus on the prize, Mister Landish. Remember what you risk should you fail. Time is short, so hurry."

The longboat faded between two ships, and Jace turned toward his companions.

"Time is short," he sighed. "We had better find an inn and begin scouting."

14

A DRESS

The hood of her cloak raised, head lowered to cast shadow across her face, Adyn Darro's gaze flicked from side to side, taking in her surroundings as she followed Jace, Hadnoddon, and Harlequin into Ryxx.

Stone buildings lined the narrow, curving streets rising from the harbor. Crates, barrels, and refuse lay beside buildings and in alleys. Holes had been patched in many of the walls, the new bricks and mortar a different hue than the old. The city itself exuded hostility, as if the very land it was built upon would fight back should anyone challenge it.

Copper-skinned Hassakani were everywhere – women wearing florid dresses with ruffles on the shoulders and skirts, necklines swooping to expose tanned skin and the hint of cleavage, the men dressed in loose tunics cinched at the waist and puffy trousers tucked into tall boots. All had black hair and dark eyes, the men often with beards thick enough to make a dwarf proud. There was a sense of toughness about the people, even the women. More than once, fierce-looking pirates nodded toward Harlequin as she walked by.

After passing a handful of intersections, they arrived at a small square, a blue fountain bubbling in the center. The square was a hub of sorts, narrow streets branching off in six different directions. It was a busy place with merchants exchanging wares for coin, women filling jugs of water, and a bard playing a lute, people surrounding him, clapping to the beat of the music. Yet Adyn saw no guards or any children.

They took a narrow street and arrived at another busy square, the Obelisk of Devotion jutting up from the center, the peak shimmering with a crimson light.

Harlequin stopped in the shade of the obelisk and turned toward Jace, a hand on her hip, sly smile on her face. "So, my little thief, how do you intend to proceed?"

His gaze went to the hillside overlooking the city. "She is surely being held in the castle. We need to find an easy way in. If I can get in and locate her, I'll come up with a way to get her out."

"Very well." The captain pointed down a street covered in shadow. "Down that route is an inn called The Serpent's Hole. It's a rough place, but they know me." She dug out a silver piece. "Procure us two rooms and wait for me there."

Jace grimaced at the coin in his palm. "I prefer to do my own planning."

"Your reputation won't get you far here. I am known in Ryxx and am far more likely to have success." She patted him on the cheek. "You just sit tight. I'll be along shortly."

The woman turned and crossed the square, her backside swaying overtly in her tight breeches.

Adyn noticed Jace watching and nudged him with her elbow. "Don't stray just because Narine isn't around."

He cast her a hurt expression. "Do you think I would do such a thing?"

Adyn watched Harlequin until she turned down another street. "She is an attractive woman, so the temptation is understandable." She flashed him a smile. "Just resist your urges, or I'll have to kick your little arse."

Jace sighed. "Why is everyone threatening me today?"

"I haven't," Hadnoddon said. "Not yet anyway." When Jace rolled his eyes, he grinned. "Let's find this snake place and see what's on tap."

Jace leading, they walked down the street indicated by Harlequin. Although curving and leading uphill, it was narrow and contained enough refuse to feel like an alley.

They passed a group of men huddled behind a building, one speaking in a hushed tone. The man stopped talking, watching them as they walked past, before resuming their conversation. Adyn had the feeling the group was up to something illegal and wondered what laws, if any, were enforced on the island.

Rounding a bend, they came to a stone building with a red door, a small window at the front. The sign above the door depicted a picture of a viper rearing up from a hole in the ground.

"This must be the place," Jace said. "Try not to cause trouble."

"I will if you will," Adyn replied, following him inside.

Torches mounted to posts running down the middle illuminated the dark interior. The room smelled of sweat and stale ale. It was mid-afternoon, only seven chairs occupied in a space large enough for ten times that number. None of the patrons appeared welcoming, scowls and dark eyes beneath heavy brows aimed at the newcomers.

Jace stepped up to the bar, the heavy-set man behind it glowering. He was bald with a scar across his cheek – a pale trail leading to a black patch over one eye. The man leaned against the bar, his visible eye glaring at Jace.

"You have the look of trouble."

Jace blinked, placing a hand against his chest. "Who? Me?"

"I ain't talkin' to the runt."

Hadnoddon growled, "Who you calling a runt?"

The barkeep's gaze flicked to Hadnoddon, then back to Jace. "It would be best if you left. Your coppers ain't worth risking broken furniture."

Jace grinned and flipped a silver into the air, the coin landing on the bar. "No copper here, my good sir. Take the silver and trust me when I tell you we have no intention of causing trouble."

The man glared at the coin, as if considering a deal from a demon. Finally, he scooped it up.

"Wonderful," Jace said. "We need a room for the night. Three ales, as well, if you would."

Scowl still in place, the barkeep turned to the shelf, grabbed three tankards, and filled them. He set the full mugs on the bar and turned to help another patron.

Jace lifted his mug and headed for an open table beneath the only window. Adyn and Hadnoddon joined him, her sitting carefully, fearful of the chair breaking. It was something she was still getting used to, as was hiding her flesh. *Is it considered flesh any longer?* She slipped a glove off and ran her metal fingers over her face, which had become a habit. And not just her face, but her entire body. Much like the rest of Adyn, her face felt warm but hard, the surface smooth. She squeezed her cheeks and found slight give. Other parts of her had retained a softness, parts she preferred remain soft, but most of the sensation was lost to her.

Can I ever have sex again? she wondered. Such urges seemed to have fled, leaving only a faint memory of what once was. *Will I ever want to?* The oddest part? She was unsure if she cared.

Lifting her mug, she took a drink. The taste was muted, even the sensation of the bubbles on her tongue and throat dulled to the point where it was barely noticeable.

Seeing a looming shadow out of the corner of her eye, she turned to find a large man standing over the table, his arms crossed over a barrel chest, stance wider than his broad shoulders. A red swath of material was tied to his head, his tanned face covered by a curly, black beard.

The man glared down at Jace. "I don't like the look of you."

"Do I know you?" Jace asked nonchalantly.

"I'm Bast the Bold."

He shrugged. "Never heard of you."

"I'm well-known in Ryxx. If you ain't heard of me, you must be an outsider. I suggest you go before it's too late."

Jace snorted. "I'd love to leave this forsaken island, but fate landed me here, at least for one night." Lifting his mug, he took a drink and wiped the foam from his lips. "In the meantime, I'm enjoying an ale with my friends."

Bast looked back toward his companions across the tavern and huffed. "Trouble will find you if you don't leave." The man narrowed his eyes at Jace. "When I look at you, I don't like what I see."

The thief looked the man from head to toe, even leaning around to check out the newcomer's backside. "To tell you the truth, you aren't my type, either. But don't worry. If you keep searching, I'm sure you will find a man who loves you properly."

A cloud passed over his face, his expression darkening. "I will tear your head off and feed it to the goats in the square."

Adyn leaned forward and whispered, "You were supposed to stay out of trouble."

Jace seemed ready to retort, his expression softening before he nodded and looked up at the man. "I'm sorry. I thought you were interested in me romantically. I face the problem often because I am so loveable." He stood and clapped a hand on the bigger man's shoulder. "To make up for the misunderstanding, let me buy you a drink."

The man growled, "Get your hands off me."

Jace did so hastily. "I'm just trying to be friendly."

"Get out before I smash your head in."

The thief frowned. "I am to meet someone here, so I cannot."

The two men at Bast's table stood and stalked over, flanking the big man. If he was built like a building, the other two were towers. One had a shaved head, goatee, and hoops dangling from his ears. The other man had long, black hair tied in a tail, arching eyebrows, and a hook nose with a ring in one nostril. Both were well over six feet in height.

"Are these three bothering you, Bast?" the bald man asked.

"Yeah, Jokal," he sneered. "They refuse to leave, even though I can't stand the sight of 'em."

The man with the ring in his nose grinned. "Perhaps we should show them proper manners."

Things had clearly spun out of control, the three pirates obviously intent on starting a fight. Rather than wait on Jace to get them in deeper, Adyn took things into her own hands.

She stood and removed her other glove, whipping it into Bast's face. The big man flinched, and her fist followed, metal knuckles connecting with his chin. He stumbled backward, the other two men dodging as he fell over a chair and to the floor. The man with the nose ring lunged at Adyn, a dagger flashing. It tore through her tunic and clanged off her torso, the effect feeling like no more than an insect bite. She chopped down with her hands, striking his forearm, bone cracking. He cried out, the blade clattering to the floor.

Hadnoddon roared and charged the man, grabbing the much taller pirate by the waist and lifting him off the floor. The pirate pounded against Hadnoddon's upper back, having no apparent effect. The dwarf flipped his assailant forward while going to one knee, driving the pirate's back into his other, a frightening *crack* resounding.

Jace ducked a punch and drove his fist into the bald man's groin. As the pirate doubled over, Jace chopped his wrist into his windpipe. The man staggered backward, clutching his throat. Jace stepped on a chair, then the table-top, and leapt. He came down hard, driving his elbow down upon the top of the choking man's head. He collapsed, falling backward onto another occupied table, smashing it, ale splashing everywhere.

Chaos ensued.

The four men seated there came at Jace. The thief dodged the first punch, the next hitting him in the mouth and knocking him over a table. Adyn grabbed a chair and threw it, striking two of Jace's attackers. Hadnoddon charged past, arms swinging as he met the other two men. His first punch struck one in the kidney, the other in the groin. The latter pirate staggered, and Hadnoddon shoved him into the two trying to get to their feet. The dwarf then dove on top of the three men and began exchanging punches.

Still lying on the table, Jace brought his knees to his chest and kicked out. The last pirate standing took the blow to the chest and stumbled backward. He righted himself and came toward Jace, but Adyn's forearm struck his collarbone, knocking him off his feet. The pirate landed flat on his back, striking his head on the floor, lying still.

Adyn stood back and took measure, while Jace rolled off the table and Hadnoddon climbed back to his feet.

Seven pirates lay on the floor, three unconscious, the other four moaning, one squirming as he held his throat and tried to breathe.

Harlequin crossed the room from the doorway, sighing. "You three were to *avoid* trouble." She stopped beside Adyn and looked down at the men on the floor, her eyes rising to meet the thief's. "I see you cannot be trusted to obey orders."

"I *tried* to play nice. They wouldn't have it." Jace gingerly touched his lip, bloody and already swollen. "The fat one over there said he didn't like my face. He's not the first to feel that way." He shrugged. "Sometimes that's just how it goes."

Harlequin shook her head, dug out a silver, and turned toward the bar. "Sorry about the mess, Arik." She tossed the coin to the barkeep. "Save us a room. I'll pay for any broken furniture later."

Arik caught the coin. "Welcome back, Harley. I hope you can keep this lot out of trouble."

She snorted as she walked to the door, speaking over her shoulder. "Fat chance of that, I fear."

Opening it, she stepped outside. Adyn, Jace, and Hadnoddon followed, finding Harlequin waiting, arms crossed.

"If you are finished playing, we have work to do."

"Honestly, it wasn't our idea," Adyn said.

The woman narrowed her eyes. "Perhaps. I know locals sometimes take issue with those outside our profession lurking about."

She turned toward Jace. "I have found a way into the castle, but it requires some compromise on your part. You see, the two of us are going to a party."

Jace grinned. "I adore parties."

"You won't enjoy this one so much." She smirked. "First, we need to find you a dress."

15

MASQUERADE

"**O**uch." Jace winced. "That stings." His lips remained swollen from the fight, the cut tender, his face and neck still raw from shaving.

"Oh hush, you big baby," Adyn said, pausing from painting his lips.

He pursed his lips again, waiting while she finished, trying to think of something else, his thoughts turning toward Narine. *She had better be safe, or Chandan will discover my sadistic side.* If all went as planned, he would be back on the ship before dawn.

Stop thinking of her, he told himself. *Focus on the objective.*

Once done, Adyn stepped back, her liquid silver eyes sparkling in the light streaming through the window of their second-story room.

"What do you think?" she asked.

"When painted red, his swollen upper lip actually adds to the effect," Harlequin replied. "Put the wig on him so we can see how it looks."

Adyn grabbed the black wig off the coconut on the table and slid it onto his head, pulling it down until it covered his own hair, twisting it so it aligned with his face. "He looks adorable."

Harlequin sauntered over, tilting her head as she examined Jace. She gripped his jaw, turning it. "Has anyone ever told you that you make an attractive woman?"

Hadnoddon snickered from his spot on the bed, the dwarf lying on his back, arms behind his head, grin on his face. He clearly enjoyed Jace's transformation.

"In truth," Jace said, "I have heard it once before and from a very pretty girl." He smiled, recalling the evening he had stolen the bracelet from High Wizard Montague. It had been among his more famous escapades, having occurred while the wizard's castle was filled with guests. The wizard being discovered naked and tied to his own bed likely added to the popularity of the tale.

"All right," Harlequin said. "Strip and slip into the dress."

Jace considered a quip but decided to comply. In truth, he did not care if she or anyone else was watching. He was already bare from the waist up anyway.

He pulled off his boots and set them aside. His breeches came next, Jace folding them and placing them with his boots. He then lifted a black skirt with red ruffles from the bed, eyeing it. Harlequin arched a brow, a wry smile on her face.

"What?" he asked, glancing down at himself wearing only his small-clothes.

"Nothing," she replied, mouth turned up in a smirk. "It's just novel to watch a man don women's clothing."

He frowned. "Aren't you supposed to do the same?"

Her eyes widened in feigned surprise. "Why yes, I am."

Hat removed in a flourish, she shook out her long, dark hair, outlined in the amber glow of the setting sun. She then uncinched her belt, Jace unprepared for what came next.

The woman unlaced her tunic and pulled it over her head to expose a fit, tanned torso, naked as the day she was born. A sunburst was tattooed just above her left breast. With a long, lean build and enough curves to capture his attention, Jace didn't realize he was staring until Adyn nudged him, breaking him from his trance.

I had better not tell Narine about this, he said to himself as he stepped into the skirt.

The ship captain pulled a ruffled blouse over her head, slipping her arms through and pulling it down over her chest. She then stepped into her skirt, not bothering to remove her boots or breeches.

"You're wearing your boots?" Jace asked.

She smirked. "It's common enough for women to wear boots on Ryxx. In fact, many men find it sexy."

"What about your breeches?"

"Nobody is going to see them, so why take them off?"

He blinked at her. "Why didn't you say so earlier?"

Her smile grew lecherous, her focus on his lower body. "Perhaps I wished to see how far you would strip."

"Blasted woman," he grumbled as he dropped the skirt and bent to grab his breeches, muttering to himself while he pulled them up.

Once his boots were back on, he stepped into the skirt and pulled it up to his waist before donning a white, sleeveless blouse, the low neckline ruffled across his chest. He had been forced to shave that, as well.

"You will have to remove the amulet," Harlequin said. "While stylish in a way, it doesn't suit your new look."

He gripped the amulet hanging from his neck, turning it over in his hand. Removing the Eye meant giving up his protection from magic. Reluctantly, he unhooked the clasp and pulled the cord from around his neck, the amulet spinning in the amber light streaming through the window. He stuffed it into his pack and turned as Adyn dug through the bowl of fruit on the table.

She held up a grapefruit and turned toward him. "Use this to fill out your corset."

"I think not." He grabbed a pair of oranges from the bowl. "I have had poor experiences with grapefruit in the past. Better if I use something more modest. Less weight and less...you know."

Adyn grinned, a black corset in her hands. "Good idea. Slide them into place and turn toward me."

With two oranges stuffed beneath his blouse, Adyn wrapped the corset around his waist and laced it together. He marveled at how fast her fingers moved.

"You have stellar dexterity," he said. "With those hands, I could teach you to pick locks."

She grinned as she worked. "I prefer to break down doors. Much faster and far less tedious."

He chuckled. "Fair point."

With the laces in place, Adyn cinched the corset tight. "It's a good thing you have a slim waist."

He groaned, the corset restricting his breathing. "Does it have to be so tight?"

Harlequin chuckled from across the room. "It's high time you men got a taste of the lengths we go through."

He turned toward her to find her similarly dressed. She looked stunning.

"My, my." Harlequin smiled, methodically scanning Jace from head to toe. "You do make a fetching woman."

"As do you."

The reply slipped out before he realized it. He paid the price when Adyn elbowed him. Wincing as he rubbed his ribs, he turned to her. "Your elbows are incredibly hard."

Adyn's look was unreadable, her silvery eyes staring at him. "Remember who is waiting for you on the ship."

Narine. "How could I forget?"

Harlequin moved close to Jace and held out a glass vial filled with a dark liquid. He accepted it while she tucked an identical one into her cleavage.

"What is this?" he asked, holding it up and turning it, scrutinizing the contents.

"The same drug you drank when you boarded my ship."

He glanced at her. "Langiun?"

"Very good, Jacira."

"Jacira?" Adyn asked.

"Yes… His name for the evening." Harlequin turned back to Jace. "Now, store the vial safely. You may need it before the night is through."

Jace stuffed the vial between the oranges on his chest, snuggly held in place by the corset.

"Come along." Harlequin opened the door and stepped into the corridor. "We must procure a carriage."

Beneath the darkening skies above Ryxx, Jace gripped his ruffled skirts to keep them from dragging in the dirt as they climbed the uphill road. The largest homes were built on the hillside surrounding Ryxx, the only homes likely to have a carriage.

The road leveled as they came to an intersection. To the right, the road led toward Ryxx Castle. Harlequin, who was in the lead, turned to the left and followed the gravel along the rim above the city. Walled compounds lined the uphill side, each home large enough to house three families, the view of the city and the bay beyond well worth the climb.

Even dressed as she was, Harlequin exuded toughness, her arms lean but muscular, eyes defiant, jaw firm. Jace had to admit, despite his feelings for Narine, he was drawn to her. *She is just another challenge,* he told himself. If he had met Harlequin a year earlier, he would have made every effort to bed her. Based on the not-so-subtle clues she had given him, such a conquest was likely to succeed and even more likely to be worth the effort.

He shook his head. *Stop thinking about her, Jace. Remember Narine. She needs you to focus on the mission.* The words repeated in his head, talking his ego and urges down from the precipice.

Even with evening upon them, the sea breeze was warm, of which Jace was thankful. He was unused to having his shoulders and chest bare to the elements. *It has been a while since I portrayed a woman without the use of illusion,* he thought. The last time had been as a maid in the Enchanter's Tower back in Marquithe, back before the world had gone mad.

Harlequin stopped beside an open gate and peered inside.

Past the gate was an uphill drive leading to an impressive manor, a carriage parked beside a fountain in front. A man sat in the driver's seat, his head resting on his chest as he dozed, his black, brimmed hat down over his eyes. Nobody else was in sight, amber light coming from multiple windows in the manor.

"Come along," she whispered as she strode inside.

The other three followed. Adyn wore her black cloak, Hadnoddon dressed in a white tunic and black trousers, both supplied by Harlequin. The sleeves and pant legs had been too long for the stout dwarf, both needing to be rolled up to fit properly.

Stopping beside the carriage, Harlequin tapped Adyn on the shoulder and pointed toward the driver before tucking both hands against her cheek, closing her eyes, and tilting her head. Adyn nodded and climbed up, the carriage rocking.

The man woke. "What?" He lifted his head, straightening his hat as he turned toward her. "Who are–"

Adyn's fist struck the man's skull with a metallic thud. His head drooped to the side. She pulled him from his seat, handing him down to Hadnoddon, the driver's hat falling to the ground. The dwarf dragged the unconscious man behind some shrubs, while Jace and Harlequin climbed into the carriage.

With the unconscious man's hat on his head, Hadnoddon joined Adyn in the driver's seat, grabbed the reins, and snapped them. The horses pulled the carriage down the driveway and onto the road. At the same moment, a beam of red light arced across the sky over the bay, the Obelisk of Devotion blooming. Hadnoddon stopped the carriage and gazed toward the red light above the city. The chant of Devotion arose, the citizens of Ryxx praying to Hassaka and feeding the power of their wizard lord.

Adyn kept her hood raised as she rode beside Hadnoddon, the horses pulling the wagon at a trot. Torches lined the street and bracketed the open gate outside the castle. The carriage slowed. Two men dressed in long, red tunics and black, billowing trousers approached. One had a short-cropped beard, the other's reaching his chest. Each wore a black turban on his head, dark eyes glaring beneath a heavy brow.

"State your name and reason for your visit," said the guard with the short, black beard.

Per instructions, Adyn and Hadnoddon remained silent.

Harlequin stuck her head out the window. "It is Lady Quin of Jinakka and my sister, Jacira. We have an invitation for High Wizard Kalzon's betrothal."

"I don't recognize you or the name. Show me your invitation," a guard demanded.

"Welcome back, milady." The other man gave her a deferential nod, then clapped a hand on his companion's shoulder. "Let her pass, Hazzal. I recognize her from an event three years ago."

"What about him?" the first guard pointed toward Adyn.

"That is my new bodyguard, Adonis," Harlequin replied. "He will remain with my carriage to escort me back to my ship tonight, after the event. One cannot be too careful in Ryxx."

One guard grunted, the other waving them along. Hadnoddon snapped the reins, and they entered the castle grounds, passing another cluster of guards standing just beyond the gate.

The road turned from gravel to cobblestone, the wheels rumbling noisily as they rode up the winding drive. Palms and ferns lined the roadway. After two sharp turns, the ground leveled, and the castle came into view. A dozen carriages waited outside the building, the area illuminated by torches on six-foot-tall posts. At one end of a two-story-tall wall, guards in red and black stood on either side of an open doorway, amber light and the hum of a chatter emanating from inside.

When the carriage stopped, Adyn climbed down and opened the door, holding it while Harlequin and Jace climbed out.

Harlequin raised her voice. "Thank you, Adonis. Remain with the carriage until I return." She then whispered, "Be ready in case we must make a hurried escape." The pair crossed the courtyard, passed the armed guards outside the entrance, and faded from view.

Adyn sighed and glanced toward Hadnoddon, who looked sufficiently ridiculous in the hat he had stolen. "I don't trust her."

He grunted. "I know what you mean. She is like the thief. Hiding more than she shares."

"Yeah, but at least he has heartstrings tying him to Narine. She holds no such allegiance. If I knew why she was helping, I might feel better about this. As it stands, I fear she might betray us."

16

RESCUE

J ace, as Jacira, walked beside Harlequin, the pair entering an open bailey occupied by men holding cups filled with ale, wine, or even swoon. There were women, as well, each surrounded by a cluster of males. Everyone was dressed in loose fabrics – tunics, doublets, dresses, and robes in a variety of solid colors, accompanied by leather belts, boots, and corsets on the women, some on the verge of overflowing.

Square turrets jutted above each corner of the bailey. Men in red and black stood upon them, gazing down at the crowd. Some held crossbows, others wore scimitars on their hips. In contrast to the city, with no guards at the gates or soldiers patrolling the streets, the castle appeared surprisingly well-guarded.

Harlequin scanned the crowd in the bailey before heading inside.

The entrance hall was grand, easily the most impressive thing Jace had seen since arriving on the island. Orange, green, and gray slate tiles covered the floor. Three stories above, a painting of a naval battle covered the ceiling. A thick, black chain hung down from the ceiling, supporting a circular chandelier holding dozens of lit candles. A stairwell divided the large, open area, rising a full story before splitting and rising another flight to the right and to the left. To each side of the ascending stairs in front of him, a half-flight of downward stairs led to a recessed ballroom filled with guests.

Jace and Harlequin stopped and stared out across the ballroom, him assessing the situation, her seeking their quarry.

The woman pointed toward a tall man in red-trimmed white robes. His long, dark hair was combed back, his beard neatly trimmed across a square jaw. He had a bright, engaging smile, laughing at something that was said.

"That is the High Wizard."

Jace nodded. "What about the girl?"

"I don't see her. Perhaps she is upstairs. I will go find her. You keep Kalzon busy."

"Me? How?"

"You are supposed to be the clever one." She patted Jace on the cheek. "Men are easy to manipulate, of which I am sure you are aware."

She proceeded up the stairs, leaving Jace to himself…until an arm slipped around his waist. He turned to find a tall, thin man with curly, dark hair smiling at him. The man's teeth had gaps, gums visible. His eyes were too close together, bracketing an over-sized nose.

"Hello," he said. "I am Wilzon, Kalzon's brother."

Jace stepped back to create more space. He glanced toward Kalzon again, noting his handsome features. *How are these two related?* "Nice to meet you," he replied in a dulcet tone.

"And your name is?" Wilzon pressed.

"Jacira."

"Ah. A beautiful name for a beautiful woman."

Jace glanced toward the ballroom and saw Kalzon crossing the floor, pausing to speak to a couple. He turned back toward Wilzon. "It was wonderful to meet you. Please, pardon me. I wish to congratulate your brother before I miss the opportunity."

He turned away, but the other man grabbed his arm and pulled him close. "Don't worry about Kalzon. He will be around all evening."

His hand went to the wig on Jace's head, brushing a stray hair aside. "Can you not feel it? We are like two stars colliding, destined to become one, distantly outshining anything else in the sky."

Jace stifled his laughter, coughing into his hand to hide it. *Do men truly believe women will swoon from such ridiculous lines?*

Wilzon continued speaking, Jace tuning it out as he watched Kalzon approach, climb the stairs from the ballroom, walk past his brother, and continue his ascent toward the upper levels. When Jace tried to pull away,

Wilzon firmed his grip on his arm. The man pressed his other hand against Jace's lower back, forcing their bodies together. Jace worried the man might feel parts that didn't belong on a woman.

The wizard's voice was filled with lust. "I want you, Jacira. I must have you."

Once again, Jace tried to slip away. "I…" *Need to go after Kalzon.*

"I am a wizard." Wilzon leaned forward and whispered, his breath tickling Jace's ear, "Have you ever had a wizard's magical staff inside you?"

It took everything Jace had to not burst out laughing. He turned away, calming himself. Wilzon misread the reaction.

"Ah," he whispered, his hand caressing Jace's shoulder. "You are overwhelmed. Do not worry. I will be gentle."

Another glance toward the stairs, and Jace caught a glimpse of Kalzon rising toward the left corridor, the same direction Harlequin had gone.

I need to get up there.

He looked at Wilzon, deciding it would be easier to lead the man in the direction of his desire.

Jace put a hand on the man's chest and trailed it down his torso until he gripped Wilzon's sash. "Come with me," he whispered. "I can wait no longer." Still gripping his sash, Jace pulled the man toward the stairs. "Let's find someplace private."

Wilzon grinned as they climbed the stairs, his hand on the small of Jace's back, soon slipping down until it cupped his arse. Jace ignored it and focused on catching up to Kalzon.

At the top was a long corridor lit by enchanted lanterns secured to the wall. Wilzon led Jace to the second door on the right and opened it to a lavish chamber with ornate furniture, a white, fur rug, and a four-poster bed draped in red silks.

"Come with me, my little flower," he purred as he gently pushed Jace inside.

Shouts came from down the corridor, a man's voice, a woman crying out.

Jace spun from Wilzon and raced down the hallway. He reached an open door to a sitting room occupied by two red velvet sofas, a pair of padded chairs, and a low, wooden table lacquered with a black finish. Across the room, Kalzon stood just inside the door to a connecting chamber, the wizard's back to Jace, arms extended before him. The man advanced deeper into the room as Jace followed.

"What have you done to her?" Kalzon growled in a deep voice. "If she is harmed, you will die a slow, painful death."

When Jace reached the doorway, he saw what had the man so upset.

On the bed in the center of the room lay a beautiful young woman, finely dressed, with long, black hair and coppery skin. Her eyes were closed, apparently unconscious. Three women lay sprawled on the floor, two with their throats slit, empty eyes staring into infinity, the third with a dagger in her chest, upper body leaning against the foot of the bed. Above it all, hovering over a tall, pointed bedpost, was Harlequin, her back pinned to the high ceiling, arms spread. One of her hands was covered in blood. The other gripped an empty vial.

Kalzon spun toward Jace, eyes red with anger. "Who are you?"

Jace's mind raced through his options.

A blade was hidden in each of his boots, another strapped to his leg, all covered by his skirt. Reaching any of them before the man attacked would be difficult. Even if he were successful, Harlequin would be skewered by the bedpost if the man's magic faltered. He made a quick decision.

His hands went to his cheeks, eyes round as he cried out in his best womanly voice, "My sister!"

He rushed past the man and knelt beside the woman with the dagger in her chest, his hand caressing her cheek, his back to Kalzon.

"I didn't know Yira had a sister," Kalzon said.

With his back blocking the man's view, Jace eased his other hand to the dagger in her chest, fingers wrapping around the hilt. He tensed, preparing himself.

"Guards! Guards!" Wilzon's voice came from the neighboring room.

With a sharp jerk, Jace pulled the blade free. Rising and spinning in one fluid motion, he threw, the blade crossing the room in a flash before plunging into Kalzon's throat. The wizard staggered backward, eyes bulging as he emitted a gurgling sound. Jace lifted his knee and spun again, driving his heel into the bedpost. The post cracked near the bedframe and tilted toward the bed but did not break off. The wizard's magic faltering, Harlequin fell, collided with the angled post just below the tip, bounced off it, and tumbled into Jace. He tried to catch her, but her momentum was too much. Unable to stop himself, Jace stumbled backward, tripped over a dead woman, and fell into Kalzon just as Wilzon reached the doorway, all going down in a heap.

Harlequin rolled off Jace, and he scrambled to his feet, spinning to find

Kalzon's eyes bulging, blood bubbling from his mouth. Wilzon lay beneath him, a streak of blood on the marble tiles near his head, eyes closed. The man moaned, his eyes slowly blinking open.

Jace leapt over Kalzon, gripped Wilzon's head, and lifted it, slamming it back down. His skull struck the floor with a sickening *crack*, and he fell still, Jace panting over the man.

"Your timing was fortuitous," Harlequin said.

He spun toward her. "What happened in here?"

She ran over to the bed and pulled the unconscious woman to the edge. "Kalzon called out from the room next door right after I had drugged her. I shouted back that the princess was changing, but he demanded to see her. I killed the other three just before he opened the door."

Jace frowned. "This was your plan?"

Shouts and the thunder of running came from the corridor. Jace hurriedly rolled Kalzon off his brother and dragged the two wizards inside. Three guards brandishing scimitars rushed into the sitting room just as Jace slammed the bedroom door closed. He locked it and rushed over to the wardrobe, grunting as he pushed it in front of the door.

Jace turned toward Harlequin, who hoisted the unconscious Sariza over her shoulder. "We need to get out of here. Now." He raced over to the window and peered outside.

They were a half-story above the bailey wall. Some of the guards rushed along the wall and toward an entrance at the far end, likely hearing the call to arms. Four armed men remained, two on each outer turret. Not ideal, but he had faced worse odds.

Jace spun away from the window and spotted a chair beside a black vanity covered in jars, vials, and brushes. He grabbed the chair, lifted it over his head, and charged the window, throwing it. The chair crashed through the glass, shards spraying out over the bailey. Shouts and screams came from the crowd below.

"Ditch the skirts. It'll be easier if they aren't in our way." He pulled his skirt down and kicked it off. "I'll climb out first. When I am ready, you hand her down to me."

Using the pommel of his dagger, Jace broke the remaining pieces of glass from the frame, then quickly ducked when a crossbow bolt sailed through the window, narrowly missing him.

He peered outside, the sky dark, the full moon shining down, torches lighting the towers above the bailey. Two guards raced from the nearest tower and along the wall, straight toward him.

Dropping his dagger, Jace snatched the throwing blades from his boots, stood, and threw. The first blade buried deep in a man's chest, but the second guard ducked, the knife sailing past. The first guard fell into the bailey, while guests urgently vacated the area. Jace scooped up his dagger and jumped out the window to land on the three-foot-wide wall.

The remaining guard rushed toward him, scimitar slashing. Jace dodged backward just beyond the blade's arc and followed with a swift kick, his boot striking the man's hand, the sword spinning out toward the waiting carriages. The guard threw a fist, Jace ducking and ramming his dagger into the man's groin. Screaming, the man stumbled off the wall and fell into the bailey, clutching his bloodied crotch. Jace stood and stored his dagger while turning back to the window.

Harlequin stood above with Sariza draped over her shoulder. She leaned forward, the princess sliding into Jace's arms. Although Sariza was a small woman, like Rhoa, Jace stumbled backward and nearly lost his balance, righting himself as Harlequin jumped down to the wall. He turned and ran toward the tower, his gaze sweeping over the carriages, searching for Adyn and Hadnoddon.

～

Seated on the carriage seat with Hadnoddon at her side, Adyn stared toward the castle. Their carriage was one among dozens, the area smelling of horses and manure.

There were too many people inside for her to feel comfortable regarding the situation. She knew Jace was clever, but the plan had been hatched by Harlequin, and the woman was difficult to trust.

Cries arose from inside, guards on the bailey wall rushing toward the castle. A crash of breaking glass, followed by a chair spinning through a window. Unsurprisingly, Jace peered through the broken panes.

"Hadnoddon! It's Jace." Adyn pointed toward the window. "Circle around!" The carriage lurched into motion, and Adyn climbed onto the roof, shouting down to the dwarf. "Get us near the wall!"

When Jace jumped out the window, a guard on the wall rushed him. At the same time, a cluster of guards emerged from a door just to the side of the carriage, the men running toward the bailey. Adyn drew her swords and jumped down. She landed on the rear of the pack of soldiers, taking three down with her weight. The other five guards stopped and turned toward her, scimitars flashing.

Adyn lashed out, her sword opening a gash across the first soldier's stomach. Another man swung, but she blocked the strike with her forearm, the sword tearing through her sleeve and clanging off her skin. She countered with an underhand thrust, skewering him before she moved on to the remaining three.

Swords came from both sides. She blocked one with her blade, another with a forearm, a third clanging off her exposed hip. Adyn swept a broad stroke, blade tip tearing through cloth and flesh. The next swipe took two of the men down, a fist to the jaw felling the final assailant.

She raced after the carriage, her gaze going to the top of the wall where another fight ensued.

～

Jace stood on the tower roof, Sariza held against his chest, while Harlequin fought two men with a scimitar she had claimed from a fallen soldier. Their blades collided in a rapid staccato, Harlequin holding her own. She kicked, forcing one man back to the wall.

Jace shifted Sariza's weight and threw her over his shoulder. One hand freed, he dug an orange out of his corset, cocked, and threw. The fruit struck a guard in the face, the man wincing and lowering his guard. Harlequin slashed. Her scimitar struck the side of his neck, and he spun way in a spray of blood. Able to focus on a single guard, she dispatched him quickly, slicing a nasty gash in his leg, followed by a kick that sent him off the wall. He fell outside the bailey and struck the ground just before a carriage wheel ran him over. The carriage stopped, Hadnoddon climbing onto the roof.

"Throw her down," he shouted.

Jace stepped out on the wall, lowered Sariza into his arms, then tossed her forward, her red skirts whirling as she flew through the air. Hadnoddon caught her with a grunt, staggering but not falling. Adyn raced up. alongside the carriage. The dwarf handed Sariza down to Adyn, and she stuffed her into the carriage.

"Jump down!" Hadnoddon shouted as he climbed back onto the driver's seat.

A cluster of guards burst out of the entrance and turned toward the carriage, swords ready. Jace leapt toward the carriage and landed on the top, nearly falling off. Harlequin landed on the roof and barreled into him, knocking him over the edge as the carriage lurched forward.

He hit the cobblestones and rolled, injuring his shoulder in the process. Twenty guards in red and black raced toward him. He rose to his feet, spun, and chased after the carriage as it turned onto the snaking drive, toward the gate to the castle grounds.

Horses at a run, the carriage hit the sharp switchback, two wheels leaving the ground, and faded from sight. Jace turned and charged into the foliage, arms in front of him, swatting away ferns, tall grass, and palm fronds while stumbling down the steep hillside.

He burst out into the open just as the carriage sped past, leaping and grabbing a rail on the side, his legs dangling dangerously close to the wheels. Fighting through the pain in his shoulder, he pulled himself up, able to plant a foot on the step.

He held on tightly, Adyn on the other side and Harlequin holding on to the roof, as the carriage raced toward the gate. Two guards began pulling the gate closed, while eight others created a human barrier across the road. Hadnoddon put the reins between his teeth, stood, and opened the driver's seat. He pulled out two loaded crossbows, turned, and fired.

The first bolt struck a guard in the back, another in the leg, the gate stopping halfway closed. Now too narrow an opening to make it through, the dwarf pulled on the reins, the carriage slowing as it approached the line of guards.

Adyn grasped the rail, her feet on the carriage step. When it slowed, she jumped off, rolled, and rose to her feet. She drew both blades and charged past the horses, straight toward the eight guards barring the drive.

She blocked the first strike, spun, and countered with a slash of her own. Two others found their way past her blades, one striking her thigh, another hitting her raised forearm. Both bounced off her hardened flesh, the men unprepared for her ability to respond. She cut through them and spun with arms extended, blades cutting through flesh. Jace and Harlequin joined the fight, cutting down the last two guards from behind before racing past her.

Jace charged the guard with the bolt in his leg, kicking the man in the midriff as he tried to stand. He then jerked the gate back, smashing the guard in the face, as Harlequin pushed the other side open.

Twenty armed guards came rushing around the bend, racing downhill toward them. It quickly became clear they would reach the carriage before it could regain speed. Adyn realized she was the only chance for escape. Rather than jump back onto the carriage as it lurched forward, she began pushing one gate closed behind it.

"What are you doing?" Jace shouted as he jumped onto the side of the carriage.

"Saving your arse," she shouted back as she ran toward the other gate.

Before she could close it, the guards were upon her.

Jace watched the receding castle gate as the soldiers converged on Adyn. Swords slashed at her as she fought back, but there were so many. The scene faded into the darkness, a lump solidifying in his throat. *What am I going to say to Narine?* He dreaded the pain it would cause her even more than the loss of his friend.

He turned and looked forward, the horses racing along the moonlit, hillside drive. Hadnoddon remained alone in the driver's seat, Harlequin having climbed inside with the princess.

Two men in red appeared from the trees on opposite sides of the road. Each held a sword high, ready to strike. Exposed, Jace readied himself, unsure of how to react. As the horses sped past the guards, they chopped down, the blades severing the harnesses from the carriage. Jace kicked out, his boot striking the head of the guard on his side.

They hit a bump and the horses pulled away, the carriage wobbling. First, it turned toward the uphill side, then the wheels sharply turned the other direction.

Jace pinned himself against the carriage as it shot down the hillside, branches swatting at him as they plummeted toward the city below. The ground was bumpy, the carriage shaking mightily. His grip came free and he spun away to fall into a fern, sharp leaves cutting him before he rolled down the hill. Again and again, he spun, before finally catching hold of a vine and stopping his momentum.

When he sat up, the carriage was already fifty feet away and barreling toward a stone building. Hadnoddon stood and leapt off, disappearing into the shrubs just before it hit a low wall. The front wheels shattered in a spray of splintered wood, the carriage flipping over the wall and rolling once before it crashed into the building.

Jace scrambled down the hillside, fearful of what he might find. Just before he reached the wall, Hadnoddon emerged from the shrubs, a streak of blood across his cheek, his shirt sleeve torn off, shoulder bloody. The two of them climbed over the waist-high wall and approached the broken carriage. Jace tore open a door, and Harlequin's upper body fell out, dangling, a nasty gash across her forehead. He pressed his fingers to her neck and blew out a breath, feeling a pulse.

"She's still alive." He stepped back. "Pull her out, and I'll check on the princess."

The dwarf grabbed Harlequin beneath the arms and dragged her from the carriage. With her out of the way, Jace entered the dark interior. Sariza remained unconscious, her leg bent at an awkward angle, but she was still breathing. Like Harlequin, her head was covered in blood. He picked her up and draped her over his shoulder before carefully climbing from the carriage.

"We need to return to the inn," Jace said.

"We need to get off this bloody island," Hadnoddon replied.

The thudding of footsteps and rustling of brush came from the hillside above them. Groaning, Jace turned toward the noise, fearing the guards had caught up to them. Metal flashed in the moonlight, slick with blood. Adyn emerged, her cloak gone, tunic and breeches shredded to meager strips of cloth hanging from her body. Only her belt, sheaths, and boots appeared intact. She climbed over the wall, tired but whole.

"You're alive," Jace breathed out in awe.

"It's a bloody miracle," Hadnoddon added.

Panting, Adyn said, "I'm glad you survived." She shook her head, taking two deep breaths. "I came across a guard on the road staring down this way. After I killed him, I followed the wheel tracks down the hillside. I feared..." She frowned down at Harlequin. "Is she dead?"

"No," Jace said. "They are both alive. At least for now."

Adyn took a deep breath. "We need to return to the ship so Narine can see to them."

Jace furrowed his brow. "I have to go back to the inn first."

"Forget about our things," Hadnoddon grumbled. "They are bound to come after us."

"The Eye is in our room." Jace shook his head. "I'll not leave it behind."

Adyn stepped close to him, grabbing the woman slung over his shoulder. "I'll carry Sariza." She slid the unconscious princess onto her shoulder, making it appear far too easy. "You stop by the inn while Hadnoddon and I head to the docks. We will meet you there."

Jace nodded and turned to leave.

"Jace?"

He looked over his shoulder. "Yes?"

"As we already discovered, Ryxx is a rough place. I suggest you revise your clothing; otherwise, you might end up in another fight."

He looked down at himself. One orange remained in his lopsided corset, which was torn down one side. Wearing his breeches, skirt long gone, blouse strapped to one shoulder, and wig missing, he could only imagine how he must appear. And he was still wearing makeup.

"You have a point. I must look ridiculous."

Hadnoddon snorted. "A massive understatement."

17

THE FLAME WITHIN

The ice-blue flames settled as Priella released her connection with her crystal throne, her magic refilled. She climbed off the wagon and commanded her soldiers to reassemble the cover, as they did every evening since leaving Illustan.

It was dark, campfires dotting the surrounding hillsides, clouds blocking the moon. The journey back from Tiamalyn had taken longer than anticipated, her party finally catching up with the army sixteen miles north of the Farrowen border. By then, camp had been struck, meals consumed, and Thurvin had conducted Devotion. Traditionally, it took place not long after sunset. Tonight, hers had been much later.

Bosinger emerged from the gloom to walk at her side, silent and vigilant as always. The pair headed toward the white pavilion positioned between the two throne wagons. A ring of six-foot-tall torches surrounded the area, a full complement of guards standing among them. She passed the soldiers and paused, waiting for Bosinger to enter first. The man had been at her side most of her life, always entering before her, his methods becoming ingrained habits for them both.

The interior was well-lit, the sprawling tent housing Farrowen and Pallanese officers seated around a long table, Thurvin at the far end, the opposite chair open. Priella sat, a full plate of food waiting for her. She had not had time for a meal prior to Devotion. Without a word, she began to eat. The food was cold, but she did not care.

Kollin, seated between Theodin and Quiam, watched her as she ate, his dark eyes unreadable. He had said little since she'd forced him to leave Tiamalyn. Each time they had stopped during the journey, she found him gazing at her, looking away when she turned toward him. She wondered why. *Is he attracted to my appearance? Is he angry for being torn from his home? Does he miss his father?* She frowned. *Does he miss Grenda's embrace?* The latter had not been difficult to discern, but she doubted if Kollin suspected others knew of his affair with the queen.

Motion at the tent flap revealed Lieutenant Garvin and his sidekick entering, the soldier's gaze resolute, the thief's shifting nervously. When Garvin reached the table, he bent to one knee.

"Greetings, Lord Thurvin. I have returned to report."

Thurvin sat back in his chair and smoothed his mustache. "I am cognizant of your efforts, for the prayers from Tiamalyn feed my power. Congratulations on your success. However, it did take longer than anticipated."

"Claiming the tower through guile, consuming far less resources than doing so with force, requires extensive research and a detailed strategy." He glanced at the thief beside him, who fidgeted. "Once Rindle and I gathered the necessary intelligence, we executed the plan and swapped the gems." He extended a hand toward Thurvin, an eight-faceted emerald resting in his palm. "This is for you."

Thurvin smiled. "Excellent." He lifted the gem, gazing upon it with greed-filled eyes.

Priella swallowed her mouthful and sat back with an arched brow. "Tell me, Lieutenant Garvin, why were you in the palace garden interrogating Kylar Mor rather than returning to your master?"

Thurvin cocked his head to the side. "Yes. I would like an answer to that, as well."

The soldier pressed his lips together, a flicker of anger in his eyes before he replied. "Kylar Mor was present during the assassination of Lord Horus. I had hoped to discover what had become of Captain Despaldi."

"What did you learn?" Thurvin asked.

"First, one of Despaldi's men died in the skirmish, leaving him with three, plus himself."

Frowning, Thurvin waved it off. "The loss of one soldier, regardless of how special, is a small price to pay for killing a wizard lord. What else did you learn?"

"Apparently, Jerrell Landish was in Tiamalyn at the time."

Thurvin jumped to his feet, eyes bulging. "Landish? Tell me you found and killed that conniving thief."

"We did not. Landish was long gone, heading for Cor Cordium with Despaldi and his men in pursuit."

"So that's where Despaldi went." Thurvin gripped the emerald tightly, his knuckles whitening. "I hope they catch the thief and turn his insides out. One way or another, Despaldi must reclaim the amulet."

Priella perked up. "What amulet?

Thurvin scowled. "It is called the Eye of Obscurance. With it in his possession, Landish killed Lord Taladain."

"How so?"

"The amulet makes the bearer immune to magic."

Priella gasped. *With it, even compulsion would be useless.* The idea of such an object lurking in the world... She took a calming breath and spoke in an even tone. "We must find this amulet and destroy it."

"Why head to Cor Cordium?" Thurvin mused. "Does he believe the Enchanters can replicate it?"

"By the gods, that would be disastrous," Priella exclaimed.

Garvin asked, "Do you wish me to pursue Landish and Despaldi?"

Thurvin shook his head. "No. Too many days have passed since Horus died. By now, Despaldi has either dispatched Landish or the thief has gone elsewhere." The wizard sat with a grunt. "No. I would rather you remain with the army. I may have need of your unique skills. For tonight, you are dismissed."

Garvin bowed and turned toward the tent entrance, the thief mimicking the man before the pair ducked outside, Priella's gaze following them the entire time. Always seeking assets, she found the pair intriguing.

Thurvin stood again, eyeing the emerald. "We will reach Fralyn in a few days. It is the last Orenthian city we will pass before entering Balmoria. As agreed, it will be mine."

Priella nodded. "As agreed."

"Very well. I will return to my tent and transform this stone into a sapphire. I shall turn the others into aquamarine."

She nodded. "We depart at first light."

Thurvin waved for Quiam to follow, the two men heading outside, leaving Priella alone with Kollin and her captains – Theodin, Shellock, and Iberson. It took her a mere moment to decide she wished to be alone, turning to her commanders.

"It has been a long day. Please, leave me for the evening. I will see you at first light."

Theodin and the other three officers stood and headed toward the exit, leaving her alone with Kollin and Bosinger.

She whispered to her bodyguard, "I will be safe alone with him. You can retire to your tent. Tell the guards I am not to be disturbed."

Bosinger arched a brow, rising and giving her a brief bow. "Good night, My Queen."

The man left, the tent falling quiet. Priella waited, sensing tension from Kollin. *He remains as gorgeous as ever.* Many nights in Tiadd, she had fantasized of them being together. Now, she could force him to love her. It would be simple. But she hesitated to do so.

"Why did you bring me here?" he eventually asked.

"You were among the most skilled wizards at the University. You are valuable to my campaign."

He scowled. "The man who just left is responsible for the death of my wizard lord and for what happened to my father."

"Your father has been healed – mind and body." She sighed. "As for Lord Thurvin, his men attacked Horus before my involvement. However, the result was inevitable. Horus was to die."

"Why?"

"I...cannot say."

He scowled. "What happened to you, Priella?"

She drew herself up. "I claimed my birthright as ruler of Pallanar."

"No. I mean..." He looked down at his hands. "I know we were never close."

"You hardly spoke to me." *Although when you did, it was nice.*

His eyes lifted, defiant. "Nor you to me."

The response surprised her. "I-I wanted to, but..."

His expression darkened. "You didn't wish to associate with the boy who publicly bloodied his manhood?"

"No." She looked away. "While an unfortunate incident, it didn't affect how I felt about you. I had already spent a lifetime having others loathe or ridicule me behind my back." She shook her head. "In truth, I wished to reach out to you many times, but I was shy, and you were so…handsome."

He leaned back, blinking in surprise. "Which brings me back to my first question. Why did you bring me here? Why not my father?"

Rather than reply, Priella stood and smoothed her skirt. She peered down at her plunging neckline, exposed cleavage, and trim waist. "Do you think I am beautiful?"

"You were already a master wizardess, skilled in illusion. With the power of a god, it is no wonder you can maintain one with ease."

She set her jaw. "Women wear makeup, wigs, and corsets. We have long been creatures of illusion, doing what we must to attract mates…or make other women jealous." She circled behind him, running her hand from one shoulder to the other. "I have merely taken it to the next level, presenting my exterior as it would be if the gods had been kinder to me."

Continuing past him, she crossed the thick rugs and stopped beside the pallet upon which she slept. It was covered in luxurious furs and pillows. She refused to leave such niceties behind, not when she had waited so patiently to attain her position.

Steeling herself, she reached around and undid the laces at her lower back. She then unhooked the collar behind her neck and pulled the top of her dress down, exposing her torso, her back to him. A glance over her shoulder brought Kollin into her peripheral vision, watching her. Swaying her hips, she eased her skirts down until they fell to the ground. It was the first time she had stripped in front of a man, bringing opposing emotions – the thrill of baring her new body and the fear of rejection.

She turned toward him, his gaze raking over her body. "Do you like what you see?"

His eyes narrowed. "What would you have of me, Priella?"

Frustration arose. "I could force you to love me, but I would prefer otherwise." She strode toward him, hips swaying. "I could make you happy, Kollin. You could have anything you wished."

He turned away. "I don't know…"

With a thought and the twist of her wrist, she altered the illusion she constantly wore, reshaping her image to appear as Grenda – dark hair, dark eyes, tanned skin, obscenely voluptuous curves.

"Is this more to your preference?" Priella said in her most sultry tone.

He looked at her, his expression darkening. "Not in the least."

She shifted the illusion, changing it back. "You clearly have been sleeping with her."

"That was a matter of survival – Tiamalyn politics while my father wallowed in madness and self-pity."

She arched a brow. "You did not enjoy it?"

Kollin stood. "Despite her appetite, the woman is cruel and manipulative. She ridiculed my...damaged body as much as she took joy in it. Her endgame was obvious, for she saw me as the most likely candidate to assume the throne." He turned away. "With my father recovered, Grenda would discard me like yesterday's breakfast."

Priella placed her hand on the side of his head, running her fingers through his hair, down his cheek, and to his jaw, turning it toward her.

She whispered, "I have never been with a man, Kollin. I have long wished for you to be my first. From the first time I saw you, I have dreamed of you and I together." She swallowed. "Would you have me?"

His pained, brown eyes stared into hers as he replied in a hushed voice, "You could have any man you wish. I...would disappoint you."

She shook her head. "I doubt it."

Kollin looked down. "It's not that I do not wish to..." He closed his eyes. "After what happened, I have never been able to...perform."

Priella smiled. "Is that all?"

He frowned, backing away. "It is not funny..."

"No." She gripped his shirt and pulled him close. "I am not laughing. I believe I can help."

"How?"

"In case you've forgotten, I wield the magic of a god."

She slid her hand into his breeches, gripping his manhood, delving with her magic to examine what ailed him. With a construct of repair, her magic flowed into him. The results were miraculous, his eyes bulging, jaw dropping. He quickly recovered, his lips meeting hers, the world melting away as he swept her up in his arms.

For the first time in her life, Priella gave in to her desires, finally with the man she had wanted for so long.

18

RACE

Drawing a breath of courage, Rawk donned his tinted spectacles and stepped from his cabin into the corridor.

Eight days had passed since departing Illustan, each with the same routine. After breakfast, Rawk would wage war with himself, battling against his fears, seeking to bury them for good. Some days he failed and remained in his room. Those days were filled with self-loathing when he talked to nobody, not even Rhoa. Today would not be one of those days.

Filled with determination, his armpits damp, heart racing, Rawk strode toward the stairs, refusing to succumb to his demons. Unlike the gemsongs, this voice could be ignored. He had proven so already. All the while, Algoron remained in the dark cabin, wanting no part of his personal battle or his visits above deck.

Rawk forced himself to walk up the stairs, rising into the bright sunlight, his eyes protected by the tinted spectacles Salvon had given him many weeks earlier.

He kept his gaze on the deck as he walked to the rail, grasping it tightly while his pulse thumped in his ears, drowning out the rush of the surf. He took a few deep breaths and lifted his head.

As far as Rawk could see, open water surrounded the ship. To be so far from land terrified him. He just could not understand why Captain Helgrued chose not to remain close to shore, making it easy to reach should anything go awry.

He spun around, searching for land, squinting through his tinted lenses. Finally, he spotted a dark mass off the port side of the ship, the white sails of two ships between them and the island. Judging by the position of the moon, those ships and the strip of land were north of *Sea Lord*.

We have changed direction again. He recalled the map Rhoa had shown him two days prior, depicting the route the ship was to sail. *We must be entering the Ceruleos Sea.* The realization stirred a sense of relief at the fact well over half the journey was now behind them. *Just a few more days,* he told himself. *Hold on for a few more days.*

When he spied his companions and four sailors clustered below the quarterdeck, he gathered his will and set off to join them.

With a widened stride, he crossed the ship, stepping carefully against the gentle rocking. An image of him falling over the rail surfaced. He shook his head to clear it, focusing on the view ahead. Rhoa was there, as were Brogan, Blythe, and Tygalas, who seemed to live on deck. There was no sign of Lythagon or Filk, of which Rawk was thankful. He did not exactly dislike the two dwarfs, but he felt the most out of place when among them.

He spotted Brogan speaking to Elrin, *Sea Lord's* first mate. He was a big man, nearly Brogan's size. Rawk was not surprised to see them together. The two had grown close during the journey, spending more than one evening drinking in Brogan's cabin while tossing dice. Their laughter was easily heard through the walls, making Rawk wish he could join them. Another fear he had yet to tackle.

As he drew close, Brogan's words became audible.

"...two silvers she can win."

Elrin scoffed. "There is no way a land-loving slip of a girl will beat Chark at his own game. He is the fastest on the ship, has been climbing rigging since he was a lad."

Brogan turned to Rhoa, cocking his head. "You are confident?"

Rhoa gazed up at the sails high above and shrugged. "I don't see why not. It's a fair bit easier than the stunts I performed in the menagerie."

Standing beside Rhoa, Blythe's golden eyes stared up at the mast before she turned to Brogan. "I have never known Rhoa to boast. If she says she can do it, I believe her."

The big man grinned. "Good enough for me." He glanced at Rhoa while holding out the coins to Elrin. "I just hope you are right. I need to win some coin back, or we are going to be staying in a dump when we reach Balmor."

Taking the silvers, Elrin laughed while clamping his hand on the shoulder of a smaller, wiry sailor. "Chark, you are about to earn yourself a silver."

"Fine by me." Chark's grin revealed a missing tooth. He appeared around ten years Rhoa's elder, his skin tanned and weathered, dark hair cropped short and sticking up in all directions.

The first mate pointed toward the bow. "Chark will take the forward mast, Rhoa can scale the main mast." He looked at her. "Remember, you must untie the lines to drop the sail. Don't cut them, or Helgrued will have my hide."

Rhoa grinned. "I'll try to restrain myself."

"You do that." Elrin then raised his voice. "You both start with my call. Whoever unfurls the topgallant sails and returns to deck the fastest wins."

A grin on his face, Chark turned and crossed the ship.

Rhoa approached Rawk, her smile alone worth his difficult journey on deck.

"I'm glad to see you," she said.

"What is going on? I heard something about a bet."

She grinned while removing her coat, an auburn, sleeveless tunic beneath it. "I am going to show these sailors what a seasoned acrobat can do."

The way her eyes lit up as she spoke was mesmerizing. The last time Rawk had seen the expression on her face was after riding the dragon. Whatever she was about to do, she radiated excitement. As she walked over to the portside rail, he noted the fulgur blades still strapped to her thighs, wondering why she had not removed them.

Beside the rigging parallel to the main mast, Rhoa stood ready. Toward the bow, Chark confidently stood near the foremast rigging. Elrin stood between them, hand raised in the air. Sailors stopped what they were doing and watched in anticipation. Even Captain Helgrued grinned from his position behind the wheel.

The first mate brought his hand down. "Lower the sails!"

Rawk's gaze fixed on Rhoa, anxiety sent his stomach fluttering when she jumped on top of the rail and began climbing the rigging. She scurried up as if it were nothing, quickly rising a hundred feet above deck. Impressively, Chark matched her pace, the two competitors simultaneously climbing each mast.

Scrambling up another twenty feet, Rhoa climbed onto the wooden yard just below the sail. Arms extended, she balanced along it and reached the topgallant sail lines seconds before Chark. However, she struggled with the knot, while Chark loosened his in a flash, one side of his sail dropping free. He then balanced himself as he walked back the other direction, toward the far end of the yard.

Brogan cupped his hands to his mouth. "Hurry, Rhoa!"

Rhoa finally got her knot untied, turned, and rushed along the yard far faster than Rawk might have wished. By the time she reached the far end, Chark had his line loosened, the sail dropping, the wind catching and filling it with a snap. Rhoa struggled with the other line, her sail fluttering in the breeze. Chark scrambled back to the mast and began his descent as Rhoa's knot released, her sail dropping and catching in the wind. She hurried across the yard, but Chark was already to the rigging, descending with practiced ease. Stopping near the mast, Rhoa drew her fulgur blades and stepped off.

"Rhoa!" Rawk cried out.

She plummeted toward the deck, racing past sails, yards, and lines, certain to splatter upon the deck. Three quarters of the way down, she jammed her blades into the mast, sparks flying as they cut gouges down the thick, wooden cylinder, slowing her momentum. She came to a stop eight feet above the deck and yanked the blades free, landing on her feet just before Chark dropped from the rigging to land on the bow.

Rawk released his breath, unaware he had even been holding it. He had seen Rhoa use her enchanted blades to slow a fall during his short stint with the menagerie, but he had forgotten how daring and skilled she was with them.

"She wins!" Brogan bellowed. The big man laughed heartily, clapping his hands, Blythe and Tygalas joining in.

Rhoa walked toward them, sheathing her blades. "Those knots were frustrating. Despite Elrin's warning, I was close to cutting them."

The first mate approached the main mast, glaring up at the gouges made by Rhoa's blades. "Helgrued is not going to like this."

Worry crossed Rhoa's face. Brogan rested a hand on her shoulder, addressing Elrin. "The mast is massive, at least three feet in diameter. Two little gouges won't cause any issues."

Elrin looked at Rhoa, slight awe in his eyes. "Regardless, I have never seen anything like it."

"You were wonderful, Rhoa," Blythe said with a grin. "I knew you could do it, although your finish was a bit...frightening."

Rhoa shrugged. "It was nothing I hadn't done before."

Chark reached them, scratching his head. "I thought I had you beat for sure, yet when I dropped on deck, you were already there."

"She cheated," said the scowling Elrin, four silvers in his palm.

Rhoa's nostrils flared defiantly. "I did not. There were no rules against me using my knives to stop my fall."

"Your fall?" Chark asked, confused.

Elrin snorted, pointing toward the long gouges in the main mast. "She leapt off the yard and stabbed her daggers into the mast to catch herself."

The other sailor's face went pale. "She did not."

Brogan laughed. "She did."

Elrin looked at Rhoa. "Can I see those blades?"

She pulled one out, showing him the unusually shaped weapon, the hilt at an angle from the blade, the blade itself a cylinder with a pointed tip.

"It looks more like an ice pick." Elrin reached for it.

Rawk warned, "I wouldn't–"

Blue sparks sizzled, burning Elrin's fingertips before he jerked his hand away. "Ouch! What the blazes?"

Brogan chuckled. "The blades are enchanted, Elrin. They shock anyone who touches them. In fact, you'll find we own a few enchanted weapons. You and the other sailors had best take care."

Blythe rolled her eyes. "Never mind him, Elrin. Brogan has become a bit melodramatic in his old age."

"Old age?" Brogan asked with a pained expression. "That is hurtful."

"It's not my fault you are *so* much older than the rest of us."

"Wait. I'm only forty-two." Brogan thumbed toward the elf. "Tygalas here is centuries old."

Tygalas shook his head. "You are correct, Blythe. He *has* become melodramatic." He turned toward Brogan. "I am only ninety-three years of age. Still young for my people."

His gaze suddenly swinging to the north, Chark's eyes widened. He scrambled up the main mast rigging and stopped thirty feet above deck. "Pirates!"

The grin slid off Elrin's face as the sailor ran to the port side rail. The two ships Rawk had spotted earlier were far closer, red and black flags visible atop the main mast of each vessel.

"Captain Helgrued!" Elrin shouted. "Make haste!"

Just when the fear in Rawk's belly had settled, the storm resumed, crashing with fury.

~

Augur in his grip, Brogan raced out of his cabin, up the stairs, and emerged on deck, ready for a fight. The bright day was even brighter than before, his augmented vision forcing him to squint. Blythe came up behind him, her enchanted bow in hand. Tygalas was a step behind with his staff, Lythagon and Filk stomping up the stairs last.

Sailors rushed around the masts, furling sails, the ship slowing. *Sea Lord* had altered course, now angling toward the pirate ships. With a growl, Brogan rushed off to confront Helgrued.

He passed Rawk and Rhoa, the dwarf obviously fighting his fears, Rhoa standing with her hand on his shoulder. As he drew close to the quarterdeck, he shouted at the man behind the wheel.

"Why are you slowing?"

"They man cutters, both faster than *Sea Lord*. We cannot outrun them."

Brogan climbed up the stairs. "You wish to fight?"

Helgrued chuckled. "Not unless they give us no choice."

The two ships were close enough for Brogan to see sailors moving around, easily two dozen on each vessel, the pirates outnumbering the crew and passengers on *Sea Lord* two to one...maybe more.

"What will they do to us?" Blythe asked from the quarterdeck stairs.

Helgrued narrowed his eyes at the approaching ships. "Even pirates are businessmen. Despite the stories, they do not sink ships or kill their quarry for no reason." He turned the wheel, the remaining sails rippling as the wind ran across them, the ship slowing further. "Our only cargo is food, and we have little coin. Once they discover we have nothing of value, they will leave and find more suitable targets."

Brogan grunted. "You sound sure of yourself."

The captain shrugged. "As sure as I can be." The lead ship drew even with them, called out, and threw a line. Elrin caught it and began reeling it in. "We will find out soon enough."

Other lines were thrown, the two ships pulling even with one another until they floated only strides apart. The pirates dropped a plank over their rail, the opposite end landing on *Sea Lord's* rail. Moments later, a swarthy man wearing a turban climbed on, scurried across, and dropped on deck. A dozen pirates followed, some carrying scimitars, others armed with spears or crossbows. They wore grim scowls, faces bearing scars, tattoos, and even rings through their noses or brows. The last man to cross wore robes of black and red rather than a tunic and loose trousers like the others. Brogan's scowl deepened.

A wizard.

Helgrued descended to the main deck, Brogan and Blythe following as he crossed the deck to meet with the wizard. He was a tall, thin man with dark, curly hair and a big nose. The other pirates surrounded the wizard in a half-circle, blades ready, dark eyes wary.

"Are you the captain?" the wizard asked, eyes scanning the area.

"I am. My name is Helgrued. Welcome aboard *Sea Lord*."

"My name is Wilzon Oratazzi, brother of High Wizard Kalzon. Where did you come from and where are you headed?"

"Most recently, we departed Illustan eight days past. We are bound for Balmor, intent on selling the food filling our holds and hoping to secure new cargo at the Bazaar."

"If you have nothing to hide, as you say," Wilzon growled, "you'll allow my men to search your ship."

Helgrued gestured toward his sailors scattered around the deck, some still upon the masts, all listening. "If I do, you will allow us to sail off without issue?"

The wizard nodded. "I will."

"Very well." Helgrued shouted, "Allow these men to search the ship. Comply, and they will be on their way!"

Wilzon waved his hand, all but two of his men rushing off.

Brogan had done his best to remain quiet but could no longer do so. "What is this about?"

Wilzon sneered, "This is about subterfuge, betrayal, and murder."

Helgrued blinked. "Whose murder?"

"My brother's."

He sucked in a breath. "Someone murdered a high wizard?"

"Yes. In Ryxx. Last night, during his betrothal celebration. They also kidnapped his future bride, Princess Sariza."

Brogan whistled, causing Helgrued to throw him a scowl.

"We are simple traders and travelers," the captain replied. "Ryxx is an island of pirates. Wouldn't *they* be more likely to conduct nefarious affairs such as murder and kidnapping?"

One of the two remaining pirates replied, "We'd not cross our high wizard. If we did, Ryxx would become a target of Hassakan and other wizardoms rather than a place to avoid. Besides, since Kalzon took control, business has been so good we rarely end up killing each other."

Blythe asked, "Do you have any description of these murderers? Perhaps we can assist your search."

"One is a female pirate named Harlequin. She sometimes portrays herself as a Hassakani noble named Lady Quin. The other is a thief, small of stature and bold beyond belief."

Brogan's eyes widened. "A bold thief?"

"Yes. He snuck into the party dressed as a woman." The wizard's eyes bulged as he bellowed, "A woman!" He shook his head. "Can you believe it?"

That sounds like something Jace would do. Brogan glanced at Blythe. "I can believe it."

"The assailants accosted me, as well. I nearly died!" Wilzon clenched his fists in frustration. "After murdering my brother, they fled the castle, killing dozens of guards during their escape. It appears they were assisted by a woman made of metal." He threw up his hands. "*Metal*! Lethal and impossible to kill." His gaze swept the area. "Has anyone ever heard of a woman made of metal?"

Silent, startled expressions stared back at the wizard.

Helgrued scratched his chin. "While that sounds rather…outlandish, I can assure you, we have no such characters on board."

Wilzon rubbed his eyes and exhaled. "They cannot have gone far. Dozens of pirate cutters seek them as we speak. I will find them. If not today, then very soon."

Pirates returned from all directions, converging on the wizard, none finding anything of note.

The wizard pointed toward his ship. "Disembark. We make haste, in search of the next ship." The pirates began scurrying across the plank.

Wilzon turned toward Helgrued. "Thank you for your compliance, Captain. If you happen upon Sariza or the vile snakes who killed my brother, please deliver them to Ryxx." He grinned. "I will reward you well."

"I will," the captain replied.

Wilzon floated up and sailed over the gap, landing on the other ship while the plank was removed, lines drawn in. In moments, the sails were unfurled, the ship sailing off to the northeast.

19

SARMAK

E yes closed, Narine extended her awareness through the construct. Sariza's wounds had been healed, but swelling remained on her brain, residue of the sleeping drug lingering in her bloodstream. *I thought the drug had been expended.* Rather than attempt a mental manipulation construct to wake the woman, she decided to let her sleep. They remained at sea, so there was no need to rush.

She opened her eyes to the dark captain's cabin, daylight seeping through the small window above the lone bed.

Harlequin sat in a chair, elbows on the table. She looked tired, likely a lingering side effect of her head wounds. The woman stuffed a chunk of bread into her mouth and washed it down with water. Chandan sat across from her, the man's brow furrowed as he watched Narine.

"She will not wake." Narine stood. "Despite my earlier efforts, traces of the drug remain in her blood."

"Is she in any danger of dying?" he asked.

"No. Just continue to get her to swallow water and she should wake, perhaps as soon as tomorrow."

"Tomorrow," Harlequin said, "we will land at Sarmak."

"Yes." Chandan nodded. "Sarazan will be relieved to see his sister returned safely."

Narine sighed. "We will wait until morning. If she does not wake on her own, I will attempt to force it."

The man stood and walked to the door, opening it, light streaming in. "Thank you again, Princess."

Narine walked to the door, pausing to glance toward the drawer where her book was stored. "May I borrow it again?"

He chuckled as he crossed the room. "I suppose you can do little harm while we are at sea." He dug out the book and held it toward Narine, who accepted it eagerly. "You will return it before we land."

"Yes." She nodded. "Of course."

She walked out and made her way toward the forward deck, clutching the book to her chest with one hand, the other gripping the starboard rail. A cloud obscured the sun, others floating across the blue sky. Azure waters stretched across the southern horizon, the white sails of a distant ship miles to the south. Across the deck, a brown strip of land was visible, perhaps ten miles to the north.

Hassakan, she thought. It was the northernmost and hottest wizardom. The exotic nature of the land, people, and culture had been a curiosity to Narine for years, but she had never imagined seeing it for herself. *Fate twists yet again*. It left her wondering what surprises awaited.

A pair of sailors stared at her, dark eyes leering, subtle smiles amid their thick, black beards. They always seemed to be watching. It made her uncomfortable and left her longing to hide in her cabin.

Releasing the rail, she made her way to the open hatch, nearly stumbling as she began her descent down the steep stairwell. Her heart raced as she imagined falling. If she were seriously hurt, nobody on board could heal her wounds.

She reached the cabin door and opened it. Adyn, Jace, and Hadnoddon sat at the table in the heart of the room, each with playing cards fanned out in one hand. Coins sat in the middle of the table...all copper, save for one silver.

Jace looked up, eyes toward her chest.

"My eyes are up here," she chided.

Adyn chuckled, and Jace gave her a wry look.

"I was looking at the book," he said.

Narine looked down, the book of magic still clutched against her breasts. "Oh." She lowered it and smiled. "Sorry."

He sat back with a grin, focus clearly not on her face. "Ahh… Much better without the book in the way."

Narine gasped. "You letch!"

Adyn laughed harder.

"I simply say aloud what goes on in men's heads. Consider it blatant honesty from someone who appreciates your beauty, and not just the bumpy bits in front."

Laughing, Narine shook her head. "I can't believe I am saddled with such rogues."

"Yeah. Who would have thought the dwarf would be the proper one in the bunch." Hadnoddon grinned. "That includes you, *Princess*."

She prepared a retort, then decided she enjoyed the accusation. "Not so long ago, before the influence of these two, you might have thought differently. However, I am happier now than I've ever been. If others are bothered, it is their problem, not mine."

"Well said, Narine." Adyn's prideful tone struck a chord.

Narine gave her friend a warm smile.

Hadnoddon arched a brow. "Are you through interrupting? I would like to play out this hand."

"What are you playing anyway?" she asked.

"I borrowed a deck of cards from Quiarre and was teaching these two how to play Hanapuli," Jace responded. "The Fastella upper-class play the game, but it has Hassakani roots. I figured it might be a good idea if they learned it in case the opportunity arises while we are in Sarmak."

Narine put her hand on her hip and glared at Jace. "You are just looking for a reason to gamble."

He shook his head. "Not true."

She arched a questioning brow.

"When you *know* you are going to win…" He grinned, "it's not a gamble."

"You won't win this hand," Hadnoddon said.

Jace sighed. "If you aren't bluffing, you just gave away leverage. You could have drawn more coin from us. If it *is* a bluff, it's too early and you won't win much."

The dwarf grunted. "Just play."

Adyn passed, Jace doing the same. Hadnoddon laid down his cards.

"Highcastle." Jace nodded. "A winning hand in most cases. You should have pushed us to throw in more coin before you gave it away."

The dwarf scowled at Jace and scooped the coins from the table.

"Jace," Narine interjected, "since the hand is finished, I thought you and I could spend some time on the next augmentation. Three remain undiscovered, and we are due to land in Sarmak mid-day tomorrow."

Setting the cards on the table, Jace rose to his feet. "You two can continue to play. The more you practice, the more you learn the subtleties of the game."

Adyn shook her head. "No. I think I'll go on deck and train with my blades."

Jace snorted. "You defeated twenty guards on your own. I doubt you require practice."

She smiled. "Those men had no chance. Blades do not harm me. By the time they realized it, they were dead." Rising, she grabbed her belt and blades from her bunk. "However, magic *can* harm me, and blades can hurt any of you. Best to be prepared, for I fear danger lurks on the path ahead."

Adyn slipped outside, but her statement remained, repeating in Narine's mind. *I fear danger lurks on the path ahead.*

$\sim$

Hassaka's Breath sailed into Sarmak Harbor, Narine clinging to the rail, connecting the learnings from the University to the view ahead.

The walled city crowned a hilltop on a point along the northern edge of the Ceruleos Sea, the gate miles from the harbor. Given the otherwise treacherous desert climate covering most of Hassakan, it, like most other cities in the wizardom, had grown far beyond the original city walls.

At the water's edge, buildings painted in pastels of yellow, peach, pink, and blue speckled the hillside to the tall, tan walls encircling the great city. Curving roads filled with carts, wagons, and people on foot led up the hillside toward the entrance. Narine spotted strange animals loaded with packs walking among them. They had long, bent necks and humps on their backs, hooves moving at a plodding pace.

"Camels," she said aloud.

"What?" Jace asked from beside her.

She pointed. "Those animals must be camels."

"Very good, Princess," Quiarre's voice came from behind. She turned toward him, and he bowed. "Camels are an important part of Hassakani culture. They are beasts of burden, such as oxen or horses, but are better equipped for the prevalent heat, the desert climate, and can travel for days without water."

"Yes. I recall learning about them at the University."

"They are odd-looking," Jace noted.

"'Tis a matter of perspective," Quiarre said. "Some might say they are beautiful."

Jace snorted. "Some might be crazy or blind."

Narine nudged him with a well-placed elbow. "Are we heading to the palace when we dock?"

"Yes. There will be two carriages waiting."

"What about the princess? She still has not awoken."

"Which is why I came to see you. Chandan wishes you to try again."

She turned toward Jace. "Will you join me?"

He shrugged. "I have nothing better to do."

They crossed the deck, following Quiarre as he led them to the captain's cabin. Harlequin was at the helm, the woman's gaze following Jace, stirring Narine's jealousy. Jace did not know it, but Adyn had told Narine about Harlequin flaunting herself in front of him while in Ryxx. She'd also said, despite the woman's blatant flirting, Jace hadn't responded – which was a relief to Narine. She glared up at Harlequin.

Just land us safely on shore so we can be done with you.

Quiarre knocked on the cabin door, waited a beat, then opened it, standing aside as Narine and Jace entered the dark quarters. Chandan sat at the desk beneath a lantern, writing something in the scrawling script of Hassakani. Narine found herself wishing the translation augmentation she had applied to Jace remained in effect, but it had worn off an hour earlier, after he had helped her decipher the final augmentation spell. The possibilities of the new discovery were tantalizing, but she had not dared to try it. Not yet.

Chandan sat back. "I will take the book now."

Jace held it out to the man. "I suspected as much."

"It is best to ensure it doesn't fall into the wrong hands." He accepted the book and turned toward Narine. "I pray the notes you took remain a secret, as well."

"Don't worry," she replied. "Others will have a difficult time deciphering them without the constructs themselves."

"True."

Chandan gestured toward the bed where Sariza lay. "Try to wake her again, Princess. Her brother is anticipating her arrival."

Narine crossed the cabin and sat on the bed. She gathered her magic, wove it as she had been taught, and placed her palm on Sariza's forehead. Eyes closed, she delved into her brain. The swelling had receded, and she sensed only a trace of the drug in her blood. Narine got the impression something had changed, subtle and undefinable. She probed deeper but found nothing wrong. At least nothing she felt a construct of repair would heal.

Altering the construct to one of mental manipulation, she implanted the sensation of shockingly cold water. Sariza jerked and gasped. Narine opened her eyes to the woman blinking, panting, a shiver wracking her body.

"It's all right," Narine crooned. "You are safe, Sariza."

The woman stared at her, confusion on her face. "Who are you? Where am I?"

"It's your friend, Narine." She frowned. "You and I were at the University together and lived on the same floor for years."

"What University?"

"In Tiadd, of course."

Chandan stood at Narine's side. "Hello, Sariza."

"Chandan?"

"Yes. You are safe. We are on a ship in Sarmak Harbor."

"A ship? What of my family? I wish to see my father."

Chandan looked at Narine before replying. "Your father died six years ago."

She sat up. "No! It cannot be."

"I am sorry, Sariza, but it is true."

"Who... Who is wizard lord?"

"Sarazan has risen to wizard lord. He awaits your return."

"My brother?"

"What is wrong with her?" Narine asked.

"Her memory appears affected. I have heard of such things. The memories often return over time." The wizard put a hand on Narine's shoulder. "You may leave. I will see Sariza to the carriage."

Narine stood and crossed the room while Chandan knelt and took Sariza's hand.

"Do not worry. We will bring you to Sarazan shortly." The wizard reached toward the table beside the bed, grabbed a cup of water, and held it to Sariza's lips. "Here. Drink."

Jace opened the door, Narine casting one last look toward the bed before following him outside.

Once the door closed, she whispered, "Something is wrong."

Stopping, Jace glanced toward the closed cabin door. "She has lost her memory. As Chandan said, it sometimes happens with head wounds."

"No. There is more to what I felt. There is something…" She struggled to articulate the problem. "Something odd has happened to her mind. It has been…divided."

His brow furrowed. "I don't understand."

"Neither do I."

A shadow slid across the deck, and Narine looked up. Harlequin stood above them, leaning over the quarterdeck rail.

"The carriages are waiting," the ship captain said. "You had better gather your things."

With Jace at her side, Narine headed toward their cabin, all the while wondering how much Harlequin had overheard. Narine's itch of distrust grew intense whenever that woman was around.

The carriages were lavish, nearly equal to the ones they had ridden back in Tiamalyn. With a black-lacquered exterior and red velvet interior, the ride was comfortable and left Narine thankful she did not have to climb to the hilltop city, especially with the hot, mid-day sun beating down upon them. Inside the carriage, the heat steadily grew worse as they rode farther from the harbor.

Jace sat beside her, Adyn and Hadnoddon on the opposite bench. The dwarf had donned his armor, his massive hammer resting on the floor between his boots, the handle leaning against one leg. Adyn wore another of Harlequin's outfits – a cream-colored tunic, black breeches, and charcoal gray cloak. Narine glanced at Jace as he stared through the window, watching the square, pastel buildings pass by. He toyed with the amulet beneath his tunic, something he seemed to do when lost in thought.

She leaned against his shoulder. "What are you thinking about?"

He turned toward her. "Quiarre. Sariza. Chandan. Harlequin. This entire thing has felt off from the start, from them drugging us, to holding you hostage, to rescuing Sariza." He shook his head. "Chandan claimed to require my expertise, yet it was Harlequin's plan we followed to free the princess. Why me? Why us? They could have hired anyone to do the job. Even so, we were beyond lucky to escape Ryxx alive."

"Perhaps that is why. Perhaps anyone with lesser skills would have failed." She looked at Adyn. "From your story, Adyn's armored body was the only thing that saved you from capture...or worse."

"It still feels off."

She rested her hand on his thigh. "Well, once we return her to Sarazan, the entire thing will be behind us."

Jace arched a brow. "Will it? I don't recall Chandan making any promises."

The carriage passed through the tall city gate guarded by soldiers in loose, red tunics, baggy trousers, and heads wrapped in black turbans. Inside, the buildings were all made of the same tan rock, lacking the colors of those outside the walls. People, carts, wagons, and camels filled the streets, the traffic even heavier than in the outer portion of Sarmak.

The concern Jace expressed fertilized already existing seeds of distrust. Narine's worry began to fester – her doubts about Harlequin, the mystery surrounding Chandan, the oddity she had found within Sariza's mind. It was a jumbled mess that left her in a cold sweat, despite the oppressive heat.

The carriage stopped and door opened. A man dressed in all white, from turban to shoes, stood waiting.

"Greetings," he said. "I am Yartan, personal servant to Lord Sarazan. Please, exit the carriage so I may escort you to my master."

Narine glanced toward Jace, seeking reassurance but not finding any. Adyn climbed out first, followed by Hadnoddon, then Jace, who extended a hand back toward Narine. She took it and stepped out.

A dozen armed guards stood in an arc behind Yartan. Unlike other Hassakani soldiers, these were dressed in all black, a red bird stitched on their lapel. In addition to wearing black turbans, a black veil covered their faces, leaving only their eyes exposed. Based on build and stance, some appeared to be women.

"Redwing Guard," she whispered just loud enough for Jace and Adyn to hear. "Sarazan's private army."

"I am aware of their reputation," Adyn said.

Chandan, Quiarre, and Sariza emerged from the other carriage, the wizard in the lead as the trio walked over to join them.

Yartan bowed to Sariza. "Welcome back, Princess. Your brother is expecting you."

"I–" she started.

Chandan interrupted. "Please, Yartan. Let us meet with Sarazan directly. It would be best to reunite him with his sister so our guests can be on their way."

The guards in black parted as Yartan turned and led them toward the palace.

It was a big structure with towers at the corners, each capped by a bulbous, pointed dome. The tallest tower stood in the heart of the palace, topped by a pointed dome, red, shimmering flames visible through arched openings.

They climbed a flight of stairs, passed columns encircled by painted murals, and entered a tall, arched doorway. A long chamber with a marble-tiled floor stretched out in front of them, the red and black tiles alternating, giving Narine the impression of a giant gameboard. Yartan led them across the chamber, their footsteps echoing off the stone walls and high ceiling.

Four of the Redwing Guard bracketed a doorway at the far end of the room. Yartan bowed to the guards, two of them opening the doors and holding them as he led the procession inside.

The throne room was long and narrow, like the entrance chamber, the floor lined with padded mats, a red stripe of carpet down the center. At the end of the carpet was a dais where Lord Sarazan lounged on a throne, his leg draped over one arm, face tilted toward the ceiling and mouth open as a woman fed him grapes. She was stark naked, her coppery skin flawless, body lean, yet with the unmistakable curves of a female. Her face was covered by a thin, red veil, soft, black slippers on her feet.

Yartan stopped a few strides before the throne and bowed, the Redwing Guard fanning out, Chandan, Sariza, and Quiarre stopping beside Yartan.

"As requested, Your Eminence," Yartan announced. "Master Chandan has returned with your sister, Princess Sariza." He stepped aside and backed away.

Sarazan gestured to the woman at his side. "Leave us, Trilla. Join the others. I will come and play with you after I am finished with my sister."

The woman bowed, turned, and hurried away, disappearing through a door at the side of the room.

The wizard lord sat upright, his angular eyes peering over the group before him. He had strong features marked by a black goatee cut to a point below his chin. A golden turban with a large ruby at the front rested upon his head. His robes were a deep red, trimmed in shimmering gold with a gold sash.

"Welcome back, Chandan. I see you have proven as capable as promised." His gaze shifted to Narine and her companions. "Who are these...foreigners?"

Chandan bowed. "Considering the situation, retrieving Sariza required special skills. The individuals standing before you are more resourceful than one might think."

The wizard lord frowned. "Your fee remains as agreed, regardless of the number of participants required to bring her home."

"As we agreed, Your Eminence." Chandan extended a hand toward Jace. "Meet Jerrell Landish, thief extraordinaire. At his side is Princess Narine Killarius of Ghealdor. These other two are their guards."

"Ahh... Princess Narine. Your beauty exceeds the flattering description shared by my sister."

Narine dipped her head. "Thank you, Lord Sarazan."

"However, we are not here for niceties."

The wizard lord stood and descended. He was tall with broad shoulders and a trim waist. Narine might guess him to be a warrior, if not for the robes and crown. He stopped before Sariza and glared down at her.

"What do you have to say, sister?" His tone carried a challenge.

Her brow furrowed. "Are you...angry with me?"

He looked at Chandan, brow furrowed. "What's wrong with her?"

"Bringing her in without resistance required...special care. Besides, these people did you a favor. Kalzon is dead."

The wizard lord grinned. "Excellent."

Chandan approached Sariza. "Give me a moment to remove the block."

The glow of magic surrounded him, an unfamiliar construct forming around his outstretched hand. Although unknown to Narine, it was clearly a construct of mental manipulation, a skill men could barely manifest. The man lifted the hand with the odd chains running from his wrist to his small finger and placed his palm against her forehead.

Sariza's eyes opened wide and she gasped. "No!"

Her arms lashed out, the glow of magic flaring. She attacked her brother with a construct of mental manipulation. Sarazan stumbled backward, hand to his forehead as the crimson power of his god enveloped him. Her attempt to strike him proved unwise.

Sarazan lashed out, ropes of red light wrapping around Sariza and lifting her into the air. She squirmed, arms pinned to her sides.

"There is the response I expected!" Sarazan's eyes were filled with madness as he stared at his sister, elevated five feet in the air. "The traitor has returned."

20

TWISTS

Jace warily watched the scene in the throne room unfold, the family reunion quickly shifting to something sinister when the wizard lord used his magic to bind Sariza and lift her into the air.

Chandan spun away from Sarazan and approached Jace and Narine. As he drew near, back to the wizard lord, he whispered softly, "You must save her."

Another twist in a series of turns.

Jace hesitated, gauging the situation.

A wizard lord, a man who commanded unknown magic, having the ability to heal himself instantly, stood before him. Twenty of the Redwing Guard surrounded the dais, Jace and his three companions caught in the middle. In Chandan, Jace had another wizard on his side...assuming the man did not remain apart from the conflict. Sariza was also a wizardess, able to assist once freed. What role Quiarre played, Jace was unsure.

Jace, Adyn, and Hadnoddon had retained their weapons, Sarazan likely believing himself beyond harm. *Bless the arrogance of youth.* He measured Sarazan, a man near his own age. His eyes lit with vengeance, a confident grin covered his face as he stared at his sister.

The wizard lowered his hand, his sister dropping to the floor with a cry of alarm. She stumbled but remained upright, her arms still bound to her sides as he twisted his hands, preparing some dire magic.

Sarazan grinned. "You will now die, sister!"

Jace darted forward, arms spread as he leapt in front of Sariza. Red bolts of lightning blasted forth, striking Jace, the amulet on his chest turning ice cold. The electricity fizzled, leaving him unharmed, the room falling silent.

The wizard lord scowled, outraged glare focused on Jace. He thrust his hands out, a beam of blinding light blotting out the world.

~

With Sarazan distracted, Narine grabbed Sariza by her skirts and pulled her backward. The wizard lord released a blinding beam of foulfire toward Jace as the Redwing Guard rushed in from both sides. Part of the magic blasted past the thief, vaporizing one of Sarazan's own guards.

Adyn charged past Narine and met one cluster of attackers, Hadnoddon following. Narine gathered her magic, prepared to fend off the others. Chandan pushed her backward, an eruption of hardened air bursting from him and launching ten warriors across the room, some losing their swords, blades falling with a clatter. The enemies landed twenty feet away and skittered across the floor.

Chandan turned toward Narine, his hand gripping Sariza's arm. "You must help Jerrell. He is our only hope."

The doors from the entrance hall burst open, and six guards rushed in. Chandan, still gripping Sariza, gathered his magic and prepared to face them.

~

Adyn charged toward the Redwing Guard, slashing at the first, her blade missing when the man flipped backward. Another attacked, her forearm blocking his scimitar. A third swept in low, blade connecting with her metal shin, the force of it knocking her off balance. She landed on her hands and knees as a hammer swung over her, striking her attacker's chest with a crushing blow. The guard flew backward, taking out one of his companions.

Scrambling to her feet, Adyn lunged with both swords, forcing her enemies backward. She then stepped beside Hadnoddon.

"You don't get to have all the fun this time," he said.

She turned, speaking over her shoulder as the enemies in black surrounded them. "Watch my back. I'll watch yours."

"This will be entertaining," he replied with a grin.

Standing back to back, Adyn and Hadnoddon stood ready. As one, the enemy warriors attacked.

Still blinded by the beam of white magic, spots dancing in his eyes, Jace drew his dagger and lunged toward where he had last seen Sarazan.

The blade struck true, tearing through the man's robe, leaving a gash across his stomach. The wizard lord's attack faltered, and he fell backward.

Sarazan's hand went to his stomach and came away bloody. His expression shifted from shock to a scowl, his wound healing instantly. "I don't know how you survived foulfire, but you have made a fatal mistake."

The man raised his hands, and lightning blasted from his fingers, striking the floor at Jace's feet in a blast of broken marble. Jace covered his face, sharp shards of tile pummeling him, cutting his legs, arms, torso, and hands. He stumbled backward into Narine, the two of them falling in a heap.

When Jace collided with Narine, she toppled over, the back of her head striking the marble floor. She winced in pain and blinked, her blurred surroundings slowly coming back into focus.

Jace sat up as Sarazan stepped off the dais, the wizard lord's body gleaming with the crimson magic of his god.

"So, you are impervious to magic, but physical attacks can harm you," he said.

Desperate, Narine grappled for her magic, but the injury to her head left her thoughts too muddled to form a construct.

The wizard lord's arm lashed to the side, magic extending toward three scimitars lying on the floor. With a sweeping motion, he launched the weapons toward Jace and Narine, blades first.

Quiarre dove in front them, the scimitars plunging into his body. He crashed to the floor, eyes bulging, mouth gaping in shock and pain. Convulsing, he coughed blood, head lolling to the side.

Jace scrambled to his feet and threw his dagger. The wizard lord swept his arm, magic sending the knife across the room. Jace charged, but the distance was too great and took too long to close the gap.

Sarazan sent ropes of magic past Jace, the tendrils wrapping around Quiarre's corpse and yanking the man forward. The body smashed into Jace's back with tremendous force. The wizard lord dodged to the side as Jace and Quiarre tumbled into the dais, the cracking of bones echoing in the chamber.

Narine's heart leapt into her throat. Still on the floor and holding her magic, she watched Jace to see if he moved. Forcing herself to turn away, she gauged the rest of the room.

Chandan defeated the last of the guards who had rushed in from the entry hall. The wizard turned toward Sariza as Sarazan lashed out with ropes of magic, binding the wizard and wizardess tightly, hands to their sides. The pair suddenly jerked up into the air, hovering there, helpless.

"You broke my trust, Chandan. Betraying me in favor of my sister," Sarazan snarled. "You shall pay the price."

Six of the Redwing Guard had recovered from the initial assault, weapons in hand as they stood beside their master. On the other side of the room, Adyn and Hadnoddon finished with the last of their attackers and turned toward the wizard lord. The dwarf was covered in blood, the bodyguard's clothing torn, her metal skin showing through.

Narine stumbled to her feet, still holding to her magic, her head clearing as she considered what to do.

Sarazan turned toward her. "You chose the wrong ruler to cross, wizardess."

With his free hand, Sarazan formed an energy construct, prepared to unleash his fury. Lacking any other choice, Narine crafted a shield of grounding. Lightning struck the shield, the energy redirecting to the floor, blasting tiles to bits. A chunk hit Narine's forehead. She stumbled backward, her shield collapsing with her lost concentration, the room spinning as she toppled over.

Grinning, the wizard lord prepared another blast.

~

Adyn glanced toward the dwarf at her side, Hadnoddon covered in cuts and gashes, hammer in his grip.

"Go see about Jace," she whispered, hoping the wizard lord was distracted.

As Hadnoddon limped toward the dais, Sarazan launched crimson bolts of lightning toward Narine. Adyn tensed in fear. Just before hitting her, the bolt bent and struck the floor, sending marble in all directions. A chunk struck Narine, and she stumbled backward, falling to her back.

Adyn darted forward and leapt as the wizard lord launched another attack. The lightning struck her in the chest, the power far greater than she had anticipated. It blasted her backward, her body locking up before she even hit the floor. She crashed to the marble tiles, skidded, and rolled, sparks sizzling across her metallic body. Her muscles spasmed violently as she came to a stop, facing the wizard lord, unable to move.

Sarazan strode toward her, his brow arched. "A warrior made of metal? Interesting."

His hand lashed out to the side, a sword lifting from the floor and sailing into his open palm. He raised it and slammed it down on Adyn's neck, her head striking the floor and cracking the tile. The blow hurt but didn't cut through her flesh.

"Very interesting indeed," Sarazan said.

Jace was in agony. His entire body hurt beyond anything he had ever experienced. Someone shook his shoulder, sending sharp stabs of pain through him, making him gasp. He opened his eyes to a bloody face with a bulbous nose and thick, black beard.

"Are you all right?" Hadnoddon asked in a hushed voice.

"I am...broken," Jace muttered, speaking requiring extreme effort. "Take the amulet."

"What?"

"Sarazan...," he gasped. "Won't expect it."

The dwarf lifted his head and pulled off the necklace. The movement was too much, the pain overwhelming, Jace's vision fading to black.

Narine opened her eyes, wincing, blood running down her face from a gash in her forehead. She raised her head and the room spun, her stomach roiling. Turning to the side, she vomited. With effort, she slowly sat up and took stock of the situation.

Chandan and Sariza were eight feet in the air, hands at their sides, bound by ropes of crimson magic. Guards dressed in black lay dead near the entrance, bodies smoldering.

In the other direction, Sarazan stood over Adyn with a sword in his hand, the bodyguard curled in a ball. Six of the Redwing Guard stood beside Sarazan, weapons ready.

Her gaze went to the dais where Jace lay unmoving, Quiarre's body draped over him. Hadnoddon knelt at Jace's side, the dwarf slipping the Eye of Obscurance off Jace's head, which then fell limply to the floor. Shock struck, Narine gasping in dread. *No!* she screamed in her head, tears blurring her vision. Jace was dead.

Grief left her sobbing, the sobs quickly ceasing as raw fury flooded in. Discarding all care for herself, she rose to her feet and gathered her magic, despite her increasing weariness, drawing it through her enchanted anklet.

Sarazan stared at her, his brow arched. "While I admit the strength of your gift is impressive, you are no match for a wizard lord. Why die for no reason, Princess? Think of what we could accomplish if you ruled by my side."

"Never," she growled.

Narine formed a construct and unleashed her magic. The man cast a shield to protect himself, but it did not matter. She had targeted his six remaining warriors.

The soldiers staggered, choking when threads of magic wrapped around their throats and constricted. She yanked her hand back, snapping their necks, the guards collapsing. The flow of magic expended, Narine staggered and fell to her knees, the pain of striking the hard floor muted by the agony of her broken heart.

Sarazan shook his head. "Now that was just murder for no reason. Killing them will not save any of you."

The man did not see Hadnoddon sneaking up from behind, arms and face covered in blood, hammer ready.

"You killed the man I love." Narine's voice was filled with loathing. "You deserve to die."

Hadnoddon lifted the massive hammer, the head casting a shadow at Sarazan's feet. The wizard lord spun and launched a fireball at Hadnoddon, the swirling blaze engulfing him.

Narine hung her head, all hope dying with the dwarf.

The flames dispersed to reveal Hadnoddon, teeth clenched, the hammer crashing down upon Sarazan's skull. A revolting *crack* echoed in the quiet chamber. The wizard lord crumpled to the floor, brains oozing from the cavity in his head. Where his sparkling blood touched the floor, the tiles crackled, turning to crimson crystal. The wizard lord's magic died with him, sending Chandan and Sariza crashing to the floor, both crying out. The room fell silent.

21

TRICKS

Narine knelt there, wobbling, woozy from expending so much energy on the physical manipulation spell. The wound to her forehead made it even worse. A numbness came over her, the floor around her littered with corpses, the area near Sarazan's head covered in glowing, red crystal.

Hadnoddon dropped his hammer and knelt beside Adyn, her body still shaking. "Are you all right?"

"I...," Adyn growled through a clenched jaw. "My muscles...cramping."

Chandan climbed to his feet, his nose bleeding as he stumbled toward Narine. "Well done, Princess."

Tears blurred her vision, hatred flaming in her heart. "You killed him. Jace is dead because of you."

"Dead?" Hadnoddon looked back toward the throne, Jace and Quiarre lying beside it. "He was alive just a moment ago."

Narine swung her head toward him. "What?"

"He told me to take the amulet." The dwarf wiped blood from his brow. "Good thing, too. The wizard's fireball scared me so bad, I think I soiled my breeches."

Laughter came from Adyn as her muscles slowly relaxed and she was able to push herself upright.

Narine rose to her feet. "A-alive?"

She stumbled across the room, stepping over several corpses dressed in black. The way Quiarre's body lay made it obvious he was dead, three scimitars sticking out of his chest, his neck bent in an unnatural manner. Jace lay beneath the man, his body twisted, one arm bent beneath his back, a shin bone jutting through his breeches just above his boot.

Narine knelt and reached toward him, hesitating. His eyes were closed, the side of his head covered in blood. Forcing herself, she touched his neck. There was a pulse, but it was weak. She grappled for her magic, wishing she had not expended so much in killing the guards. Delving into Jace's body, she found broken and dislocated bones, but that was the least of his problems. His ribs were broken, the tip of one of the scimitars through Quiarre piercing his lung, collapsing it. His skull was cracked, brain swollen.

She gripped Quiarre's arm and pulled the man off Jace. Desperate, she returned to Jace's side and tried to gather more magic, but she was too tired. Even with the added strength of the object on her ankle, it would not be enough. Her chin dropped to her chest and she leaned forward, hugging his head as she sobbed.

Chandan said, "The path of destiny is a harsh road, Princess."

Narine lifted her head and looked at him through a curtain of tears. "Why did you do this? To what end?"

The man stopped at the foot of the dais. "The ruby throne must sit vacant. If there were another way, I assure you, I would have pursued it, but prophecy demanded your presence."

"This was all to see Sarazan dead?"

"It was the only way." He dropped to one knee. "We must all make sacrifices to ensure the future."

"And what sacrifice have you made?!" she shouted.

The man unlatched the clasp on his wrist and pulled the golden array of chains from his hand, slipping the ruby ring off his finger in the process. "My sacrifice began long ago, this just another in a sequence of possessions I have conceded for the Order." He extended his hand, the jewelry resting in his palm. "This is now yours."

She stared at it in confusion.

In a gentle tone, Chandan said, "Take it and save him."

Her eyes widened. She grabbed the chain and slipped it onto her hand, ring over her middle finger. She secured the clasp on her wrist and turned her hand, the ruby glimmering as she drew in her magic, the power flooding in, her skin glowing with a brilliance augmented by both the object on her hand and one around her ankle. Through a construct of repair, she wove threads unlike anything she had crafted before – shifted bones back into place, patched holes in flesh, eased the swelling on his brain. She had no idea how long it took, but she did not stop until every part of his broken body was fully healed.

Jace gasped, jerking in her arms. She looked down at him, his eyes flickering open.

He muttered, "I must have pleased the gods to have been gifted with the likes of you."

Tears of relief flowed down her cheeks as she hugged him close and kissed his forehead.

Sweet breath filled Jace's lungs, his stomach growling with a vast hunger. He allowed Narine to hold his head to her chest while he savored the embrace. In truth, there was no place he would rather spend time.

Her tears dripped onto his face as she released him. With effort, he sat upright, groaning. Quiarre lay at the foot of the dais, dead. In fact, corpses were strewn around the throne room. Chandan and Sariza stood a few feet away, him with eyes narrowed at Jace, her staring toward her dead brother. Hadnoddon helped Adyn to her feet, the dwarf covered in blood, Adyn shaking as she stood, her clothing shredded.

Groans came from nearby, two of the guards in black moving, still alive. Chandan walked over to the first man, produced a dagger, and slit his throat before moving on to the other, veil and turban removed to reveal a woman's face. He slit her throat, as well.

"Why did you do that?" Jace asked.

"We cannot have witnesses." Chandan wiped the blade clean and slid it into his sheath. "Sariza must assume rule unchallenged."

Her eyes widened. "Me?"

He turned toward her. "Since your brother has exiled or eliminated any would-be challengers to the throne, you should have little trouble. The only wizards remaining in Sarmak are either old and feeble or too young to rise."

"I..." She hesitated. "When you betrayed him, I assumed you intended to take his place."

Chandan shook his head. "My destiny lies elsewhere."

Jace slowly stood, his joints sore from the skirmish.

Narine put her arm around his back to support him. "Are you all right?"

"I am fine...except for the hunger."

He faced Chandan, anger stirring. "I am tired of you pulling strings, wizard. You manipulated this entire thing, leading us here, claiming we were returning Sariza to her brother's care."

The wizard nodded. "I did what required doing."

"Why?" Jace asked.

"The wizard lord had to die. It was the only way."

Narine shook her head. "I still don't understand."

"The answer lies in prophecy, Princess." Chandan's tone grew distant, detached, as he recited the words. *"Seek the Charlatan of Ages and reclaim the Crimson Lord's sibling. In the presence of his own blood, the wizard lord shall fall to he who bears the Eye of Obscurance."* He shook his head. "I would have never guessed the thief would turn the amulet over to the dwarf, who then landed the killing blow."

"This entire thing, from rescuing Sariza to coming to Sarmak, was about assassinating Sarazan?" Jace growled. "Have you told us nothing but lies?"

"Rescue?" Sariza exclaimed, tears in her eyes. "I'd finally escaped my brother's wrath and was to marry the man I loved. Only on Ryxx could I live safely beyond Sarazan's grasp." She shook her head. "You killed Kalzon and destroyed my life."

Chandan put a hand on her shoulder, but Sariza shrugged it off. "I am sorry, Sariza. Kalzon's death was not part of the plan."

Jace glanced toward Narine, guilt twisting his stomach. He had not intended to kill Kalzon but had thought little of it...until now.

Sighing, Chandan turned to Jace and Narine. "I regret masking the truth from you, but it was required to ensure the future. Not everything I told you was false, for I am, in truth, part of the Order of Sol, as was Quiarre."

He held his hands out in supplication. "Let us return to *Hassaka's Breath*, and I will answer your questions."

"The ship again?" Jace muttered.

Narine asked, "Where are we bound?"

"Our next port is Antari, but our destination is farther inland."

Jace rolled his eyes. "Spit it out, man. Where do you intend to take us?"

"We journey to the Valley of Sol to confer with Master Astra. Urvadan rises, and a dark future fast approaches. You people are our only hope, the fulcrum point upon which the scale of destiny balances. With the assistance of the Order, we pray to tip fate in our favor."

After Narine healed Hadnoddon's wounds and failed in an attempt to assist Adyn's recovery, they exited the throne room. As they crossed the entry hall, Yartan burst in with several Redwing Guard. The servant saw them and froze, the guards spreading out behind him, prepared to attack.

Yartan said, "The Tower of Devotion has gone dark. The crimson flame no longer burns."

"Lord Sarazan is dead," Chandan replied.

Kneading his hands, Yartan stared toward the closed throne room door. "What... What will we do? The Darkening is many weeks away. Who will guide us?"

Chandan grabbed Sariza's arm and brought her in front of the man. "The same blood as Sarazan and his father flows through Sariza's veins. She is a skilled wizardess, trained at the University and raised here in the palace. Support her rule and others will fall in line, at least until the Darkening. If someone else wishes to challenge her right to the throne, they may present themselves to Hassaka then."

Yartan's concern melted away, replaced by a weak smile. "Very well, Master Chandan. With you at her side, as you supported Sarazan, all will be well."

The wizard shook his head. "I cannot remain in Sarmak. I have matters of import to address elsewhere."

"But...we have no wizards to protect us."

"You have Sariza, who now controls the Redwing Guard. That must be enough."

Chandan led them across the hall, leaving Yartan and Sariza behind.

22

CHALLENGES

From a hilltop at the edge of an orange grove, Garvin stared down at the city of Fralyn and the structure from which the name originated. An oft-studied subject in military circles, Fralyn Fortress was the most famous bastion in the Eight Wizardoms.

Larger than any other castle, the citadel dwarfed the neighboring city, looming as a big, dark monolith in the heart of a river valley. Even from miles away, the stronghold was impressive – three hundred feet wide and eight times the length, blocky, square towers rising above.

The fortress also acted as a bridge since it spanned a narrow point on the Serpent River, physically connecting Orenth to Balmoria. Maker-built, the structure was larger than some cities. More importantly, whoever controlled the fortress controlled the river. With the wealth of resources coming out of Zialis and various inland mines, having such control was worth the heavy price paid to claim the stronghold. *I wonder why Orenth has allowed Balmoria to hold it for so long.* At various times in the past, both wizardoms had controlled it, but Balmoria had held it unchallenged for the past century, taking it soon after Lord Jakarci claimed the throne of Bal.

"There it is," said Quiam, the recently promoted captain sitting on the horse beside Garvin's. "Our scouts report the portcullis on each riverbank is closed, the fortress held by thousands of armed soldiers."

"It appears High Wizard Greehl monitored our approach," Rindle noted.

The thief had asked to ride with Garvin and the officers to survey the area ahead of the marching army. Garvin didn't mind. While not a soldier, Rindle's different perspective had proven useful in the past.

Rindle added, "The obelisk stands within the city. I suspect Lord Thurvin will have little trouble capturing it."

"True, but Queen Priella wishes to push into Balmoria." Eyes narrowed, Garvin stared toward the citadel. "We have little choice but to find a means to cross here."

"Isn't there another bridge?" Rindle asked.

"There was, fifteen miles upriver," Quiam replied. "Lord Jakarci ordered it destroyed eighty years ago. Land traffic must pass through the fortress, guards collecting tolls from anyone wishing to enter Balmoria."

The thief whistled. "I had heard the Bals were a greedy bunch."

Garvin snorted. "You have no idea how much they earn from the tolls collected at this crossing."

"Our fleet waits downriver. If the ships landed in Fralyn, we could board, and they could carry us to the next port."

Garvin shook his head. "The nearest port is Lamor, a hundred miles north. The shoreline is treacherous between here and there with no place to land. Based on the size of our army, horses and all, it would take weeks to move everyone. Splitting our forces would also leave us vulnerable to attack." He grimaced. "Priella insists we continue north and do so quickly."

Closing his eyes, he rubbed them wearily. "Yet another assault for a power-hungry wizard. How did I end up right back where I started?"

Rindle snorted. "I was thinking the same thing. After we left Henton behind in Ghealdor–"

Garvin flashed Rindle a stern glare, cutting him off.

Quiam gave Garvin a questioning look. "You are a military man, Garvin. Where else would you be?"

Sighing, he shook his head. "Apparently, nowhere else."

Garvin pulled the reins, turning his mount. "I've seen enough. The army will catch up soon. Let's plan the camp deployment and assign stations before they arrive. Once the command pavilion is ready, we shall meet, for we have plans to discuss."

Along with their escort of eight Midnight Guard, Garvin, Quiam, and Rindle headed back to the road, following it down the hillside as it wound its way around a vineyard. They came to an open field a mile from the fortress, still hundreds of feet above it. While not level ground, it was an ideal distance from the fortress to set up camp, placing them above any approach from the city, the stronghold, and the river.

There, they settled, the horses gnawing on the long, yellowed grass. Garvin sat and stared toward the fortress, lost in thought. By the time the wagons with the tents appeared, the sun was past the midpoint in the sky, giving them plenty of time to set up camp before nightfall.

～

Garvin, with Rindle a step behind, ducked inside the command tent. Theodin, Shellock, and Iberson were already inside, as were Quiam and Lieutenant Voltan, the leader of the Farrowen scouts, all surrounding a table covered in maps, the one on top a freshly drafted sketch of the immediate area.

Voltan pointed toward the map, finger running along it as he spoke. "As you can see, the fortress spans the width of the river at its narrowest point. Don't let the drawing deceive you. The banks are still a half mile apart."

A long, narrow structure ran down the middle of the river on the sea-facing side of the stronghold.

Never one to hold back, Garvin pointed. "What is this?"

"The fortress is a Maker-made structure, and this is an extension of the building. It is a pier running down the center of the river, connecting the core of the fortress to an island a quarter mile downstream. The Balmorian naval ships dock along the pier. There are currently twenty-four moored there, protected by a string of manned towers along the pier." Voltan tapped on the chunk of land at the end of the pier. "This entire island is covered in battlements. We counted sixteen catapults and twenty ballistae on the island, all facing outward, ready to wreak havoc on any enemy ship attempting to approach either the city or the fortress. Since it is connected to the stronghold, soldiers can easily migrate from one structure to the other."

Rindle asked, "How do boats coming down the river reach the city? It looks like the fortress blocks the way."

Voltan shook his head. "Four massive, arched openings exist beneath the fortress, two on each side of the shipyard. Any boat passing through must pay a toll, as does any wagon passing through the fortress when traveling between Orenth and Balmoria."

"That's extortion," Rindle muttered. "Orenth must make a fortune off those tolls."

"Indeed," Priella said as she entered the tent with Bosinger and Kollin. All fell quiet as the wizard queen approached. "Have you identified a means to take the fortress?"

Theodin shook his head. "Not yet, My Queen. Voltan was just giving us a lay of the land so we might better understand what we face."

She turned toward Voltan and arched a brow. "What do you suggest, Lieutenant?"

The man's easy manner changed noticeably. "It... It is a daunting task, Your Majesty. I had hoped for suggestions after the briefing."

"You have no suggestions yourself?"

"Well... We have superior numbers, but the fortress is large enough to house thousands–"

She interrupted. "How many do you believe are stationed there?"

"Our best guess says at least two thousand. Three at most."

"Our infantry alone is six times their numbers already, and our ranks will swell further when we unload the transport ships. How large is our fleet beyond the harbor?"

"Thirty-two ships, My Queen."

She turned toward Theodin. "What if we attack by sea and land at the same time?"

The man rubbed his chin. "It might work, but our loses would be great."

"How many?"

"Half. Perhaps more."

Priella gave the man an icy glare. Bosinger put his hand on her shoulder, brow arched as she glanced at him. The woman sighed, visibly relaxing. "You are experienced military experts. I trust you will come up with a solution. However, the sands continue to collect in the hourglass. We must reach Balmor before the grains expire."

What drives her schedule? Garvin frowned, eyes narrowing at the woman. *She is hiding something.*

Priella walked to the tent flap and glanced backward. "You have two days to think of something. We need to reach Balmor with our force intact, and we need to do it soon."

She left, Bosinger and Kollin trailing, the tent falling silent.

~

Once Priella exited the command tent, her expression relaxed. She stared toward Fralyn Fortress for a moment, guards visible on the sunlit battlements. She sighed and headed uphill, toward two white tents. Above hers, waving in the breeze, was the banner of Pallanar, white with an ice-blue diamond in the center. A midnight blue pennant with a silver lightning bolt stood over the other tent. She headed toward the latter with Kollin and Bosinger trailing.

The guards outside did not challenge her as she approached, but their eyes flicked toward the tent nervously.

What is going on? Concern of betrayal swirled.

"Remain out here," she said over her shoulder to the two men escorting her.

Ducking inside, she stuttered to a stop, her eyes widening. Thurvin sat in a copper tub, half-filled with water, rubbing soap beneath an armpit.

"My Queen." He smiled. "Since you did not bother to announce yourself, perhaps you would care to join me?"

"I…" Priella turned toward his table as she gathered herself. "I came to discuss Fralyn."

"What of it? The tower should be easy enough to claim. I intend to do so tonight, after Devotion."

"No. Not the city. The fortress."

"I assume High Wizard Greehl views us as a threat to Balmoria and does not intend to let us cross."

She frowned, her gaze shifting toward him. The man seemed to be scrubbing his crotch, which was thankfully obscured by the foam-capped water. "Of course, he views an army exceeding ten thousand troops as a threat. However, he is likely to underestimate us. When has he ever faced one wizard lord, let alone two?"

He shrugged. "So, what's the problem?"

"Anything we do here reduces the chance of surprise when we reach Balmor, where Lord Jakarci awaits."

"You can't expect to reach Balmor without him realizing two wizard lords ride at the head of this army."

"I suppose not, but it doesn't mean we can't hope for him to underestimate us."

Thurvin snorted. "What does it matter? My power dwarfs his. He cannot win."

"Have you faced a wizard lord in combat before?"

"No."

"History has proven they are incredibly difficult to kill, especially without the advantage of surprise. He knows we are coming and has time to prepare." She shook her head. "I cannot believe it will be easy."

Thurvin stood, his naked body exposed above the water, which came to his knees. He was a scrawny man, lacking both muscle and fat, but was surprisingly well endowed. Priella realized she was staring and turned toward the tent flap, her cheeks flush.

He chuckled. "See anything of interest, Priella? Perhaps you would like to try riding a wizard lord rather than the young pup you rescued from Tiamalyn. I may know a trick or two he has yet to learn."

Her embarrassment turned to anger. Setting her jaw, she spun back toward him. "You are my subject and will treat me with respect."

Thurvin blinked, eyes narrowing. "My power outstrips yours."

Steeling herself, she stalked toward him. "The power I *allow* you to wield."

His magic flared so intensely, she flinched away. Ropes of it wrapped around her and lifted her off her feet, drawing her close.

He glared at her with a madness in his eyes and sneered, "I could destroy you here and now."

The magic ropes binding her were too tight for her to inhale fully, her response rasping out. "You forget what I offer."

The man blinked, the madness fading as he frowned. "What did you offer? I cannot recall."

She tried to speak but had no breath to do so. Frantic, she debated attacking him but knew it would spiral, his strength too great for her to face directly. Her mouth moved, no sound coming from it.

"Speak up, woman," he growled.

Spots began to dance before her eyes from the lack of air. She tried again, a strangled word coming out. "Power…"

He pulled her closer. "I still cannot hear you."

With her arms bound to her sides, she could not reach out, even though he was just a few feet away. However, her hands were free. Desperate, she kicked off her slipper and cast a spell of compulsion, channeling it from the hand on her hip and down her leg as she kicked out. Her bare foot grazed the part of him closest to her – his manhood. At the same moment, she released the spell, attacking his mind with a sharp strike.

The man stiffened, eyes bulging and then rolling up in his head. She dropped to the ground in a heap while he stumbled backward and collapsed into the tub, his head striking the copper lip, water splashing over the carpets.

Priella gasped for air as she stared at the unconscious wizard lord. There he lay, naked, wet, and vulnerable. For the first time since assuming the throne, she felt fear. The man's power was too great for her to control, at least for any meaningful length of time. He had one more tower to claim. Fralyn was a small city but would add to his might, nonetheless.

She climbed to her feet, one still bare, and stood over the tub, chewing her lip. Killing him while unconscious would be a simple thing. Doing so while awake? Nigh impossible. Yet the man's power was too useful to dismiss. Not enough time remained for her to reclaim all the thrones for herself. Besides, she had sensed a madness in him and wondered if it was the result of the immense magic at his disposal.

I cannot afford to go mad.

With her breathing slowing, she set her jaw and circled the tub to kneel beside him. She cast a construct of repair and healed his injury. The man began to stir. Urgently, she used another construct, one long forbidden, and erased a small slice of his memory.

Eyes blinking open, he looked around, confused. "What happened?"

"You slipped and hit your head on the tub. Thank the gods I was here to heal you before you drowned."

Thurvin sat upright and shook his head as if to clear it. "I... I don't remember. Where am I?"

"Outside of Fralyn. We just arrived hours ago." She subtly planted more seeds in his mind before removing her hand from his shoulder. "If you are all right, I will leave so you can dress. You must prepare for tonight, when you claim the Fralyn Obelisk of Devotion."

"Yes." He gave her a weak smile. "Thank you, My Queen. I will capture the obelisk, then we will see what we can do about taking the fortress."

With him once again under her control, Priella ducked outside. Bosinger and Kollin stood there, both staring at her in concern. She stormed past them, unwilling to even allow them to ask what had happened.

23

A GIFT

A line of soldiers in front of him and far more behind, Rindle waited with a bowl in hand, the line into the mess tent slowly advancing. He stepped inside, an almost appetizing scent wafting through the air.

Stew again, he thought. He had discovered army food lacking in both taste and variety, the meals doing little else than filling his stomach. *Perhaps the military intentionally sucks the joy out of eating.*

From across the tent, a man approached, eyes intense and fixed on him. He recognized him as the queen's bodyguard. Rindle prepared to address the man, but he walked past without stopping, Rindle watching the bodyguard leave the tent.

Shrugging, he turned back toward the line, now a three-stride gap to the soldier in front of him, the man's bowl being filled. He quickly closed the gap and lifted his bowl, frowning when he noticed a folded piece of paper in it. Grabbing the paper and squeezing it into his fist, he stood there while a cook filled the bowl. He slid to the next station and accepted a hard, dry biscuit before turning and heading outside.

The sun had dropped below the horizon, the sky the purple of dusk, the hillside speckled with campfires. Rindle made straight for the tent he shared with Garvin, the larger command tent not far beyond it. He lifted the flap and ducked inside, the interior dark and empty, his tentmate still meeting with the commanders. A grunt escaped as he sat on his bedroll. He set his bowl down and fumbled around until he found the enchanted lantern, activating it with the twist of a knob, casting the tent interior in pale blue light. Palm open, he stared at the folded piece of paper before unfolding it to reveal crisp handwriting.

Thief,

You and your colleague possess unique skills, as demonstrated by your success in Tiamalyn. Those abilities would be of use to me. Fetch your partner and visit my tent after Devotion. I have a gift to bestow should you prove amenable to my request.

-P

He frowned while staring at the message, thoughts churning in his head. *The bodyguard made sure to catch my attention before dropping the note. He counted on me knowing who had sent him.*

Sighing, he muttered, "How do I get myself into these things?"

He reread the note and wondered about the gift. Caught between the alluring prospect of her offer and fear of disobeying her request, he resigned himself to visiting her tent once he lured Garvin away from the other soldiers.

Reclaiming the bowl and spoon, he set his mind to the task while he ate.

Bright beacons pulsed upon the hilltop, one ice blue, the other deep azure. Queen Priella sat upon one throne, Lord Thurvin upon the other, soldiers chanting prayers to both at the same time. Beams like bridges of light blazed across the sky from both shimmering thrones.

Rindle knelt outside his tent, mumbling the chant while waiting for Devotion to end – twenty minutes that sometimes seemed like hours. The throne of Pallan dimmed first, the throne of Farrow continuing on for a full five minutes before it, too, ceased.

The moment the second throne fell dark, Rindle stood and rushed toward the command pavilion, intent on interrupting before Garvin was drawn into another long conversation. He ducked in as the officers gathered around the map-covered table.

Rindle sidled up to the man and nudged him. "A messenger arrived. It's urgent."

Garvin waved him off. "Whatever it is, it can wait."

He rolled his eyes. "The message is from Despaldi." He hoped the lie caught the man's attention.

The lieutenant's head turned in a flash. "Despaldi?"

"Yes." Rindle tugged the man's arm. "Come."

"If you will excuse me," Garvin said to the commanders. "I must see to something."

They stepped outside, and Rindle rushed up the hill, forcing Garvin to follow before he could ask questions. A shape rose into the air ahead of him, dark blue robes rippling in the breeze. The wizard sped off into the night, flying over the camp and toward the city below.

"That was Lord Thurvin," Garvin said.

"He can fly," Rindle said in awe.

Garvin looked at him. "How observant."

"I didn't know wizards could fly."

"The man is hardly a wizard any longer. He may be closer to a god by now."

Rindle stared toward the city. "What do you think he is doing?"

"My guess? He is about to convert the obelisk from Oren to Farrow. As you can see, he no longer needs us for such tasks."

"Come on," Rindle said as he continued up the hill.

Rather than heading directly for the queen's tent, he angled toward Thurvin's, slowing as he drew close, looking around to see if anyone followed. Satisfied, he turned sharply and looped around the back of the tent. Garvin remained quiet, watching as Rindle knelt and pulled on a stake. It did not move.

"Help me," he whispered.

"Why?"

"I don't want anyone to see us enter."

Pressing his lips together, Garvin knelt and jammed his dagger into the turf, loosening the earth around the stake. He then pulled it up, freeing the line.

Rindle lifted the edge of the tent and peeked in.

Bosinger stared at him, sword in hand. "Hurry up, thief."

After waving for Garvin to follow, Rindle crawled inside and stood, dusting himself off. Garvin slipped in and stood beside him, gaze sweeping the tent. The queen sat at a table near the middle, Kollin Mor standing over her like another bodyguard. *As if she needs such protection.* Rindle suspected Priella could snuff him out before he could draw his blade.

A meeting conducted in secret meant Rindle could paint outside the lines, so he chose to skip titles and other niceties. More so, the queen wanted something of him, placing him in either a position of power or one of peril. Direct questions would reveal which one more quickly.

"What is this truly about?" he demanded.

"This…" Priella rose from her chair, her gaze going from one man to the other, "is about loyalty."

A snort slipped out before Rindle realized it. Garvin gave him an even look, making it clear he was to remain quiet. The man turned to Priella.

"Go on," he said.

She strolled toward Garvin, hips swaying overtly, finger running down her throat. "Are you loyal to Lord Thurvin?"

Garvin inhaled deeply, jaw set. "I have been a Farrowen soldier since I was sixteen years old. Even when I served in the Murguard, it was under a Farrowen captain."

"Despaldi."

He grunted. "You have done your research."

"In truth, little other than what Lord Thurvin has been willing to share."

"Yes, I served under Despaldi. He is the reason I joined the Midnight Guard after leaving The Fractured Lands."

"It sounds as if he had a significant impact on your life."

"You could say that."

She stepped closer and adjusted Garvin's coat. He had yet to switch back to his armor. Rindle wondered if he would ever wear it again.

"In that case, you have my condolences."

He blinked. "What?"

"Didn't your wizard lord tell you? Despaldi is dead."

"How?" Garvin's voice was strained.

"It seems he met his demise while attempting to kill a thief named Landish."

Rindle leaned back with a start. "Jerrell Landish?"

She smirked. "The very same."

"Let me get this straight…" Garvin licked his lips. "Despaldi and his men somehow killed a wizard lord, only to later fall victim to a thief?"

Rindle thought the same thing. *Will Jerrell's well of luck never run dry?*

Her smirk remained as she turned away, speaking over her shoulder. "Did your vaunted wizard lord ever tell you how it was possible for Despaldi and his men to kill a wizard lord?"

"No," Garvin growled.

She grabbed a book off the table, eyeing it as she turned it over in her hands. "This book contains secrets no other wizard knows. Using this knowledge, your wizard lord imbued Despaldi and four others with his magic, gifting them abilities far beyond mortal men. With these abilities, they attacked and killed Lord Horus, at Thurvin's command, one of Despaldi's men dying in the confrontation.

"Also at your wizard lord's behest, Despaldi tracked Jerrell Landish to Cor Cordium. There, he and the three other enhanced soldiers battled Landish and his companions. In the end, Despaldi died and Landish escaped. Only one of his men survived. That soldier, a man named Ferris, was captured by Cordium soldiers and imprisoned. He escaped from his cell and returned to Marquithe after we departed. A messenger reached us a few days ago, informing Lord Thurvin of what had occurred." She shook her head. "It's a shame he didn't care to share the passing of your captain with you, Lieutenant."

The man stared toward the carpeted ground, his fists clenched, breaths rapid.

Priella strolled toward them again, her finger lifting Garvin's chin until his eyes met hers. "What has your loyalty earned you, Lieutenant?" She turned toward Rindle. "Or yours, thief?"

She spun around and walked away again, stopping to look over her shoulder. "Pledge your loyalty to me, and I will reward you." Cocking her head, she added, "If you think about it, you are not even betraying a past promise, for Lord Thurvin has plead fealty to me. Through him, you two are mine, as well. I offer you the opportunity to gain something in exchange."

A beat later, Garvin asked, "What do you propose?"

Priella finished her turn, smiling while tapping the book in her hand. "I will gift you both with abilities unlike anything you imagined. With your new skills, you will execute a mission for me. One I hope will spare the lives of thousands."

Rindle could not hold back any longer. "What kind of abilities exactly?"

She turned to him. "Imagine if you could enter any room undetected, sneak into any building without anyone aware, even if occupied by thousands." She strode closer, and Rindle felt himself drawn into her green eyes. Her voice dropped to a whisper. "I could make you a shadow come to life."

He knew his skills as a thief were good, but not enough to squash the ever-present ghost of Jerrell Landish. *I could be the best.* The idea was beyond tantalizing.

"There must be more," Garvin said.

"I will give you more." She turned toward him. "You will rise as I rise, which will be beyond anything you can imagine. Just remember, I will require your loyalty, for your abilities will not last, not without my magic reigniting them...or altering them from time to time."

Garvin nodded, his jaw set. "Do it."

She smiled. "I am glad we have come to an accommodation."

Turning around, she set the book on the table, opening it and paging through it beneath the light of an enchanted lantern. Her face took on a look of concentration, hands held above the book, fingers wiggling, wrists turning.

Finally, she said, "Thief, come here."

Rindle turned toward Garvin, the man's hardened gaze fixed upon the wizardess. Magic had never been a friend to him, but a source of fear. Now he was to have some unknown spell placed upon him in a bargain struck by someone else. He swallowed hard, fear dropping down his throat to settle in the pit of his stomach, sending it roiling like a stormy sea.

"*Now*, thief," she growled.

He forced himself forward, his feet as heavy as lead. She held her hands toward him, eyes narrowed as she placed a palm on his chest. A wave of nausea struck, the world tilting. He stumbled, reaching for the table to right himself. His hand slid through it, the sensation similar to reaching into water. Landing on his hands and knees, he gasped when he saw the ground through his hands. Lifting them before his face, he flexed translucent fingers that had the dark tint of shadow. He looked down at himself, body appearing like a phantom.

"What have you done to me?" he asked, his voice lacking substance, coming out as a breathy rasp.

Priella smiled. "You have become a shadow of yourself. Rise."

He stood and floated before settling, his stomach twisting.

The queen stepped closer, eyes alight as she gazed at him. Slowly, hesitantly, she reached for him, her hand pressing lightly against his chest. Then she pushed forward. He gasped, her finger raking his heart and causing it to skip a beat.

"Truly remarkable," she said. "Your very physical nature is as ghostly as you appear." Stepping back, she gestured to him with a flick of her hand. "Try jumping."

"Jumping?" Rindle rasped.

"Yes. Try it."

With a thrust, he floated toward the top of the tent, slowing as his head and upper body passed through it. The wind struck and pushed him backward, his lower body still in the tent as it slid past, his arms waving in panic, fearing he might be swept away. Slowly, his body sank back into the tent, his head dropping inside just before he reached the tent outer wall.

The interior reappeared and he drifted to the ground, the people inside all staring at him.

"Why did you do this to me?" Rindle's shout sounded more like a forceful whisper.

Priella waved the comment aside. "Do not worry. It is temporary. How long it will last, I am unsure, but I made the opening large enough for a proper effect, so it will pass more quickly than otherwise."

"Not permanent?" Rindle did not understand the rest of her statement, but he was thankful to not remain a ghost forever.

She returned to the table and paged through the book, stopping and tapping on a diagram with a smile. "All right, Lieutenant. It's your turn."

24

GREEHL

Garvin rowed toward the middle of the river, the massive fortress blocking the moon, casting the rowboat in shadow. The current caught hold, drawing them toward the arched opening beneath the fortress. When it slipped beneath the massive structure, he guided the craft toward the brick wall.

"Climb onto my back," he said.

Rindle's shadowy arm reached around Garvin's neck. The slightest pressure, akin to a silken scarf, pressed against his chest, the thief weightless. He pulled the oars in as the tunnel wall drew closer, flexing his fingers in preparation.

When the boat struck the wall, he leapt. His fingers grasped the damp brick, dozens of tiny claws upon each fingertip digging in. He brought his bare feet beneath him, toes latching onto the surface. Like a spider, he crawled up the arched ceiling until he was upside down, craning his head back to watch the rowboat float out of the tunnel and into the moonlight. Undoubtedly, the Balmorian soldiers would find the boat and investigate. Scrambling back the way they had come, he crawled toward the tunnel entrance.

He slunk around the corner and up the outer wall. Ten feet up, he reached the first battlement, a narrow walkway with a low wall patrolled by pacing archers wearing the black and yellow leathers. Pausing, he waited until the nearest archer turned his back, then he scurried past.

The sound of running water faded as the river grew more distant. A backward glance revealed the water over a hundred feet below. He slowed and peered between two merlons. Again, the battlements were patrolled, many of the soldiers wearing chainmail and armed with halberds. The torchlit parapet wrapped around the entire structure, twenty feet deep with thick, blocky towers rising up along the middle.

Garvin crawled back down a few feet and whispered over his shoulder, "Go search for him. He is reported to occupy the tallest tower, the one in the center of the fortress. If you find him first, look for me outside."

"Got it," Rindle whispered.

The thief climbed up and stood on Garvin's shoulders before his shadowy form slipped over the wall and disappeared.

Garvin climbed back up and peered through the gap, waiting while two guards spoke to one another. A door opened, the soldiers turning toward it as a man with wings on his helmet stepped outside. He called them over, warning them of an empty boat found in the shipyard. Soldiers currently inspected the lower reaches in search of possible intruders.

Their backs to him, Garvin slunk over the wall, padded silently across the parapet, and scrambled up the tower.

Rindle had spent a significant portion of his thieving years lurking in shadows. Now he *was* a shadow, moving among the Balmorian soldiers unaware, although he was only an arm's reach away. A euphoria filled him – a sense of invincibility and supreme confidence. But when he entered the amber aura of a burning torch, a soldier's eyes followed him.

The man tapped a fellow soldier on the shoulder and pointed toward Rindle. "Havmor, did you see that?"

Reacting, Rindle slipped into a shadowy recess and froze.

Havmor looked right toward him. "See what, Torrey?"

"Um…" Torrey pulled his helmet off and scratched his head, squinting. "I thought I saw a shadow."

The other man chuckled. "Of course, you saw a shadow." He approached the wall and pointed toward his own. "I see one right here, and another at your feet." Laughing, he stepped beside his companion. "We all have them, Torrey. If yours goes missing, be sure to let me know."

Torrey laughed and slipped his helmet back on, the two men turning to gaze out over the river.

Exhaling in relief, Rindle slipped from his hiding spot and continued, hugging the wall, mindful when approaching torchlight. No other soldiers appeared aware of his passing.

He reached the center tower and crept along the wall but found no door. Placing his palms upon the brick wall, he gathered himself and pushed. His hands slid through, his head and body following. Passing through the brick felt like striding through mud, thick and resisting. When his hands broke through, he pulled himself the rest of the way until he emerged in a small, dark room with a single bed. A snore arose, but he ignored it. The room was far too small to suit the man he sought, so he walked to the door and pushed his head through, peering up and down the torchlit corridor. Empty.

Slinking down the corridor, he came to a stairwell and began an ascent toward the upper levels.

The central tower stood five hundred feet above the river, Garvin clawing up the outer walls, slowing to peer inside windows. None of the rooms contained his quarry.

He crawled to the corner and peered around the moonlit side of the tower. A balcony bulged out near the top. A downward glance revealed a guard parapet five stories below. Farther down, dark silhouettes moved along the pier in the center of the river. Three lookout towers were spaced along the pier, hundreds of feet apart, each lit by torches. At the end of the pier was a dark island encircled by battlements, amber torchlight flickering upon the top of the wall.

The defenses are impressive. It would be impossible to approach the fortress by ship without paying a steep price.

Dismissing such thoughts, he rounded the corner and scrambled along the moonlit side of the tower.

Garvin reached the uppermost balcony, climbed onto the railing, and landed lightly on the balcony. Both pairs of glass-paned doors were closed. He peered through into a sprawling chamber, dark save for a flickering candle on a stand beside the bed. A man with dark, shoulder-length hair and a goatee hanging below his chin lay there. Garvin watched for a full minute to ensure the man was asleep, breaths deep and even. He needed to get close before the wizard could wield his magic. Carefully, he tested the door, the handle turning. As quietly as he could, he eased it open and stepped inside.

A shadow came at him from one side. He ducked, a blade speeding over his head. Rolling forward, he rose and spun. Another shadow came from the opposite side and smashed into him, driving him to the floor. Garvin rolled with his momentum until he was on top, his assailant pinned to the floor. A third shadow lunged with a kick, and he dodged, the boot flying past his face. He caught the attacker's heel and lifted hard, sending him crashing to his back.

The room lit up, a globe of light above the bed, the yellow-robed wizard standing on the mattress.

"Stop!" the wizard shouted. "Or die."

Eight other soldiers stood in the room, five men and three women, each wearing black leathers with a yellow arrow on each shoulder. Six held weapons ready, short swords with narrow blades and an odd hilt. Another climbed back to his feet, while Garvin knelt over the last – a woman with short, black hair and angular eyes.

He held his hands up and stood, the woman scrambling from beneath him and straightening her leathers with a glare.

The wizard climbed off the bed but did not approach. He scowled as his gaze swept Garvin from his bare feet to raised hands.

"High Wizard Greehl, I presume," Garvin said.

Greehl sneered. "I suspected the queen might send an assassin. Too bad for you, Bals respond poorly to treachery. When she sees your head upon a halberd outside the Orenthian gate, she will understand we will not be denied. Balmoria is not hers to conquer!"

"If I meant to kill you, would I have come unarmed?" Garvin had left his sword and dagger in his tent.

"What do you want then?"

"I came to arrange a meeting."

"Lies!" The wizard extended his hand toward Garvin, ropes of magic lashing around him, lifting him off the floor. "I will not listen to your lies!" The rope slid around Garvin's neck. "As I said, your head is now forfeit." The man squeezed his fist, the rope around Garvin's neck tightening.

~

Slinking from the stairwell, Rindle peered down the torchlit corridor. Unlike the others, this one was guarded, a pair of soldiers standing beside a closed door halfway down the hallway. The men wore chainmail over yellow tabards, heads protected by pointed, metal helmets.

Rindle slid along the wall, toward the room. Rather than enter the torchlit area near the guards, he pushed himself through the brick wall and emerged into a well-lit chamber. Garvin was inside, surrounded by armed warriors dressed in black. His bare feet were above the floor as he squirmed, hands grasping at his throat. A wizard in yellow robes held an outstretched hand toward Garvin, the wizard's back to Rindle.

He rushed the wizard from behind and slid his hand into the man's chest, concentrating as he squeezed his heart, partially solidifying at the same time. The wizard stiffened and gasped.

Rindle's voice came out as a hiss. "Release him or die, Greehl."

The wizard lowered his arm, Garvin falling to the floor and gasping for air.

"Now, I will release you, but you must listen," Rindle rasped.

At the man's nod, he withdrew his hand. Greehl stumbled to a nearby chair, leaning on it as he turned around.

"A shade?" he panted, a hand on his chest. "What dark magic has she embraced?"

"No," Garvin warbled, voice weak as he stood. "Not a wraith. What you face is a man augmented by Queen Priella's magic."

One of the warriors in black flipped the short sword in his hand and threw. The missile passed right through Rindle's chest, causing his heart to flutter for a breath before the blade struck the wall and fell to the floor with a clatter.

"You cannot kill me," Rindle laughed, voice scratchy. Even to himself, it was a frightening sound. He turned to the wizard. "However, I could have ended you, wizard. It would have been easy...if that were the reason for our visit."

Garvin nodded and took a step toward Greehl. "As I said, we are not here to kill you. Priella does not wish you or anyone else in the fortress dead. She does not intend to conquer Fralyn Fortress or Balmoria."

"What does she want?" Greehl asked, seemingly recovered.

"She wishes to meet with you, face to face. Come to the Orenthian gate at sunrise. She will be there with only her bodyguard, no others. Once you listen to her proposal, you may decide how you wish to respond."

The wizard scowled at Garvin before finally nodding. "Very well. I will meet her at sunrise."

"She will be there alone, as promised." Garvin turned and walked toward the open balcony door. "Come along, thief."

Rindle crossed the room, startled gazes following his ghostly form. He latched an arm around Garvin's chest, concentrating to keep it solid, and the man leapt. They flew over the edge, the fall a terrifying one. Twenty feet down, Garvin latched onto the moonlit wall and scrambled across it.

Rindle glanced backward to find a shocked wizard leaning over the balcony railing, watching until they rounded the tower and faded into the night.

25

INFLUENCE

Priella sat upon her horse while staring toward Fralyn Fortress, draped in predawn gloom. A fur-lined cloak rested over her shoulders against the chill. It would surely warm once the sun rose, but at the moment, her breath stirred in the air. Bosinger sat on his horse beside her, the bodyguard in full armor, helmet in place, expression stoic. Soldiers covered the hillside to her left and right, dressed for battle but standing at ease, curious. They seemed unsure of what to expect, which was no surprise. Nobody knew the truth of her plan, not even Bosinger. Even so, he obeyed, ready to play the part he had been given.

At least I can always rely on him.

Theodin approached on foot and bowed. "Will you not accept an escort, My Queen? Twenty Gleam Guard soldiers should not be perceived as a threat."

She expected he might try to talk her out of this meeting. Kollin had tried and failed. If the man who shared her bed could not sway her, she doubted anyone else could. She looked back toward her tent, the white pavilion visible in the distance. His tall, dark silhouette stood outside, watching her. If she had not demanded he remain at the tent, he would now be at her side. She could not afford such distractions.

"No," she replied, eyes fixed on the brightening horizon. "I must get Greehl to lower his guard, or this will not work. I intend to cross without losing any soldiers...ours or theirs. Those lives are required for the fight ahead."

She glanced at Bosinger. Although he appeared fierce in his gear, it would be inevitable for others to underestimate his abilities. None would grasp his augmentation until it was too late. *I pray he need not test those abilities today.* She remained wary of betrayal. It was her greatest fear, the most likely thing to deny her future.

Her hand went to the saddlebag and patted the contents. *It is still there.* She counted on Greehl's greed. A thin thread of hope to cling to, but it was something.

A line of yellow light bloomed on the horizon, the sun creeping over the foothills to the east. *Finally.*

Speaking to Theodin, her gaze fixed on the fortress, she said, "I will soon return. Be ready to march." She kicked her horse into motion, Bosinger riding at her side.

Down the hillside they went, turning at switchbacks twice before nearing the river, the ground leveling. The dark fortress loomed over them before they even drew close. It was massive, easily four times the size of Illustan Palace.

They came to a fork, one path continuing northwest to the city of Fralyn, the city wall a quarter mile away, the Obelisk of Devotion thrusting above it, burning with the blue flame of Farrow. *The last tower I will allow Thurvin to claim.* The wizard lord concerned her, the strength of his magic requiring her to frequently reinforce her influence to keep him in check. She wondered if he were going mad. *Can compulsion control a broken mind?* The question could not be answered. She was the only person alive who knew the spell, so there was nobody else to ask.

Turning, they followed the gravel road toward the river until it veered to a brick ramp rising to the closed portcullis. Towers stood on both sides of the opening, the open tops three stories up, a narrow parapet running between them. Priella counted sixteen archers staring down at her, all dressed in black and yellow leathers. None had arrows nocked.

She dismounted, Bosinger doing the same while she removed her prize from the saddlebag. Together, they walked toward the gate. Through the gaps in the bars, at the far end of the dark tunnel through the fortress, she spied the dimly lit archway leading to the far bank. From within the gloom in between, two silhouettes appeared – one a tall man in robes, the other short and athletic with broad shoulders and a narrow waist. Priella stopped two strides from the bars and waited, watching their approach.

The wizard's robes were yellow with black symbols around his cuffs and down the seam, his sash black. He had shoulder-length hair and a long, dark goatee, matching Garvin's description of Greehl.

The warrior beside him was a woman dressed in the garb of the Black Wasps, the Balmorian Special Forces. She had a blade on each hip, throwing knives on her boots and upper arms. Woman or not, the abilities of the Black Wasps were widely respected.

Like Priella, Greehl stopped two strides from the portcullis, just beyond her reach.

"Thank you for meeting with me, High Wizard," Priella said firmly.

"You are Queen Priella?"

"I am."

He frowned. "You are not what I imagined. How is it a woman holds the power of a wizard lord? It is forbidden."

She embraced her magic, gathering power only a wizard lord could manage, skin glowing to anyone with the gift. "The magic of Pallan is mine to wield. As for whether it is forbidden, why should I be presumed guilty for the crimes of a woman centuries dead?"

Greehl set his jaw. "You hold your magic, but will it save you? If anything should happen to me, my soldiers will attack. Regardless, the portcullis will remain closed."

"I have no intention of attacking, but if I did, I could destroy every soldier above me in the blink of an eye."

The man grimaced. "I am here. What is this about? Why have you brought an enemy army to our border?"

Priella smiled. "I am not your enemy, Greehl. In fact, I wish to form an alliance."

He sneered, "I will not betray Jakarci or Balmoria."

"I speak not of betrayal." She held up the book of magic, opening it to a page depicting a diagram. "This tome reveals constructs unlike anything taught at the University. With the knowledge in this book, I have been able to extend my power, gifting it to others. The two men who visited your chamber last night were imbued with but two examples of what is possible."

The wizard stared at the book with narrowed eyes. "The book reveals a new family of constructs?"

"It does. The construct of augmentation."

"I see."

She held it out and stepped up to the portcullis. "I wish to gift it to you, for you to share with Jakarci."

"Why?"

"I fear what the future holds and wish Balmoria to be prepared." At least that part was not a lie.

The wizard gestured toward the woman at his side, waving her forward.

"No," Priella said. "This prize is too great for any ungifted to hold. Accordingly, I have placed a unique spell of protection against any non-wizard." She knew of no such spell but prayed Greehl believed her.

He scowled, but his gaze remained fixed on the book, eyes filled with longing. "All right."

Greehl stepped forward as Priella took a half-step, extending her hand through the gate. The wizard reached for the book, and she let it slip from her hand. His eyes grew wide and he lunged to catch it, his head coming within her reach. The construct of compulsion formed as she slapped her hand against the side of his head. The connection lasted only a second, but by then, her control over him was complete.

With the book in hand, Greehl stumbled backward, the warrior at his side drawing her blades, ready to strike.

"Stop!" Greehl commanded. "I am fine. No harm done." He clutched the book. "I have the book, a gift worth far more than gold."

"Perhaps you will consider it worth the price of passage," Priella suggested. "As I said, I have no wish to wage war against Balmoria. I only wish to enter and cross the wizardom."

"Why?"

"I know you hold no love for your neighbors to the north, nor the Kyranni for you."

Greehl blinked. "You plan to attack Kyranni? Why do so?"

"Let us just say they possess something I wish to have."

The man stood silent for a breath before saying, "I must meet with my captains to ensure there are no misunderstandings. Return at noon with your forces. The gates will open, and you may proceed."

"I have troops on ships, waiting at the mouth of the river. I would have them disembark in Fralyn to join my march."

Greehl nodded. "You may do so. I will ensure they are not attacked." He then turned and faded into the shadows, his bodyguard at his side.

Priella spun and walked back to her horse, considering the transaction and possible outcomes.

While Greehl was powerful for a wizard, his magic was a pale imitation to her own and vastly less than Lord Thurvin's. Her control over him was complete, and he did not even know what had occurred. Undoubtedly, he would comply with her request, ordering his troops to obey.

Priella had done the impossible, guaranteeing entry into Balmoria without losing a single soldier. She climbed upon her horse and rode back toward her army, a smile upon her face.

When Priella and Bosinger arrived back at camp, the tents had been struck, wagons being loaded as she had commanded. Only her own and Lord Thurvin's tents remained standing. She headed toward the prior while staring at the latter, debating how she was going to explain her success to Thurvin without him realizing the influence she had been exercising against him. Controlling the man had turned out to be a constant challenge.

The guards outside her tent bowed, eyes appearing wary, neither saying a word as she ducked inside.

Thurvin sat in her chair, feet crossed upon her table.

Teeth and fists clenched, she fought her anger and stuffed it behind a forced smile. "Why, Lord Thurvin. I am so glad you are here."

"I see you return empty-handed. Will you now allow me to unleash my magic? A sufficient display would quickly slay the army, allowing us to cross the river while sending a message to Jakarci."

Priella walked past the table and stopped, her back to the other wizard. "I struck a bargain with Greehl." She could not reveal her ability to influence the man's mind. Not without risking her position with Thurvin. "I gave him the book on augmentation in exchange for passage, promising his soldiers would be left unharmed in the process."

Thurvin snorted. "You expect me to believe he capitulated for so little?"

She turned toward him. "He will join us with the promise of becoming High Wizard of Balmor once we remove Jakarci and convert the Tower of Devotion. Think on it. Charcoan gave you Starmuth for less." In truth, she had not yet offered the position to Greehl, but the lie made her story more plausible.

He frowned. "You know how we took Starmuth?"

Priella smirked, sensing his faltering confidence. "You are not the only one who understands the value of knowledge." Crossing the tent in slow, sensuous strides, she said, "Not only will we cross unchallenged, but our army will swell further. In addition, the Orenthian Army from Tiamalyn will arrive within the hour. By the time we reach Balmor, we will be twenty thousand strong with forty ships at our disposal."

"What then?"

With feigned nonchalance, she rounded his chair. "Then we will crush Jakarci, and I will claim the Balmor Tower of Devotion. My magic will increase, and the remaining Bal cities will follow suit. With our combined power and the strength of our army, nothing can stop us."

She ran her hand along his shoulder, touching his neck and embracing her magic. The spell struck, attacking his mind, bending it to her will. The man's magic had grown too powerful, overcoming her influence far too quickly. She could no longer afford to hold back, for there was too much at stake.

26

BETRAYAL

The Pallanese and Farrowen soldiers stood ready, tents struck, riders mounted, wagons loaded. The infantry was lined up in ranks beside the road, cavalry waiting on the gravel, wagons at the rear. The Pallanese fleet from Norstar had unloaded additional infantry at the city docks, as had the Farrowen fleet carrying Captain Henton's troops. Those two forces, four thousand additional troops, waited between the city and the fortress, swelling Priella's army to an excess of fifteen thousand when counting the recent arrival of those from Tiamalyn and Yor's Point. Once unloaded, the ships had sailed back out into the bay – another fifteen hundred soldiers spread across twenty-four vessels.

From her saddle high on the hillside, Priella watched the activity surrounding the fortress below.

Ships flying the black and yellow flag of Balmoria slipped out from the fortress pier and floated down river, toward the Novecai Sea. On the far bank, soldiers poured from the fortress, preparing to march. Priella smiled, pleased with herself for executing her plan with such precision. She glanced up, the sun high overhead.

It is time.

Waving her arm above her head, she caught the attention of her captains, the men issuing orders to begin the march.

"If I hadn't seen it myself," Bosinger said from the horse beside her own,

"I wouldn't have believed it." He shook his head. "The fortress has only changed hands a dozen times in two thousand years, none without extreme bloodshed. To have done so without losing a single soldier, and to augment your forces in the process... It is a massive victory."

A warmth filled her chest. Bosinger's praise was a rare and precious commodity – something to revel in.

From the horse to her other side, Thurvin added, "I, too, am impressed, My Queen. While I had hoped to use Greehl and his soldiers as targets to test my might, this is a better alternative. Balmor and Lord Jakarci are sure to crumble when our hammer strikes. Once you possess his magic, nothing can stop us."

Led by Theodin, the cavalry at the fore of the army began the advance – six hundred mounted soldiers. Another six hundred waited with her, fourteen thousand soldiers on foot sandwiched in between. Far out at the mouth of the bay, her naval fleet waited, the Balmorian fleet joining to create a force exceeding fifty ships.

It was all coming together as Vanda had shown her. She just hoped it had happened in time.

~

Garvin held the reins loosely in his palm, careful not to use his fingertips. He was still getting used to his augmented abilities, fingers and toes easily sticking to things unintended.

His horse advanced toward Fralyn Fortress at an easy walk at the rear of the forward cavalry. Theodin, Shellock, and Iberson – the three Pallanese captains – rode at the front, along with the flag bearers. Three pennants, each marking a different wizardom, rippled in the breeze. It was an odd sight. Just when Garvin had grown used to a Pallanese flag beside Farrowen's, the emerald green of Orenth was added to the mix. Soon, the yellow of Balmoria would join them.

As he passed the last infantry squadron waiting beside the road, Henton shouted orders, calling for his soldiers to march. The captain met Garvin's gaze, Henton's scowl a reminder of their last exchange in the mountains of Northern Ghealdor.

I had thought to never see him again, Garvin thought. *Odd how destiny has its own plans.*

In ranks six men across, Henton's squadron of three thousand stomped down the road, slipping between the leading cavalry and the trail of soldiers strung out along the snaking hillside path. The timing and order to march was a thing of beauty – at least for a lifelong soldier. Looking over his shoulder, Garvin spied the wagons pulling onto the road far up the hillside, two covered wagons among them – one carrying Lord Thurvin's crystal throne, the other Priella's. Rindle hid in the shadows of her wagon, Priella demanding he keep his abilities a secret. Thus far, only the queen, Kollin Mor, and Bosinger knew of the magic she had gifted to Garvin and the now ghostly thief.

Garvin chuckled. *After all those times Rindle grumbled about long days in the saddle, he has been given another means to travel. We shall see how much he likes it after a few days.*

The cavalry turned at the fork, the captains and the flag bearers at the fore slowing fifty feet from the closed portcullis. The battlements above were empty, deserted, while Balmorian soldiers continued to gather on the opposite side of the river.

A horn blew, echoing across the valley. The portcullis began to rise, revealing the shadowy, empty tunnel, the distant opening at the far end a tiny oval of light.

Calls came from Theodin, the standard bearers waving their flags, the cavalry advancing, entering the shadows of the fortress. Six horses astride, hundreds of horsemen advanced until Garvin reached the opening – the arched ceiling twenty feet high at the apex, the walls thirty feet apart.

Inside, the clopping of hooves on the paved ground echoed like thunder. Garvin eyed the brick walls, narrow, rectangular openings spaced every six feet. Undoubtedly hidden passages intended to house archers who would loose through those openings and lay waste to enemies caught in the tunnel. With a portcullis on either end, it was a perfect trap, the realization leaving him restless. A backward glance showed the infantry, ten soldiers astride, running at an easy jog as they entered the tunnel, likely to speed the crossing.

As he turned forward, the standard bearers emerged from the tunnel and into Balmorian lands. The sunlight beyond the tunnel beckoned as his unease grew more intense. His free hand went to the hilt at his hip, eyes gazing at the dark openings in the wall. He fought the urge to kick his horse into a gallop, to be away from the closed confines.

Pallanese and Farrowen riders continued to pour out of the far end of the fortress, the rising anxiety twisting Garvin's innards. He turned to look at the infantry ranks behind him, two thousand bobbing helmets now within the tunnel.

Hearing a clanking sound from ahead, alarms went off in Garvin's mind. He spun around to see the portcullis crashing down, the iron spikes impaling soldiers and horses in a spray of blood, shrieks filling the air.

Garvin pulled on the reins and drew his sword, turning his horse as the portcullis on the other end slammed shut, cutting off the soldiers and wagons yet to enter the fortress.

A spear thrust out from the slot in the wall to his left, impaling his horse, narrowly missing his leg. Arrows began to fly from the openings, men screaming, people around him dying. Desperate, Garvin dove off his stumbling horse, free hand extended toward the wall, fingers latching on to catch him, keeping him from falling to the ground. As an arrow sailed from the opening beside him, he drove his blade into the dark maw, a scream coming from the other side. When he pulled the blade back, it was slick with blood. A wounded horse tripped over the body of another, the animal falling toward him, forcing him to dive out of the way lest he be crushed.

He rolled and rose in a crouch, the chaotic confines of the tunnel filled with blood, screams, and death.

Priella, Thurvin, and Bosinger rode down the hillside at a walk. They trailed the latter half of the cavalry, horses easing forward as the infantry jogged ahead – thousands of soldiers disappearing into the fortress tunnel. The two covered wagons hauling the thrones followed directly behind her, dozens of supply wagons bringing up the rear.

Priella took a deep breath of the salt air blowing in from the west. She felt at ease, enjoying the warm, spring weather, the bright sunlight shining upon the river where it met the sea beyond the city of Fralyn.

Noise arose from the fortress, the advancing infantry suddenly stopping when the portcullis crashed down. Shouts and screams came from within the dark tunnel. Archers appeared on the ramparts, arrows raining down upon her soldiers. At the same time, the Balmorian force on the far side of the river attacked her lead cavalry, loosing arrows from the rear while the front line rushed in with shields and halberds. Catapults on the river island began launching huge stones toward the three Farrowen ships still in the city harbor. The stones struck with frightening force, smashing massive holes in each ship.

"We have been betrayed!" she shrieked, pointing toward the fortress. "Unleash your fury, Thurvin. Kill anyone attacking our soldiers!"

With a growl, the man bloomed with magic, floated up inside a spherical shield, and sped off.

She then turned toward Bosinger. "Open the gate!"

The man launched his mount into a gallop, racing along the road, past the others. Thurvin drew near the fortress and began launching lightning bolts, blasting one archer after another, quickly clearing the parapet of soldiers.

"Greehl will pay for this!" Priella spun around and pulled her horse beside the wagon holding her throne. "Thief!" she shouted. "Get out here."

A shadow slipped from beneath the opening, the wagon driver reeling backward, eyes wide as he stumbled and fell from the wagon.

Priella turned her mount and gestured behind her. "Get on, Rindle."

Rindle's ghostly form floated over, his arm wrapping around her waist. She kicked her horse into a gallop and raced toward the battle.

More Balmorian guards emerged upon the ramparts, the archers loosing at Thurvin, who hovered fifty feet above the ground. Arrows shattered against his shield, and he released a blast of air, the force of it striking the archers, lifting them off their feet and smashing them against the tower walls with terrifying force. Those on the sides of the tower were blown right off the battlements, arms flailing as they fell to their deaths.

When Bosinger neared the closed gate, he leapt off his horse, rushed to the portcullis, squatted, and heaved. The strength augmentation Priella had gifted him with two nights earlier had boosted his strength beyond that of twenty men. Even so, the gate was made of wrought iron and weighed tons.

Slowly, the portcullis rose to his knees, then his waist. Finally, with a roar, he squatted beneath it and thrust up, holding it above his head. Soldiers rushed out, many covered in blood, some with arrows jutting from arms or legs.

Priella pulled her horse over to the side of the road, not far from the fortress. "Hold tight," she said over her shoulder. "I am going after Greehl, and you are going to tell me where to find him."

She gathered her magic and lifted herself off the horse while standing upon a platform of solidified air. "Where is he?"

The thief pointed toward the center tower. "There," he hissed into her ear. "Near the top."

While rising upward, she cast another spell, a rope of magic lashing toward the tower a thousand feet away. She wrapped the other end around her waist, pulling taut, and launched herself forward, the phantom-like Rindle clinging to her back.

~

With his back to the wall, the corpse of his horse at his feet, Garvin tore off his boots. Arrows were flying, men dying, and he was trapped.

He turned to the wall, lifted a foot, and leapt, toes clinging to the brick as he scrambled up, following the wall into the arch until he crawled upside down along the apex. Ahead, he spotted an opening in the ceiling, arrows flying through it, impaling soldiers below. He paused just before the opening to await the next volley, then twisted and swung feet-first through it, bringing him into another tunnel, much smaller than the one below.

Startled, the three archers cried out and stumbled backward. He kicked out, hooking one by the heel and sending the man to the ground. Another nocked a bow. Garvin leapt with a roundhouse kick, his foot striking the soldier's arm, knocking it aside. The arrow sailed past and plunged through the throat of another enemy soldier. Eyes bulging, the man fell to his knees, tipped forward, and disappeared through the hole in the floor.

Garvin kicked again, striking the soldier in the groin, the man bending forward. He grasped the man's shoulder, fingers clinging to the leather armor, and fell to his back, pulling his attacker's upper body downward while thrusting his feet into the man's torso. His momentum took the soldier forward, sending him through the opening and into the tunnel below.

By then, the third had regained his feet, bow raised and nocked. Garvin rolled, the arrow striking the floor. He drew the knife at his hip and threw, the blade burying in the enemy soldier's chest. Eyes wide, both hands clutching the hilt, the man collapsed. Garvin rushed over, pulled his dagger free, and peered down the tunnel.

It was half the width and half the height of the tunnel on the first level. Enemy soldiers rushed toward him. In the other direction, the tunnel ended less than twenty feet away, a sturdy door along one side. He darted to the door and pushed it open to find the portcullis winch in an otherwise empty room.

He slammed the door shut and barred it just before the attackers reached it. Fists pounded against the door, but it was solid and would hold against anything less than magic or a battering ram.

Garvin rushed to the winch, flipped a lever, and began cranking the wheel. To one side of him, the black bars of the portcullis rose, the counterweight lowering to his other side. He did not know how many of his fellow soldiers survived in the tunnel below, but at least they now had a means to escape.

Priella soared over the battlements, toward the central tower. Below, Thurvin had turned his attention to the catapults on the island, the wizard lord launching a flurry of fireballs, setting the siege engines ablaze.

"The balcony," Rindle hissed into her ear. "There."

She headed toward the balcony five hundred feet above the river and lowered herself to it. The ghostly thief slipped off her shoulder, waved for her to follow, and slipped through the glass-paned door. Dismissing her shield, construct of protection ready, she stepped inside.

The spacious chamber seemed to be empty, until she looked at the four-poster bed. Blindfolded, Greehl lay against the headboard, arms spread, ropes attaching his wrists to the bedposts. Black cloth was wrapped around both hands, his head slumped to one side.

He lifted his head. "Who is there?"

Still holding to her magic, Priella lashed out, the blindfold splitting down the middle, the wizard jerking with a start.

He blinked, a smile of relief stretching across his face. "My Queen. You have come to save me."

She stalked toward the bed while Rindle slid into the corner, melting into the shadows. Her fists were clenched, but she held her anger in check. *It would be easy to destroy him, but I must know.*

"Why did you betray me?" she growled.

The man shook his head. "I tried to stop them, but the Wasps are trained to handle wizards."

"Explain. How did this happen?"

"Scouts warned of your approach days before you arrived. When we discovered the size of your force, my officers and I knew we must take it seriously. Then I heard two wizard lords led the army – Lord Thurvin, now powered by the prayers of Farrowen and Ghealdor, and you, the first female since Pherelyn to wield the magic of a god.

"We were fearful of what we faced. Never before had two wizard lords formed such an alliance. Until now, not even a single wizard lord had ever led a military campaign. I shared the legend of Pherelyn with them, disclosing her ability to control the minds of others. I told them I was fearful of you possessing such ability, and I begged them to prepare for the worst."

Priella's eyes widened, her stomach souring. "The worst?"

"When Lord Jakarci learned of your approach, he sent a message instructing us to slow or prevent your advance at any cost. His instructions included a warning – should you march into Balmoria unchallenged, our wizardom and the entire world would be lost."

A chill ran down her spine. The way he said it made it sound as if she were the Dark Lord incarnate. "You still have not explained why you are tied up and why those soldiers had to die."

"Oh, but I have." He shook his head. "If anyone were likely to be targeted by your magic, it would be me. Accordingly, I removed myself from all planning and set up a trap in my room should you try to assassinate me or convert me with your magic. Your men sprang the trap last night but convinced me to meet with you. The gift you offered was too tempting.

"However, my soldiers planned a surprise and initiated that secret plan after you and I met this morning. When I issued the command to allow your army to pass, the Black Wasps attacked me. The fracas was costly, and I killed dozens before someone knocked me out." The man sighed. "When I woke, I was blindfolded and tied to my bed, incapable of using my magic. I only pray their trap did not go as well as they had planned."

"Why didn't you warn me?"

He shook his head. "I could not tell you what I did not know."

"Where are these officers?"

"Two led a force to the Balmorian side of the river, ready to ambush your soldiers once the trap was sprung. The others sailed out with my fleet on ships bound for Balmor." He frowned. "You are upset with me."

She growled. "Thousands died today. I needed those soldiers."

Greehl began to cry. "I am so sorry, My Queen."

"Apologies will not bring them back."

Sobbing, he asked, "What would you have of me?"

Priella sneered. "I want you to die."

The man stopped crying, eyes bulging, mouth working without a sound emerging. He fell against the headboard, head drooping against his shoulder, dead eyes staring into space.

Rindle emerged from the shadows and slunk toward her. "What did you do to him?"

"Nothing," she replied. "He died to please me, nothing more."

Fires burned, black smoke filling the air, rising from bodies piled along the river. The sun was low on the horizon when Garvin and Quiam led the remaining cavalry along the roadway on the Balmorian side of the river. They rode at a trot, five hundred exhausted soldiers trailing, emerging from the long shadow cast by the fortress and up the grassy hillside. The parapets stood empty, the ramparts barren. Not one ship occupied the garrison pier, nor were any visible in the bay beyond, all either at the bottom of the river or departed for Balmor.

A melancholy as thick as the black smoke from the mass funeral pyres filled the air. Nothing outside of Fralyn moved, the fortress abandoned and left behind as a testament to the men who had died. In his years as a soldier, Garvin had experienced many things. None could compare to the disaster the men now called the Fralyn Failure.

To have so many soldiers killed by so few enemies... Thank the gods the day is nearly over.

The horses crested the hilltop, the roadway passing through a grove of figs. Rolling hills stretched into the distance, rounded mountaintops farther north. Leaf trees draped in shadow slipped past as they rode north along the gravel road, stirring up a trailing swirl of dust.

Nearly an hour later, the last remnants of daylight in the western sky, they arrived at the new camp location. Garvin slowed his horse to a walk and turned off the road, navigating toward the three white pavilions pitched upon the hilltop in the midst of a field filled with thousands of tents.

"I must report to Lord Thurvin," Quiam said.

Garvin nodded, focused on the pavilion with the Pallanese flag above it.

"I will update Priella. She lost her captains today, so the duty must fall to someone else."

"Very well. May Farrow be with you, Lieutenant."

When Garvin had last seen her, Priella had been livid. Few things frightened him, but an angry wizard lord was near the top of the list, a vengeful woman not far behind. But an angry female wizard lord? Garvin shuddered.

I hope her anger has cooled.

He stopped outside her tent and dismounted. As always, guards in gleaming plate armor stood outside, the two men thumping fists to their chests. *They no longer challenge me before I enter.* It was just as well. While typically even-tempered, the day had worn him down, so he was likely to snap if pushed too far.

Priella was inside with Kollin, the pair lying on her pallet, her in his arms. Garvin was thankful they were clothed. Oddly, Bosinger was absent. His eyes swept the shadows in search of Rindle.

The queen pushed up onto one elbow, her legs exposed from the knee down, feet bare. The deep neckline of her dress drew his gaze. *She is an attractive woman*, Garvin admitted. *I understand how the young man is drawn to her.*

"I am here to report, My Queen," he said.

"Very well, but be brief. I must soon begin Devotion." She swung her feet down to the rug and slid them into her slippers. "I pray you have some good news. I don't know if I can handle more disappointment."

She sounds as worn by today's events as I am. "The dead – horse, men, and a few women – were removed from the fortress. We found a barrel of naphtha and used it to ignite the pyres. They were burning when we departed."

"How many?"

"Eleven hundred enemy soldiers. Two thousand of our own, along with five hundred horses. I cannot say how many died with our three lost ships."

Her hands went to her head, holding it, as if the weight of the world were crushing her. "So many," she sobbed. "Lost for nothing."

The reaction was unexpected. Until now, she had appeared hardened, conniving, commanding.

He continued. "The messenger must have reached the fleet, for they departed right after you left. The Balmorian ships have a lead on them, but I suspect all head for Balmor."

She lifted her head, eyes bleary as she wiped the tears away.

Kollin placed his hand on her back, the corners of his mouth drawn down in concern. "You could not have anticipated Greehl's betrayal. It is not your fault."

Her head snapped around. "Anticipating betrayal *is* my responsibility. I was too confident in my ability to twist the wizard in my favor. I never suspected he might allow his own officers to betray him."

The wizard frowned. "I don't understand how you could have possibly predicted such a thing."

She sighed, her hand going to his cheek. "Perhaps I could not before, but I must remain vigilant. It cannot happen again. I have lost too much already."

Garvin's mind raced, in search of better news. "Your quick action did save some. As far as we can tell, five hundred soldiers escaped the tunnel. Had the gates remained closed, those men would be dead, as well."

"Five hundred." She stood, smoothing her skirts. "Well, that is something."

She walked toward the exit and paused beside Garvin, her hand resting on his shoulder. "Thank you for what you did today. With Theo and the others gone, I need a man of your experience and abilities. I am going to tell Thurvin you are being raised to commander. You will report to me and nobody else, Henton, Quiam, and the remaining officers reporting to you."

When she stepped out, Garvin stared at the tent flap, thinking it odd how, after all this time, he had attained such an exalted rank but no longer desired the position.

27

DECEPTION

The barge moved slowly upstream, green palms along the shoreline of the Rintari River easing past. To the west, fields of green crops fed by irrigation ditches lay just beyond the foliage growing along the river. Tan, barren hills stood beyond the fields, marking the edge of the Hassakan Desert. A few miles to the east, mountains of rock, sand, and scrub formed the barrier between Hassakan and Kyranni, the two northernmost wizardoms.

Narine stared out at the passing scenery as she sat beside Jace on a shade-covered bench, their backs to the cabin wall. Neither had spoken much during the day. She remained angry with him, he with her. *That damn woman,* she thought. *This is her fault.* She had not seen Harlequin since their morning departure, yet the flirtatious ship captain was still causing her trouble.

After Lord Sarazan's demise, the sea journey had been torturous, even though it was brief, *Hassaka's Breath* arriving at the new port a day after departing from Sarmak. The wound on her forehead left Narine with an almost constant headache. Coupled with the choppy waters, she had been ill the entire voyage. Hoping to fare better once on land, she was happy to disembark when the ship docked outside of Antari.

Chandan had led them to a harborside inn with the plan to rest for one night, then depart on a barge the next morning to head upriver. The wizard purchased rooms, meals, and drinks for everyone before retiring to his own private room. The situation had quickly soured. Narine reflected on the evening, trying to determine why Jace had betrayed her trust.

Empty plates before them, Jace, Adyn, and Hadnoddon downed tankards of ale as they shared small talk. Most of Narine's dinner remained uneaten, her hand continually going to her aching forehead. Chandan had healed the gash but could do little else for her, his talents lying elsewhere.

"I am going to bed." Narine rose to her feet.

"Are you all right?" Adyn had asked in concern. "I thought you would feel better once you were off the ship."

"I had hoped so, as well. Perhaps a good night of sleep will get me past this headache."

Jace stood. "Do you want me to join you?"

She shook her head with a wince. "No. You should enjoy yourself. Right now, I would rather be alone."

"I understand." He handed her the key. "Lock yourself in. I'll pick the lock and take care not to wake you when I come in."

"Thank you." She looked down at Adyn and Hadnoddon. "I will see you in the morning."

With that, Narine went upstairs to the third-floor room she was to share with Jace. Alone in the darkness, she lay there, her head pounding. She missed having his arms around her, but she did not wish him to suffer in silence, and she certainly was not in the mood for anything other than sleep.

Better to let him have a fun evening with the others. It was her last thought before she had drifted off.

The inland breeze was warm, the air growing hotter as the barge was rowed upstream. Jace was thankful for the shade and the breeze coming off the water, but he dreaded the moment they would dock and the journey to follow, suspecting the heat would quickly become unbearable. Even without looking at her, he remained aware of Narine sitting beside him. From the corner of his eye, he spied her hair fluttering in the breeze. His arms crossed, he stared into space, the prior evening running through his mind...or as much as he could recall.

After Narine had retired for the night, he, Adyn, and Hadnoddon continued to drink and tell stories. It was a subdued evening, a relaxing and enjoyable break from the persistent danger and death surrounding them. He soon lost count of the ales, each somehow tasting just a tad better than the one prior. Finally, his head fuzzy and the hour well past nightfall, the three of them agreed it was time to go to bed.

Jace followed the dwarf and bodyguard up to the third floor, stopping outside the door to his room. It was locked, and he recalled giving Narine the key.

He groaned. "My coat." His picks were in his coat, but he had taken it off because of the heat. He turned toward Adyn as Hadnoddon unlocked the door to their room. "I left it on the back of my chair."

He spun and rushed down to the taproom, four tables still occupied. As he crossed the room, his surroundings tilted, making him feel as if he were still on board *Hassaka's Breath*. His chair came into view and a lump stuck in his throat. The coat was gone.

Jace made for the bar, slapping his palm on the top. The small, coppery-skinned barkeep turned toward him. "Did someone find a coat?"

The man's brow furrowed as he said something in Hassakani.

Jace sighed in frustration. "Coat," he said, pretending to put his arms into the sleeves of an imaginary coat. He tried again, speaking slowly. "Did... someone...find...a...coat?"

The man shrugged.

Closing his eyes, Jace muttered, "Why me?"

A hand rested on his shoulder. "Are you all right?"

He opened his eyes to find Harlequin standing beside him with an arched brow, lips drawn up in a smirk. She wore a loose, leather vest over a white tunic, unlaced to expose coppery skin and the hint of cleavage, a bead of sweat running down from her collarbone, his gaze following until it faded from view.

He forced himself to turn away. "My coat. I left it on a chair by the wall, and it's gone."

She leaned over the bar and spoke in Hassakani, the barkeep shaking his head as he responded. The woman held up two fingers and said something else, Jace only catching the word swoon.

Turning to him, she said, "He hasn't seen your coat, nor has anyone turned it in."

Jace rarely removed his coat in public and counted it as a prized possession, the interior lined with hidden pockets for his lockpicks and weighted dice. "This place is too blasted hot," he complained. "I only took it off because I was sweating profusely."

The barkeep slid two small cups across the bar.

"If you believe this is hot, wait until you journey inland." Harlequin lifted the two cups off the bar and held one out. "This is for you. Nothing like a shot of swoon to make your troubles seem less so."

Jace took the cup, tapped it against hers, and downed it. Their empty cups slammed down on the bar simultaneously. He recalled Chandan stating they would depart at sunup.

Running his hand cross his damp forehead, Jace muttered, "This is horrible. I don't have a key or my picks, and I don't wish to disturb Narine."

"Is she still unwell?"

"Her headache persists. She didn't sleep well on the ship last night, so I thought to let her get a good night of rest. Now I will have to wake her to get into our room."

"There is an extra bed in my room. You can sleep there."

"I don't know..." He frowned, eyes narrowing. "Why are you here anyway? I figured you would remain with your ship."

"It's not *my* ship. It belongs to the Order and will remain in port until the next time they require it."

"What of the sailors on board?"

She shrugged. "They remain in port, as well. Come along. I would like to get a good night of sleep. We leave early tomorrow."

"You are coming upriver with us?"

She laughed and slid an arm around his shoulders, guiding him toward the stairs. The room tilted mightily this time and he stumbled. Without her, he would have surely fallen.

Somehow, he had made it up the stairs, because he vaguely recalled the dark corridor. That was the last thing he could remember until morning.

The next memory came with the haziness of sleep, his head pounding, another pounding echoing in the room, somehow amplified in his skull. His eyes flickered open to morning light streaming through a gap in the curtain, his mouth dry, sticky, and tasting like a cat had used it as a litter box. The light made the ache in his head even worse. He then heard movement, feet padding across the floor. Another knock sounded, and he rolled over to find a nude woman opening the door to a corridor filled with people.

Not even attempting to cover herself, Harlequin pulled the door open farther and stood with a hand on her naked hip. In the hallway, Chandan arched a brow. Narine stood at his side, Adyn and Hadnoddon behind her.

Startled, now fully awake, Jace sat up, the room tilting, his head throbbing. Like Harlequin, he was completely naked, his bare leg sticking out from the covers, torso fully exposed.

With a growl, Narine's hand extended toward the room, the hair on Jace's arms standing on end. Harlequin shot up, her back slamming into the ceiling. There she remained while Narine strode in, cheeks flush with anger.

"What have you done?" Her eyes bulged with fury as she glared at him.

Jace stammered. "I didn't... We... I can't remember, exactly. I lost my coat and couldn't pick the lock."

Narine bent and picked his coat up off the floor, waving it in his face. "This coat?"

He shook his head. "I swear, Narine. I forgot it downstairs and went back. It was gone."

Adyn spoke from the corridor. "The thief did forget his coat. He went down to retrieve it, which was the last we saw of him."

Narine looked up at Harlequin, the tall woman's lean, copper-skinned body still pinned to the ceiling, her black hair hanging down, a smirk on her lips.

"What happened? Tell me," Narine demanded.

"The thief and I had a drink at the bar. Afterward, we returned here. You might guess at what happened next."

Jace gripped Narine's wrist, his fingers clamping around the enchanted chains Chandan had gifted her. "Don't do anything rash."

"He is correct, Princess," Chandan said in a firm tone. "Harlequin is an asset to our cause and killing her would do nothing to help secure our future. Besides, we have little time and must reach the docks before the barge departs."

Narine jerked her wrist from his grip and stomped out of the room. Harlequin fell face-first to the floor with an "Oof". Wind knocked from her lungs, she curled up on her side and fought for air.

Adyn entered the room, her liquid metal eyes narrowed and focused on Jace. "I thought you were better than this. I did not believe you would ever hurt her." She spun and left, Hadnoddon trailing after flashing Jace a condemning look.

Chandan said, "You two must dress quickly and hurry to the docks."

The wizard walked away, leaving the door open as Jace sat on the edge of the bed, trying to understand how things had gone so wrong.

The same thought remained with him now as he sat on the barge, a half-day later.

Thuds from the cabin behind Jace drew him from his reverie. Female shouts and a scream followed. He and Narine turned toward the wall at the same time, their eyes meeting for a moment. Hers were red and puffy. When she turned away, the lump in his throat returned, the noises from the cabin forgotten.

Adyn finished strapping Harlequin to the oar, the woman's wrists and ankles bound like a pig on a spit. She grinned at the thought and considered it fitting.

The door opened, and Hadnoddon burst into the cabin. "I heard shouts!" His brows shot up. "What's this?"

Adyn glanced toward the scowling woman lying on the floor. "This is a solution to a problem."

He smirked. "What are you going to do with her?"

"Where are Jace and Narine?"

"Last I saw, they still sit on the bench around the corner, neither talking, both appearing as if they could chew rocks."

"Take one end of the oar. Let's bring this conniving wench outside."

He grabbed the flat end and they both lifted. Harlequin dangled from it, scowling, her nose bloody, eye already swelling closed.

Adyn clenched a fist at her. "Remain silent until I say. Then you will tell the truth. All of it." She waved Hadnoddon forward. "Let's visit our star-crossed lovers."

The dwarf backed through the door and outside, a pair of deckhands watching in wide-eyed shock. He turned the corner, Adyn following, Harlequin dangling between them. They settled in the gap between the outer rail and the bench where Narine and Jace sat.

Narine pressed her lips together and glared at Harlequin. "Thank you, Adyn. It was kind of you to bring me a present, but I am no longer angry with *her*." Her tone shifted as she snapped toward Jace, "The fault belongs with someone else."

He held his hands up in appeal. "I told you, I don't–"

"*No!*" she yelled. "Don't you dare use the fact you don't remember as an excuse."

"Narine," Adyn said softly, drawing her attention. "You need to hear this."

The princess crossed her arms over her chest. "All right."

Adyn nudged Harlequin with her boot. "Spit it out, wench."

Harlequin sighed. "Nothing happened."

"The entire story. Tell it. Now." Adyn left no room for argument.

"When I entered the inn last night, I saw Jace with Adyn and Hadnoddon, the three of them heading upstairs. The way he stumbled, he was obviously drunk. I spotted his coat on the chair, so I took it, rushed up to my room, and left it there. When I descended, Jace was at the bar, asking about his coat. I… I bought us each a cup of swoon."

Hadnoddon snorted. "He was already drunk, and you added swoon?"

"Yes. He told me he was locked out of his room and didn't wish to wake Narine. I offered him the extra bed in mine. He declined, but I insisted. I was able to get him inside, but he collapsed onto the bed before I'd even closed the door. I helped him out of his clothes and did my best to get him to respond, but he was too far gone to be of any use to me. So, I slept in the other bed and remained there until you woke us this morning."

Narine glared at Harlequin with undisguised loathing, her lips and knuckles white.

"Don't do anything rash, Narine," Adyn said. "As you can see, I beat her a bit already and tied her up. Perhaps we can do something less permanent than killing her."

Taking a deep breath, Narine nodded, her hands relaxing. "What do you propose?"

"Hurt her pride," Hadnoddon suggested.

"How so?" Adyn asked.

"She uses her looks as a weapon," the dwarf said. "Make her less attractive. That should sting sufficiently."

Adyn grinned. "I know just the thing."

With the sun below the western horizon, the dry, desert air cooled rapidly. Ropes tied to palm trees on the riverbank ran to cleats at the tips of both front keels. The people on board, including the sixteen crewmembers who manned the oars, gathered on the front deck.

Narine stood beside Adyn, Jace and Hadnoddon nearby. She glanced toward Jace, his expression unreadable. *Once this is over, I will apologize. I need to apologize*, she thought.

Chandan and Mohan, the captain of the barge, rounded the corner, appearing from the rear of the vessel.

The wizard said, "All right. Everyone is here. What is this about?"

"This is about justice." Adyn gripped Harlequin by the arm and led her to the forward rail. "This woman sought to twist the truth in her own favor. By doing so, she caused unnecessary pain to her companions."

Chandan frowned. "Is this about last night?"

"It is," she replied. "The entire thing was intentional, made to appear as if far more had occurred than what was reality. For her betrayal, she must pay."

"You cannot kill her," Chandan said. "She is a valuable asset to our cause, regardless of her questionable morals."

"We are not going to kill her."

Adyn returned to Narine's side, waving her forward. "Go on. Do it."

Crossing the deck, she stopped in front of Harlequin, the taller woman's expression defiant. Narine reached up and removed Harlequin's brimmed hat, freeing her black mane, wavy curls flowing over her shoulders. Placing a palm on the woman's head, Narine gathered her magic and inverted a construct of repair, one applied for a very specific purpose. She channeled the spell into the woman.

Harlequin's eyes grew round as she gasped, her hands going to her head, drawing back a fist full of hair in each palm. Wisps of black hair began fluttering away in the breeze, clumps of it falling to the deck, some dropping into the river. Even her arching eyebrows fell off as if plucked simultaneously.

In the span of a few breaths, the woman was completely bald. In fact, her entire body was bereft of hair. Narine pulled away and released her magic, the spiteful woman's appearance reminding her of Adyn's hairless form without the metallic flesh.

"What have you done to me?" she cried.

"Justice," Narine replied. "Do not worry. It will grow back...in time. Until then, you will find it far more difficult to manipulate others toward your own ends."

She spun away and approached Jace, stopping a stride away. "I should have known. Should have trusted you. Will you forgive me?"

Jace shook his head. "No."

Her heart sank.

"*I* am the one who should seek forgiveness. I should have not placed myself in a vulnerable position. Even now, I cannot tell you if anything happened because I cannot recall it myself." Gripping her hand, he brought it to his lips and kissed it. "Please, forgive me."

Narine glanced around, seeing everyone watching them. She pulled him by the hand. "Come along. We should discuss this in private." As she walked past Adyn, she whispered, "Give us an hour alone."

She heard Adyn snickering as she led Jace to their cabin. They both had cause to make amends, and she knew just how to do it.

28

HEAT

Jungle surrounded the small village, thick, broad, green leaves everywhere. The buildings were made of bamboo, as were the docks. Tall mountains stood to the east, a dirt road heading in the same direction marked by a sign in the shape of an arrow, the word *Nintaka* inscribed on it. Narine recalled the city from her studies. Near the Eastern border of Hassakan, Nintaka was a mining town nestled in the mountains bordering Kyranni.

Is Nintaka our next destination? she wondered.

She stepped off the barge and followed the dock to shore, climbing the riverbank to the flat, sandy area where Adyn and Hadnoddon waited. Jace, Chandan, and Harlequin came last, the barge then pushing from the dock and drifting back into the river, oars turning as it began the return trip to Antari. A sense of trepidation arose, Narine feeling like she had been abandoned in the middle of nowhere without a means of returning. Jace gripped her hand, and she turned toward him, flashing a smile as her worry slipped away.

Chandan began down the road. "Come. Our outfitter is this way."

They passed through the quiet village, Narine gazing at her surroundings with curiosity.

An old Hassakani woman dressed in loose, cream-colored dress hung wet clothes on a line strung between two buildings. Beside the old one, a younger woman in a chair busily stitched fabric. Three children ran past, laughing as the one in the rear chased the other two.

Narine counted eleven buildings, one of which had a sign above it, jugs of water and other supplies resting on benches beneath an awning out front. A section of jungle enveloped the road for a span before a twelfth building came into view. It also had a sign, a fence stretching from the building and bordering the road before turning and running up a hillside. The fenced area consisted of a dirt clearing with scattered palms, shrubs, and a bamboo awning in the middle. Camels stood in the shade of the awning, drinking water and chewing on dry grass.

A smiling man, tall and thin with oversized teeth, emerged from the house. He said something to Chandan in Hassakani. Chandan replied, the two speaking briefly before the other man headed toward the gate.

"Come," Chandan said. "Korsu says our mounts are ready."

Narine threw a questioning look toward Jace, who shrugged. They followed Chandan and Korsu through the gate and around the house. At the rear were six camels, brightly colored blankets over their humps, ropes running from a bridle on their heads. Two more camels stood among them, both bearing loaded packs.

Korsu stood before Narine and said something in Hassakani, gesturing toward the pack on her shoulder. She frowned, lowering it and handing it to him. The man took it and waved for the others to do the same. With all packs gathered, he approached the already loaded camels and used ropes to secure packs on top of packs.

Chandan walked up beside one of the camels, tugged the reins downward, and said, "Genua!"

The camel bent its front legs, kneeling, then doing the same with the rear. Chandan then waved to Narine. "Climb on."

She frowned at the idea but saw little choice. Lifting her skirts, she rested her stomach on the camel's hump and rotated to kick a leg over. She sat up, palms on the hump, legs exposed from her knees on down, golden band visible on her exposed ankle.

"Stabit!" Chandan commanded, the camel rising. Narine shifted so as not to slide off, somehow holding in a squeal.

The wizard turned to the others. "Just like this, you will mount, and we will depart."

The process continued, each rider climbing onto a camel, the beasts rising to stand until all were ready. Korsu opened the gate, and Chandan led them out, each tethered to the one before it, a chain of lumbering animals, their rider's heads bobbing back and forth with each step.

Chandan waved to Korsu, who called out and waved as they rode past. The caravan followed the road and turned at a bend, the roadway rising toward a hill to the north. Narine wondered how long she would have to ride the smelly, lumbering creature.

~

With the hills behind them, nothing but dry sand lay ahead. The heat was intense, Narine riding with a wrap on her head, a thin veil over her face. Her legs were covered in cloth, hands tucked in the folds of her skirts to remain out of the sun. She longed to shed her garments and was willing to ride naked at this point, but direct sunlight carried too much risk. *At least the sweat evaporates quickly,* she thought. Even that offered no relief from the heat.

The caravan continued across the dunes as it had for hours, the shade of the jungle long forgotten. Dry, barren mountains lay to the southeast. Nothing but sand, never-ending sand, spanned to the north and west.

From time to time, they would stop and drink water, but nobody ate. Nobody wanted to. Thirst and weariness consumed all other thoughts, the heat leaving Narine woozy, her stomach roiling.

Finally, when the sun reached the horizon and long shadows stretched across the desert, Chandan turned and led them into a gully at the foot of two peaks. A small area of green hid there, palms and brush surrounding a pool of water. The air felt noticeably cooler, partly because the sun was no longer visible, partly from the proximity to water.

They dismounted and tied the camels to posts near the water's edge. Two tents were assembled, white canvas supported by waist-high poles at the center and stretched out by stakes, the sides open, an unrolled rug to sleep upon. After eating trail rations without a fire, the air turning cold enough to force Narine to don her cloak, she crawled beneath the tent she was to share with Jace and Adyn and fell asleep.

~

Narine had thought it impossible, but the second day of riding was hotter than the first. The oppressive, stifling air seemed to sear her lungs with each breath. Camping at the oasis had allowed them to drink and refill their waterskins, but they were once again instructed to ration what they had. Chandan had warned them if anything went wrong, water defined the thin line between death and survival.

Time seemed to pass more slowly than the plodding pace of the camels, the endless swaying motion lulling Narine to sleep. Repeatedly, she would wake with a start just in time to catch herself before she slipped off her mount. On one such occasion, she did not wake until it was too late. Fortunately, Jace rode near enough to grasp her arm and stop her from a long fall to the hot sand.

It was late afternoon when Chandan turned his mount toward a narrow canyon bordered by steep walls of rock. When they entered the shade, the temperature dropped dramatically. Narine pulled the wrap and veil off her head, then the thin blanket off her back and legs. She sighed in relief and took a drink from her waterskin. It was warm, but still soothed her dry throat. Then the last drops dribbled out, the waterskin empty. Worry began to claw at her. It was her backup, the first also empty. How had she drunk it all?

The canyon narrowed further until they rode through a gap so slim, Narine had to pull her legs in so as not to scrape them against the rock. It curved and ran beneath an arch before widening to expose a valley. Chandan stopped his camel, the others settling and surveying the view.

Green foliage covered much of the valley floor, a meandering river flowing from a lake in the center. Tall, narrow spires of tan and orange rock jutted up here and there, appearing like towers, the upper portions illuminated by the late afternoon sun. Peaks and rocky cliffs surrounded the valley, forming a gorgeous backdrop. All of this would have been worth the journey on its own, but it was not what captured Narine's attention.

In the heart of the valley, beside the tranquil lake, was a massive pyramid, the peak standing hundreds of feet above the valley floor. The crystalline tip reflected the sunlight, sparkling like a massive diamond. To the other side of the pool was a city of sorts, filled with stone buildings of ancient and exotic design. Tall pillars, arches, domes, and obelisks filled the space, and a stone bridge arched over the river at the near end of the lake.

"Behold," Chandan said. "The Valley of Sol, home of the Order."

29

THE ORDER

T he valley floor was pleasantly cool, making Jace wonder if the water
flowing through it affected the air temperature. Green, lush, and full of
life – lizards on the riverbank, birds in the trees, fish visible in the water – the
valley was the antithesis of the sweltering, dead wasteland of the Hassakan
Desert. The difference made Jace feel mentally out of phase, and he had to
remind himself how little time had passed since he was near exhaustion from
the intense heat.

The camels followed a well-worn trail along the river, the clear water
appearing aqua blue against the pale riverbed, a school of orange and black
fish lazily swimming past. They rounded a turn, the foliage parting to reveal
the city they had seen earlier.

A bridge arched over the river, people dressed in golden robes crossing
from the far side where the massive pyramid resided. Two men stood
outside an entrance at the foot of the pyramid, appearing puny in the
shadow of the towering monolith. The structure was larger than it had
seemed from a distance, the men standing no taller than one row of stone
blocks, dozens of rows rising above them, making the peak easily four
hundred, perhaps five hundred feet up. Past the pyramid, the shoreline
trimmed until the lake butted against the cliff. Water ran down the steep rock
to become a waterfall, dropping into the far end of the lake.

Chandan led them past the bridge, the camels approaching a cluster of men in gold robes. All had shaved heads and walked with hands clasped at their waists. As they passed, Jace got a closer look.

Two had the delicate facial features of women, their chests filling out the robes differently than the others. *Women with shaved heads?* He glanced back toward Harlequin. Even with her wide-brimmed black hat, it was obvious she was bald. The way her unlaced tunic exposed her chest to her sternum, it was just as obvious that she was a woman. *So much for her penance. She will fit in well here if all the other women are also bald.*

They rode through an archway and into the city itself, people moving around, all dressed in the same gold robes. Each had a white sunburst on one shoulder, an exact match to the tattoo on Harlequin's breast. He considered mentioning it to Narine, then quickly reconsidered.

No need to rekindle that fire.

Chandan turned and rode into a stable yard, two young men in gold robes emerging, both with shaved heads. After a brief exchange in Hassakani, Chandan dismounted and motioned for the others to do the same.

"Do not worry about your supplies. They will be brought to your rooms in short order." He motioned with his hand and turned away, speaking over his shoulder. "Follow me. Lord Astra will wish to meet you."

The man returned to the paved street and led them deeper into the city. Jace took Narine by the hand and walked beside her while examining the surroundings.

Every building was built of pale stone blocks, the same as the pyramid, but in an odd mismatch of shapes and styles. Here and there stood round towers, some with flat roofs, others with cone-shaped peaks, and two with the bulbous tops reminiscent of those at Sarmak Palace.

Many of the buildings were simple, rectangular structures with flat faces, but some of them had external pillars like what he might expect in Tiamalyn. A couple were topped by the same peaked roofs prevalent in Illustan, while others had arched entrances and domed roofs similar to the palace in Fastella. Second- and third-story walkways spanned overhead, connecting buildings on opposite sides of the street.

Every person he saw, whether with farm tools or books in hand, wore the same golden robes with the starburst emblem. While every person was bald, their appearance varied – the pale skin of Pallanese and Farrowen, the tawny flesh of Ghealdans, Orenthians, and Bals, the brown skin of Kyranni, and the coppery skin of Hassakani. Then he noticed a pair of dwarfs, both shaved bald like Rawk, yet retaining their long, shaggy beards. Even then, he was not prepared for what he saw next.

Two citizens walked toward them, gray-skinned with almond-shaped eyes and pointed ears. With sharp facial features, slight builds, and fluid movements, he knew the pointed ears and gray skin were more than a human oddity.

Jace tugged on Chandan's robes, slowing the wizard. "Are those two elves?"

"Drow, actually. Dark elves. They live north of here, in a mountain city created by dwarfs long, long ago."

Hadnoddon asked, "A dwarven mountain city to the north?"

"Yes. Domus Argenti."

"That cannot be," Hadnoddon snorted. "Domus Argenti was destroyed in the Great Cataclysm."

Chandan stopped and turned toward him. "Not true. It was abandoned, and for good reason. Creatures of darkness invaded and occupied those tunnels for centuries before the drow drove them out."

Hadnoddon's scowl deepened as he turned back to stare at the two elves. "Why would elves live in a Maker city?"

"Much like their brethren to the south, the drow were once Silvan, bound to their forest and their forest to them. With the Cataclysm, those trees now lie beneath the sea, much of their magic lost. In time, their skin changed color, magic evolving, along with their very nature. Those elves are no longer Cultivators but are something else. Something unique. Therefore, they call themselves drow."

"Cultivators?" Jace asked. "Elves are Cultivators?"

Chandan smiled. "You might be clever in the ways of man, but you have much to learn of the broader world."

Chandan continued, the roadway coming to an aqua-colored creek trickling toward the long lake between the city and the pyramid. They crossed a short bridge spanning the creek and turned toward a miniature version of the pyramid, this one made entirely of crystal. A small, stone structure stood before the pyramid, the door at the front painted black, a golden sunburst in the center. Chandan led them to the door, opened it, and entered.

They walked into a small room leading to a descending stairwell, light filtering in through glass panels on the roof. They walked down a long flight of stairs and stepped through a doorway, Jace pausing to examine his surroundings.

Light shone through the crystal pyramid above, the interior of which was hollow, the high ceiling giving a spacious impression to the chamber. Water trickled down one of the side walls, feeding the clear, blue stream meandering through the room. Plant-covered mounds grew along the stream and made the interior feel as if they were outdoors. Through it all was a curving, mosaic path made of blue, red, yellow, and white tiles, each colored cluster creating symbols unfamiliar to Jace.

Chandan led them along the path and across three separate arched bridges over the winding stream. The palms parted to reveal a tiny, elderly man sitting cross-legged on a circular dais, eyes closed, expression placid. Like the citizens of the valley, his head was bald and polished. Unlike the others, the man's robes were white, the starburst on his shoulder gold. The surface of the dais beneath him was marked by a mosaic inlaid in glittering gold, the lines forming a sunburst.

The group gathered at the foot of the dais, nobody saying a word. A full minute passed before the man opened his eyes. His gaze swept across the six people before him, mouth turning up into a smile.

"Welcome back, Master Chandan."

Chandan bowed. "I am pleased to return successfully, Lord Astra."

"Ah, yes. The Crimson Lord is vanquished, joining the others. Soon, only one will remain, the balance shifted, the stars aligned."

Jace frowned. "Why did you wish Lord Sarazan dead?"

The man looked at Jace, his gray irises reminding him of Salvon's, but in this case, it felt as if the man peered into Jace's soul. "The Charlatan. I am not surprised. Suspicion is in your nature, among the traits shaping you into the tool destiny requires."

"I am nobody's tool." His grimace deepened. "You didn't answer the question."

"Sarazan's death was not required, but rather the vacancy it created. The Thrones of Power will soon lie empty, all save one. With each, the imbalance is corrected, the power of the old gods returning to its full glory."

"The old gods?" Jace narrowed his eyes. "What is this about, and what do you want with us?"

"Ahh. Straight to the heart of the issue." The old man nodded. "Very well." He rose to his feet and stepped off the dais, standing no taller than

Hadnoddon but lacking the dwarf's stout, muscular build. "Come. We will dine, and I will explain further."

He led them down the path to the far end of the chamber. A corridor stood to each side of the room, the old man walking down the one on the left. The underground tunnel was well-lit, every other floor tile made of crystal, glowing with a warm, golden aura. Astra opened a door and entered a room occupied by a long table surrounded by eight chairs. Cups full of red liquid and plates piled high with food sat before each chair, the smell of freshly baked bread filling the air.

Astra strode to the far end of the table and gestured toward the chairs. "Please. Sit. Eat." He sat in the end chair, the others gathering.

Jace stared at the table, one seat without a plate, and frowned again. "How did you know six people would be joining you?"

Astra grinned and tapped the side of his nose, the gesture familiar. "How observant, my young thief. I knew you would arrive today because I saw it happen."

He sounds like Xionne, Jace thought. "Is this about prophecy again?"

Astra laughed, his high-pitched tone like a chime. "What you call prophecy, we call possibility."

"You sound much like the Seers."

The man nodded. "They are our counterparts. We serve similar capacities with different objectives."

"What is your objective?" Narine asked.

"You have traveled far and must be hungry." The man picked up a basket of rolls and handed it to Jace. "Please, eat and listen while I tell you a story."

Jace grabbed a roll, finding it still warm, and passed the basket to Narine. He bit into it and turned toward Astra as the old man began his tale.

"Long, long ago, before time itself began, there was a presence. You might call it a god, but this was far larger, for this presence gave birth to the universe itself. The universe is vast beyond our comprehension, filled with many worlds. Each was left in the care of a god made from a piece of this presence. However, with our world, something went wrong. Rather than a single god, we were under the guidance of two entities – one known as Vandasal, another known as Urvadan.

"This was never meant to be, and the very nature of these beings placed them in contention with one another. For many years, Vandasal held sway, the god's power greater than that of his brethren. Jealous and ambitious,

Urvadan sought to shift the balance in his favor, doing so by capturing the moon and holding it over his center of power for eternity.

"The act of capturing the moon, of course, came with significant consequence, triggering an event later called the Great Cataclysm. The seas, drawn by the pull of the moon, rushed in, flooding the lowlands, leaving only areas of higher elevation dry. Cracks formed in the land, plates shifting, volcanoes raging. When this activity settled, a mountain range of towering peaks split the land, dividing east from west. In the middle of that range, chasms remained... What you now call The Fractured Lands.

"From this shift, Vandasal's might was greatly reduced, vast numbers of his followers destroyed. The god journeyed to Murvaran to confront Urvadan, demanding he undo the damage he had caused. Urvadan refused, instead striking his brother down. Still, one cannot kill a god so easily, for Vandasal remained...albeit as a shell of his former self.

"The young gods, those worshipped today, rose up in power to fill the vacuum created with Vandasal's loss and Urvadan's contentment to hide in Murvaran, disconnected from mankind."

When the old man quieted, Jace asked, "What does any of this have to do with us?"

"Oh. Yes." Astra pointed a finger into the air. "The Order of Sol was formed many, many centuries ago as a secret organization in the pursuit of truth and knowledge. However, our core objective, which has eluded us for millennia, is to repair that which was broken."

"Which is?" Narine asked.

"The young gods were never meant to be. They are constructs of mankind rather than beings of creation itself. The magic of wizards and prayers of Devotion are the core of their being. At the same time, those beings are connected to one another, the power of their fellow gods supporting them when a wizard lord dies. If we can eliminate all wizard lords at once, the prayers of Devotion ceasing, the young gods will wane and allow Vandasal to return."

Jace glanced at the others, his brow furrowed. "The Seers seemed certain Urvadan was behind the wizard lords' deaths."

The old man smiled. "Perhaps they follow false prophecy. Perhaps such prophecy was created to steer them from the truth."

"Which is?"

"The recent sequence of wizard lord deaths has been a long time in coming, carefully planned and executed. This could only be possible with the collective knowledge and abilities of the Order."

A stunned silence fell over the room, food remaining untouched as Jace and his companions exchanged startled glances.

The old man stood and stepped back from the table. "I must now bid you a good evening. Master Chandan will show you to your quarters. I will see you again tomorrow at mid-day in the Temple of Sol."

He bowed and walked away, leaving everyone at the table to their own thoughts.

The tower where Chandan lived was round with a bulbous dome at the top, the roof supported by a ring of arches. He led them into the building and up a curved stairwell. The main level was open, save for a ring of pillars and a bubbling fountain in the center. The second level contained a kitchen, a brick oven, counters, cabinets, and shelving along the outer walls, a long, black table with six chairs occupying the middle. Again, a ring of pillars supported the floor above.

The guest apartment was on the third level – three bedrooms and a bathing room occupying half the floor, the other half consisting of an open sitting room and two stairwells, one going up, the other down. The man bid them good night and continued his ascent, his personal quarters consisting of the upper three levels.

Narine peered into the first bedroom and saw an enchanted lantern on a table near the door. She activated it, the soft, blue light illuminating the room to reveal a single bed, a nightstand, a wardrobe, a vanity with a washbasin, and a narrow, arched window.

Adyn, who stood in the doorway, said, "I'll take this one."

The next room was identical and claimed by Hadnoddon. The last room was slightly larger than the others, the bed big enough for two. Jace walked past her, dropped their packs onto the bed, sat, and pulled off his boots, setting them aside. Narine closed the door and kicked off her slippers. She then turned her back to him.

"Can you undo my dress?"

He did so without comment. She slipped it off one shoulder, then the other, easing it down and dropping it to the floor. Her shift smelled of sweat, as did her body, which was unsurprising considering the journey through the desert. She had never been so hot in her life.

"Ugh. I stink," she said. "I am in desperate need of a bath and a change of clothing."

"Yeah," he muttered, still staring into space.

Narine furrowed her brows. "What's wrong?"

"What?" He did not even look at her.

Concerned, she turned to the mirror and smoothed her shift. Her hair was greasy and coated with dust, her cream-colored shift stained from sweat. Yet her body had become leaner over the past two seasons, her waist trimming, her backside tightening.

She tried again. "I said, I need a bath. You could use one, as well."

"That's nice." Still, he didn't look at her.

Her hand on her hip, she stood in front of him and leaned forward. "Jace!" When he jerked with a start, she asked, "What's wrong?"

"What do you mean?"

She stood upright and gestured toward her body. "I am standing in front of you, half-naked and suggesting a bath. Based on past experience, I anticipated more enthusiasm. Usually, the mere mention of such activity would raise your flag and have you waving it about as if on parade."

He sighed. "Sorry."

"It's not..." She swallowed. "It's not me, is it?"

"Nothing of the sort." Rising to his feet, he placed his hands on her hips. "I cannot stop thinking about what Astra said. About this entire, exotic scheme."

"Scheme?"

"The wizard lords. How each died. The circumstances behind each death were markedly varied, as were the players involved. How could the Order, *anyone* orchestrate something so elaborate without us aware of what was happening?"

Narine frowned in thought. "I don't know."

"And the Seers... They were convinced the Dark Lord was behind everything. But these people claim it was their doing. However, that does not explain the darkspawn attacks or the goblins in the dwarven tunnels."

"No. I guess not."

"And what of Salvon? Is he part of the Order?"

She blinked, taken aback. "I hadn't thought of that." When looking upon it in a different light, the man's role in past events certainly appeared intentional, scripted. "If he were part of the Order the entire time, it would explain so much."

"Except for his...magic or whatever it was in the end." Jace shook his head. "I thought only a wizard lord was capable of such things, but now I am not so sure." He cocked his head. "Did you ever sense any wizard magic from him?"

"No. Never. Not even in Oren'Tahal."

"That's what I thought. However, it is frustrating to have three questions surface for every answer we are given. Soon, we will be buried in them." Again, he stared into space.

She gripped his chin and kissed him. Then she stepped back and took his hand. "Come on. We both need a bath, and you need something else to occupy your thoughts."

He arched a brow as she pulled him toward the door. "Such as?"

Narine smiled. "Oh, I am sure we will think of something."

30

THE PAST

S ea Lord sailed along Bal's Sound, having slipped through the Harkan Straits at sunrise, leaving the Ceruleos Sea behind. Other boats sailed ahead and behind them, some heading inland, others toward the sea. Both shores were miles from the ship as it floated down the heart of the waterway.

It was mid-afternoon when Blythe found herself on deck, standing between Brogan and Tygalas on the bow, the wind in their faces as they watched the passing scenery. Nearly an hour passed without anyone speaking, as if mesmerized by the surrounding beauty – the dark blue waters, the green, tree-covered hillsides, the puffy, white clouds floating overhead.

The ship eased around a bend and the harbor came into view, long piers and smaller docks running for miles, beginning at the south bank and continuing around the east end of the sound. It was, by far, the largest harbor Blythe had ever seen, hundreds of ships moored at the docks, masts jutting up like a forest bereft of leaves.

The tall, gray walls of Balmor stood just inland, warehouses, small in comparison, occupying the gap between the docks and the city. East of the city, a sea of white tents shone in the late afternoon sun. The Great Bazaar was world-renowned, known even to a girl who grew up in the woods of Northern Pallanar. Despite the stories, though, Blythe never imagined the Bazaar would approach the size of the city itself.

"Finally, our journey comes to an end," she said.

"Once we reach the Bazaar, what then?" Brogan asked. "Xionne's prophecy mentioned the past meeting the future, but it did not say what we should do once we arrived."

"Perhaps destiny will find us," Tygalas ventured.

Snorting, Brogan shook his head. "I prefer not to go in blind. As a soldier, rushing into battle without knowing what you face is a good way to get yourself killed."

Blythe arched a brow. "Like when you attacked a wyvern by yourself?"

"That was different."

"How so?"

"I didn't care if I died back then."

"What is different now?" she asked softly.

He put his arm around her shoulders. "Please don't make me say it."

Blythe chuckled. "I'm just teasing."

Tygalas turned toward Brogan, hood covering his ears. "We have seen wyverns outside our wood. They are big, vicious monsters." The elf gave Brogan a questioning stare. "You tried to kill one by yourself?"

"It was attacking our horses."

"How did that turn out?"

Brogan shrugged. "The beast is dead, and I'm still here."

Blythe added, "Thanks to Narine. If not for her healing magic, you would be dead, as well." A pang of loss twisted her stomach as she recalled the aftermath of the fight. "Phantom was not so lucky."

"Phantom?" the elf asked.

"Her dog," Brogan replied sadly as he squeezed Blythe against his side, his chainmail scratching her.

She wrinkled her nose. "Do you have to wear that? You smell like sweaty metal."

"We are going into battle, Blythe. Armor is important. It can mean the difference between life and death."

A worried male voice came from behind. "Battle? Who said anything about a battle?"

Blythe turned to find Rawk and Rhoa standing behind her. "There isn't going to be a battle." She nudged Brogan in the ribs. "He only says that because we don't know what to expect."

Rhoa sighed. "I can tell you I expect a hot meal and a soft bed tonight." She shook her head. "I thought living in a boxed wagon was difficult, but twelve days on a ship has made my time in the menagerie feel like a pleasant vacation." Rubbing her neck, she added, "We are stuck on a floating chunk of wood with nowhere else to go. It is far too limiting."

Rawk snorted. "It's unnatural. No stone to feel, no earth to touch... Just endless miles of water."

The elf sighed. "No trees, no plants, no grass...no life other than humans. I agree, Stone-Shaper. It is unnatural."

Blythe noticed an odd look cross over Rawk's face, then it was gone. She stared at him a moment longer and decided it was nothing, turning her attention to the passing harbor. They had already passed three piers, half the slips occupied. *Sea Lord* slowed as the sails were furled.

Elrin approached with a nod. "We are about to dock." He pointed ahead. "See the fourth pier out, the man with the flags? He waves them to tell us to land there."

Brogan nodded. "Thanks, Elrin. We had best retrieve our things."

He led the group toward the stairs while Blythe cast another glance at the city of Balmor.

A square, gray tower thrust up from the heart of the city, the top shimmering with the yellow light of Bal. *At least Lord Jakarci remains in power.* After three wizard lords had died in rapid succession, the world seemed to have righted itself. Two of those thrones had been reclaimed, which gave her hope. As she returned to her cabin, she wondered if any others had succumbed to the chaos.

Twelve years had passed since Brogan had last been to Balmor. Surrounded by his friends, Blythe at his side, he walked down the dock while staring at the tall, gray walls of the city ahead. The color seemed appropriate, marking the dark period of his life.

After his disgrace in the Murguard and subsequent exile, he spent the next six years migrating from city to city, working as a hired sword for anyone with coin. A brief stint in the Kyranni city of Nandalla was followed by a longer stay in Balmor.

Nearly three years wasted working for that slime, Teskin.

Those years were a blur – long, boring days spent protecting the man's wares, earning just enough coin for nights filled with an overindulgence of ale and women whose names he could never recall. Somehow, Brogan had put up with Teskin's greedy behavior and verbal abuse longer than most of the man's hired guards. When he had finally had enough, the result left Teskin without an appendage, and Brogan without a job.

I was lucky to escape Balmor alive.

From there, he had moved on to Tiamalyn. Another two years wasted before settling in Fastella. Working for Cordelia had been unpleasant, but less so than his other jobs. *Of course, that also ended when Jerrell approached me with a ridiculous proposition.* Funny thing was it earned Brogan enough coin to retire.

He chuckled at the memory, shaking his head.

"What's so funny?" Blythe asked.

"I was just recalling my first adventure with Jace, known as Jerrell at that time." He gave her a sidelong smirk. "Did I ever tell you about the time he shoved a great sword up the arse of a ten-foot-tall monster?"

"He did what?" Blythe laughed, the others chuckling, as well.

Brogan grinned broadly. "He was hired to retrieve an item from an ancient castle guarded by a monster, which turned out to be a minotaur – half-man, half-bull. During a fight, one which I was quickly losing, Jace came up behind the monster and thrust with a sword nearly as tall as himself. The blade went right up the monster's arse..." He held his hands a few feet apart, "burying this deep."

A hearty bout of laughter followed.

As her chuckles settled, Rhoa said, "When Salvon first recited the tale, I was skeptical. However, the more I got to know Jace, the more plausible it became." She shook her head. "He is the only person I can imagine doing such a thing. Anyone else would likely get killed attempting it."

"I know what you mean," Brogan replied. "The thief might be annoying, but he possesses a flair for schemes and seems to twist luck in his favor more often than not."

They turned and walked along the docks, the harbor to their left, warehouses and the city wall to their right. When they came to a city gate, Brogan stopped and turned toward his companions.

"It's getting late. Should we go into the city and find an inn?" The idea of ale was appealing.

Blythe wrapped her arm around his. "Perhaps we could go see the

Bazaar, just for a bit. Xionne said we would find our destiny there. What if we need to do it tonight?"

Brogan frowned, his stomach growling.

Lythagon said, "Blythe makes a good point."

Tygalas looked toward the sun, low in the western sky. "The sun will meet the horizon in an hour. Perhaps we could investigate until it does."

Sighing, Brogan said, "Fine." He turned, waving them along. "Come on. I will show you around."

A quarter mile farther along the coast, the wall turned, and the view opened to expose a settlement outside the city.

A half-mile deep and twice the length, the area had been worn to gravel, unlike the surrounding grasslands. Row upon row of white tents covered the Great Bazaar, the gaps between filled with wagons, carts, horses, and people on foot. It was often said a hundred gold pieces exchanged hands every day in the Bazaar. Brogan knew better. Most days, the number was two to three times that amount.

He led them down one row, gazes examining the wares displayed in the shade of awnings. The first housed woven rugs piled waist high, the tent walls hidden behind massive tapestries. Another tent held paintings upon easels, the artwork exquisite. The third tent sold an array of odd trinkets, some made of metal, others wood, yet others clay. In the next tent, sheets of fine silks billowed gently in the breeze coming off the water, the shimmering fabric an array of colors.

Blythe and the others gaped in awe as they passed one tent after another, each containing a wealth of items worth more than most people earned in a lifetime. Of course, each tent was also guarded, usually by large men dressed in armor, weapons at their side, scowls upon their faces. Some tents had as many as six or even eight guards.

They arrived at a pavilion three times the size of any other, a dozen armed guards standing along the outside, just as many within. Glass display cases held fine jewelry – necklaces, rings, bracelets, headdresses, pendants. Shelves and tables were covered in exquisitely crafted statues of various materials – wood, ivory, clay, silver, and even gold. The center of the tent contained ornate furniture made of dark wood, lacquered and polished in the style of the Northern wizardoms.

Blythe broke away and entered the shop, heading directly toward a pedestal. Upon it was statue of a dog, standing proud. It was carved of black onyx, eyes blue sapphires, claws encrusted with gold.

"It's marvelous." She looked back at Brogan. "This reminds me of Phantom."

Brogan knew she missed the dog. Truth be told, he missed him, as well. "I bet it costs a fortune."

A familiar voice came from behind a tent wall, a man emerging. "It is a mere eight gold pieces. Surely a small sum for such fine craftsmanship."

The man was short and portly, his dark hair braided with beads, rings adorning every finger, necklaces sparkling on his loose robes. He had a hooked nose over a black goatee, and a jewel-encrusted black patch covered the eye facing Brogan.

"Teskin," Brogan growled.

The man turned toward him, his remaining eye widening. "You!"

Scowling, Brogan replied, "I'm not thrilled to see you, either."

Teskin sneered, "You cost me an eye." He held up his hand. "And my thumb!"

"You refused to pay me what I was due. I took your thumb as justice. Your eye, well… That was an unfortunate accident."

Teskin shouted, "Guards! Kill this man!"

In a flash, Brogan's sword was out, ready to defend himself. Rhoa appeared at his side, her blades ready, Lythagon and Filk at his other side – one armed with a sword and shield, the other with a battle axe. Blythe slid her bow off her shoulder and held it ready, the cover still over it. Weaponless, Rawk and Algoron stood behind them, facing outward to protect their blind side.

Guards entered the tent from the front, others converging from the rear and sides. With a quick scan, Brogan counted twenty-two, all armed, none wearing armor. Half the men had swords, a handful with cudgels, the rest with an array of weapons, including crossbows and daggers.

Brogan raised his voice for all to hear. "We might be outnumbered, but you'll find us difficult to kill. I know how little Teskin pays you. Consider if it is worth dying for just so he can sate a thirst for revenge for something that occurred twelve years ago."

The guards stopped, exchanging glances, all eyes finally settling on a man as big as Brogan. He was roughly ten years younger and in better shape, a nasty scar on the side of his shorn scalp. When the man sheathed his sword, half the others did the same.

Their leader. Brogan was aware of how it worked, having held the same position at one time.

The man turned to Teskin. "We were hired to protect your wares, not kill on command."

Teskin's face turned red. "I pay you well, Reagor. You–"

Reagor laughed. "You pay just enough for us to survive while you reap excessive profits."

Turning toward the other guards, Teskin growled, "What of you?" He pointed toward Brogan. "I will pay five silver pieces to whomever kills this man."

Brogan snorted. "Who would risk death for five silver pieces? I see nothing has changed, Teskin. You are still a miser who cares only for himself."

The remaining guards sheathed their weapons and slunk away, save one. He was tall and lanky with greasy hair and an unshaven face. The man held a crossbow in his hand, bolt loaded and pointed at Brogan.

"You might get a lucky shot, killing me instantly," Brogan growled, glaring at the guard. "Anything less and your head will take a permanent vacation from your body." He grinned. "Is it worth the risk?"

The man lowered the crossbow and backed away, but his hate-filled glare never left Brogan.

Turning toward Brogan, Teskin pointed toward the exit. "Out! The entire lot of you. I want you out of my tent, or I'll call the city guards to arrest you for trespassing."

Brogan shrugged, slid his falchion back into the sheath, and backed away. "Best be off before I break everything I see." He grinned when Teskin's face grew pale. The man had always cared more about coin than anything else. Having his inventory destroyed was likely to wound him worse than losing a thumb and an eye.

The group gathered in the aisle between tents lit by the orange hue of the sun, now just above the horizon. With Brogan and Blythe in the lead, they resumed their journey away from the city, passing dozens of other tents before they reached the outer edge of the Bazaar.

A few hundred feet away, on a patch of trampled grass, was the largest tent Brogan had ever seen. It was well over a hundred feet tall and two hundred feet in length. Boxed wagons painted in garish colors, impossible to miss, were parked behind the tent. One of them was bright red with yellow trim, yellow wheels, and a yellow star on the side. He frowned in thought, staring toward it, then he heard Rhoa gasp.

"I can't believe it," she whispered, tears in her eyes. "That is Stanlin's wagon. The menagerie. I am home."

31

REUNION

Applause could be heard outside the performance tent, roaring cheers marking the end of the show. A longing swelled inside Rhoa, reminding her how much she had enjoyed performing – the audience on the edge of their seats, holding their breath as she performed acts most people could not, or would not, ever attempt.

She stood on the gravel roadway, her companions surrounding her as she wiped tears from her eyes. A big hand gripped her shoulder, drawing her attention.

Rawk gave her a smile. "Destiny brought you back to your family. They will wish to see you, if even for just a while."

Blythe stood at Rhoa's other side. "This is the troupe you mentioned? The people who raised you after your parents died?"

She nodded and turned toward the wagons behind the tent, one painted bright red with a yellow star on each side. There could only be one such wagon in the world. She recognized the others, as well, all painted in bright colors.

The crowd began to emerge from the tent, smiles on their faces, many commenting on what they had witnessed, laughing at the spectacle. Again, Rhoa was surprised how much she missed being the topic of those conversations. She had been so focused on the troubles surrounding her, she had lost a sense of her own needs and desires. *Do I wish to rejoin them when this is over?* It was a question she could not answer. Not now. Not yet.

Through gaps between the wagons, she spotted the crew heading into the tent to clean and prepare for tomorrow's show. Moments later, performers filed out and headed to their wagons, likely to change into more comfortable clothing. When she saw Sareen and Juliam, she sucked in a breath, tears blurring her vision again.

"It's all right, Rhoa," Blythe said in a gentle tone. "You should go and see your family."

She was torn, excited to see them but fearing them rejecting her for running off without an explanation. "What about our quest?"

Blythe smiled. "We were to meet our destiny at the Bazaar, where the past intersects with the future. Encountering your troupe here is likely more than coincidental." She squeezed Rhoa's hand. "If you like, we will come with you."

Rhoa looked at the others, all eyes on her, heads nodding.

"Yes. We will come along, and if they have food..." Brogan grinned, "we will stay as long as you like."

She laughed and wiped a tear away. "Thank you."

Inhaling a deep breath of resolve, she headed toward the wagons. As usual, they were arranged in a multi-layered circle, the wagons used to haul supplies on the outside, those housing the crew coming next, the performers' wagons near the middle. At the heart of it all was an open area with chairs, tables, and a firepit.

Rhoa and her friends stood near the firepit, smoldering coals waiting to be fed fresh logs. There, she waited, biting her lip, wondering what she should say, worried about how they might react.

A door opened and a massive, muscular man stepped out, holding it for a tall, lean blonde woman.

"What are you–" Juliam stopped mid-sentence and stared in surprise, eyes wide. "Rhoa?"

"Rhoa!" Sareen bolted past him, arms spread as she engulfed her in a fierce embrace, Rhoa's head held to her chest.

Suddenly, her worries were gone, replaced by a warmth she had not realized was missing until that moment.

∾

Night had claimed the sky, the round moon shining, the pale light mixing with the glow of the campfire. The air had cooled but was comfortable with a coat on. Per Blythe's request, Brogan had removed his chainmail. While he felt less protected, he did not miss the smell or the weight. Regardless, it was worth it just to have her head on his shoulder, his arm around her as they listened to Rhoa's tale. Having Blythe beneath his arm made life worth living.

Niles Bandego, one of the jugglers, filled Brogan's cup with wine before moving along to fill Lythagon's. The entire menagerie, an odd collection of twenty-eight performers and crew, listened intently while Rhoa shared the wild adventures surrounding her since she had last seen them. Many sat on benches, some occupied chairs, and a few stood, all clustered around Rhoa and the fire.

As he sipped the wine, Brogan listened to her rendition, one excluding many sensitive details. Even with a watered-down version of the story, it was a tale landing somewhere between amazing and outlandish. *How did we survive all this craziness?* Even for a soldier, a man who had lived much of his life on the edge, the realization brought him a sense of wonder.

When Rhoa finished, explaining they had come to Balmor at the behest of an ancient prophecy, she asked, "What about you? After I fled from Starmuth, I heard you were in Lionne. How did you end up here?"

Stanlin, dressed in an obnoxiously bright red coat, his mustache waxed and curled, stood. "When you disappeared, of course we feared for your life. Malvorian's men were obviously searching for you, but we had no idea why." He glanced toward Juliam. "Until Juliam finally came clean and told us of the item you stole from the Enchanter's Tower. Do you still have it?"

Rhoa shook her head. "No. The thief I mentioned retains it. Or he did when I last saw him."

Stanlin twisted the end of this mustache, nodding. "Perhaps it is for the best. The amulet might place us all in danger once again." He extended his arm. "Did you know the Despaldi character broke my arm while interrogating me?"

Rhoa looked down at the ground. "I'm so sorry."

He shook his head. "You know I am tougher than such things."

"Oh please," his wife, Purdi, said. "You whined about your arm for four weeks." She put a hand on her broad hip and looked at Rhoa. "You would have thought he was crippled for life."

Rhoa laughed. "I bet."

Stanlin, wounded look on his face, continued his story. "Without you, Rhoa, the show just wasn't the same. We tried another night in Starmuth, but it went poorly, so we decided not to go on to Fastella and made for Lionne instead.

"We spent only two weeks there, working on a new performance in front of small crowds before moving along. Our next stop wasn't until Fralyn. Again, we performed for small crowds and made adjustments until I felt we were ready. By then, we were sapped of funds and needed a big payout. Where to find one?" He held his arms out to his sides, grinning. "The Great Bazaar, of course."

Rhoa nodded. "I recall we did well the last time we were here. That was...three years ago?"

"Sounds about right."

Sareen stood from her chair, the tall blonde slipping an arm around Rhoa's shoulders. "All right. We are caught up with your story, you with ours. Now, I think it's time to celebrate." She smiled at Rhoa and raised her voice. "One of our own has returned, and by the sounds of it, the gods were looking out for her."

"Right you are, Sareen!" Stanlin held out his cup. "More wine, Niles! We drink hardy tonight."

The band began to play a lively tune, many troupe members rising to dance around the fire. Brogan emptied his cup again, the wine warming his throat, his head abuzz, so Niles could refill it. Now back on land, his stomach full, drinks flowing, and Blythe at his side, he realized he was happier than he had been in a long time, even if he was to sleep on a hammock in a tiny wagon for the night. Still, he had slept in far worse.

"Stop the music!"

A soldier emerged from the gloom, dressed in chainmail over a black and yellow tabard, wings on his helmet marking him as a Balmorian Army officer.

Brogan shot to his feet, his hand going to his hip. *My sword. I left it in the wagon.* All of their weapons were stored in the wagon Rhoa used to share with the other acrobats.

A host of armed guards assembled behind the squad leader as a short, portly man in loose robes appeared at his side.

"That's him, Sergeant." Teskin pointed toward Brogan. "This man and his seven companions robbed my shop. Arrest them!"

Brogan counted the soldiers behind Teskin. Eight of them, all dressed in standard Balmorian Army gear. The wagon where the weapons were stored was in the opposite direction of the guards. He looked toward it, turning the odds over in his head, liking his chances. He made to rush to the wagon, but Rhoa jumped in the way, her palm pressing against his chest.

"Don't, Brogan," she hissed. "These people are my family and have suffered enough because of me. I don't want anyone hurt or killed because of your eagerness to fight."

"Wise choice," the sergeant said. He then stuck two fingers into his mouth and whistled.

A dozen additional soldiers emerged from between the surrounding wagons, all bearing loaded crossbows. Another man was with them – the lanky, surly guard from Teskin's tent.

"Those are the right people," Teskin's guard said.

"Why are you lying for this slime?" Brogan asked.

When the guard just grinned, Brogan knew he had been paid.

The squad leader's eyes swept the crowd. "Which are the others we are supposed to arrest, Teskin?"

The man pointed toward Blythe, Rhoa, Tygalas, and the four dwarfs. "These two women, the one with the hood up, and the four short ones."

The eight guards who had arrived with Teskin approached, each carrying shackles, the other soldiers standing ready, weapons in hand. Many stood within arm's length of one or more troupe members, ready to kill should the call be issued. Despite his powerful preference to fight and escape, Brogan allowed a guard to spin him around, shackle his wrists behind his back, and usher him toward the city.

The Balmor Jail was a dark, blocky, stone building near the heart of the city. The sergeant led the procession past the guarded outer door and into a torchlit corridor. Although worried for herself and her companions, Rhoa was relieved the soldiers had left the troupe unharmed.

They passed a room with guards playing cards at a table, others sleeping in bunks. The next room contained a desk, a burly man with shorn hair sitting behind it, arms crossed over his barrel chest, eyes closed.

The sergeant kicked the desk, startling the guard.

He jumped to his feet, thumping a fist to his chest. "Sergeant Odama. Good evening."

"Don't 'good evening' me, Thad." He jabbed a finger in the big man's face. "You fell asleep again. How are you supposed to guard the keys if you are sleeping?"

"Um…" Thad stroked his oversized chin. "I had a big dinner, sir. Sometimes it makes me sleepy."

"Don't give me excuses. What are you going to do to solve the problem?"

The man scratched his head. "Um… Not eat too much for dinner?"

Odama rolled his eyes. "Yes, you idiot." He released a sigh. "I need to place these prisoners into cells to await trial."

Thad's lips moved as he pointed from person to person, counting to himself. "There's eight of them, Sergeant."

Speaking through clenched teeth, Odama said, "I know there are eight of them."

"Do they all need their own cell, or can they share?"

"When do we put more than one into a cell at a time?"

"When there ain't no cells left, Sergeant."

Odama pressed his lips together, nostrils flaring, but his tone remained even. "How many cells remain open, Thad?"

"Just two."

"*Two*? Why are so many full?"

"Well, far as I can see, none have been tried, freed, or executed for near two weeks."

"Two weeks?" Odama exclaimed. "What are Jakarci and his magistrates doing?"

A man in black robes, head covered by a hood, appeared in the corridor. "*Lord* Jakarci." He flipped his hood back to reveal a tanned face, short gray hair, and a trimmed, gray beard. The man was average height with a lean build, perhaps sixty years of age. "You will refer to him by his title, *Sergeant*."

Odama scowled. "What are *you* doing here?"

The man smiled, his attention on Rhoa. His intense, gray eyes sparked a memory.

Her eyes grew wide. "It's you."

"So, you do remember our meeting." The man smirked.

While brief, meeting him had been among the most impactful moments of her life. "You are the one who told me about the amulet."

"You are welcome." He rubbed his chin. "Since Taladain's throne sits empty, I presume you were successful in your quest."

She frowned. "How did you know about that? I never told you why I was interested."

"Ah. Straight to the heart of it, I see." The man shook his head. "However, the question must remain unanswered for the moment. We have more pressing issues to address."

Sweeping his arm at the prisoners, he declared, "You are to release these people, Sergeant."

Odama's scowl deepened. "They were arrested upon claims of thievery and are to be tried."

"The claims are false, made by a man with a vendetta against a former guard. If anyone should be arrested and tried, it is Teskin Odette."

The sergeant blinked. "But Teskin is among the wealthiest merchants in the Bazaar."

"My point exactly," the other man said. "Regardless, I must insist. Remove their shackles and place them under my care."

Again, Odama's nostrils flared, but rather than argue, he waved his hand. "Release them."

When a guard removed Rhoa's shackles, she rubbed her wrists, happy to have them freed. Once the others were unshackled, the man with the gray beard stepped back into the corridor.

"Come along," he said, fading into the shadows.

The others looked at Rhoa, who shrugged. "I don't even know who he is."

"Doesn't matter," Brogan said. "We are leaving."

They hurried out and found the man waiting for them in the square, arms crossed over his chest, hood covering his head. A dozen Black Wasps stood behind him, dark silhouettes wearing leathers, hoods up, faces covered by veils. Each had two short, thin swords on their hips and a band of throwing stars across their chest. The area was otherwise eerily quiet.

As they drew near, the Black Wasps spread out, encircling Rhoa and her companions, making it clear they were not free to leave.

"Follow." The mysterious man in robes turned and headed toward a street.

"Wait," Rhoa called out.

He stopped and turned to her. "What?"

"Where are we going? We don't even know your name."

"My name is Solomon Vanda, and we are going to meet your new benefactor."

Brogan rolled his eyes. "Who is?"

Vanda pointed toward the west, his intention unmistakable. Anxiety twisted Rhoa's innards as she stared at the shimmering yellow light at the top of the tower Vanda headed toward.

They were being taken to meet Jakarci, Wizard Lord of Balmoria.

32

RITUAL

Narine, Jace, Adyn, and Hadnoddon stood in the common area outside their rooms in Chandan's tower, each wearing black robes. The robes hung loose, lacking the sash usually worn by wizards. As instructed, they were naked beneath the robes, which felt odd. Jace made an inappropriate comment about how "free" his parts felt, eliciting laughter from Adyn and Hadnoddon, while Narine shook her head, trying to hide her smile.

Dressed in the golden robes of the Order, Chandan appeared in the stairwell, waved for them to follow, and descended to the ground level. He led Narine and her companions outside, sweltering air hitting them the moment they stepped into the sunlight. She looked up, the tall cliff walls looming over them. The gap where the sky was visible ensured the sun only reached the valley floor for a few hours a day, leaving it cast in shadow from mid-afternoon until late morning the following day.

"Raise your hoods," Chandan said as he donned his own. "The dark fabric might absorb heat, but the shade it provides is better than nothing."

Narine and her companions did as instructed, the hood shading her face from the intense sunlight. The breeze slipped through the thin material, but it was a hot wind and did little to cool her. Ahead of them walked a steady stream of robed figures in all shapes, sizes, and skin tones – from stout dwarfs to lean elves, dark-skinned Kyranni to even pallid-skinned Frostborn.

There were a few hundred in total, all marching toward the bridge at the south end of the lake.

Chandan fell into line, Narine and her companions strides behind him as they passed through the quiet city. As they crossed the arched bridge, Narine peered over the edge into the clear blue waters flowing past. The moment reminded her of crossing the bridge over the lava river in Oren'Tahal, even though the scenery and situations were starkly different. Part of her remained amazed that they had survived the skirmish with the goblins and ogres. Her thoughts then turned to Salvon and the man's calm demeanor after the giant scorpion's stinger pierced his chest.

If Salvon is part of the Order, can others here survive something similar?

Jace was right. Questions mounted faster than answers received.

They followed a path along the far side of the lake, leading directly to the massive pyramid. The closer they drew to it, the larger the building seemed to grow. Built of pale, stone blocks, each taller than a person and twice the length, the crystal tip of the structure, which was hundreds of feet above the valley floor, gleamed in the sunlight.

Upon reaching the open doorway, Chandan led them inside, shadows engulfing them, the temperature dropping dramatically. A simple, torchlit corridor led straight forward, intersecting tunnels leading off it in both directions. They came to a stairwell and descended, the temperature dropping further, yet not cold. The stairwell ended at a short corridor, an open doorway leading to an enormous chamber.

Walls made of stone blocks encased a square-shaped room hundreds of feet across. The floor was covered in a complex mosaic of colored tiles – symbols of power and patterns of constructs, giving Narine the impression that all existing knowledge of magic was represented within the room. Peering up, the ceiling came together at a square section of crystal, sunlight refracting through it in a beam of color, continually growing wider until it reached the floor five hundred feet below.

"A rainbow," Adyn breathed out. "It's beautiful."

"It is a spectrum of light." Chandan turned toward them. "While sunlight appears white, it is, in truth, all colors, from violet to crimson." He looked up. "The peak acts as a prism and separates the light as you see it, just as sunbeam passing through water can create a rainbow."

The members of the Order arranged themselves in a large circle, the colored light near the center.

"Come. It is nearly time." Chandan headed toward the middle of the room, Narine and the others trailing him.

As they drew close, the symbol of a golden sunburst became visible in the center of the floor, directly below the crystal at the peak. A cluster of seven robed figures stood on the sunburst, all facing the newcomers. Four were women, three were men, all with varying appearances and skin color. Chandan addressed them in Hassakani. He then turned, his gaze sweeping from Hadnoddon to Adyn to Jace and to Narine.

"The ritual will soon begin."

Jace asked, "Just what is this ritual?"

"You seek knowledge. Here, you will receive answers."

"Do we get to ask questions then?"

The man laughed. "Nothing of the sort. Your answers will come through experiences, each unique to yourself."

The thief frowned. "Why are your responses so cryptic?"

Astra, wearing his white robes and gripping a clay jug capped with a cork, emerged from the crowd, the petite man approaching. "Because we do not possess the answers you seek. Rather, they exist in future versions of yourself." He then turned toward Chandan, speaking to the wizard in Hassakani.

Jace muttered, "I changed my mind. These people are worse than the Seers."

Hadnoddon grimaced, while Adyn chuckled.

Narine felt self-conscious standing beneath the spectrum of light, surrounded by a ring of strangers dressed in gold robes, all staring. Her gaze swept across them, again struck by the myriad of appearances, as if they represented all peoples in existence. It left her wondering just how far the Order extended, for it sounded as if those standing in the temple were a mere sample of their numbers. She then spotted Harlequin among them, the woman's bald head blending with the others.

Astra finished speaking and turned toward Narine and her companions. "You must remove your robes."

Narine's eyes widened at the idea, her stomach fluttering.

"Um..." Jace looked down at his robes. "We aren't wearing anything under these."

The man smirked. "I am aware."

Jace flashed Narine a sidelong glance, shook his head, and undid the laces at his neck. He pulled the robes up and over his head, leaving himself naked.

Narine turned toward Adyn, who had already disrobed, her charcoal metallic skin illuminated by the streams of light. Beyond her stood Hadnoddon, the dwarf grumbling under his breath as he pulled his robes off. That left only Narine.

The idea of being naked in front of so many people terrified her, heart racing as she undid the laces. She began lifting the robes up, her breath coming in shallow gasps as she paused, the hem at her thighs.

"Do not worry," Jace whispered. "Your body is a thing of beauty, equal to a stunning sunset or a gorgeous vista. If anything, I am jealous of these people, for they get to appreciate a work of art I am loathe to share."

She gave him a smile of thanks, took a deep breath, and pulled the robes over her head. *Nothing to hide behind now.*

Astra took the robes from each of them before walking off.

Feeling everyone's eyes on her, Narine resisted the temptation to cover herself, instead standing proud, chest and chin thrust out while she held her stomach in. *I can do this.* She glanced at Jace, who leered at her, a smirk on his face.

"Perhaps we can get some time alone later," he whispered.

Narine smiled, then noticed how his body had reacted. "Can you not keep that thing under control?"

He looked down. "It's not my fault. I've told you before... Your body makes me eager."

"It seems I'm not the only one made of metal." Adyn snickered. "Or is that wood?"

Narine turned toward her, aghast. "Why are you looking?"

The bodyguard shrugged. "I've seen naked men before, you know. All things considered, you should be happy...and proud."

"We are *not* having this conversation right now."

Adyn laughed again.

Chandan and three others approached, two women and a man, each taking position in front Jace, Narine, Adyn, and Hadnoddon. Narine stared at the woman before her. Tall with pale skin and red brows. *Pallanese,* she thought. The woman placed her palm just above Narine's left breast, the cold hand causing her to flinch. An aura of magic surrounded the woman. Narine gasped in pain, jerking backward, her hand going to her chest. She looked down at the fresh, raw brand burnt into her skin – a sunburst like those on the robes, the same mark she had seen on Harlequin's left breast. Jace, Hadnoddon, and even Adyn had been similarly marked.

Jace rubbed his chest, a scowl on his face. "Why?"

Chandan replied, "It is required."

The man and seven other members of the Order each took position on one of the eight points of the sunburst. They also then removed their robes, tossing them backward.

Narine's eyes bulged in shock.

Chandan's body was covered in tattoos – symbols and twisting script she had seen only once before. The bodies of each of those standing on the sunburst points were covered in the same.

"Sorcery," Jace growled.

Astra approached, the man still wearing his white robes. "The young gods proclaim sorcery as evil because they wish to control you. I told you before. The Order was founded on the pursuit of truth. One truth we determined millennia ago was that sorcery was nothing but a tool, no different than a hammer, a sword, or even wizardry. The tool itself is not evil. How you utilize the tool determines whether it be for good or ill."

Astra uncorked the jug in his hands and stepped before Jace. He poured sparkling, crimson liquid into his palm and rubbed it onto the starburst burnt into the thief's chest. "Blood is a conduit for sorcery." The man then moved on to Narine and held up his hand. "The blood of a wizard enhances the conduit." He rubbed the liquid across the sunburst on her breast and moved on to Adyn. "Augmenting sorcery in this manner enables us to circumvent the limits placed upon us by the young gods." After applying blood to her sunburst, he moved to Hadnoddon. "It allows access to truths those gods prefer remain hidden."

The small man then crossed to Chandan, handing him the jug. Chandan poured blood across his chest and handed the jug back to Astra before rubbing it across symbols marking him from collar to knees. Astra continued around the sunburst, each person pouring the blood across their chest and rubbing it on his or her nude body.

Jace whispered, "This is disturbing and freakishly sensual at the same time."

Narine nudged him. "Hush."

Finally, Astra took the jug and departed, the ring of gold robes parting to allow him past.

Chandan hummed loudly and began to chant, the others in the temple joining him. It reminded Narine of her Trial at the University. The situation was eerily similar – the chamber with light shining down, the symbol on the floor, the eight people surrounding her, stirring some unknown power. At the same time, the differences were stark – sunlight rather than moonlight, the points of the symbol outside the circle rather than contained within, the bodies naked and covered with markings coated with blood.

The surroundings began to blur, her and her companions' feet lifting off the floor. They floated upward, into the light, the spectrum of color swirling to white until it was too bright to see. Then she was alone.

33

ANSWERS

J ace stepped through the doorway and looked around. He stood inside a study, shelves filled with thousands of books covering the walls. The ceiling was high above, a ladder hanging from a rail near the ceiling used to reach the upper shelves. Scattered here and there were gadgets and contraptions of odd design. Two brown leather sofas and a complement of chairs created a seating area around a glossy black table, upon which were stacks of books. He entered the sitting area, picked a book from one of the stacks, and opened it. The words inside were scrawled in a foreign text – the same text found in the books beneath the Oracle in Kelmar. He stared at the words, wishing he had the advantage of the language augmentation, before closing the book.

He left the sitting area and crossed the marble floor to two sets of stairs. Down a half-story was a bedroom, the four-poster bed unoccupied, the room dark. Not seeing anything interesting, he chose the ascending stairs instead.

A brief climb brought him to a loft, separated from the library by railings made of dark, glossy wood. The loft exposed a curved outer wall, giving Jace the impression he was in a circular tower. Small, diamond-shaped windows faced outward, the light from the muted sun and bright moon combining to create an odd, green hue. The frosted windowpanes blurred the landscape from view.

Situated in the middle of the room was a long, ornate desk and another sitting area surrounded by pedestals displaying a myriad of objects made of metal, wood, and rock. One such item drew Jace's attention. He walked toward it and leaned close for a better look.

It was a round medallion engraved by an eight-pointed star with an eye in the center, each point marked by a unique symbol. Jace clutched at his chest. The amulet was not there, but this could not be the Eye of Obscurance. It was safe in his room within Chandan's tower. Besides, this one was different. The eye in the center was open, staring at him.

"No," said a familiar voice. "That is not the amulet you have claimed."

Jace turned as Salvon crossed the library floor and climbed the stairs. The old man stopped at the top, narrowed eyes sweeping Jace from head to toe.

"Very little surprises me," Salvon said. "Yet your presence here is...quite unexpected."

The man walked past Jace, circled the desk, and sat in the ornate chair. He gestured toward the brown leather chair in front of the desk. "Please. Sit."

Jace sat, his mind reeling as he tried to gather his thoughts.

Salvon leaned forward and rested his forearms on the desktop, fingers intertwined. "I am curious. What brings you here?"

"I... I do not know," Jace said hesitantly.

The man tilted his head. "Do you even know where you are?"

Jace shook his head.

"Ah." Salvon leaned back. "What do you last remember?"

He frowned, sifting through his memory. "We crossed a desert and found a pyramid. They made us remove our clothes and...smeared blood on us."

Salvon smiled. "That is your story?"

Jace grinned. "Crazy, right?"

"It does sound outlandish, but I know something of the Order of Sol."

"That's it!" Jace exclaimed. "The people in the golden robes. Are you one of them?"

"You could say that." Salvon stroked his beard. "So, you have come here seeking answers."

The image of Salvon and the giant scorpion flashed in Jace's mind. He sat forward, elbows on his knees as he stared at the man. His chest appeared whole.

"What happened, Salvon? The last time we saw you... Did you truly jump into the lava?"

Salvon chuckled. "I did not, but I did hope to make a flashy exit. At times, I prefer flamboyance. It is a guilty pleasure, but we all have our bad habits."

"You are not an ordinary man."

"No."

"What are you?"

The old man smirked. "You pose a question even I cannot answer. Not exactly."

Jace sighed, rolling his eyes. "I thought I was supposed to get answers."

"What am I?" Salvon tapped on his chin. "I guess you could say I am a memory, akin to the afterimage you see when you stare at the sun, then close your eyes. You are no longer looking at the sun, but the image remains for a time, regardless of where you look."

Sighing, Jace sat back. The answer was useless. He was about to complain, then decided it would do no good. Instead, he realized he needed to ask better questions.

~

Light beckoned at the end of the shadowy tunnel. Narine glanced backward. Only darkness waited in that direction. Her slippered footsteps were silent as she padded into the light and peered into the cavern.

A man stood over a long table, open books spread out before him. He wore the robes of a wizard, black fabric with bands of silver symbols around his wrists, neck, and hem. A silver headdress held his long, white hair from his face. The smooth cavern walls were covered in colored tapestries depicting great battles. The one nearest to Narine showed men, elves, and dwarfs fighting side by side against creatures of darkness. Wizards wielding lighting, fire, and ice stood on the battlements, looking down upon the conflict.

Across the room was a long rack divided into hundreds of small slots, a roll of parchment occupying all save one, which was noticeably empty.

Narine entered the room and noticed a parchment unrolled in front of the wizard, books resting on the outer edges to hold it flat. A construct marked the parchment – a construct unlike any she had ever seen. Drawn to it, Narine approached the table.

The wizard spun around, glow of magic flaring. Narine gathered her own magic and formed a shield just in time, the fireball smashing against it, bits of fire scattering throughout the room.

"Stop!" Narine cried before the man released another attack. "I mean no harm."

The wizard frowned, his lined eyes narrowing. He had a long, white beard and was so thin, she feared if he stumbled, he might break.

"A wizardess? Who are you? Why are you here?"

Narine blurted, "My name is Narine Killarius. My father was Wizard Lord of Ghealdor." *Why did I tell him that?* She tried to recall why she had come. "I seek...answers?"

The man's eyes widened. "My tapestry!" He scurried past Narine, arms waving as he cast another spell. A section of the tapestry glowed orange, flames spurting from it, smoke rising. A dome of magic covered the tapestry, all air sucked from it before the dome sealed shut. The flames died out, smoke filling the encapsulated area. A moment later, the man released the spell and leaned against the wall, panting as if he had run a great distance.

"Are you all right?" she asked, tentatively stepping toward him.

The wizard waved her off. "Yes. I am fine. It's just the years." He paused and tilted his head. "Perhaps the miles, as well."

"I gave you my name. Might I have yours?"

"Oh. Yes. Right." He hobbled past her, returning to the table. "My name is Barsequa. What are you doing in my study?"

Narine's jaw dropped. She had heard the name many times while at the University. After all, Barsequa Illian had founded the institution two thousand years before Narine was born.

"You cannot be him."

The old man turned back to her. "Do not tell me who I am or am not. Now, answer me. Why are you interrupting my work?"

She gathered herself and tried to recall how she had arrived there in the first place. Images flashed in her head – camels, a gorgeous valley, a pyramid, standing naked in front of others.

Answers...

"I have come for answers."

The man snorted. "If you wish to study magic, do so at the University. I am busy."

"I attended the University for eight years. Not all I seek can be found there."

Barsequa turned toward her, eyes narrowed. "Eight years?"

"Yes. I graduated as master nearly a year ago."

He stalked toward her, face drawn in a scowl. "Liar!" he bellowed.

Narine jerked back with a start, quickly recovering. "I am not."

"The University only began accepting students three years past."

"What?"

"Surprised? You should do more research before you craft false stories."

Confused, Narine fell silent, the man turning back to the parchment. *How could I be speaking with Barsequa? He has been dead for two thousand years, passing sometime after the University opened.*

The answer struck, and she realized the impossible had happened. *Either I have been cast back in time or am speaking with a ghost.* Either way, she knew it was an opportunity to gain the answers she craved.

"What is the eighth major construct?"

The man spoke over his shoulder. "The University only teaches six."

"I know. I studied them, learned them well, and passed my Trial." Approaching, she stopped beside him. "The seventh construct, I know, as well. Augmentation."

He spun toward her. "Where did you learn that?"

"I studied a book. *The Compendium of Applied Research Regarding Constructs of Augmentation.*"

His eyes widened. Without a word, he scurried through the door at the side of the chamber, the neighboring room blooming with light. Narine walked to the door and peered inside. It was a library, also windowless. Shelves lined all the walls, two tables in the middle littered with books. The man walked to a shelf and pulled a black tome from it, the cover gilded at the edges. He caressed the book and opened it before sighing in relief.

The wizard spun toward her. "Show me."

"Show you what?"

"You claim to have studied this book. Show me a construct from it."

Narine's brow furrowed, preparing to retort, but she opted otherwise. Instead, she gathered her magic and held out her hand. Eight connecting ovals materialized, each made of an intricate pattern. She brought her hands together, wrapping the ovals into a loop and turning them over, bending the ends in to form a ball of light, the surface a repeating pattern. With her arm extended, the sphere hovered above her palm while the old man peered into it.

Finally, he stepped back. "Celerity. Well done, too. You may dismiss it."

He returned to the other chamber, Narine following. The man stopped at the table and turned toward her.

"How many years have I been dead?" he asked.

"Two thousand. Perhaps longer."

"Ahh." He nodded. "At least man has not destroyed one another yet."

"No. However, I fear the Dark Lord intends to succeed where mankind failed."

"Urvadan." He pressed his lips together in disgust. "What of the young gods?"

She shook her head. "Wizard lords are dying, and the younger gods seem to wane without them."

"So, the time has finally come."

"You knew?"

"I suspected."

"Can you help me?"

"You have already discovered the seventh major construct. I was reluctant to share it should the ability be misused."

Narine thought of Despaldi and his men. From the start, she knew their magic had come from augmentation. She wondered how Lord Thurvin had discovered it. "I fear another already misuses it."

He frowned. "Who?"

"Lord Thurvin, Wizard Lord of Farrowen."

Barsequa sighed. "Is he a good man?"

She shook her head. "No. He seeks to rule the world."

The old man collapsed into his chair. "As I had feared." He lifted his gaze to Narine. "He does not possess the eighth construct, does he?"

"I... I do not know. I have no idea what it is."

Barsequa rubbed his eyes, the man appearing tired. He waved his hand, the other chair sliding across the room before stopping in front of him. "Please. Sit. I will share my secret, but beware. Others will seek to abuse the power, so use it wisely and share it with no one."

Jace rubbed his chin in thought. "After the parents fled from Hassakan, it took you years to find her?"

"Yes. Seven years, hope waning with each. But I have developed patience few others could fathom. Even then, our paths crossing was a serendipitous encounter, occurring when I had grown weary of the search."

Seven years, Jace thought, his mind spinning at the complexity of the scheme.

"So, you played a part all along?"

Salvon nodded. "Yes."

Another thought occurred to Jace. "What about the contract I took to recover the Eye of Obscurance from Shadowmar?"

The old man chuckled. "I informed Olberon of the Eye's existence, then gave him the map."

"How did you know his man, Brenshaw, would seek me out?"

"Another carefully placed suggestion."

Jace narrowed his eyes. "How did you know I would succeed?"

"After your success in altering the lottery a few years earlier, I chose to place my faith in you."

"You knew about that?"

The old man smiled. "I paid for it."

Jace's jaw dropped. "Do you know what happened as a result?"

Salvon's smile melted. "You altered the address to the building where Rhoa lived."

Jace turned away, regret coiling his stomach. "It was random. I had no idea."

"Not as random as you might believe."

He turned back to the old man. "What do you mean?"

"The lottery was fixed, drawn for 18 Harper Street. You changed it to 618 Harper, where Rhoa's family lived." He leaned forward. "Why a six, Jace? You could have changed it to anything, but you chose to add a six."

Jace frowned in thought. "The event occurred ten years ago, so it's hard to be sure. I vaguely recall the number six popping into my head, so I wrote it in."

"How much did you earn on that contract?"

Swallowing hard, Jace muttered, "Six gold pieces."

The old man smiled. "Six gold. A large sum. A *memorable* sum, particularly for someone so young. You were... What? Eighteen at the time?"

Jace nodded.

"Perque was paid well to hire Cordelia to alter the lottery results. You were her obvious choice, the sum she was to pay you dictated up front by Perque."

The old man turned and peered out the window. "Little in life is actually random chance. I wish it were otherwise, but to mold Rhoa into the person she is today, her parents had to die. Placing the blame upon Taladain ensured the rest would fall into place."

He turned back toward Jace. "Once Rhoa learned about the Eye and what it could do, she was bound to go after it. Her unique skillset and immunity to the enchanted traps protecting the amulet aligned perfectly, nearly ensuring her success. Sending you after the amulet at the same time was a question of timing."

He smiled again. "I believe it went quite well. It required effort to not pat myself on the back the day you, she, and Rawk entered Fortran's Inn with the Eye in your possession. From that point on, I was able to take a more direct hand in guiding the lot of you toward the desired outcome."

The depth of Salvon's scheme was mindboggling, a plot spanning decades or more. Jace tried to focus on one question at a time, but Salvon had led him to one that burned with a brilliance.

"What, exactly, was your desired outcome? Why do all this?"

"I cannot answer your question in full, but I will give you a portion of it." He sat forward, eyes intense. "Think, Jerrell. What events have occurred thus far?"

Jace shook his head. "There has been so much…"

"Summarize it."

He scowled. "Fine." With a deep breath, he recalled the events since obtaining the Eye. "First, Taladain died. Then Malvorian and Raskor. Horus and Belzacanth followed, and finally Sarazan. While two of those wizard lords have been replaced, four thrones remain vacant."

"Very good."

"You…wish the young gods to fail." It was a guess, but an educated one. Salvon smirked. "I do."

"The Order of Sol seems to feel the same."

"As I said, I know something of the Order."

"They claim the young gods do not belong, that Vandasal and Urvadan must return."

The old man rose from his seat. "We have reached the end of the answers I am willing to share, Jerrell. It would be best if you left."

Jace glanced toward the door across the room. "I would, but I don't recall how I arrived here."

Salvon gestured for him to stand, then put his arm around Jace's shoulders and walked him toward the stairs leading down to the library. "Do not worry, my boy. Returning is simple."

When Salvon stopped, Jace turned toward him, his back to the stairs.

The man shoved Jace in the chest. Stumbling backward, he grappled for the railing, but Salvon slapped his hand away. Jace fell, arms flailing as he tumbled helplessly downward.

"It is...incredible," Narine muttered as she stared in wonder.

Barsequa held the construct before her, the pattern unlike any she had ever seen, yet vaguely resembled one of Illusion. He expanded it into a three-dimensional disc, bulging in the middle, edges of the two surfaces contacting one another. It was the second construct he had shared with her, both able to bend space beyond the limits of science.

"Memorize it well," the old man said. "As with the construct of spatial transmission, limitations apply. While with the first you may only contact persons with whom you are familiar, the construct of spatial transference is limited to destinations you have visited in the past. You see, much like an illusion, you must fully visualize your destination while you expand the construct. It requires one to be strong with the gift, the size of the portal proportional to the scope of the caster's abilities. One who is weak with the gift could do little more than transport a small rodent or a piece of fruit."

Awestruck, Narine sifted through the questions in her head. "These skills... Are they better suited to men or women?"

The old man nodded. "Another excellent question. While most skills are dependent on one's chemical makeup, constructs of augmentation and those of spatial shift appear equal when cast by male or female wizards, relying purely on the strength of the caster."

Despite her desire to absorb as much knowledge from the wizard as possible, Narine knew Jace, Adyn, and the others would be waiting on her return. "I have been here for hours and must leave soon." She frowned. "The patterns you have shown me are intricate, too complex to memorize in a short time. I fear I will forget them."

"Ahh." He smiled. "I have just the solution."

The man stood and returned to the chamber with the scrolls. Narine followed as he led her to the dark corridor from which she had arrived.

"Did you come in through the seaside entrance?" he asked.

"Seaside? I don't even know where we are."

He stopped, his face covered in shadow. "You are on Tiadd, my dear. The University is on the other side of the island."

She frowned in thought. "The other side of the island? I was told this side was uninhabitable. Nothing but steep cliffs and sheer drops."

"Quite true. Therefore, it is perfect for a secret study. Once the University was complete, the Makers crafted this for me. You are my first visitor." He grew quiet, tone taking on a quality of regret. "You may also be my last. I fear my time is short for this world."

On impulse, Narine hugged the man. He stiffened briefly before relaxing, his arms wrapping around her. Tears tracked down her cheeks for the kind old wizard – a legend in her own time, many centuries later. Finally, she released him and wiped her cheeks dry.

Barsequa cleared his throat and straightened his robes. "Well. We had best get you back. How did you arrive?"

"I… I do not know. I was in a temple in the mountains of Hassakan, then I was here."

"Transference across time." His tone was filled with wonder. "What construct made it possible?"

"It was, well…sorcery."

"Sorcery? Does such a thing exist?"

"It does in my time, but it is very rare."

"Very well." He nodded. "I suspect you will return the same way you arrived." The man tapped on her forehead. "The way back is in here, for your mind is the vehicle that brought you here."

He drew in his magic, skin glowing, and pressed a palm against her forehead. The constructs of spatial transference and spatial transmission appeared in her mind, filling it, burning an imprint as darkness descended.

Narine jerked with a start, her eyes flashing open to a swirl of light. The visit with Barsequa had been so real, moving…enlightening. A sense of wonder lingered, as did the two constructs he had shown her.

The spinning light slowed, white becoming beams of color. She floated down toward the sunburst on the floor, landing lightly, as Jace settled beside her, a determined expression on his face. To her other side were Adyn and Hadnoddon, the prior appearing resolute, the latter haunted.

The light dimmed, the eight nude sorcerers appearing through the blur. They lowered their arms, the chanting in the room ceasing. Those men and women reclaimed their robes and began dressing. Astra approached with an armful of robes, heading toward Narine.

"I pray you found what you sought, Princess. Given your reluctance to shed your clothing, I thought you might wish to dress."

Narine glanced down and realized she was still naked, as were Jace, Adyn, and Hadnoddon. She accepted the robes and pulled them over her head, sliding her arms into the sleeves, the hem tumbling past her hips and dropping to her ankles.

She turned to Jace, who seemed crestfallen. "What's wrong?" she asked, worried.

"Nothing," he sighed.

She reached out, cupped his chin, and turned his face toward hers. "No. Tell me. You look so sad."

"What do you expect? The view just shifted from spectacular to ordinary, save for your face, of course."

She slapped his arm. "You had me worried. I should have guessed it was just more of your depravity."

He chuckled and slid the robe over his head.

"Perhaps you should be encouraged," Adyn said. "Based on his earlier reaction, he is enamored with your appearance. I can think of far worse addictions."

The members of the Order filtered out of the temple, quickly leaving the four of them alone.

With the robe on, Jace leaned close to Narine and whispered, "Seeing you strip in public sparked an idea I think you'll like."

She smiled. "What are you up to now?"

A grin stretched across his face. "Tonight, when it's dark, I thought we could go for a swim."

Narine laughed and took his arm, the couple following the robed figures out.

34

SHIFTING WINDS

Rhoa woke to the smell of food, savory and inviting. She sat up in the bed as a servant placed a tray on her table. He was thin with gray hair and tanned skin, dressed in a black coat over a yellow doublet.

"Good morning, miss," he said, gesturing toward the table. "Your breakfast awaits. Do not dally. Lord Jakarci will be meeting with you shortly."

He walked over to the window and pulled open the drapes, bright sunlight streaming in.

"Thank you," she replied, running her hand through her hair, still groggy.

"My pleasure." The man turned and left the room, closing the door quietly.

She slid out of bed, still wearing her breeches and tunic. While she had been able to wash when shown to her chamber the prior evening, she had no other clothing to wear. Padding across the room, the marble tiles hard and cold beneath her bare feet, she peered out the window.

In the heart of a massive arboretum was a dark monolith jutting up into the sky. The yellow flames of Bal shimmered at the top of the tower, a reassuring sight after seeing other Towers of Devotion fall dormant. Her gaze swept the area as she considered the design of Balmor Palace, where she and her companions were held.

Unlike other castles she had seen, this one had no outer wall separate from the structure itself. Instead, the lower stories had no outward facing windows, and a moat wrapped around the square complex with a hollow center. The arboretum was filled with greenery, water features, statues, and patios, all surrounding the Tower of Devotion – a square, gray pillar topped by golden light.

Rhoa turned from the window, sat, and began to eat. As she had discovered in prior visits to Balmoria, the local fare was different than Southern wizardoms. Her meal consisted of spiced meat, blended beans, and flat bread, a bowl of fruit on the side. It reminded her of the Hassakani meals her mother used to make when she was young.

She ate with fervor, finishing quickly, then headed to the washbasin. After cleaning her hands, face, and scrubbing her teeth, she donned her boots and coat. Fully dressed, she stepped out into the corridor.

Four guards stood at the far end, the bulky men obscuring the stairwell. They had been told it was for their protection, but it felt more like they were prisoners. At least the accommodations and food were far better than they would have received at the city jail.

She knocked on the door across the hall.

"Come in," Blythe's muted voice came through the door.

Rhoa opened it to find Blythe and Brogan seated at the table, plates cleaned.

"Good morning, Rhoa," Blythe said, a smile on her face.

Rhoa noted Brogan smiling, as well. "I trust you two slept well."

Blythe's grin stretched wider. "Eventually."

"Oh." Rhoa's cheeks grew flush.

"It was nice to have a proper bed," Brogan said. "I didn't even break it."

Her face warmed further. "*That's* how you broke the bunk on *Sea Lord*?"

The couple laughed.

Blythe patted Brogan's hand. "You should have seen him, scrambling about our cabin, naked as the day he was born, trying to fix the thing."

"Seen him?" Rhoa blanched.

"Well, it *was* funny."

Brogan grunted. "I eventually gave up and pulled the mattress onto the floor and slept there." He shook his head. "Those tiny bunks aren't made for someone my size. I couldn't imagine the two of us trying to share one all night."

Footsteps drew Rhoa's attention. She turned to find Vanda coming down the corridor, relieved for the diversion. It felt odd to see him during the day. He seemed much less mysterious than at night.

"Gather your companions, Rhoa," the old man said. "Lord Jakarci is waiting."

She frowned, not recalling giving the man her name. *Perhaps he overheard someone say it last night.*

Dismissing the thought, she headed down the hallway and knocked on a door, Blythe and Brogan each doing the same. Moments later, they were all in the corridor, following Vanda down the stairs. After descending three flights, he led them through a set of doors and out into the arboretum.

The warmth of the sun was inviting, but it was still early, likely to be uncomfortably hot later in the day. They entered the shadows of the trees, following a paved path. The trees parted to reveal tall, neatly trimmed shrubs. Vanda led them past the shrubs, turned, and entered a maze. As Rhoa followed, the scent of flowers tickling her nose, she tried to keep track of the twists and turns. It was not long before she lost track. The center of the maze opened to a pergola-covered patio. A long table and ten chairs sat in the shade of the structure. Near the table, a man, one of the most obese people Rhoa had ever seen, sat on a bench.

He was dressed in voluminous white robes marked by yellow symbols on the cuffs and lapel. His head was bald, his goatee black with gray streaks. With tanned skin and dark eyes, he appeared to be in his fifties. Rhoa got the feeling he was much older.

Vanda bowed. "Your Eminence." He gestured toward Rhoa and the others. "As seen in my vision, I have located the tools of destiny."

Tools?

Arm outstretched, Vanda gestured toward the wizard. "I present to you Lord Jakarci, ruler of Balmoria and soon to be savior of the world."

Jakarci released a grunt as he pushed his tremendous weight off the bench and stood. He waddled toward them, stepping out from the shade of the pergola. "Welcome to my garden. I thought it a more pleasant location for a chat than a stuffy throne room." He grinned, cheeks bulging. "Besides, there are no spies out here. Well... None I don't trust completely."

"Spies?" Rhoa muttered.

Jakarci chortled. "Of course. Spying is among Balmoria's greatest indus-tries. That, and trade, of course. Information and commerce go hand in hand." The man gestured with a broad sweep of his arm. "The palace is riddled with secret tunnels and bolt holes, thick with spies at all times."

Blythe's eyes widened. "They can see in all the rooms?"

Jakarci tilted his head, a smirk on his face. "Yes. If you are wondering, you did have an audience last night."

Her cheeks flushed, she looked at Brogan, who shrugged.

"Why allow this?" Rhoa asked.

"Because they work for me," Jakarci said. "However, some are double agents, paid by another ruler or some wealthy merchant."

Brogan grunted. "If you know they are double-crossing you, why not have them killed?"

Jakarci waggled a thick finger. "If I did so, it would only alert my counterparts of my knowledge. They would replace their lost agent with another, and I would, once again, have to ferret out who is loyal and who is working for another party." He shrugged. "Still, I do kill some from time to time, often to send a message or to annoy a competitor."

"That sounds horrendous." Brogan scowled. "I'd just kill the lot of them and be done with it."

Jakarci laughed, chins wobbling. "Where is the fun in that?" The man turned and walked toward the table, each step requiring visible effort. "No. It is better to play the game as it is meant to be played." He stopped beside a wide chair, the wooden arms over three feet apart. "I have been doing so for a hundred twenty years and have developed some skill."

Gesturing toward the other chairs, he said, "Please. Sit."

Led by Vanda, they all approached the table and sat, the wizard lord at one end, Vanda at the other.

"Vanda, would you care to introduce me to our new allies?"

Brogan arched a brow. "Allies?"

The wizard lord grinned. "Once you understand the truth of it, you will see."

Vanda gestured toward Brogan. "As you may have guessed, this is the *Redeemed Warrior*, Brogan Reisner, formerly of the Gleam Guard, the Murguard, and various other positions in numerous cities. At his side is Blythe Duggart, the *Golden Huntress*. Those two are Lythagon and Filk, both Guardians from Kelmar. The two across the table are Rawkobon and Algoron Kragmor, stone-shapers from Ghen Aeldor. Beside them is Tygalas, the *Silvan*

Prince." He grinned. "Lastly, I present to you Rhoa Sulikani, *She Who is Blind to Magic."*

Jakarci stared at Rhoa. "Amazing."

She and her companions exchanged startled looks.

"How do you know our names?" she asked.

Vanda grinned. "Much of this information could have come through our spy network, but I must confess, I have other means."

"Such as?"

"I am a sorcerer."

Brogan gasped. "Blood magic?"

Jakarci laughed. "Vanda is too modest. He is no mere sorcerer, but the greatest sorcerer to have ever lived."

Vanda shrugged. "Perhaps. Such titles are meaningless. Only results matter." He then turned to Brogan. "Yes, blood is often used in sorcery, but why should such a simple and natural resource make it inherently evil? Is it because it comes from living beings? Acquiring blood does not require the host to die. In the end, intention makes all the difference."

"All right," Brogan said. "With the niceties out of the way, what is this about? Why are we here?"

"You are here," Jakarci said, "to help me save the world."

Rhoa looked to her companions, who exchanged confused glances.

"Allow me to explain," the wizard lord said. "Last year, a dispute arose between Kyranni and Balmoria after I asked for Kelluon's support in a private matter. He refused, so I raised the import and export tariffs between our two wizardoms." Jakarci spread his arms. "Kyranni needs Balmoria more than we need them. We are a far richer wizardom with the largest trade market in the world."

Arms crossed over his chest, Brogan said, "We care nothing for squabbles between wizard lords."

"Have patience," Jakarci said. "I am getting to the point.

"The dispute escalated this winter when I shut off all land traffic to and from Kyranni. Even the Murguard must receive supplies via water transportation unless the shipments come from Hassakan."

Rhoa's brow furrowed. "How do you close off a border?"

Vanda replied, "A river divides the two wizardoms, a bridge connecting them. By destroying the bridge, the only means across is by boat."

"My troops patrol the river, limiting such crossings." Jakarci grinned.

"However, the entire thing was a ruse. In truth, I sought a reason to destroy the bridge."

"Why?" Blythe asked.

Jakarci leaned forward, smile gone, gaze intense. "Because an army approaches. Rather than allow the force to invade unhindered, we needed to buy time to ensure your arrival."

Our arrival? Rhoa's head spun. It was all happening so fast. She felt like a ship caught in a storm, struggling to remain afloat, her life at the mercy of something beyond her control.

A man dressed in a black cloak entered from the maze, interrupting the conversation. He pulled his hood back and bowed. "Pardon the interruption, Your Eminence," the man said. "You wished to be alerted when the remnants of Greehl's force arrived."

"How many made it?"

"Six hundred."

The wizard lord released a heavy exhale. "What of Priella's army?"

"They will reach the basin before nightfall."

Jakarci looked at Vanda. "Time appears to have expired."

He nodded. "As I envisioned."

Brogan pounded his fist on the table, the noise startling the others. "Will someone tell me why we are here?!"

The wizard glared at him, lips pressed together, nostrils flared. Then his expression relaxed. "A monster rides at the head of Priella's army. She believes she can control him, but she is wrong. Even now, the chains connected to him weaken, for his power is too great, the links too brittle. When he sees the flame of Bal, he will wish to claim it for himself. If his power increases further, our world is doomed."

"A monster?" Blythe asked. "What sort of monster?"

"The worst kind," Jakarci replied. "A wizard lord whose ambition is insatiable, the magic he wields unequaled."

Blythe's voice dropped to a whisper. "What is his name?"

"Thurvin Arnolle."

Rhoa flinched, although she had suspected the answer all along.

"With Farrowen, Ghealdor, and Orenth in his grasp, Lord Thurvin wields the magic of three wizardoms. Soon, he will come here, intent on gaining a fourth." He gestured toward the tower looming above them. "It cannot be allowed."

"Orenth, as well?" Blythe asked, eyes wide. "He killed Lord Horus?"

"Yes."

Brogan leaned forward, eyes narrowed. "You want us to kill a wizard lord?"

Brow raised, Jakarci said, "One of you has done so before." He turned to Rhoa.

She recoiled, memories of the encounter with Taladain flashing in her head. It had not been easy, but in the end, the wizard lord lay dead, his blood on her blades. The skirmish with Taladain had included a frightening display of his might, and his magic was a pale shadow of what Thurvin now wielded.

"Sire," the sorcerer interjected, "with the army approaching, we must evacuate the Bazaar. Anyone remaining outside the city walls when the sun sets does so at their own peril."

Rhoa stood, alarmed. "My family is out there!"

Jakarci nodded. "You may go to them, then return here to prepare. Tell them to find shelter inside the city walls, but they must do so before sunset. Once the gates close, they will not reopen until the threat is removed."

35

BREAKING STORM

Standing inside the boxed wagon she once shared with the other acrobats, Rhoa strapped her sheaths to her thighs. A sense of relief accompanied the reclamation of her fulgur blades, an odd sense of comfort from weapons that had killed more than once.

They are just tools, Rhoa, she told herself. *You use them as you must, nothing more.*

When she thought about those deaths, she felt a hollowness, as if a piece of her had been destroyed with each person she killed. Now she was being asked to kill another.

Thurvin is a bad man. From the moment you met him, it was obvious. You can do this. The words felt hollow, as well.

The door opened, Rhett peering in, holding a crate filled with trapeze ropes and bars. The young man's handsome face was one she knew better than most. Back when he first joined the troupe, she spent many evenings dreaming of his striking blue eyes. However, she had been merely thirteen at the time, him three years her senior. Of course, he never noticed her attempts to flirt or her longing stares. Over time, those feelings had settled, the two becoming close friends…as happened when living and performing together every day for nearly seven years. Rhett was among those she had missed the most since her abrupt departure in Starmuth. Nearly half a year had passed since then, the time filled with adventures, trials, and momentous events. Her perception of the world had altered as a result.

"Rhoa." He stepped inside. "I didn't expect to find you in here."

"I came to retrieve my blades."

"I am not surprised." Rhett set the crate down and dusted himself off. "I know how much they mean to you."

She smiled. "I have little in the way of possessions. These blades…" She patted her thighs, "are the only thing I can truly claim as my own. Of course, it helps that nobody else can use them."

Rhett stood in front of her, staring down into her eyes. He was short for a man, but still a half-head taller than Rhoa. "I…," he stammered, running a hand through his cropped, brown hair. "I didn't get a chance to talk to you last night."

"Is now the best time?" she asked. "Only two hours remain until sunset, and I must return to the city."

"Please."

"All right."

He rubbed his muscular arms – arms honed from years of trapeze work. "We have known each other for a long time."

"Seven years."

"Yeah. You were young when I joined… We both were. At first, I guess we were like siblings thrown together by this exotic, oversized family."

She chuckled. "*Exotic* is an interesting description."

"As time went on, particularly the past couple years, I began to feel something different." He looked away and rubbed his eyes. "What I am trying to say is…" Lifting his gaze to hers, he said, "I like you, Rhoa."

She smiled. "I like you, as well, Rhett."

He stepped closer, placing his hand on her upper arm. "I mean, I thought… I hoped you and I would end up together. Forever."

Rhoa blinked with a start. Her heart fluttered. "I… Um…"

He leaned in and kissed her. She tensed at first, palms against his chest as if to push him away. Then she melted into the kiss, the flutter in her chest quickening. His lips were soft, chiseled chest firm. The world spun, pulse thumping in her ears. He pulled away, her eyes flicking open, breath coming in gasps.

He cupped her cheek with his hand as he stared into her eyes. "You don't need to reply right now. I just needed to tell you how I feel. More so, I had to kiss you…just once. If I didn't take the chance now, I feared I may never get another."

He turned to the door and spoke over his shoulder. "Think on it. When this is over, come find me and we will talk."

Hurriedly, he slipped outside and closed the door behind him. Rhoa stared at it, feeling more confused than she could ever recall.

The door opened, Rawk peering in. "Oh. There you are. We were looking for you."

Heart still racing, mind a jumbled mess, she grasped for a response. "I, um…" She patted her thigh. "I was just getting my blades."

He smiled. "I know you are attached to them. I'm sure you are happy to have them returned."

She nodded, relieved he had avoided asking further questions. "You know me too well, Rawk."

"Come on." He pulled the door open and stepped back. "We are ready to head back to the palace."

She stepped outside and followed him to join her friends, lips still tingling with the memory of Rhett's kiss.

~

A flurry of activity filled the area as Brogan waited outside the menagerie camp. Blythe, the elf, and the dwarfs gathered beside him, while Rhoa lingered behind, shouting reminders for the troupe to make for the city before sunset. When she reached the road and gave a nod, Brogan resumed the trek back to the city.

If the menagerie troupe looked busy, the Bazaar was outright chaos.

Everywhere Brogan looked, workers and armed guards loaded carts and wagons. Shop owners scurried around, shouting orders and appearing on the edge of losing their sanity. The journey was slowed by the need to weave between people, around carts, and to pause for workers carrying loads from one side of the aisle to the other. When Brogan reached Teskin's tent, he stopped and grinned, crossing his arms, the others stopping beside him.

After a moment, Teskin turned in Brogan's direction, his lone eye bulging, face reddening. "What are you doing here?" he growled.

"I wanted you to know your twisted scheme failed."

"I will get you eventually, Reisner," the man sneered, "but I currently have bigger issues to address."

"Yes. An army will arrive soon." Brogan gestured toward Teskin's tent. "I can't imagine how much stress you feel right now. After all, there is nothing you care about more than your money." He strode closer to Teskin, the shorter man backing away as Brogan leaned toward him. With a growl, he said, "How much gold would you lose if this were all destroyed?"

Teskin began gasping, his hand to his chest.

"Oh, do you still have a heart condition?" Brogan asked in an innocent tone. "I totally forgot."

Teskin dropped to the ground, landing on his backside, his back to a shelf, hand on his chest as he panted.

Brogan chuckled. "One day, you will get what you deserve, Teskin." He spun and walked away, leaving the greedy merchant behind.

Blythe walked beside him, brow arched. "Did you really have to do that?"

"He is a snake."

"What if he dies?"

"We all die, Blythe. However, I doubt he will go so easily. If the gods have any sense of justice, he will suffer before he meets his end."

They continued toward the city, moving through the chaos of people loading wagons and carts. When they reached the gap between the Bazaar and the city wall, Tygalas stopped and pointed toward the hills to the south.

"The army approaches."

Brogan stopped and stared, spotting a string of riders coming down the road through the pass. Behind the cavalry were thousands of soldiers on foot. It struck him as odd to see his own people, led by Queen Priella, this far north. He recalled the toddler version of her from long ago – green eyes and red hair, the girl staring up at him while tugging on his armor. *That was back when I was so sure of myself. Prior to my mistakes. Prior to the wounds to my pride.* His regrets had piled up over the following two decades and had come close to consuming him. He glanced at Blythe as she stared toward the approaching army. *She saved me. Perhaps I can save Priella.*

36

ATTACK

Four long days after the disaster at Fralyn Fortress, Queen Priella and her army marched over a mountain pass and were blessed with the first sighting of Balmor, trade capital of the Eight Wizardoms.

Marquithe, at the hub of the Southern wizardoms, paved roadways connecting it to other cities and borders, often staked claim to the same title. However, it lacked three major elements Balmor had. First, the weather was forever pleasant, seldom too hot in the summer and never worse than mild in the winter. Second, it was situated at the end of Bal's Sound – a long, wide waterway connecting to the Ceruleos Sea. The sound was simply the world's premier natural harbor. Last, and most importantly, Balmor was home to the Great Bazaar.

Priella's gaze swept over the basin before her, the tall, gray walls of Balmor nestled beside the waterway. The late afternoon sun shone upon the white sails of ships floating in from the sea, others sailing out for some distant port. Just east of the city, a sea of white tents sprawled across the basin. Although miles away, she could tell the Bazaar was filled with activity, people appearing like ants in the distance. Carts, wagons, and horses filled the aisles between tents.

A sigh of relief slipped out, and she ran her hand through her hair. "Thank Pallan, we made it in time."

Kollin looked over from his horse next to her. "In time for what?"

"I...cannot say. Not yet." When he frowned, she reached out and took his hand. "You must understand, certain events must occur, and I dare not risk altering fate. We have but one chance."

His brow furrowed, frown deepening.

She squeezed his hand. "I ask you to trust me and wait just one more night. If we wake tomorrow morning and all is well, I will disclose my secret."

He nodded and gave her a smile, which set her heart racing.

He is so beautiful.

"Thank you."

"They are evacuating the Bazaar," Bosinger said from the horse on her other side.

Priella turned her attention back toward the tents, all activity seeming to flow toward the city.

"Why?" Kollin asked.

Bosinger grunted. "A foreign army approaches. Preparations are being made. They expect a siege."

She stared toward the city, the tower in the center shimmering with a yellow flame. "It is just as well. Those people are safer inside the walls."

They rode down the hillside, the valley floor miles below, the front of her army now reaching the grass-covered basin floor. *Garvin is down there, assigning tasks, outlining the camp defenses.* Meeting with him privately earlier in the day, she had made her orders clear. The commander was to take the utmost caution against attack, for they could not relive betrayal like what occurred in Fralyn.

Garvin stopped his horse at the bottom of the hill and gazed over the field between him and the Bazaar – two miles of waist-high grass bending in the breeze coming off the harbor, giving the appearance of waves upon land. Behind him, the hillside was covered in grass and clusters of leaf trees that became more prevalent the higher he looked. A full forest covered the top of the hill.

Some of the open areas on the hillside were level enough to pitch the command tents, allowing a view of the basin. He would ensure the wagons also remained above the plains. No need to risk their supplies to theft or vandalism.

He spotted Quiam talking with one of his sergeants and rode over, slowing as he reached him.

"Captain Quiam."

"Commander," Quiam said with a deferential nod.

"We make camp here, at the foot of the hill. Commander tents and wagons are to remain up there." He pointed toward the hillside. "Out of harm's way and where we can properly see any approach."

Quiam nodded. "Agreed."

Garvin nodded toward the Bazaar and the city. "Although we have space, we are in enemy territory. We will maintain an active perimeter defense at all times. Assign three hundred of your men per shift starting at sunset and changing every three hours. Find Henton and have him do the same with his troops. You take the eastern flank, him the west."

"Yes, Commander." Quiam pounded his fist to his chest, turned his horse, and began issuing commands.

Garvin turned toward the Bazaar, the white tents painted orange in the light of the setting sun.

Years had passed since his last visit to Balmor. Even then, he had barely entered the city, sleeping for a night at an inn near the eastern gate before departing.

I need to know how they are preparing.

He kicked his horse into a trot, gaze sweeping from horizon to horizon. During the day, it would be impossible to approach the city unnoticed unless doing so at a crawl, below the height of the grass. As he drew closer, the Bazaar came into focus.

Most of the tents were empty, only a smattering of people and a half-dozen wagons remaining, bodies moving around with a sense of urgency. A long line of wagons and carts waited outside the city gate, slowly inching forward. Five hundred feet before reaching the tents, Garvin turned to circle the Bazaar as he headed toward the city.

Dark gray walls a hundred feet tall surrounded Balmor, likely eight feet thick and impenetrable, the same as every other great city he had visited. The east gate stood open, dozens of guards visible, many gazing in his direction. Dozens more patrolled the top of the wall, many holding bows, likely waiting for him to draw close enough.

Sorry to disappoint, he thought as he continued west, at the edge of the grass, remaining distant. Hundreds of feet of blackened earth lay between him and the city walls. *They burned the grass to prevent anyone from approaching unseen. Clever.*

By the time he reached the western end of the city, the sun had dropped below the horizon, the walls darkening further. As he suspected, there was no gate here, confirming that the only ways inside were through the harbor gate to the north or the eastern gate outside the Bazaar.

He filed the information away, turned his horse around, and rode back to camp at a walk, taking care to avoid any holes or obstructions in the failing light. *A fall out here, alone, with enemies on the walls, could be fatal.*

By the time he circled the city and neared the Bazaar, the gloom was thick, the hills a dark shade of purple beneath the fading light in the sky.

Screams came from the Bazaar, followed by familiar hoots, the sound sending chills down Garvin's spine. He slowed and peered toward the tents, dark shapes darting around. A man burst out from a tent. He was overweight and dressed in loose, pale robes, eyes round with fear. Two dozen gray, wiry attackers, weapons in hand, chased after the man. He was clearly in poor shape and rapidly losing his lead. Instantly, Garvin knew the man would not outrun the pursuing goblins. He turned his horse and kicked it into a gallop, racing down the road, eager to return to camp.

He then noticed movement at his side, a wave of monsters rushing across the open fields, straight toward him.

The last vestiges of daylight lingered in the western sky, the moon to the east shining between two clouds, stars visible where clouds were not present.

Priella stomped through the parked wagons, Bosinger at her side. "Where is it?"

"We will find it, Priella," the bodyguard replied. "Getting angry won't help your cause."

"It's nearly dark, and I have yet to find my throne. I have every right to be upset. I am to face Jakarci tomorrow. I need my full magic."

The sky to the north lit up, beams of yellow light shooting from the Tower of Devotion inside the city walls.

She flung her arm out in that direction. "See. Jakarci gathers his magic as we speak." She continued peering through the wagons, not finding the one she sought.

"There is Sergeant Haim." Bosinger pointed toward a stout, middle-aged man in a Pallanese Army uniform, a pale blue diamond on the shoulder of his coat. "He's in charge of logistics. He'll know where it is."

Lifting her skirts above the long grass covering the hillside, Priella marched up to the man.

Haim turned toward her, his eyes widening. "Your Majesty."

"Don't, Haim," she growled. "Where is my throne?"

He rubbed his balding head, "Um, well… The wagon broke an axle about four miles back."

"*What?*"

The man stepped backward, holding his hands up. "I have my best men on it. They'll have it repaired quickly. They are likely done by now."

She closed her eyes and took a deep, calming breath before opening them. "Send a man to find out when it will arrive, then have him report to my tent immediately. If the wagon does not reach camp soon, I will go to my throne. Devotion cannot be missed."

The sergeant dipped his head. "As you wish, My Queen." He backed away, spun around, and shouted. "Chessing! Get over here!"

A thin man in dark messenger clothing rushed over.

Haim pointed south. "Get on your horse and backtrack until you find the wagon carrying Queen Priella's throne. Find out how soon it will arrive, then report to her tent immediately. I want you back here within the hour, or your head is forfeit!"

"Yes, sir!" The messenger thumped his chest and rushed off, into the gloom.

Priella turned away with a sigh, heading for her tent, Bosinger shadowing her. Another light bloomed in the night – the blue, shimmering flame from Thurvin's throne, the wagon positioned on the hilltop above the command tents. *The man recharges his power*, she thought. He had become increasingly more difficult to control. Numerous times a day, she would find a reason to touch him and plant seeds of influence. She shuddered to think what would happen should he turn on her. The power he wielded seemed to be pushing him toward madness, her magic repeatedly having to bring him back from the brink.

A distant cry drifted from the front edge of camp. "We are under attack!"

Shouts came from across camp, orders called out, cries of surprise followed by screams.

"Who would dare attack us?" Priella asked in shock.

"Who, indeed." Bosinger drew his sword.

She stalked toward her tent as Kollin emerged, their eyes locking. "We are under attack."

"I am with you," he said.

"Good. Let us find out who is behind this."

The three of them headed down the hillside as shouts and the clang of weapons colliding echoed in the darkness. She embraced her magic and wound her hands together with a construct of illusion, a globe of light appearing. With a thrust, she launched the light over the tents, toward the outer edge of camp. What she saw made her gasp.

Gray-skinned monsters swarmed the swath of grassland between camp and the Bazaar. They were wiry, armed, and frenetic, attacking her soldiers with abandon.

"What are they?" Bosinger muttered.

"Goblins," Priella breathed. "It has happened. *This* is the war we came to fight." Her stomach twisted, regret and failure making her wish to vomit. "I was to claim Jakarci's magic before it happened, but it is too late."

Bosinger put a hand on her arm. "Steady, Priella. If this is our battle, we fight, regardless of the circumstances."

She nodded. "You're right." Setting her jaw, fists clenched, she said, "These are darkspawn, evil and twisted, monsters of the worst kind. They must be stopped. This is why I appointed Garvin commander. He will know what to do."

"What about us?"

"Come. We are going to fetch Thurvin. It is time to unleash the weapon he has become."

37

THE ULTIMATE WEAPON

S till upon his horse, Garvin called out orders while riding parallel to the rushing monsters.

"Shields, form a line, pikes ready! Swords behind pikes, ready to strike!" He watched the goblins closing the distance. "Archers, raise bows!" He waited a beat. "Loose!"

A rapid staccato of twangs sounded in the night, hundreds of arrows sailing toward the attacking horde.

"Cavalry! Mount and split. Pallans to the east, Farrowens to the west. When the horn sounds, sweep the enemy flanks!"

The arrows landed, goblins falling with squeals, arms flailing as the front of the force struck the line of shields. Hundreds of goblins died, bodies impaled upon pikes or with arrows, but the onslaught continued.

One monster slipped through the ranks and charged toward Garvin. He drew his sword, turned his horse, and slashed, lopping off the monster's head. The headless body stumbled past him and collapsed.

A cloud slid in front of the moon, the gloom thickening. *We need light... and magic. Where are those wizards?* He glanced up the hillside to where the azure flame of Farrowen shimmered a quarter mile away.

A globe of light bloomed on the hillside and flew across the sky, sailing directly over him. It stopped over the field, revealing a grassy plain thick with thousands of goblins.

With the targets again visible, he called for another volley.

~

The world was pure bliss, Thurvin's back arched in the throes of ecstasy while prayers rushed in, filling his magic. His body shook with the power, fists clenched, eyes bulging. It was so overwhelming, he could not breathe. Minutes went by with him held hostage by the incoming prayers, but he did not suffocate, did not die, for his magic continually healed his body, his power great enough that it now happened without thought.

As time went on, the incoming prayers dwindled, the grip of the thrall loosening.

"Thurvin!" a distant voice called.

He dismissed it, unwilling to end Devotion until he could gather no more power.

"Thurvin! We are under attack!" The voice was female and familiar.

In the back of his mind, he recalled the army camped just outside Balmor – home of Jakarci, a rival in more ways than one. *Does he dare strike? What if he attacks while I am receiving Devotion? Am I vulnerable?* Reluctantly, he released his connection to the throne, the bright azure light receding, the incoming magic ceasing to feed him.

He gasped, sweet air refilling his lungs as he stood upon the wagon. Priella and her bodyguard stood below him.

"You had better have a good reason for interrupting Devotion," Thurvin growled.

The queen pointed toward the Bazaar across the basin. "Darkspawn attack our army!"

He frowned at the distant globe of light, gray bodies moving in the dark grass below, soldiers engaging. "Darkspawn?"

She strode closer. "Goblins. Thousands of them. Our men need your magic." She pointed. "Go and destroy them!"

Thurvin floated off the wagon to land on the ground, brow furrowed. *My power vastly outstrips hers. Why am I listening to this little girl and her feeble magic? Why would I allow her to take the Balmor Tower of Devotion and gain more power when I could take it myself and rule the world?*

His mouth turned up into a sneer. "*You* fight the goblins. I only care about Jakarci." He made a fist. "His magic will be mine. With the Bazaar, Balmor is the largest city in the world. Imagine my magic once those prayers are mine!"

He took a step, embracing his gift, prepared to fly off to the city to confront the Wizard Lord of Balmoria. Priella dove at him, her hand grasping his before he could react.

Thurvin stiffened, eyes bulging as she attacked his mind with a psychic barrage, assaulting his will. Despite his magic, he felt his defenses whittling away until something broke. He collapsed, bringing her down with him, the darkness crashing in.

Thurvin's head hurt, temples throbbing. He blinked, opening his eyes to Priella kneeling beside him, her hand on his cheek. The sky was dark, moon covered by a cloud, the silhouette of a wagon and his throne upon it looming over him.

"What happened?" Thurvin mumbled as he sat up, holding his head.

"When you completed Devotion, you grew dizzy and fainted," she said. "Your power is too great. If it grows further, you might destroy yourself."

He nodded. "You might be right."

"Come." She gripped his hand. "Rise. Help us fight these monsters."

"Monsters?"

"Yes. Darkspawn. Goblins. Thousands of them are attacking our army." She held his hand to her chest, her skin soft and warm against his knuckles. "I need you, Lord Thurvin. Our soldiers need you." Her other hand went to his cheek, cupping it, her smile a welcoming beacon in the darkness, warming his heart. "It is time to unleash your power," she crooned.

He smiled. "Yes, My Queen. I will make the monsters pay!"

Turning toward the battle, he embraced his magic, a shield wrapping around him and lifting him off the ground. He sped toward the basin, in search of targets.

Priella sighed in relief. "That was close."

"You are losing him," Bosinger warned.

"I know. His magic... It is doing something to his mind. It is as if there is a madness to the power, especially right after Devotion. If his mind breaks altogether, I may not be able to control him." She set her jaw and gathered her own magic, using it to lift herself off the ground. "I must watch over him, ensure I do not lose control."

"What should I do?" Bosinger shouted from below.

"Go to my tent. You and Kollin are to protect it. If my throne arrives, come find me."

She turned and floated off, toward her army.

The light in the sky faltered, plunging the battlefield into darkness. Breaks appeared in the shield line, the second, third, fourth, and fifth lines of soldiers engaging with the attacking goblins. It was a bloodbath, goblins dying by the hundreds while hundreds more replaced them, clangs and cries arising from weapons colliding with metal and flesh.

Garvin shouted from his saddle, "Naphtha!"

The archers to his left and right wrapped wet rags around their arrowheads before nocking the bow.

"Torches!"

Dozens of soldiers with torches in hand rushed forward, using them to light the rags.

"Loose when ready!"

Streaks of amber shot through the evening sky, falling hundreds of feet away. Flames flickered in the murk, the grass catching fire, goblins screaming and flailing as they burned. The light, although distant, gave additional clarity to what they faced.

Well over a thousand goblins lay dead, but the horde numbered many times that, the field thick with angry monsters. From his time in the Murguard, Garvin knew goblins were mindless and, as long as they remained under control, would continue to attack without regard for their own lives. Despaldi's words echoed in his mind.

Cut the head off the snake, and the rest will crumble.

He searched the horizon until spotting a distant glow to the northeast, far beyond the reach of his army. Upon a small hill, a fire burned, shapes moving around it. The fire surged to an inferno, a ball of it launching into the night sky, arcing toward camp.

He kicked his horse forward, slowing as he reached Quiam. "I am transferring command to you."

Quiam looked at him. "What? Why?"

"I need to stop this fight."

Without waiting for a reply, he kicked his horse into a gallop and headed up the hill toward camp as the fireball crashed down, killing a dozen soldiers and setting two tents ablaze.

Priella soared over her camp, some of the tents having been abandoned before fully assembled. The attack had come before they had fully settled. She hadn't eaten dinner yet and suspected most, if not all, of her soldiers suffered from the same hunger.

She peered down at the dark shapes on the battlefield as a flash of blue lightning sizzled across the fields, immediately followed by a boom of thunder. She lowered herself and focused on the source of the strike. When she saw him, she drew closer, careful to remain behind the wizard lord as he fired another blast. Using care, she extended her influence upon him, turning his anger against the darkspawn, reinforcing his loyalty, aligning his cause to hers.

Thurvin laughed as he stalked through the long grass and released two simultaneous bolts of lightning, the electricity arcing from monster to monster in an expanding chain of destruction, dozens exploding into flames as their bodies fried. He strode through the enemy horde, blasting again and again, reveling in the moment. The ease with which he destroyed, the enemy helpless to stop him. He was death incarnate – a single man able to take on an entire army. Since they were darkspawn, he could kill with abandon and without fear of regret. It was glorious.

He wrapped a shield around himself and floated up, arrows bouncing off harmlessly as he sped above the burning grass, deeper into the horde of monsters.

Slowing his mount as he neared the command tents, Garvin spotted Bosinger and the young wizard from Tiamalyn.

"Bosinger! I need your assistance!"

The bodyguard rushed over. "What is it, Commander?"

Garvin pointed to the east. "See the fire on that low hill?"

"Yes. What of it?"

"It has the look of shaman magic. Those goblins control the others. If we can kill them, the rest will crumble."

He frowned. "Crumble?"

"They turn into thoughtless beasts, easily killed and often running away, afraid when not driven by shaman influence."

Kollin said, "I will come, as well."

Garvin narrowed his eyes at the young man. "Have you been in combat?"

"Well... No, but I was among the most powerful students while at the University."

"Let the boy join," Bosinger said as he turned toward his horse, unhooking the reins from a post. "He can ride with me."

"All right." There was no time to argue, and Garvin figured the young man's magic might be useful. "Has anyone seen Rindle?"

From atop his horse, Bosinger clasped Kollin's hand to help the younger man into the saddle. "He was riding in the wagon with Priella's throne. It broke an axle today and has yet to arrive."

A horse approached at a trot and entered the torchlight, the rider dressed in plain clothes. The man drew his mount to a stop. "Where is Queen Priella?"

"Out there." Bosinger pointed toward the basin. "Fighting a battle against darkspawn."

The man peered toward the fight, thunder rumbling as bolts of lightning arced across the fields. "I was to report when her throne would arrive."

"You found it?"

"Yes." The messenger pointed toward the road. "It was in the pass when I reached them. It'll be here within minutes."

Garvin had heard enough. "Perfect." He turned to Bosinger. "Follow me."

He reined his horse around and rode through the upper portions of camp, emerging on the gravel road. Sure enough, a lonely wagon, two enchanted lanterns dangling from the lead horses, rolled downhill, toward them.

Blocking the road, Garvin held his hand up. "Stop!"

The wagon came to a halt, the driver asking, "What is this about?"

Ignoring the man, Garvin pulled beside the wagon and called out, "Rindle! Come out and climb on my horse!"

A shadow flickered, slipping past the driver and floating over to Garvin's horse. "What is happening?" Rindle hissed.

Garvin turned his mount. "We ride to kill some monsters."

He kicked his horse into a gallop, riding along the ridge with Bosinger following.

Priella remained airborne, hovering above the fracas. Occasionally, goblin arrows struck her shield and shattered, but she otherwise appeared unnoticed. Below, Thurvin lay waste to the monsters, fireballs, lightning bolts, and ropes of magic lashing out as he strode through the enemy host. He killed with rapid efficiency in a display of frightening power.

A glow arose at the eastern edge of the battlefield, a swirling ball of red energy rising, arcing through the sky, and dropping toward Thurvin. In his mad bloodlust, he did not see it coming.

Just before it struck, Priella thrust her shield toward the ball of angry magic. Redirected, it struck the ground ten strides in front of Thurvin and separated, bits of sizzling, red energy splashing in all directions. It struck dozens of goblins, their bodies convulsing violently as they collapsed. The wave of malevolent magic hit Thurvin before he could react, his body seizing up as he fell to his knees, shaking, fists clenched.

Priella lowered herself and prepared a construct of repair, intent on helping the wizard lord, when he suddenly bloomed with bright, blinding light.

With a roar, Thurvin rose into the air. "You darkspawn cannot harm me! I have become immortal!"

Swirling his hands, he drew in the surrounding air and crafted a twisting construct. Powerful wind buffeted Priella, forcing her to drop to the ground. She shielded herself and stood, backing away as the tornado took shape, Thurvin at the heart of it. The cyclone grew increasingly more powerful, picking up goblins, alive and dead, and tossing them around like leaves. The roaring storm grew, the long grass bending mightily until chunks of earth also lifted into the air. Finally, Priella turned and ran for fear of being swept away.

∼

Garvin rode down the hill, descending behind the shaman bonfire, a dozen of the goblin magic users dancing around it, waving their arms and hooting. Another ball of red, deadly magic arose and launched toward the battlefield. The magic missile struck the tornado and exploded, sending crimson sparks in all directions. The tornado dissipated, hundreds of bodies falling toward the ground. For a brief moment, Garvin wondered if Thurvin had fallen, as well. He banished the thought, focused on the true enemy while forming a plan.

Bosinger rode at his side, the two mounts and four riders just outside of earshot from the fire.

Slowing to a stop, Garvin turned his mount toward Bosinger's, lowering his voice. "We must strike hard and fast. Their magic takes time to manifest. Even small spells take a few seconds to appear. If we can surprise them, we can kill them and end this fight."

Bosinger nodded, drawing his sword. "I'll attack from the right. You take the left."

"Agreed."

Garvin turned toward Kollin on the back of the other man's horse. "They don't do well with light. If you can blind them, it will buy us more time."

Kollin nodded. "I can do that."

"Good. Let's go kill some darkspawn."

Garvin turned his horse, circling to the left. As it picked up speed, he drew his sword, speaking over his shoulder. "Rindle, when we reach them, slide off and do your thing."

"Do what, exactly?" Rindle hissed into his ear.

"These monsters have hearts just like men. Stop the hearts and you stop them from attacking."

"Got it."

The goblins surrounding the fire turned toward the approaching horses and began shouting, waving their arms. A bright, white light bloomed above Bosinger's horse, the goblins raising their arms to shield their eyes as Garvin's horse closed the gap.

He swung, lopping off the head the first monster as Rindle slipped off. The horse ran another over, the creature crying out. Bosinger struck from the other side, launching himself off the horse, his thick, armored body crashing into three monsters, one falling into the fire, screaming.

Garvin turned in the saddle and spotted a shaman waving its hands, a chain of human bones around its neck. Before the shaman could release the spell, it stiffened, eyes bulging at the shadowy arm in its chest. The goblin shook and fell to its knees, blood gushing from its mouth as Rindle crushed its heart.

Another monster rushed from behind Rindle, and Garvin threw his blade, the sword spinning through the phantom-thief, the hilt striking the goblin in the head. The monster stumbled, and Bosinger picked it up with one hand, smashing it into two others in a shrieking mess of bloody bodies and broken bones.

Kollin turned Bosinger's horse and released a blast of ice, coating the last two goblins in white frost. The monsters stiffened and stumbled. Bosinger leapt and brought his fists down onto the back of each enemy, his augmented strength shattering their backs.

Suddenly, the area grew quiet. Three goblin corpses lay in the fire, burning, two others in a single, twisted heap. Two were headless, two with crushed spines, and one lay on its chest, neck twisted in a grotesque manner, empty eyes staring up at the sky.

Garvin turned toward the battlefield. Goblin shrieks and squeals had replaced the angry hoots of battle. The surviving darkspawn turned and fled, heading northeast and fading into the night.

38

RUIN

Priella floated above a sea of corpses, some human, most goblin, her magic taking her toward the heart of the eerily quiet battlefield. Here and there, fires remained, black smoke rising from burning grass and smoldering bodies. When she spotted a man in torn, blue robes rising to his feet, she lowered herself and landed before him, her slippered feet sinking into the churned earth.

"Lord Thurvin, are you all right?" she asked.

He turned toward her, fire reflecting in his eyes, a madness within. "I am immortal. Their best magic could not kill me." He sneered and laughed, his arm sweeping toward the surrounding ruins. "Behold the ease with which I destroyed thousands of darkspawn."

She reached out and touched him, using her magic to influence him. "Come. Let us return to camp."

The man's expression calmed, madness slipping away. He wiped his brow and nodded. "Yes. Of course."

They each rose on a platform of air and sailed across the battlefield. Ahead, her troops gathered in clusters, sorting through the wounded and the dead.

Priella then spotted two horses riding through camp, both heading toward the command tents. She lowered herself until she was able to make out Bosinger and Kollin upon one horse, Commander Garvin upon the other.

She floated past them, heading up the hill and landing outside her tent. Thurvin settled beside her, the man frowning.

"Are you sure you are all right?" she asked. "I can heal you, if needed."

As she reached for him, he backed away. "I told you, I need no healing. I am invincible!"

She then spied the covered wagon beyond her tent and sighed in relief. "Thank the gods. My throne has arrived."

The ache to initiate Devotion tugged at her, but she resisted, deciding she would wait for Garvin and Bosinger to report first. The two horses emerged from the gloom, slowing as they drew near. Garvin leapt off his mount, a transparent shadow flickering beside him as he strode toward Priella and Thurvin. Bosinger stopped and helped Kollin off before dismounting.

"Why did you leave the command tent?" Priella demanded.

Bosinger gestured toward Garvin. "Commander Garvin needed our assistance." He grinned. "We chopped the head off the snake."

Priella turned toward Garvin. "What is this about?"

"You made me commander for a reason, Priella." Garvin had never before used her name rather than title. "Goblins are a frightened, mindless lot when not tightly controlled by their magic users. A single shaman can control a thousand of the monsters." He pointed northeast. "When I spotted a shaman fire at the edge of the battlefield, I did what I had to do. With surprise on our side, Bosinger, Kollin, Rindle, and I killed them, ending the fight."

"*I* ended his fight!" Thurvin growled. "Without my magic, you all would have been slaughtered. I, alone, destroyed this enemy."

Kollin retorted, "I am sick of your blowhard nature, Thurvin. Don't delude yourself into believing you don't need others. *We* killed the leaders and ended the fight, while you put on a meaningless display of magic." He stepped closer and sneered at the shorter wizard. "Without Devotion, you are nothing but a tiny little man whom everyone despises."

Thurvin's entire body shook, fists clenched, face turning red as he bloomed with the strength of his magic. He thrust his fist forward and launched Kollin back forty feet, smashing him into the wagon holding the throne. He struck hard, bones cracking, body breaking, before he fell to the ground, face-first.

"Kollin!" Priella cried, an invisible knife tearing through her heart. She stumbled toward him, sobbing.

Behind her, Thurvin shouted, "I will show you true power!"

The wizard lord lifted himself into the air, still glowing with his magic, and released a beam of foulfire. It struck the nearby wagon, the cover bursting into flames, the crystal throne of Pallanar lighting brightly for a few seconds before it exploded, taking the wagon with it. Shards of crystal and splintered wood sprayed in all directions. Priella raised her arms to cover her face, a fragment of crystal burying in her flesh as she fell onto her back.

She sat up, wincing in pain. With clenched teeth, she pulled the shard out, blood oozing from her arm before her magic healed the wound. Rising to her feet, she stared in shock at the destroyed throne, her means of gathering prayers. Without it, she would revert to a normal wizardess, reduced to a tiny fraction of the power she had grown used to wielding. She turned and gasped when she saw Bosinger lying on the ground. A much larger chunk of crystal jutted out from his eye, the other locked open in surprise. It was obvious. The man was dead.

Thurvin floated overhead, laughing. "Sorry, My *Queen*," he sneered. "You no longer have the power to control me."

Priella took a step backward, hand to her chest, shaking her head. *This is a dream. Just a bad dream.*

The wizard lord nodded. "Yes. I realized you were twisting my thoughts, planting false desires." His voice rose to a roar. "*No more!*" He lifted clenched fists and turned toward the city of Balmor, the yellow flame of Bal shimmering at the top of the Tower of Devotion. "In fact, it is time my rival, Jakarci, understood the meaning of true power. When I take his life, I will take his tower and the prayers of Balmor will feed me, for I am a god among men!"

The wizard lord sped off into the night, heading toward the city, while Priella fell to her knees, sobbing.

A hand touched her shoulder. "Priella."

She looked up at Garvin, a bloody gash across his cheek.

"You cannot give in to despair." He shook his head. "It will do no good. Use your mind. Use your magic. Seek an answer."

"What... What can I do?"

Garvin glanced to the side. "Bosinger is beyond saving, despite the healing ability you demonstrated with Kylar Mor. You cannot save your bodyguard, but you might save the man you love."

"Kollin!" She stood, turned, and rushed over to him.

She pulled a broken board off his back and knelt, placing her hand on his forehead. Delving into him, she found dozens of broken bones, his brain swollen, but he was still alive. A foot-long splinter of wood stuck out from his side. She pulled it free and held her hand over the wound, wet and sticky.

Her magic had not been charged in over a day, exerting much of it during the battle, but enough lingered. With it, she knitted his broken bones, sealed punctures and lacerations, internal and external, and eased the swelling on his brain.

When finished, little of her magic remained, but she knew he would live. She lifted her gaze toward the distant city and wondered if it would be a wasted effort. Raw terror filled her when she imagined Thurvin capturing another Tower of Devotion, the prayers of another great city added to his might.

EPILOGUE

The ground shook, chunks of rock falling from the temple ceiling to the rocky floor. H'Deesengar remained seated upon his throne, yellow eyes narrowed as he watched, curious. The debris could not hurt him, a being from another plane, so there was no cause for concern. From the caverns outside came the shrieks of goblins, some crying out in fear, others as they died.

The quaking ceased, the goblins falling silent. Vezkalth appeared from the side passage and approached the dais.

"Are we under attack?" H'Deesengar asked.

Vezkalth shook his head. "I do not know the cause of the quake, Master."

The demon lord's permanent scowl deepened, his attention turned toward the star on the floor surrounding the throne. Two more lights on the points of the star had dimmed. *Only three wizard lords remain.* One of those remaining lit with an orange glow. He grimaced. *Kelluon is one of them.*

He tentatively reached out, the field of energy bending easily when he applied pressure. Yes, it burned, but pain was irrelevant. Rising to his feet, he placed both hands against it and pushed. The burn ran from H'Deesengar's hands, up his arms, to his body as he moved forward, smoke rising from his black, leathery skin. Suddenly, he emerged from the prison for the first time in millennia.

Head tilted toward the cavern ceiling, H'Deesengar released a howl of victory, echoing throughout the warrens beneath Murvaran. "Free!" he bellowed. "After all this time, I am free!"

Wide-eyed, Vezkalth knelt. "What would you have of us, Master?"

"Sound the Horn of Gyradon to call the wyverns. It is time to claim this world."

Vezkalth hesitated. Of all the goblins H'Deesengar had gifted, only Vezkalth had demonstrated true intellect.

"What is it?" the demon lord asked.

"Are you not concerned Urvadan will discover your escape?"

H'Deesengar grinned. "Urvadan slumbers, unaware of the centuries of subtle influence that put him in such a state. By the time he awakens, it will be too late.

"The gods are failing, the world ripe for a new supreme being. I shall consume every wizard alive, their power feeding my own and until my might is unparalleled. When I am finished obliterating the mortals of this world, I will confront Urvadan himself."

With the chant of Devotion surrounding her, Eviara said the words she had recited every night for as long as she could recall. The orange beacon atop the Anker Tower of Devotion faded, the blaze simmering to a dull flame, ending Devotion. Anker might be the last remaining Kyranni city, but it was also the largest, the prayers of the citizens feeding the man who protected them.

She rose to her feet, gazing out over the battlements. The killing zone outside the city walls remained empty. Three weeks had passed since the last darkspawn attack. Twenty-one days, and no help had come from either Balmoria or Hassakan, the two neighboring wizardoms. She wondered if the messengers had reached either wizard lord, or maybe Jakarci and Sarazan just did not care.

Pacing along the wall, she gave words of encouragement and nods of thanks to the soldiers who spent every evening upon the wall with her. Four times, those soldiers had faced a horde of monsters born of a nightmare. Each evening, they had held the darkspawn at bay long enough for Lord Kelluon to release his magic and end the onslaught. She was proud of the men and women who protected the city, inspired by their courage, apprecia-tive of their resilience.

I pray this is another, boring evening.

As the words echoed in her head, a shout arose from a woman on the wall. "I see something!"

Eviara peered into the darkness, the tree line shadowed beyond the light of the braziers spaced along the middle of the killing zone. At first, she saw nothing. Then something moved – a silhouette, others joining.

A distant howl echoed in the night, followed by a massive wave of hoots. The monsters burst forth, charging toward the city.

"Archers ready!" she shouted, the call relaying up and down the wall. She glanced toward Halata, the messenger always shadowing her. "Tell Bogori to have his squad ready in case they breach the gate."

"Yes, Captain." The messenger spun and raced along the wall, toward the tower stairs.

Eviara turned, gazing over the battlefield, the goblins charging toward the braziers. When the vanguard passed the flaming pots, she shouted. "Raise bows!" She paused for a breath, then cried, "Loose!"

Twangs echoed up and down the wall, arrows arching high, falling in a rain of death. Goblins screamed, stumbled, and died, their brethren running over them as if they were mere doormats.

"Fire at will!" Eviara shouted before turning toward the crane to her right. "Divers ready!"

She spun and ran along the wall, calling for the other divers to prepare – women bearing naginatas, lines around their waists tied to cranes mounted to the top of the wall. The moment the goblins reached the bottom of the wall, the divers leapt, blades ready as they plunged downward.

When Eviara arrived at the next tower, she approached the wizards, eight of them clustered together.

"Are you prepared to provide support?"

Chort, the eldest in the group, replied, "We know what to do."

"Good." She turned to look over the battlefield. "Just watch for arrows." *I hope Kelluon arrives soon.*

~

Two trolls charged toward the wall, Eviara preparing to call for the ballistae to loose. The massive beasts stomped on their fellow darkspawn, goblins screaming as they were flattened by the giant trolls, intent on breaking through the wall. When the nearest troll was midway between the braziers and the wall, a beam of white light shot out, striking the monster in the chest. The beast stiffened, face twisting as it stumbled to its knees, a two-foot-wide hole through its torso.

Kelluon! she thought

The wizard lord stood fifty feet down the wall from Eviara. She rushed toward him as he released another blast of foulfire, felling the second troll.

"Lord Kelluon," she panted as she slowed. "I am glad you are here."

The tall man exhaled while staring toward the battlefield. "It appears I arrived just in time."

"Yes. And thank Kyra for that."

"How fares the battle?"

"We have killed many, two thousand or more, but they continue to attack."

"Have any reached the top of the wall or breached the gate?"

She shook her head. "Not yet, sire."

Cries came from along the wall. She spun and saw her people pointing up toward the sky, a winged silhouette sliding past the full moon, a high-pitched squeal echoing above the city. Other, similar shapes emerged from the night sky, each far too large to be a bird.

"What are they?" she muttered.

"Some sort of dragon-like creature," Kelluon replied.

"I thought dragons were just a myth."

The monsters descended toward the wall, wings outstretched, claws extended. Archers loosed, a burst of arrows striking the nearest beast, some bouncing off or shattering, others burying in its scaled flesh or webbed wings. Still, it descended and struck, knocking three soldiers from the wall, grasping two others in its claws. A burst of flames shot up from a wizard, singeing the beast. It banked and released its hold, the soldiers in its grip flailing as they fell toward the wizard, all three spinning off the wall.

Another winged creature descended, and Eviara called to the nearest soldier manning a ballista. The war machine released a four-foot-long bolt, striking the creature in the chest. It fell and struck the top of the wall, smashing through stone merlons and tumbling into the city, taking eight soldiers with it.

More of the winged monsters appeared, clashing with the city defenders. Eviara held her naginata ready as one sailed toward her. Just before it struck, she lashed out and dove, her blade lopping three massive, clawed toes off its foot. The monster squealed as it sailed past, banked, and turned back toward her. Before it could strike again, Kelluon released a lightning bolt. The blast struck the monster in the chest, sending it off course. It sank rapidly and crashed head-first into the wall, the impact rocking the ground and rattling Eviara's teeth.

Another cry came from behind, and she spun around. A blast of dark purple magic shot from the sky, instantly vaporizing a cluster of soldiers upon the wall. In the light of the magic, she noticed a humanoid form riding on the back of a winged beast. The rider pointed, the monster banking and coming directly toward her.

Kelluon thrust his arms toward the attacking monster, a beam of white light striking it, burning a hole through its body. The dragon-like creature faltered, tilted, and tumbled through the air, heading toward the city. As the beast sailed close to the wall, the being on its back leapt, twisted, and fell fifty feet. Rather than splattering, it landed upon the wall in a crouch, the impact sending chunks of broken stone in all directions.

Slowly rising, the figure stood eight feet tall, skin black and leathery. The creature was muscular and obviously male, its exposed manhood barbed. Even the head was grotesque – spikes rather than hair, fangs jutting up over the upper lip, eyes a solid yellow with black slits for pupils.

"Greetings, wizard." The creature's voice was deep and gravelly.

Kelluon stepped beside Eviara, orange and black robes rippling in the breeze. "What…are you?"

Laughter arose from the being, the sound sending chills down Eviara's spine. Two soldiers stalked toward the beast, prepared to attack it from behind.

"I am the demon lord, H'Deesengar. I was once a prisoner of the god, Urvadan, but am now free!"

The soldiers attacked, one slicing with a sword, aiming for the monster's legs, the other stabbing his spear at its back. The sword struck and buried in a calf, sticking there. The tip of the spear emerged from the demon's stomach.

H'Deesengar looked down at the spearpoint, gripped it, and jerked it forward, the man holding the shaft stumbling with it. Moving with impossible quickness, the demon lord spun, gripped the man's head, and lifted. The soldier kicked with futility, the demon lord laughing before he drove the man downward into his fellow soldier, both smashing to the wall with frightening force, bones shattering, blood splattering. Releasing a grunt, the demon kicked the sword free from its leg, its wounds healing instantly.

The demon turned back toward Kelluon and Eviara, face splitting into a horrific grin, sharp fangs white in the night. "I have come to destroy you, wizard. Soon, all of mankind will pray to me, their new god."

With a roar, Kelluon thrust his arms forward, foulfire blasting forth, the light blinding Eviara. She raised her arm to cover her eyes and reeled backward. When the light faded, she blinked and lowered her arm, the spots in her eyes slowly clearing.

Through the hole in the demon's chest, she saw dozens of dead soldiers, body parts vaporized by the blast of raw magic. Yet the demon smiled, the hole sealing in a shimmer of purple until the creature was, again, whole.

"Now," H'Deesengar said, "you die."

In a flash, the demon lord was on Kelluon, lifting the wizard over its head. It grunted, muscles flexing as it tore an arm right off the wizard. Kelluon screamed, the wound healing in moments. Ropes of magic coiled around the creature's waist, constricting. The ropes dug into the demon lord's flesh and snapped tightly, severing the beast's body, but the two pieces reformed instantly in a flash of netherworld magic.

Eviara backed away in fear, clueless as to how they could defeat something that could heal itself so easily.

H'Deesengar thrust downward, smashing Kelluon to the wall in a splatter of blood and brains. The flames on the tower faded. The demon extended a hand toward the dead wizard, a dark magic enveloping the dead wizard. Bits of flesh and sparkling blood broke off Kelluon and floated into the demon. A purple glow enveloped H'Deesengar, growing brighter and brighter as Kelluon's flesh seeped into its body until the wizard lord was gone. The demon lifted its head to the sky and roared loud enough to shake the battlements.

It has taken Kelluon's magic, Eviara thought. She knew the city was lost and feared all of mankind would soon follow.

NOTE FROM THE AUTHOR

Only one book remains in the **Fate of Wizardoms** epic, and I hope you will join me for the series conclusion. **A Contest of Gods** releases in August 2020. Fear not, for additional novels set in the Wizardoms universe will follow.

To remain up to date on my new releases, I invite you to **join my author newsletter**. There are even free gifts included because I like to reward my readers for their support.

If interested, proceed to www.JeffreyLKohanek.com.

Best Wishes,
Jeff
www.jeffreylkohanek.com

ALSO BY JEFFREY L. KOHANEK

Fate of Wizardoms

Book One: Eye of Obscurance

Book Two: Balance of Magic

Book Three: Temple of the Oracle

Book Four: Objects of Power

Book Five: Rise of a Wizard Queen

Book Six: A Contest of Gods

* * *

Warriors, Wizards, & Rogues (Fate of Wizardoms 0)

Fate of Wizardoms Boxed Set: Books 1-3

Runes of Issalia

The Buried Symbol: Runes of Issalia 1

The Emblem Throne: Runes of Issalia 2

An Empire in Runes: Runes of Issalia 3

Rogue Legacy: Runes of Issalia Prequel

* * *

Runes of Issalia Bonus Box

Wardens of Issalia

A Warden's Purpose: Wardens of Issalia 1

The Arcane Ward: Wardens of Issalia 2

An Imperial Gambit: Wardens of Issalia 3

A Kingdom Under Siege: Wardens of Issalia 4

ICON: A Wardens of Issalia Companion Tale

* * *

Wardens of Issalia Boxed Set